THE DIG

♦

Boston Low: A mistake-filled, heroic mission caused NASA's best pilot to quit the space program. Now his nation and the world need him as never before . . .

Maggie Robbins: The enthusiastic journalist was not trained for a mission like this. But in the end, she would hold the key to its survival . . .

Ludger Brink: The cool, arrogant scientist was one of the world's leading experts on meteorites and asteroids. But on the planet Cocytus, enlightenment would come through mystery . . .

Creator: Brought back from a death state, he is the ultimate engineer—and the voice of a people destroyed by their own power.

♦

ALAN DEAN FOSTER

THE
DIG™

Based on a story by Sean Clark

WARNER BOOKS

A Time Warner Company

WARNER BOOKS EDITION

Copyright © 1995 by LucasArts Entertainment
All rights reserved. Used under authorization. The Dig is a trademark of LucasArts Entertainment Company.

Aspect® is a registered trademark of Warner Books, Inc.

Cover design by Don Puckey
Cover illustration by Bill Eaken

Warner Books, Inc.
1271 Avenue of the Americas
New York, NY 10020

Visit our Web site at
http://pathfinder.com/twep

Ⓦ A Time Warner Company

Printed in the United States of America
Originally published in hardcover by Warner Books.
First Printed in Paperback: February, 1997

10 9 8 7 6 5 4 3

To Steven Spielberg
I waited forty years for those dinosaurs. Thanks.

THE
DIG™

CHAPTER

1

"It's a rock, Mr. President."

Warren Lyon Fraser—father, philanthropist, scion of a wealthy Illinois merchant family and at present leader of the nominally Free World, glanced up absently from behind his desk. From behind *the* desk, Earle reminded himself. The Chief Executive was preoccupied, his thoughts on the Cabinet meeting scheduled for one o'clock and the state dinner being readied for the Spanish Premier.

Knowing this in advance it was incumbent upon Earle, as chief science advisor to the White House, to couch his report in terms sufficiently strong to penetrate the social and diplomatic fog that permanently enveloped the President. That meant being straightforward and to the point while keeping complex scientific terminology to a minimum. Words had to be chosen for immediate impact as opposed to accuracy. Something had to be done about the situation, and done soon.

While very much aware of the President's busy schedule, Earle had insisted on the meeting. The news was too important, the need for a prompt and appropriate response too critical, for the relevant information to wend its way to the Chief Executive by means of the usual ruthlessly distilled and bowdlerized written report. Not that Earle was a particularly forceful speaker, but there was no way he was going to try to convey these particular details through emotionless print or stammering underlings.

No, not these details. They were too weighty. In every sense of the word.

So he'd used every ounce of pull he possessed to get five minutes of the President's time, confident that when Fraser was made aware of the gravity of the situation, he would perk up and pay real attention. After all, what Earle had to say would instantly render irrelevant the most important state dinner or Cabinet meeting.

"I take it you're referring to the 'object'?" Fraser peered up at his science advisor out of kindly, heavily lidded eyes that seemed never to blink. "Staff has been whispering about it since yesterday, but I didn't see any point in wasting time on rumor and speculation. Thought I'd wait for the facts." The fingers of his right hand idly rotated a formal memo in slow circles, as if he were absently polishing the desktop.

"I hope there aren't too many. Facts, that is. I've a partial Cabinet meeting in one hour. Nothing major; just the usual assortment of crises and catastrophes." Earle smiled politely as the President eyed the elegant brass clock on his desk. "It's just that I'd like to grab a bite to eat first."

"Yes, sir." The Science Advisor wasn't intimidated. His briefings were usually delivered elsewhere in the White House, but he'd spent more than a little time in the Oval Office and was comfortable in its surroundings.

"Well, come on, then, Willy. So it's a rock. What kind of rock? Big, small, purple . . . what?" The President waited, expectant but impatient.

Despite the prompting, Earle hesitated. Surely no similar report had ever been delivered in such august surroundings, with the portraits of other presidents gazing down critically. That was why it was so important for him to get it right the first time, to leave no room for uncertainty or equivocation.

"It's about a mile in diameter, Mr. President. My colleagues would chide me for not using metrics, but the details of the final report are going to be in all the papers tomorrow, and that's a convenient size reference to use. Makes it easy to come to grips with it."

"A mile-long rock," the President murmured. "Or asteroid, rather."

"That's right, sir." Warren Lyon Fraser was no scientific sophisticate. His background and upbringing had been in business and politics. But you didn't get to be President of the United States without knowing a little something about everything. Or at least not without knowing how to fake it well.

"An asteroid, sir, that's right. That's the problem."

"I take it a mile in diameter is substantial, as asteroids go?"

"Substantial enough, sir."

"I'm beginning to get the feeling, both from what I've been hearing whispered around and now from your attitude, Willy, that this isn't going to be something I'm going to be allowed to ignore."

"I'm afraid not, Mr. President." The Science Advisor's expression was solemn.

Fraser sighed resignedly and leaned back in the thickly padded chair. It squeaked ever so slightly. "Why not?"

"There are two problems with this particular asteroid, sir. The first is that nobody saw it coming. It's not big enough to announce itself boldly, but once it crossed the lunar orbit, it should have been picked up by half a dozen observatories, or at least a few of the hyperactive amateurs who do a lot of astronomy's dirty work."

"And it wasn't?" the President inquired.

"No, sir. It just kind of showed up. Solar objects don't play trick or treat. It's against the rules. This thing has broken a lot of rules. One minute the immediate terrestrial vicinity is empty and the next it's home to this rock. Somebody should have seen it coming long before it entered orbit."

"So it's in orbit?" The President's interest was clearly piqued. "Don't these comets and such just go flashing past and then disappear?"

"Normally that's just what happens, sir. But not this thing. It came barreling in at God knows what velocity, skimmed the outer atmosphere, and slowed down. Slowed down aston-ishingly fast, as a matter of fact. We're very interested in how that happened. Initial observations indicate that it's not a pall-asite or—"

"Excuse me, Willy?"

"Sorry, sir. An exotic type of metallic meteorite. Prelimi-nary analysis suggests that this one's composition is unre-markable, except for an occasional odd blip on isolated readouts."

"I'm glad to hear it." The President had a wicked sense of humor, which he chose to display only in private. Earle had been the recipient of it on more than one occasion.

"It's that occasional blip that has so many of my col-leagues intrigued, sir. They wonder if it might explain why no one saw this particular rock coming. It's not just our peo-ple either. The Russians, the Japanese, the Europeans; they all missed it too."

"Maybe it's just that nobody was looking in the right place at the right time."

Earle nodded. "That's entirely possible, sir. In fact at the moment, that's the most reasonable explanation. Especially when you consider that it came in over the Antarctic. Unfor-tunately, that doesn't help us with the second problem."

"It better be a big one." Fraser glanced significantly at the clock.

Earle squirmed inwardly, wishing some of the big boys from Houston were there to back him up. None of them could spare the time, however. They were all working furi-ously on the Problem.

"It's the orbit, sir. That's the trouble. It's a declining orbit. Rapidly declining, as a matter of fact. It really doesn't make any sense. Considering the speed at which the object must have entered the solar system, it should have zipped on past instead of letting itself be captured. The calculations . . ." He fumbled clumsily with the inside pocket of his jacket. "Here, sir: I sketched it all out for you. I thought it might make the situation a little easier to understand." He smiled hopefully. "You know: a picture's worth . . . ?"

Fraser straightened in his chair and took the drawing. With simple, straightforward lines it showed the Earth, the Moon, and a tight ellipse encircling the Earth. At the far point of the ellipse was a small dot.

The President glanced up at his advisor. "This isn't the kind of orbit the shuttles use, is it? Or any of our communications satellites?"

"No, sir. Those would be near-perfect circles, each representing a stable orbit. See how extreme this one is?" Leaning forward, he touched the ellipse where it came nearest to Earth. "If something isn't done very soon, this asteroid's orbit will decay rapidly, and it will enter our atmosphere, at which point it will crash into the surface, either in one very large piece and many tiny ones or in a number of fairly large ones. Again, much depends on its composition." He straightened. "I'm told we'll have more accurate figures later this afternoon."

Warren Fraser nodded slowly and rubbed his lower lip with the forefinger of his left hand. He no longer looked at the clock. The President of the United States, Earle noted absently, had hairy knuckles.

"What happens then? Worst-case scenario, Willy."

Earle considered. "I can't give you specifics, sir. No one can. Everything depends on the size of the pieces, their chemical makeup, and where they strike. If they come down in the vicinity of, say, Easter Island, we can expect possible tsunamis throughout the Pacific Basin. Middle of the Atlantic or Indian oceans, more of the same. If a lot of it burns up on entry, the effects could be minimal."

"I see." The President's expression did not change. "What if these hypothetical pieces don't land in the middle of the ocean? What if a big chunk were to come down somewhere near here?"

"Why, in that case, sir, no one would have to worry about which party is going to dominate the next session of Congress. Or any other phase of government, for that matter. Personally, I've always thought it would be more appropriate for the capital to be located in a more central location. Missouri, for example."

"As bad as that," the President muttered.

"Yes, sir, as bad as that. We might lose everything as far north as Philadelphia. Baltimore, certainly."

"So much for waterfront redevelopment." Fraser stared evenly at his advisor. "There's no way you can predict where it will come down?"

"No, sir. Nor in how many pieces, nor how big or small they'll be. Just that it's likely to make an awful mess of wherever it strikes. Remember, we've only been on this for less than twenty-four hours. The astronomy people have to coordinate observations with the chemists and so on. If it's mostly nickel-iron, well, that's not good. It means most of it's liable to come down in one piece. We don't have a lot of time."

"But it *could* break up into small pieces, disintegrate on entry?"

"Yes, sir. Though I don't see much of an advantage in being tagged by a shotgun as opposed to a rifle."

The President grunted softly. "All right. So much for wishful thinking. What do we do about it? Is there anything we *can* do about it?" He was reaching for the phone. The phone that could command legions, or dollars. "I'm going to get on this myself. We'll appoint a top-flight committee—"

"Please, sir." Earle put forward a restraining hand. "I'm afraid that the standard congressional speed of response isn't going to be adequate in this case. We have to do something *right away*."

Fraser left the phone in its cradle and steepled his fingers. "You wouldn't talk like that unless there *is* something that can be done. Well, let's have it. I hope it won't cost too many votes."

"Waiting is *liable* to cost voters, sir. Thousands of them." Earle swallowed. This was really why he'd sought the meeting with the President. Across the country, dozens of scientists and engineers were depending on him to sell the idea. He hoped he'd be able to. So far, it was the *only* idea.

"Preliminary modeling suggests that it should be possible to adjust the asteroid's orbit, to nudge it into a stable position."

"I see. I presume this can't be done by landing a few hundred players from the NFL on one side of the object and having them all jump up and down simultaneously?"

Earle smiled, relieved that the President was able to find some levity in such a terribly serious situation. "No, sir." Now came the difficult part. "Actually, it would involve the use of low-level nuclear explosives. Calculations show that they could be placed—"

Fraser interrupted. "Just a minute, Willy. Nuclear?"

"I'm sorry, sir. I know how controversial this is going to be. But nukes are really the only things with enough kick to affect an object of this size. There are no alternatives. And it has to be precise. We don't want to bust this thing up. We just want to adjust its attitude."

"I'm going to have the same problem with Congress. Nukes." The President shook his head slowly. "Can you see me going to a bunch of senators with this?"

"You have to, sir. Tell them that if we don't, and don't do it fast, a number of representatives are liable to lose something more than a few votes. Like entire districts, for example."

Fraser sighed. "All right. That's my job. If I can't get authorization, we'll have to do it by presidential decree. Assuming the procedure can be cleared, do we have anything suitable with which to do the work?"

"We have very little experience with anything but weapons-grade nukes, Mr. President. But the Russians have been using them for decades and—"

"Oh, wonderful. Congress is going to love this."

"It's not as bad as all that, sir." Earle tried to inject some enthusiasm into his voice. "We've been sharing information with them for years, especially as regards long-term space missions."

Fraser considered. "A cooperative enterprise could be useful to both sides." He smiled thinly. "It would also allow us to share the blame if this thing flops."

"We've already been in contact with the appropriate people in Moscow and Khabarovsk. They assure us that not only can their devices do the job cleanly and on the first try but that they have the necessary kilotonnage on hand."

"These 'devices,'" the President murmured. "They'll fit on a shuttle? With no danger to the crew?"

"Yes, sir. Fully shielded and ready to be armed. Actually, compared to some of the payloads we've been putting in orbit recently, this one will be comparatively small. I've scanned the schematics, and the mechanics are pretty basic. The Russians have always tried to keep things simple."

The President's voice was soft. "It's a long way from using cherry bombs to blow up pop bottles on the Fourth. Used to do that when I was a kid. We won't be able to hide this one, Willy."

"No, sir. Everyone will be watching. Everyone on the planet. We can do this, Mr. President. The Russians have the package, and we have the delivery system."

"Can't we just shoot the 'package' up there and avoid exposing our people to the possible consequences?"

"I'm afraid not, sir. In order for them to be maximally effective, the explosives have to be sited precisely on the asteroid's surface. It means a shuttle trip, matching orbits, hand placement. There's no getting around that."

"I'll take your word for it, Willy."

"It's not my word, Mr. President. Several hundred people have been working overtime to put this together. It's the best chance we have."

Fraser was quiet for a long moment, gazing at something unseen. Eventually he looked again at his visitor. "You know what the hallmark of a successful politician is, Willy?"

"No, sir." Earle forced himself to listen. The President had a tendency to ramble.

"It's the ability to find some good even in the most god-awful situation. For example, we're not talking the end of the world here."

"No, sir," the Science Advisor murmured. "Only a meaningful portion of it."

"That's right; encourage me. Our people are sure the Russian nukes will work?"

"Reasonably sure, sir. In science nothing is certain. But they have used them before, to dig tunnels for canals and expose large, deep ore bodies, and they've refined them over the years."

"Assuming they do, think of the possible benefits. It means that America can once again lay claim to being the world's savior. I realize that when I say something like that, it may sound unnecessarily cold to you, Willy, but as President I have to take everything into account. I do hope to be reelected in two years."

"Of course, sir." Earle kept his expression carefully neutral. In the previous election he had voted for Fraser's opponent.

"Now, let me see if I understand something correctly. If this rock can be properly stabilized, it will go into more or less permanent orbit around the Earth?"

"That's correct, sir."

"Then we could use it to replace many of our existing communications and scientific satellites, couldn't we?"

Earle smiled in what he hoped wasn't a patronizing manner. "Not entirely, sir. It would be a stable orbit but not a geosynchronous one. But it could serve as a useful base for many scientific programs. A cheap space station, and far larger than anything we could put up."

The President was nodding approvingly. "Good enough. The Earth will acquire a second moon. With potential economic benefits."

"Perhaps, sir. However, I don't think that should be our first priority."

Fraser swiveled slightly in his chair. "You don't have to justify expenses to Congress, Willy. I do. Wait and see. If we go through with this, there'll be half a dozen senators insisting we claim the rock as *U.S.* territory. Then I'll have to mollify Kubiltov and his gang, and the Europeans will sulk, and . . . well, you get the picture. There's more than science involved here."

"Yes, sir." Earle was growing impatient. "However it's handled, sir, we need to move on this right away. Falling rocks know no politics."

"Rocks and politics both involve leverage, Willy. You've worked in Washington long enough to know that."

"I have, sir. I'm just trying to emphasize the need for speed in this matter. Every moment is important. If we wait too long, the asteroid's orbit will decay to the point where no amount of explosive, nuclear or otherwise, will be able to affect it."

"I'll do the best I can, Willy. I promise I'll sign the necessary authorizations as soon as the Cabinet has been consulted. We'll clear this afternoon's agenda so we can deal with this. NASA will be the beneficiary of a presidential decree by five o'clock this evening." His eyes bored into the Science Advisor. "God help you, Willy, if your people are wrong about these nuclear explosives and they don't work properly."

Earle met the President's gaze evenly. "God help us, Mr. President, if they don't work, period." He turned to leave.

"One more thing, Willy."

The Science Advisor paused. "Yes, sir?" From the wall, Andrew Jackson seemed to be watching him intently.

"If this doesn't come off as planned, we could get the blame for whatever angle of approach the object eventually takes."

"I know that, sir. This is an unprecedented situation. There are no guarantees. The only thing we know for certain is that if we don't do something, and do it quickly, the asteroid will eventually strike the surface. It's only a question of where, and of how many will die."

Fraser nodded. "Then you'd better get going. You have people you need to talk to, and I have to make some phone calls."

"Right, Mr. President." Earle left the Chief Executive reaching for one of the three telephones on his desk. It was the direct line to Moscow. Not that it mattered what he and President Kubiltov said to each other. All that mattered now was setting off the right-size packages in the proper places on the surface of a fast-moving rock the size of a small Iowa town.

The immediate priority was finding the best people to deliver those packages.

It was Low's favorite place in the city. Down by the water, close to where the incomparable bridge spanned the inconceivable crack in the exquisitely beautiful coastal mountains. To impoverished immigrants from Asia and the Pacific Basin, it doubtless still was a golden gate. To the residents of Marin County, it was a shorter commute. To tourists from around the country and around the world, the ultimate souvenir picture.

Today the entire length was visible, devoid of mist. That would disappoint the tourists, he knew. More than a few expected the fog to perform on cue, as if the city had giant fog machines installed outside the gate to create just the right photo-op when the tour boats were cruising by.

Fog or not, Low loved the bridge. There was no more gracile public structure in the United States. Simple and functional, the Taj Mahal of the Far West. He never tired of looking at it.

Off to his right, the Alcatraz boat was just leaving. A covey of gulls swooped low in search of edible debris. Two harangued him raucously.

He held up the empty sack from the fast-food restaurant. "Sorry, guys. No more French fries. Try something radical. Go look for fish." Thoroughly urbanized, the gulls refused to believe him. They settled on a nearby wave-washed rock and eyed him petulantly, in spite of the fact that he'd finished his meal twenty minutes earlier. He didn't blame the gulls. French fries were an easier catch than tuna fry.

There weren't many people out on the point today. Besides himself, he'd seen only two couples. The point was inherently romantic, a fine place to smooch. Cold as it was, with the wind skipping in past the Farallons, you naturally gravitated to your companion in search of body heat. In contrast, Low was alone, unless one counted the fish and the crabs, the plovers and the gulls.

After morning rush hour, the bridge quieted down. He could see the first wall of fog, hovering well outside the gate, waiting for the slight change in temperature that would allow it to roll in and smother bay and city. That business about creeping in on little cat's feet was baloney, Low knew. The fog was an eager opportunist, charging forward to fill every crack and crevice the instant it was meteorologically permissible.

He settled back in his heavy coat, altogether comfortable with his solitude and cholesterol-laden lunch. He did not expect to be disturbed.

That's when he saw a familiar face coming toward him. Harry Page. The NASA representative looked the same as he had the last time they'd met, at the conclusion of some inane official function. Low's last official function. How long ago had that been? Well over a year, anyway.

Now he was here, picking his way awkwardly over the rocks, an anxious expression on his wide, bearded face. It didn't bode well for the rest of the afternoon. It presaged formal conversation, which Low wanted no part of.

He could get up quickly, pretend he didn't see the visitor, and make a dash for his car. Page could never catch him. But Low knew there would be another car somewhere up above, on the access road, probably parked right next to his own. A featureless black or white, wholly functional government car. There would be a driver waiting for Page, and perhaps an assistant.

Resignedly, he wondered what Harry wanted. It must be important for them to send him all the way out here instead of communicating by phone or fax. Important enough to disturb his retirement. He consoled himself a little with the knowledge that Page probably wasn't looking forward to the encounter either.

Then it was too late to attempt a graceful exit, because the NASA rep was waving to him and calling his name. Sensing coming awkwardness, the gulls took flight, deciding to try their luck down by the wharf.

An indifferent Low slipped the crumpled, greasy bag into a jacket pocket. It was the kind of sloppiness that would never have been tolerated on a shuttle mission, and he luxuriated in it, delighting in his Earth-bound status. He had an uneasy sensation that it was about to be disturbed.

"Boston!" Page waved again, with studied enthusiasm. "How ya doin', Boz?"

"I'm fine, Harry. Pull up a rock." Page did his best, and Low watched him squirm uncomfortably. "What brings you out to the edge of the continent?" Low already knew the answer: he waited to hear the corollary.

Page winced. The rocks didn't suit him. Though the two men were about the same age, what was left of the NASA rep's hair was streaked with gray. Low always believed the radiation in Washington was more damaging than any to be encountered in space.

"Partly the food, Boz. I had breakfast down on Fisherman's Wharf this morning. Dungeness crab omelet. Can't get that inside the Beltway."

Riding high in the water, a Liberian-registered container ship was entering the gate, steaming smoothly beneath the bridge. On its way to pick up cargo bound for Yokohama, Low thought. Or Singapore, or Djakarta. He sighed. There was no escape there either. The bureaucrats had conquered the planet, and you had to coexist with them no matter where you lived.

"How long you been looking for me?"

"Since then. I was told this was one of your favorite places." His smile, at least, seemed sincere. "We've missed you, Boston. The program misses you. I still don't understand why you didn't take that administrative position down in Houston. I'll never be offered that kind of salary if I live to be ninety."

"Same reason I opted out of the whole program, Harry." Picking up a small pebble, he chucked it bayward. It struck the water with a satisfying *splook*. "I didn't know what I wanted next, but I knew I wanted out."

Page squinted at the place where the thrusting bridge pierced the underside of Marin. Sunlight ricocheted off the chilly water, harder on his blue eyes than on Low's.

"You heard about the rock?"

Low made a noncommittal noise. "Anybody who hasn't?"

Page chuckled. "Some rice farmer in Bangladesh, maybe, or a Mongol family out on the steppe. Everybody's heard about the rock. You see people all the time, just stopping to stare up at the sky. Wondering if it's going to come down near them. Wondering if it's going to come down *on* them."

Low didn't reply. He was as guilty as anyone else. Especially at night, when you could see it pass overhead. Knowing that with each pass it was sinking a little lower, coming a little nearer. Vindication at last for Chicken Little.

A green crab was ensconced on the moist sand by his feet, using one claw to shove food into its mouthparts like a miner panning for gold. Its body was the size of a silver dollar.

"Anybody ever figure out how the whole astronomical establishment managed to miss its approach?" he heard himself asking.

"Not yet." Page didn't see the crab. Like most of his kind, Page rarely took the time to look down and see what was happening right at his feet. "They're still arguing about it. We're just damn lucky it went into an elliptical instead of coming straight down on top of Saint Louis, or something. At least this way we have a little time to try and do something about it."

"Damn right about that." Low continued to watch the crab. Unlike him, it was perfectly suited to its profession.

"You know that the rock's in a rapidly decaying orbit."

"I'd heard." Low heaved another pebble waterward. A scavenging gull darted toward it, veered off when she saw it wasn't an edible. Her rowdy cry was reproaching. Behind the two men, a young couple in dark jackets were wrapped up in each other, oblivious to gulls, bridge, water, city, and the world in general. Low envied them.

"What are they planning to do about it?"

Page shook his head dolefully. "Man, you really are out of the loop, aren't you?" When Low didn't react, the rep continued. "The Russians are providing us with some state-of-the-art excavation packages. Really sharp stuff, minimal residual rads. Only, they're not going to be used for widening canals or exposing deep ore bodies."

"Kick it out into deep space?" Low inquired casually.

Page shook his head again. "Too much bang required. Probably blow it into a thousand pieces. Big, dangerous pieces. The intent is to just nudge it, stabilize the existing orbit."

"That's asking a helluva lot of the explosives people."

"It's all been worked out." Page exuded confidence. "Even where the poppers are to be placed. Nobody expects any surprises. The operation's already been carried out a hundred times."

"Computer simulation," Low murmured.

"In Houston and at Langley. Results match up every time, to enough places to reassure even the committee people. No margin for error."

"There's always margin for error." Low frowned. The crab had moved on. "Be an awful mess if somebody's figured wrong and it comes down faster."

"They haven't and it won't." Page changed approach. "The President and Congress are kind of enamored of the rock's potential. They see it as a mile-long space station."

Low let out a derisive snort. "I'll bet the toy manufacturers are ahead of the station designers. So they could have a zero-gee bowling alley, so what? Unmanneds can do it safer, cheaper, and better." His left eye twitched, but Page didn't see it.

"Sure they can, but a big, solid platform is an easier sell. Sexier. There's a lot to be said for it, Boston." He leaned a little closer. "We've got to pacify the rock anyway. Why not try to put a favorable spin on it?"

"I suppose." Raising his eyes, Low favored his visitor with that special gaze. The one that only people who have seen the Earth as a blue-white marble possess. It didn't unsettle Page. He'd been the recipient of it many times before, from a number of men and women. Dealing with it, and them, was part of his job. He could handle complex equations and engineering problems, but he could also handle people. Which was why he had been sent to the coast instead of one of the others.

Besides, he'd known Boston Low off and on for more than ten years. As much as anyone could get to know Boston Low.

Like a point guard spotting an opening to the basket, the fog was starting to make its move. Soon both bridge and bay would be hidden by thick white mist, and the mournful howling of the foghorns would resound across the waters like a pride of homesick lions calling to one another in the night. He blinked at his old acquaintance.

"You want me to fly it, don't you, Harry?"

"Not me, Boz." Page glanced up and back toward the road, where others waited. "It's not up to me one way or the other. They wouldn't listen to me if I tried to talk to them about it. I was asked to come and tell you. I did try to tell them what I thought your answer would be."

Low looked away, welcoming the fog. "Then there's no point in my repeating it, is there?"

"It's not that simple. This is a national, an international, emergency, and this is no ordinary shuttle flight."

"No shuttle flight is ordinary," Low mumbled, for lack of a better response. "Remember the *Enterprise*?"

"Of course I remember." Everyone remembered Low's

second flight as commander. A mistake in fueling, contradictory calculations . . . to this day no one knew how the shuttle had been allowed to lift off without enough fuel to make a proper reentry. The very real possibility of burning up on approach. The near supernatural manner in which Low had adjusted, compensated, finessed and tweaked the shuttle's trajectory, skipping it into the upper atmosphere and then out again, in and out, slowing it without the use of the nonexistent fuel, making calculations and decisions without the use of a computer, until it arrived safely at Edwards missing half its nose tiles but without anyone aboard suffering anything more lethal than a deep bruise.

It was called flying, a skill half forgotten in an age of massive parallel computing and redundant backups, of ground control and preordained flight paths. It made Boston Low a national hero. He'd accepted it all quietly and gracefully while turning down all but a few of the endorsement offers. Just enough to supplement his NASA pension.

And when the acclaim had begun to die down, when the reporters no longer camped out on his doorstep waiting for sound bites, he had firmly and without fuss retired. Not to the rolling hills of Virginia or the space centers of Houston or Canaveral, nor to the glamour of Los Angeles nor the perpetual nightlife of New York, but to a simple two-bedroom condo in northwest San Francisco, proximate not to power brokers and politicos but to panhandlers, prostitutes, tourists, illegal immigrants, and the best Chinese food in North America.

Also fog and seagulls. There was a lot of both in Boston Low.

"They want you," he heard Page saying. "They want you bad."

"Who wants me?" He smiled. The crab had returned and was peering up at him from beneath a rock with eyes like black-tipped pushpins.

"The agency. The project scientists and supervisors. The President and Congress."

"I'm forty-two, Harry. I've commanded two shuttle missions and participated in five. Ever heard of pressing your luck? I've had my fill of empty space. The *Enterprise* did that to me. The only space I want to explore anymore is the one inside of me." Tilting back his head slightly, he waved at the sky.

"There's nothing up there to draw me back, and plenty to keep me here. It's dead out there, Harry. Dead and lifeless and cold. When you gaze out and see the whole Earth floating beneath you, it's beautiful, but when you look anywhere else, all you see is the cold empty. Black emptiness. Death."

"Boston, listen . . ." Page began.

"No, you listen, Harry." Low used the voice that made even multiple-term senators shut up. "I've had enough, understand? I'm not afraid, I'm not scared. I've just had enough. That's why I retired. It's called being sensible. So it doesn't matter who 'wants' me."

He looked away, and both were silent for several minutes before Page spoke again, his voice soft but insistent.

"Don't tell me you aren't even a little bit curious to see what's up there, to see what it's like? This is an extraterrestrial, probably extrasolar visitor. This isn't like you, Boz. I remember you being a lot of different things, but indifferent wasn't one of 'em."

"I know what's up there, Harry. I know what it's like. So do you, so does the rest of the establishment. It's a big chunk of rock and metal. That's all. As dead as its immediate environment and no different from the tens of thousands that are drifting around right now between Mars and Jupiter. This one's just a little closer, that's all. Interesting? Sure. Special? I don't think so."

Another moment of reflection, then, "Look, Boston, I don't know how to go about telling you this. As someone who's always spoken his mind, I'm not comfortable with it at all."

Low grinned. "You don't speak your mind, Harry. You're a government functionary and you say what they tell you to say.

You're a good government functionary, though. I'll give you that."

Page grinned back, though much of it was forced. "Okay, so I'm a professional B.S.'er. Call it what you want. As a good government functionary, listen to me. You can't get out of this one, Boz. Even the Russians want you, dammit. And everybody, they're going to get you. So you might as well get used to the idea."

Low wasn't in the least impressed. "You can make a man do a lot of things, Harry, but you can't make him fly a space shuttle. You don't *want* to make him fly a space shuttle."

Page raised both hands defensively. "I told you, it's not me. It's everyone else."

"What are they gonna do, Harry? Threaten me? What are they going to threaten me with? Death, dismemberment? The IRS?"

"I warned them they couldn't intimidate you. I told them it wasn't possible."

Low nodded slowly. "Once you've been Out There, common, ordinary terrestrial threats no longer carry much weight. They all seem pretty much"—he searched for the right description—"weightless."

"Why do you think," Page responded, "they want you to lead this mission? Nothing bothers you, Boston. You're not only not afraid of them, you're not afraid of anything. Everything you're telling me right now underscores your appropriateness for this project."

Low gazed out across the water, wishing the fog would hurry up. You couldn't hurry fog, though. "You're very clever, Harry. Too damn clever. That's why they sent you."

A diffident Page leaned back against a rock. "Just being straightforward." Reaching down, he picked up a pebble of his own and threw it. It didn't reach the water. "You ever think about where that rock's going to come down if it isn't dealt with, Boz? If it isn't pushed just right?" He gestured expansively. "It or a big hunk of it might come down right here. Right in the bay, or on the bridge. Or on your house."

"Could happen anytime in the future too. If not this rock, another."

"Yeah, but not everybody has your fatalistic outlook on time, Boston. If you won't think about yourself, think about all those others. Think about your neighbors. Think about me."

"I am thinking about all the others." Low wanted to take the crab home, but knew it wouldn't live long. "All the others who are qualified to command a mission like this. There's Terrence . . ."

"Terrence the Trance?" Page gave back a look of disbelief.

"All right, what about Woodside, or Turginson, or even Murasaki?"

Page was nodding. "Sure, what about them? Any one of them could probably handle it, and they'd probably do a good job, and they'd probably bring it off. It's all a matter of trying to put together the best package. Of stacking the odds in favor of success. Everybody, everything, says that putting you in charge gives us the best odds."

"Want to know what you can do with the odds?" Low could feel the temperature dropping as the fog began to block out the sun. "Who else would be on the mission?"

Page felt a great weight lift from his shoulders. Low hadn't agreed to come aboard, hadn't consented to participate, had not in actual fact agreed to anything, but he'd stepped over an invisible line. The representative did not pause to savor his accomplishment. He was too grateful to celebrate. That could come later.

"Before I tell you, there's something I've always wanted to know. Something that's been bugging me for years." Low turned to him. "Why *did* your parents name you after the city in which you were born, and why don't you live there instead of here? They're both seaports, both on a coast."

It was Low's turn to chuckle softly. "I grew up there. That was enough. You can grow out of a place, you know. I'm just grateful I wasn't born in Indianapolis, say, or Winnemunca."

Page grinned back at him. "The copilot will be Ken Borden."

Low's response was approving. "Should've guessed."

"I thought you would anyway." Page knew that Borden had flown with Low before and had served as copilot to other captains during the commander's third and fourth missions. Borden was always up, always cheerful, efficient and smart, one of the brightest stars in the program. All he was missing was that little extra something that led Mission Control to designate one pilot as commander and another as backup. No one ever told him that, of course.

Not that he was incapable. Quite the contrary. It was simply that he never seemed to be anyone's first choice. If he was bitter, or disappointed, or ever guessed the truth, he never let on, never complained. Borden was the ultimate team player.

"Ken's a good man," affirmed Low. "We've always been comfortable with each other." Coming from someone like Low, the word *comfortable* carried with it a raft of favorable connotations in the private lexicon of shuttle pilots. "What about the explosives? Are the Russians sending along one of their own people?"

Page shook his head. "Washington and Moscow both want someone who's had some Russian training but is more experienced in shuttle payload procedure. There's not enough time to train an explosives specialist. I'm told the packages are fail-safe and so simple a ten-year-old could set them."

"Oh, now, that's reassuring," Low responded sarcastically.

"Relax. You know Cora Miles?"

"Cora?" Low brightened perceptibly. "She's still in the program?"

"Sure is. What made you think otherwise?"

"I remember Cora as being a little too aggressive to stay with any one enterprise for any length of time. Even the space program. Last I heard she was thinking of running for a House seat."

"She is. This'll probably be her last mission."

"Cora always was good at timing." He laughed under his breath. "That's Cora: unrestrained ambition held in check only by the inability to do a hasty or bad job."

"You disapprove? Because if you want somebody else, Boz, it's your call. All you have to do is—"

"No, no. She'll be fine. You could blindfold her, plug her ears, turn her upside down and spin her around a hundred times and she'd still be able to insert a computer chip into a satellite the size of a city bus utilizing only the shuttle's main manipulator arm. Talk your ear off about her cereal-box endorsement while she was doing it." He smiled at old memories. "Cora'll do just fine.

"I can see her campaign literature now. 'Vote for Cora Miles, the Woman Who Helped Save the Earth!' That ought to snare her a few votes. Who else? Surely not just the three of us?"

Page shifted his backside on the unyielding rocks. "No one wants this mission to be crowded. There's a lot of concern about people bumping into one another or putting forth conflicting suggestions at an awkward moment. You know: the Too Many Cooks school of space travel. Once up, there'll be no time for arguing. You and Borden and Miles could do it. Plant the explosives, step back, check the results and get out. A two-day mission."

"That's something, anyway," Low offered approvingly.

"However," the rep added quickly, "there *will* be two ancillary specialists aboard. They won't get in your way, but their presence has been approved. After all, this is the first close-up look humankind's ever had of an asteroid. The international scientific community will hang us all in effigy if they're not allowed to send at least one of their own along."

"Can't they wait until after the orbit's been stabilized?"

Page shrugged. "The Russians are already talking about putting a *Mir* space station down on its surface. But everybody wants something out of this first visit besides just a big bang." His expression sought understanding. "I'm assured he won't get in your way. I can say that now, can't I? We can count you in?"

Low considered fog and gulls, wondering when he'd see them again. "I suppose." His reply was committed and unenthusiastic. For his visitor's benefit he managed a smile. The same laconic, open smile that had charmed journalists and politicians alike.

"But only because the damn thing might land on my house, and I like it just the way it is."

"Sure, right." Page was almost pathetically grateful.

Low sighed. "When do they want me in Florida?"

His friend was apologetic. "How long will it take you to pack?"

"That's what I thought," Low replied sourly. "Not that I have a lot to put in order. I mean, it's not like there's family or anything."

"I know." Page's voice was perfectly neutral, devoid of any false sympathy. Low appreciated it. "That's another reason they wanted you for this one."

"Yeah. Wrong place for a family man. This way, anything goes wrong, no wife and kids have to suffer along with the old man. The fewer there are to take the blame, the better. That's agency policy: always looking ahead."

Page observed simply, "The car's waiting. You won't have to take the bus back."

Low nodded curtly as he rose. There was no point in trying to explain to someone like Page that he liked to ride the bus, or why.

It felt strange to be back at Canaveral. Moist and steamy instead of moist and cool, the air hung heavy on him like a soggy bathrobe. It seemed to pool up in his lungs, making breathing an effort instead of a pleasure. The terrain was flat rather than hilly, the vegetation gnarled instead of straight and orderly. The gulls were a familiar presence, the alligators definitely not. Any vibration underfoot was caused by the movement of massive machines instead of the ground itself.

I've left my heaaart, in San Francisco, he sang silently to himself. Also wallet, fish, friends, and lifestyle. He hadn't brought along so much as a driver's license. Wasn't required, to drive a space shuttle.

Those who didn't know him, visitors and workers new to the program, misinterpreted his silence as stress. It was left to others to explain that Boston Low was immune to stress in the same way some people were immune to measles or whooping cough. If there existed such a thing as an antistress gene, it was intimately interwoven in the commander's DNA. Informed that a nuclear bomb was about to go off in his immediate vicinity, Low's response would most likely be a diffident, "Oh well."

He found the physical plant pretty much unchanged from the time when the spaceport had served as both home and office. He took note of new paint, matured landscaping, and the sizable new assembly building for the *Minerva Deepspace* probe. A sweeping, glassed-in observation deck to appease visitors and tourists completed the most recent renovations.

Minerva was twenty years from launch, he knew, and he wondered if he'd live long enough to see it lift off. Much depended on the development of the Russian *Proton III* launch vehicle, along with the size of NASA's budget. Easier to deal with the failings of science than the whims of Congress, he mused. At the same time he wondered why he cared.

Off in the distance were the two shuttle platforms. The ship itself would still be in the assembly building, being prepped and readied by an army of technicians. Though their components were designed to be interchangeable, each craft had its own individual superstitions, a fact that the men and women who flew them knew. As did the pilots. Low's was that he never mentioned the name of whatever shuttle he was flying until it had safely achieved booster separation.

A small superstition, quite unjustifiable in a scientifically enlightened age. Especially for a pilot like Low. On the other hand he'd survived five shuttle missions; two as commander, one a near disaster, and saw no reason to change his personal modus operandi.

Staff and visiting space buffs alike recognized him; the former staring a moment before looking away, the latter voluble to the point of rudeness. He was the hero of the *Enterprise,* and won't you please sign this for my little boy/girl/niece/nephew/Aunt Clotilde, Commander Low? His casual attire was no disguise. Frequently he paused and signed, knowing even as he did so that his signature was destined for shoeboxes and dusty drawers. His reluctance always gave way to inherent courtesy.

He'd tried and failed to get out of attending the reception. Need your presence, old chap, Page and the others had insisted. You're a reassuring influence. Good for the program. Won't you pretty-please come? Didn't anyone understand that he was better at navigating clouds than canapes, better at explaining equipment failure than at making small talk?

Small talk, small people. Clenching his jaws, he stepped into the meeting room.

It was door-to-derriere with mission specialists, spaceport personnel, hangers-on, would-be hangers-on, the privileged and friends of the privileged, a few captains (or at least lieutenants) of industry, and those ubiquitous high-profile journalists who were nominal friends of the space program but who would desert its cause in an instant in favor of a high-profile murder case, especially if a celebrity or two were involved. There were also several famous science-fiction writers trying hard to pick up women young enough to be their daughters, as well as more U.S. senators than one was likely to encounter outside a major committee meeting.

Feeling as out of place as a fern on the slopes of Erebus, Low made a beeline for the open bar. The crowd worked to his advantage: No one called out to him. With eyes only for busy bottles and the tip jar, the bartenders ignored him.

Thus safely ensconced in a relative haven, he shook a few hands and bestowed a few smiles. He'd been through worse, especially after the *Enterprise* flight. A few faces he was half glad to see: engineers, programmers, others he had worked with. The delight in their eyes when they recognized him was an embarrassment. Low wore his celebrity like a pair of two-sizes-too-small sneakers.

Each face brought back memories, not all pleasant. Memories of hard work and long days, of sacrifice mental as well as physical. Of the kind of personal, inner satisfaction a man gets from doing a job better than anyone else can. Of friendships made and lost, of laughter and violent disagreement.

Experiments, satellite repairs, spacewalks. All easy in weightlessness, weren't they? What the public didn't, couldn't, know was that the less weight a man's body has to carry, the greater the burden on the mind. In space Low became a hundred-and-eighty-pound brain. Headaches were more than inconvenient; they could prove fatal.

Better to let the mass of muscles and blood vessels and nerves and water do most of the work, he knew. That's what he'd been doing for some time now, letting the rest of the corpus lug around a tired brain. The chimps had it right all along.

The similarity of some of those populating the meeting room to man's nearest genetic relative was striking. He amused himself by inventing more direct comparisons. At least chimpanzees didn't lie.

Then why was he there? He knew the answer, as did Page and the rest. Boston Low might no longer be an active participant in the space program, but that didn't mean he wanted to see it fail, didn't mean he wished for mankind to remain forever Earthbound. Low hoped for his brethren to reach the stars.

He just no longer particularly wanted to go there himself.

Yet here he was once again, pressing the flesh in advance of the instrumentation, doing his part. While others availed themselves of the open bar, he settled as usual for carbonated liquid sugar. From the middle of the room Borden waved at him. Low nodded in response. Ken wouldn't violate his privacy, Low knew. His copilot thrived on the attention and would gladly gather it about himself, thereby freeing Low of the necessity to share.

During the previous weeks' simulation they'd meshed easily, each complementing the other, a perfect pairing in the ground-based shuttle cockpit. Other than a few hellos, they'd spoken little, not out of an aversion to talk but because there was no need. Each man understood the other, knew his strengths and weaknesses. Borden knew that Low was no fun and so let him be. Low knew the same and was aware that Borden wouldn't miss him.

He envied his copilot's easy way with a crowd, with the fawning sycophants who hovered about the space program. Technological groupies they were, and he had no use for them. Borden flaunted the nectar of his renown and drew them off, even as Low kept his petals closed.

The important thing was that Borden didn't need the adulation. He simply enjoyed it.

When the crowd briefly parted, he saw Cora Miles flanked by two congressmen from California and the senior senator from her home state of Texas. Talking campaign strategy, no doubt. Probably telling her that saving the world from looming catastrophe was all very well and good, but it wouldn't guarantee election to the House. Not that it wouldn't give her a leg up on her opponents, Low mused.

There was one man he badly wanted to meet. He was supposed to be in attendance, but so far Low hadn't spotted him. When he finally did, there was no mistaking the individual for anyone else. The striking blue eyes beneath the protruding forehead, the chiseled features, the short blond hair and stocky build, all were instantly recognizable from the photos that graced the back covers of numerous book jackets. As if that weren't enough, the tall glass of dark beer the man held like a conductor's baton was conclusive.

Recognition was simultaneous and mutual. The man pushed his way through the crowd to join Low. Swapping the beer from right hand to left, he smiled without showing any teeth and extended an open palm.

"Ludger Brink, Commander Low. It is a true pleasure. *Wie gehts?*"

"Not too bad. What do you think of all this?"

The scientist made a face. "Publicity. Personally, I prefer the times when wealthy aristocrats underwrote pure science. Politicians have no class. But then, it is not their approval that we seek, *nicht wahr?* Only open checkbooks."

Low simply smiled and raised his cola. Brink was coming along as the representative of the EEC space authority. NASA could have insisted on another one of its own, but the exigencies of good public relations demanded otherwise.

Besides, Brink was eminently qualified. Not only was he one of the world's two or three leading experts on meteorites and asteroids, with a shelf full of books and well-respected papers on the subject to his credit, he had spent months, not days, in space, as a researcher aboard the *Mir II* space station. He'd done four spacewalks and his fluency in Russian would allow him to decipher any cryptic instructions that accompanied the critical explosives packages. His other specialty was extraterrestrial seismology, with particular reference to Ionian volcanism.

Appropriately then, the small bit of colorful embroidery that decorated the front of his short-sleeved shirt was not of a crocodile or polo player, but of Mons Olympica.

Low couldn't vouch personally for the scientist's command of Russian, but his English was virtually flawless, with only the slightest suggestion of Teutonic tartness. According to his dossier, Brink was also conversant (if not fluent) in French, Italian and, of all things, Turkish. Equally important to Low, the man's handshake was firm and easy. He carried himself with the kind of confidence only those who are the very best at what they do, and know it, can manage.

That suited Low just fine. He had no use on a shuttle mission for anyone who was subject to second-guessing, or who doubted his or her own abilities. Such indulgences required time. Along with air, that was the one commodity a shuttle crew did not have to spare.

"I wish we had more time to prepare and get to know each other, Commander, but the asteroid will not wait."

Low replied approvingly. He, too, would have preferred more preflight preparation time. It was encouraging that Brink felt the same.

"I know. Nice to meet you, finally." He glanced around the crowded room. "Wish we had a day or two to talk privately."

"*Warum?* Why? You know what you have to do, I know what I have to do. If a machine is properly engineered, the parts should fit together correctly the first time it is turned on. If not, then it is the fault of the designers, not of the parts."

"Can't argue with that." Low knew that Brink would carry out his work efficiently and as instructed. He just didn't know if he was the kind of guy you'd want to invite down to the local sports bar to watch the big game.

Not that it mattered. They were only going to be living together for a few days, during which time they'd both be far too busy to worry about establishing any kind of close camaraderie. One of the benefits, Low knew, of a short mission. He was looking to get it over with, not to initiate any long-term friendships.

Brink looked as well as sounded capable. Low knew he wouldn't have been picked for this mission if it had been otherwise. But it was still good to finally meet him. As for his personality, that bothered Low not at all. He looked at it in much the same way as he did when he was choosing a doctor. Give him the crass, crabby, impersonal and efficient over the smiling, joking, easygoing and incompetent any day.

"I'm sure we'll get along fine," he told the German. "As for the mission, I've had to do much more delicate work than this out there. This is pretty much a go in, do a couple hours' work and get out. After that, it's out of our hands."

"That is the way I see it. My only wish would be for more time on the surface of the object." He shrugged. "But this is not primarily a scientific mission. There are too many political considerations."

"Yeah, I know." The longer they talked, the better Low felt about the mission scientist. Despite different backgrounds and specialties, it was clear they shared a disdain for administrative and bureaucratic interference. He wondered if the other man disliked these official command functions as much as he did.

"What about the, um, packages we're supposed to deliver?"

Brink's polite smile faded. It was hard to smile when talking about nuclear explosives, especially when you were going to get personal with them.

"They are already here. I have spent the past several days going over them with the team from Irkutsk. Among their number are two people who have been involved with the most recent utilization of such devices. You are familiar with that foolishness about melting the permafrost over the entire Khovanchi ore body?"

"Afraid not," Low responded diffidently. "I'm not much on keeping up with developments in international mining."

"No, of course not. Anyway, you should know from your own preparations that the devices are typical of Russian manufacture and design. That is to say, they are simple and straightforward. You do this, this, and that, in the prescribed order, and you get a big bang. If it works." To Low's surprise, the scientist then waved in the general direction of the room's crowded middle.

"Are you enjoying this?"

"What do you think?" Low took a sip of his cola.

The corners of Brink's mouth curled upward. "It is impossible to avoid this sort of nonsense. Big science takes big money. It is the same in Germany, in Europe. If one desires the freedom to do original research, one must pay as much attention to the media as to the microscope."

"I understand. Tell me, Ludger, what do we really know about the object? I know you've been heavily involved in the preliminary studies."

Brink shrugged. "A little. The object is fascinating for many reasons, aside from the doomsday scenario that it has precipitated. Much of the scientific community's interest lies in trying to find out where it came from, whether it is a stray from the Mars-Jupiter belt or extrasolar. If extrasolar"—and his eyes shone—"it can be a real window into the chemistry of the galaxy.

"From what we have been able to learn so far, I should say that it is a typical mesosiderite, part rock and part metal. The proportions are of great interest, as the density appears to vary."

"So it's all stone and nickel-iron?"

"Not at all, Commander. There is pyroxene and plagioglase as well as evidence of olivine crystals."

"Then it's a pallasite?"

Brink smiled approvingly. "Much too early to say. One

this size would be unprecedented. I cannot wait until I can walk upon its surface and see it in person."

"With gravity that light, you won't be doing any walking."

"A figure of speech, Commander." Brink did not appear offended by the correction. "It would be equally fascinating to study it after its passage through the atmosphere. But of course that is what we are charged with preventing." Something beyond Low caught his attention.

"Ah, I see Ms. Robbins approaching. No doubt she will want to talk with you as well."

Low frowned. "Robbins? I don't know any Ms. Robbins."

"You will, Commander. No doubt she wants yet another interview, and I have already given mine. Now, if you will excuse me, I espy a fatuous industrialist of great reputation and wealth who fancies himself an amateur scientist. I shall take it upon myself to relieve him of some of his money in the form of a grant promise while encouraging him in his harmless dementia." This time it was he who extended a hand.

"A pleasure to meet you at last, Boston Low. I have complete confidence in your abilities and in the success of our forthcoming endeavor. After all the intense preparation, I expect the mission itself to be something of an anticlimax. I look forward to it nonetheless." With a last handshake and half-smile, he broke away. Low could see him bobbing off through the crowd, his head rising and falling amid the suits like a sea otter in a bed of black and navy-blue kelp.

"Commander Boston Low?"

Turning, he found himself confronting a face that was known to him, though what lay behind it was as much an enigma as that of the personality of any complete stranger. If you lived within the boundaries of the United States, you'd have to have spent your life in a cave not to know Maggie Robbins. She was one of the most famous telejournalists in the country, a regular on a highly rated newszine, and noted for her reports from hard-to-reach, faraway places. Low had watched her himself but without making any personal connections. Up until this moment she had been nothing more than another eminent talking head.

Despite her comparative youth she had already reached a level in her profession that the majority of her counterparts would never, despite a lifetime of striving, achieve. Her rise had been, and Low had to smile to himself, nothing less than meteoric.

Her presence did not delight him. Low liked interviews about as much as he'd once enjoyed escorting groups of VIPs around the Cape, an onerous burden to which all astronauts had once been subjected by administrative fiat. He steeled himself for her questions. Lamentable though it might be, public relations was a part of his job.

If naught else, she was certainly one of the more attractive interviewers he'd been compelled to deal with.

She was pumping his hand and mouthing platitudes. Her handshake was solid; not the little half-sliding grasp so many women were fond of, the one that made you feel as if you'd been kissed by a thrush.

"Well, it's about time," she declared firmly. "I was beginning to wonder if you really existed or if they were just going to stick a cardboard cutout of you in the pilot's seat and send the ship up on automatics."

"You're half right." He was a bit taken aback by her enthusiasm and energy. "Computers do most of the flying."

"So maybe it's only your personality that's cardboard. I guess I'll find out."

"I beg your pardon?" he replied politely.

Her brows dipped slightly toward each other. "You know that I've been assigned by my network to do a comprehensive report on the whole project?" Before he could respond, she added, "You should know that every reporter on the planet wanted this assignment and that NASA gave it to me. I think that's because of my history of support for the space program and also because I'm comfortable working on what some people would call far-out stories. Far out geographically as well as in subject matter." This was all delivered at a speed that left Low slightly breathless.

Searching for an appropriate response, he mumbled, "I think I saw a piece you did last year on the latest *Viking* mission."

"Yes, that was me. Nice of you to remember. I've talked about you too."

"Oh?" he murmured, wondering whether he should be surprised.

"Part of my ongoing reporting on the space program. Of course everybody did something on the *Enterprise*." She smiled engagingly.

An odd sort, Low thought. Sophisticated and ultraknowledgeable but with the perkiness of a college senior. It was that charm, that air of harmless, girlish enthusiasm, that had allowed her to obtain interviews with reluctant and even dangerous personalities in Africa and Asia. That, and a boundless energy that was as impossible to resist as it was to ignore.

As a top-of-her-profession reporter, she also possessed the tenacity of a pit bull and the directness of a cobra. While openly friendly, he was also immediately on guard, knowing that anything he might say or let slip was likely to show up on the evening news, possibly out of context.

"Yes, everybody did." He strove to make small talk. "I'm sure you'll do a fine report on the project."

"You can bet on that. I expect it to be right up there with my exclusive interview with the chief of the Iranian underground last year and the head of the Chinese dissident movement the year before that. Those were both done on-site, you know? After wearing a chador for three months, I don't think a space suit will bother me."

"I seem to remember hearing about the Iranian thing," he told her, not at all sure that he had. "Congratulations." It sounded like she was going to try doing a report from inside a shuttle suit. You had to admire her quest for verisimilitude.

"This is going to be bigger, much bigger. I promise. And you won't have to worry about me. I'll stay out of the way, I won't touch anything or do anything unless I'm specifically instructed to, I won't interfere with operations in any fashion."

"Good of you to say so, but there really isn't much you can get into once the shuttle's off the ground." She could wander around Mission Control all she wanted, he knew. Experienced reporters did it all the time.

She wasn't through. "I've been preparing myself for this ever since they first detected the object. I knew they were going to send a ship up there. Like everybody else, I just didn't know they were going to try to move it."

"We're not going to move it," he quietly corrected her. "We're just going to alter its trajectory a little."

"Yeah, that." She shook her head as she remembered something. "Those tests they put you through are as tough as climbing the mountains in East Timor. At least you don't have to deal with torrential rain and leeches. But no problem." She smiled ingratiatingly. "I passed them all. Knew I would. Had a little trouble with balance, but nothing serious. Not enough to keep me off the mission."

Low blinked. "Excuse me. 'Off the mission'? I guess I don't understand."

She gawked at him. "You mean they haven't told you? There are five people scheduled to go aboard. Who did you think the fifth one was?"

"You?" It was his turn to gape. "I expected another specialist, like Ludger Brink." His thoughts, so arduously pacified in preparation for the party, were now stirring afresh.

For the second time in as many minutes, he found himself bathed in that ingenue-with-a-doctorate smile. "No, it's going to be me. Don't worry. Like I told you, I'll stay completely out of the way."

With difficulty he subdued his rampaging emotions. "You'll stay out of the way, all right." Raising himself on tiptoes, he searched the crowd and lifted his voice. "Page? Harry Page!" The representative who'd been assigned to Low ever since he'd committed was nowhere to be seen, having providentially vanished from sight. Though he'd seen him earlier, Low suspected he wasn't going to see him again this night.

"Come on, Commander. I know there's a difference in our ages, but surely it's not that significant. What are you going to do next: tell me that space is no place for a woman?" She eyed him challengingly.

He continued to search the crowded meeting room for signs of Page or any other high-ranking agency rep. There were none in his immediate vicinity. As opposed to this persistent, eager woman, who was practically inside his jacket.

Without looking at her he replied, "Why don't you ask Cora Miles about that? If you're trying to provoke me, you're going to have to come up with something better than ancient, discredited clichés."

She wasn't in the least nonplussed. "They told me nothing bothered you. Just checking."

Temporarily giving up on his search, he let his eyes meet hers. He didn't need to say anything. His gaze conveyed everything he was thinking: that she was unqualified, ignorant of what she was getting herself into, and that he considered her to be nothing more than excess baggage.

"Whew!" She fanned herself melodramatically. "Turn it off, Commander. You're not going to scare me or make me change my mind."

He relaxed the intensity of his gaze. "Actually, you're right, you know. Space is no place for a woman. Or for a man, or for a fruit fly. It's no place for any combination of proteins and amino acids that likes to think of itself as alive and wants to go on living. If you relax for one second, it'll kill you quickly, unpleasantly, and with all the indifference of a void. You've done reports on the space program. Ever done one on what exposure to vacuum can do to the human body? Ever wondered what it would be like to open your mouth for a breath of fresh air and have only cold emptiness to suck? You know what explosive decompression is?" Without waiting for a response, he proceeded to explain, in great detail, taking no pleasure in the recital but leaving nothing out.

All the while she waited and listened, maintaining her infuriatingly cheerful grin.

"Is that all?" she commented when he'd finished. "You know, I've studied all of it, Commander. I'm fully aware of the dangers and the hazards. All I can say is that I'd rather deal with the risks of space travel in the company of experts like Cora Miles and Ken Borden and yourself than spend half an hour in a tropical downpour trying to pry a python's jaws off my cameraman's arm with the aid of a couple of newswriters from New York, which experience I've already had.

"I once spent an entire evening watching three unpleasant, unshaven men with AK-forty-sevens slap my hostess around, trying to get her to admit to spying for the CIA. They kept threatening to start on me when they were finished with her. You're not going to frighten me off, Commander, so you might as well get used to the idea of having me around.

"No matter where I've been or what I've done, I've always come out of it in one piece. Unless you and your accomplices don't do your jobs properly, I expect to emerge from this experience in similar condition. Your own people tell me that as shuttle missions go, this should be a comparative milk run. It's short and you have only one objective instead of dozens or hundreds to carry out." She relaxed.

"If you can handle all that, I think you'll be able to deal with a few questions. You won't even know I'm around. Think of me as a large, irregularly shaped videocamera and we'll get along just fine." She eyed him expectantly.

She exuded a different kind of professional confidence than Brink, he decided. In its own way it was no less unshakable. Don't judge her by her looks or drive, he told himself. She wasn't likely to panic in a difficult situation, or quail before the unexpected. If a schoolteacher could be sent on a shuttle mission, why not a journalist?

That wasn't the problem of course. The problem was that it was *this* shuttle mission. Her presence was one more extraneous inclusion he'd have to worry about. Not that it would be the first time.

This close to liftoff he knew he was unlikely to change any minds. Page wasn't likely to be of any help, nor were any of his ilk. Someone, or several important someones, had decided to ordain her presence aboard. She was assigned cargo, and he'd just have to deal with her. She was impressive, but cargo nonetheless. He might as well make the best of it.

He eyed her anew, trying to see her as a fellow mission participant instead of dead weight. Could she help out, do anything useful? She was the modern analog of one of those elegant old cast-iron carnival fortune-tellers. Drop in a million dollars and it asks questions.

"You're either a very brave woman," he remarked finally, "or a very stupid one."

She grinned back at him. "Both hallmarks of the successful network journalist, Commander Low." She scooped a glass from a passing waiter's tray. "Drink?"

"Got one." He gestured with the remnants of his soft drink.

"Ah yes, I remember." Her tone turned Shakespearean. "The bold and resolute commander doesn't smoke and doesn't drink." She favored him with a sideways glance that could have supported a hundred different interpretations. "So what do you do?"

Low was not a particularly imaginative man, but neither was he a complete social ignoramus. He chose to ignore subtle implications. "I walk a lot. In the woods, along the beach, through the city. If you don't mind my asking, Ms. Robbins . . ."

She cut him off. "The only thing I mind is you calling me 'Ms. Robbins.' Try 'Maggie.' The Ayatollah wouldn't, but everybody else does."

"Any particular ayatollah?"

"All of 'em. You wonder how they manage to reproduce their own kind." Her smile widened. "You're trying to distract me, aren't you? I'm surprised. I thought you'd be pumping me for reasons or qualifications."

"Why?" He swirled the ice at the bottom of his glass, an intimate interlude in hydraulics and fluid physics. "You don't have any. Not that it matters. This late in the game I can't do anything about it anyway."

She nodded slowly and her expression changed to one of studied sincerity. "I meant what I said, Commander. I won't get in your way and I won't cause any trouble. Should any kind of emergency arise, I think you'll find me a fast learner. If I wasn't"—and the smile returned—"I'd have been dead a dozen times over in as many years."

"I don't doubt that."

"You're a national, no, an international hero, but don't expect me to venerate you. As far as I'm concerned, you're just the pilot and I'm only a passenger."

"I never asked to be venerated," Low snapped back. He was beginning to wish he'd accepted her offer of harder liquid. "I just wanted to do my job."

"Which you've done, better than anyone else in your highly specialized profession. That's why you're running this mission. That's why I'm going along. I'm just as good at what I do as you are at what you do." It didn't seem possible, but she managed to move a little closer. "People who are the best in the world at what they do have no reason to argue among themselves. We stand above the rest, Commander. I hope you'll find my presence complementary instead of antagonistic."

"I guess I will. As long as you remember that it was politics and public relations that put you aboard and not any particular skills that relate to the carrying out of the actual mission."

She bristled visibly, then took a healthy swig from her glass. "You know, I'm very good at reading people. Something of an expert. I think I can read you. You're tough. You'd have to be, doing what you do, doing what you've done. Right now you're testing me, trying to get a rise out of me, checking to see how I'll respond to a challenge. Even a small one, such as an oblique insult. It doesn't bother me. I've been insulted by experts." When he didn't respond, she said, "Well, do I pass?"

Reaching out with careful deliberation he took the glass

from her unresisting fingers, eyed the contents, and sipped. His face wrinkled and he passed it back to her.

"God, the swill they serve at these official functions!"

"I know, it's dreadful, isn't it?" She deliberately took another swallow. "But when you have to do as much talking as I do, anything that soothes the throat is welcome."

"Anything?" His eyebrows lifted.

She hesitated and her grin returned. "You make do with whatever's available. I fully expect, you know, to get a book out of this experience along with my daily reports. I expect to win a Pulitzer. Came close two years ago when I cracked the Mayan forgeries. You remember that?"

"Oddly enough, I do. Don't remember you, though."

"That's right, Commander, keep testing. I'll keep passing. It's good that you don't remember me. It means that the journalism carried more of an impact than any personalities. I'll take it as a compliment." She searched his face. She wasn't much shorter than he was, though it felt otherwise. Boston Low had a way of making people feel small. It was the same with the Russian cosmonauts, physically short men all.

"You could do worse than be stuck with me. Keep that in mind. I'll see you later, Boston Low."

Without waiting to give him a chance for the last word (not that he wanted it anyway), she turned abruptly and disappeared into the crowd. She was of the sort who wouldn't be happy unless they always had the last word, he knew. He tracked her until he could no longer see her.

Yes, he had to admit, he could have done worse. She was engaging, intelligent, persistent, and easy on the eyes. All that really mattered, though, was if she would prove as good as her word and stay out of the way. That and that alone would make her welcome in his eyes.

Offered a choice, though, he would have preferred to have onboard another fifty kilos of atmosphere.

CHAPTER

4

Taking into account both cargo and crew, it was well nigh the lightest shuttle load in the history of the program. There was even some talk among the more cost-conscious of including the latest backup weather satellite in the mission, or one of the two new South American communications packages scheduled to be orbited later in the year.

This practical suggestion was quickly voted down. Not because the shuttle and crew couldn't handle an additional deployment, but because on this mission, more than any that had preceded it, there could be no distractions.

Low relaxed in the pilot's chair and with his practiced, experienced eye scanned readouts he thought he'd never see again except in a movie. They'd changed hardly at all, and he'd been thoroughly checked out on the most recent modifications and additions. The calm voice of Mission Control whispered in his headset. There was a hypnotic quality to it, as there was to the complete moment.

Any minute now, he told himself. Any minute now I'll wake up, and I'll be lying on the damp banks of Redwood Creek, or waiting for the almond cookies to come out of the oven at Hung Fat's, or watching some family from Iowa trying to deal with Dungeness crab out back of Scaparelli's.

He blinked. The readouts didn't blink back, and he sighed resignedly. What to most of humanity was the opportunity for great adventure he saw only as a job to get over with. Which, although he did not consciously realize it, was the safest approach to take.

Viewed through the shuttle's windows, the sky above the Cape was a perfect cerulean blue. There were no clouds, no wind, and no incipient hurricanes waiting to ambush liftoff. There would be no weather delays, which suited Low fine. He hated delays of any kind. They got in the way of life.

People asked him if he ever became used to it. He hardly knew how to answer them. How did one become "used" to strapping oneself to the tip of a gigantic bomb and riding it into space, trying to monitor a thousand things at once while knowing that the next nanosecond could easily be the last one of your existence? One didn't grow used to such things. What people never seemed to understand was that the thoughts were always much worse than any reality.

Might as well grow used to the thought of drifting forever in the icy void, engines useless, waiting for the last breath of air to escape from your lungs, waiting for the numbness to begin in your fingers and toes, waiting for . . .

Stop that, he ordered himself. In seventy-two hours it would all be over, done with, and he could stop worrying. Stop thinking. Sequestered among more important instruments, the chronometer would count it down for him. Seventy-two hours and they would be back where they'd started. The weather was expected to hold, and there'd be no need to divert to Edwards. A short mission. A milk run.

There would be congratulations, the requisite debriefing and then he could slip away. Back to where people didn't give a damn who you were. Back to the other, wilder sea. Back to where he'd left his heart. Seventy-two hours.

"Let's get moving," he muttered under his breath.

"You say something, Boz?" Borden spoke without taking his eyes from the readouts and instrumentation that were his responsibility.

"Yeah. I was wondering if the physicists are wrong and our rock is actually made of green cheese."

"Maybe it's a cheese ball." Borden nudged a switch. "You

know: soft inside, hard and crunchy on the outside." The co-pilot was the sort who'd happily don a lampshade and dance on a tabletop to liven up a party. Later and with equal glee, he'd effortlessly calculate the spatial relationship between shade, skull, table, floor, and the chest of the nearest attractive woman. He was equally adroit at risqué limericks and differential calculus.

"Somewhere there's a guy with a degree in food chemistry who's devoted his life to cheese." Low turned slightly in his seat. "Don't you think so, Ludger?"

Behind him the scientist chuckled softly. "You are being irrelevant, Commander."

"Wish I was." Low gently caressed a small dial. He was a long way from the redwoods. A long ways from any woods. Dark and deep, he mused. "Stand by, everyone."

"This is so exciting!" Robbins's irrepressible enthusiasm bordered on gushing. Low hated gushing.

"Sure is." Beside her, Cora Miles waited patiently, counting votes as she lay back in her seat. Until they were on the job, there was little for her to do. She'd already rehearsed her work, not to mention suitable sound bites for the media.

Low was glad his copilot and Mission Control specialist were so outgoing. Like fin whales confronting a shoal of krill, they'd filter out the reporters before they could reach him. To Low, lack of attention was a blessing, not an omission.

"Everyone okay back there? Ms. Robbins?"

"Fine, just fine, Commander." Other than a slight tightness in her voice, she seemed to be doing well, he decided. Probably too busy concocting opening lines for her initial report to deal with the reality of what they were about to do. "I am having trouble with something, though."

They were very near to liftoff. Low's response was sharp with concern. "What is it, Ms. Robbins? We don't have much time."

"This won't take much time." He felt her staring at him. "If you don't stop calling me 'Ms. Robbins' and start calling me Maggie I'm going to open all my reports that quote you thusly: 'The unbendingly formal and stuffy Commander Low said today . . .'."

"Suit yourself . . . Maggie." In his ear the voice of Mission Control was beginning the ritual of counting down the remaining seconds verbally. It was an anachronism from the early days of spaceflight, turgid and melodramatic. No one had suggested doing away with it. Doing so would have sent the public-relations people ballistic.

There was something else he wanted to tell her, but the cheery Borden stole his speaking space. "Don't sweat it, Maggie. I've been on roller coasters that throw you around worse."

Me too, Low thought, *but none with the potential to blow me to bits.*

Then there were only seconds left, too few and too much to do in them, and finally not even that. A great roar, more vibration than sound, began beneath and behind them. Too overwhelming to allow for casual conversation or nervous jokes, it rose in volume until it dominated the universe.

Then they were moving, the entire complex cylindrical skyscraper rising from its foundations and reaching, clawing at the sky. Slowly at first, accelerating steadily, kept from tumbling by patient internal gyros and high-speed programs, hearing none of the cheers that accompanied their Promethean ascent, they rose into the blue as had dozens before them.

Their destination was similar but their goals very different. This time they were going not to visit the cosmos but to interact with a piece of it.

Low's entire body was vibrating like a violin string as he monitored a dozen, a hundred readouts. Beside him, Borden had begun to whistle softly. Low recognized the wordless march from the last movement of Brian's Gothic symphony. Subsequent to ignition and in defiance of her stubborn sophistication, Maggie Robbins had uttered a gasp of astonishment. She was quiet now, and Low had no time to spare to check on whether she was gaping in amazement or had lapsed into unconsciousness. Coddling would have to wait until the engines had finished firing.

No matter how much they tried to prepare you for it, no simulation could really come close to duplicating the sensation of rising atop that thundering spire of metal and plastic and ceramic alloy, a darkening sky rushing at you and burning hell at your back. The Hand was on him now, pressing against his face and chest and lower body, shoving him back into his chair, trying to keep him from doing his job. It was a rough caress, invited and familiar. Before his eyes, light blue gave way to navy, then purple, fading, like the end of a film, to black.

The stars came out, and he did not rejoice in their reacquaintance.

Though to all outward appearances he was as calm and at ease as any tourist on the rear deck of a cruise ship, he did not truly begin to relax until the two massive solid-fuel boosters had been jettisoned and the main engine had fully ignited. The bomb at his backside had been reduced in strength but not defused.

"Burn, you sonuvabitch, burn!" he murmured to himself. In the increasing absence of atmosphere, the main engine complied softly, whispering fire. Beneath his determined, active gaze the shuttle's instruments, like so many tiny electronic gnomes, peered back at him, reeking of normalcy. He relaxed a little more.

Behind him, Brink was muttering aloud in German. Low caught a few words but was too busy to go hunting for more. For the first time since he'd made her acquaintance, Robbins was silent. Whether she was awed or unconscious, it made no difference to him. Well, maybe a little, he chided himself. He was being too hard on her. Miles would be resting patiently, waiting for orbital insertion before she could start checking out the shuttle's arm. Borden had stopped whistling and was reciting a poem that began, "There was a young lady from Mars, whose husband got lost in the stars."

Low had heard it before. His copilot was behaving normally, as was the ship. To others *normal* might translate as "dull." To Low it was pure bliss. Let others "Challenge the heavens, and assail the affrighted stars!" as the quote went. Give him monotony and routine and he was a happy camper.

Mission Control barked congratulations, which Low let the effusive Borden acknowledge. Follow-ups and checkouts continued unbroken. There was no room on a shuttle flight for anything less than perfection. At least there was no room for it on a flight commanded by Boston Low.

For the first time since liftoff he allowed himself to think about their cargo. Three small, unprepossessing metal containers, any one of which was capable of vaporizing the shuttle and its occupants as instantaneously and thoroughly as a soap bubble in a blast furnace. Two had been designated for use, with the third as backup. If their initial efforts proved successful, it would be disarmed, taken apart, and jettisoned.

Far below, the President was accepting congratulations and well-wishes from representatives of the media, friends, political allies, and assorted sycophants. He smiled and waved, accepting as his due the implication that he had organized the mission, chosen the personnel, scripted their individual tasks, and built the shuttle in his backyard out of spare parts.

It all went with the political territory, Earle knew. If something went well, you could claim all the credit. If it failed, you blamed Congress, or NASA, or international terrorists. Standing on the platform watching lesser lights swarm about the Chief Executive, he was glad of his own comparative anonymity and privacy. He wouldn't have been President had the powers that be begged him to take the job, even if it came with all the money and power in the world. Not even billionaires could buy privacy, far less ranking politicians.

Someone would have to be unrelievedly ambitious to want the post, he mused. Or incredibly bored.

Then the media, having fed and been sated, moved off in search of nourishing sound bites elsewhere, herded along by snapping assistants. The President glanced around and, spotting Earle, started in his direction. At his approach the Science Advisor struggled to wrench his gaze back from the sweeping window, from the place in the sky where a tiny speck was on the verge of vanishing.

Fraser was relaxed and at ease. "Well, Willy, if everything goes as well as the launch, we'll all be heroes by the middle of next week. If not"—he shrugged philosophically—"we still have time to try again. You know that the *Independence* is being readied for backup and a crew is being briefed."

"Yes, sir." It was no secret. The President was just making conversation. "As to trying again, that depends."

The Chief Executive made a face. "Depends? What are you talking about, Willy? What could happen? I've been assured that the explosives onboard the *Atlantis* aren't powerful enough to break up the asteroid."

"I know, sir." Earle forced a smile. "You know me. I'm just a worrier. I'm paid to worry. There's very little chance of anything going seriously wrong. It's just that nothing like this has ever been attempted before, and reality has a way of pitching out surprises that haven't been anticipated in the simulations."

The President clapped a friendly hand on the older man's shoulder and stared out the window, searching the sky for that which had already disappeared from sight. "One thing you learn in politics is not to anticipate trouble, Willy."

"Tell that to my wife's brother in Bethesda, sir. He was supposed to start reroofing his house this week. He's delaying work until he knows for sure where the rock is going to end up."

The President grinned. "A fatalist, eh?"

Earle glanced at his boss. "Not really, sir. I was the one who told him to hold off."

Fraser lost the smile. "You really think this may fail and the asteroid will come down?"

"I don't know, sir. As a scientist, I'm obligated to consider and prepare for every possible eventuality." It was his turn to smile. "I feel like the coyote in the Road Runner cartoons. There's an anvil coming straight for me and all I can stick between it and my head is a dinky little black umbrella." He returned his attention to the sky. "I'd feel a lot better if we knew the exact composition of that asteroid. Some of the readings that are coming in are seriously skewed. A few are downright contradictory."

"And you're concerned that without knowing the precise composition, the planned placement of the nuclear explosives may be flawed."

Earle wasn't surprised. The President was a master of unexpected knowledge. It was a survival skill.

"That's right, sir. It isn't that I'm not confident. Everything has been carefully worked out and calibrated and rechecked via simulation. It's just that I'm not a hundred-percent positive."

Fraser smiled encouragingly. "If you were, you wouldn't be much of a scientist, Willy."

"So this is weightlessness." Contrasted with her carefully polished veneer of sophistication, Maggie Robbins's girlish delight seemed even more ingenuous. "What a gas!"

"Lack of," Miles corrected her. The payload specialist was secured in her chair, running preliminary operations checks on the manipulator arm and related instrumentation.

Up front, Low and Borden monitored the shuttle's status and position. They would come up on the asteroid from below and behind, like a white shark stalking a seal. The slower their approach, the less fuel they'd have to burn to consummate the rendezvous.

"I know you checked out," Miles observed, "but you'd be surprised how different people react. No nausea at all?" A smiling Robbins shook her head. "That's good. I'm too busy to clean up after you."

Borden glanced back at the floating journalist. "Me, I've always found weightlessness sort of a cross between approaching heaven and feeling like you're going to puke every minute. You can quote me on that."

"Not sure I want to, Ken." Using the shuttle's built-in handholds, she carefully maneuvered herself around to face the front of the ship, hovering near the ceiling so that she could watch the two pilots at work. "I've never felt anything like it."

"There isn't anything else like it." Low turned his head. "Watch yourself. There are instruments up there also. Near your left arm."

"Oh, sorry." Robbins adjusted her position, bumped her right leg and stabilized herself. "I'm still trying to get the hang of this." Her smile widened. "So to speak."

Absorbed in the swarm of readouts, Low didn't reciprocate. He'd smile later, when they'd finished the job.

Borden stepped in. "That's all right, darlin'. You're doing fine. Just whatever you do, don't hit that button right there."

An anxious Robbins twisted to her left. "What? What button?"

"That one, that one right there!" Borden exclaimed, his voice rising.

A panicked Robbins drew in her arms and legs, fearful of making contact with the dreaded switch. Clasped into a ball, she began to spin toward the back of the cockpit, extended her limbs, and finally managed to steady herself by latching onto a handle. Anxious eyes sought those of the copilot.

"What did I do? What did I almost hit?"

Borden took a deep breath and pointed. "See that red depression up there, near where you were floating? That's the emergency eject. One tap on that, and *foom!*" He spread both arms wide. "The whole canopy comes off, our parachute systems engage, and we're blown out into the atmosphere for emergency descent. Except that we're no longer in atmosphere and we'd all explosively decompress before we could freeze to death or die of suffocation."

Robbins turned slightly green. "I'm sorry, I'm really sorry. I didn't know." She eyed the ominous depression. "You'd think they'd put some sort of safety shield over a control as critical as that. There should be . . ."

She stopped in midsentence, having espied something she hadn't seen since she'd first stepped aboard the shuttle. It was Boston Low. He was smiling. Striving mightily not to, and failing. It had welled up within him and was threatening, despite his best efforts, to break free.

The sun was coming up over the terminator line, and with it dawning realization.

"Hey, wait a minute." Her gaze shifted from mission commander to copilot and back again. "Something that sensitive *would* be protected from casual contact. Hell, I bet it wouldn't work outside the atmosphere anyway. It wouldn't even be *operated* manually, because in an emergency you wouldn't have time to activate it and . . ."

Borden couldn't hold it in anymore. He burst out laughing, only to have it echoed by Miles. "Hey," she shouted forward, "pack it in, Ken. Don't you know that unrestrained levity is against NASA in-flight regulations?"

"Put me on report!" Tears were streaming down the copilot's face. That is, on the ground they would have been streaming. In the cockpit they broke away in tiny perfect globules and went bobbing off in all directions, eventually to be captured by the ship's disapproving cleaning and purification system.

"Besides, I'm being comparatively restrained. Boston's the one you need to report." A cackling Borden nodded in the Commander's direction. "You know Boz. When he hears something funny, he just can't control himself. I mean, look at him! It's positively obscene."

Low shot his friend a glance. He didn't exactly collapse under the weight of unrequited hilarity, but something not unlike a chuckle did finally escape from his quivering lips.

Robbins actually blushed slightly, then nodded portentously. "That's right, have your little joke. I'll see that this is reported appropriately."

"See that you do." Borden wiped at his eyes with the back of one hand. "I always like to see credit given where it's due."

The last of the tension broken, Low called back to the others. "Cora, Ludger, how are you two doing?"

"We're fine, Boston," Miles responded. "The arm system checks out perfectly. Other than that, I just want to go on record as saying how much I enjoy shepherding such a nice, safe cargo and to remind anyone listening that my will and testament can be found in my safe-deposit box at the Bank of Galveston, Second Street and Houston.

"Unofficially, I'd rather deal with nuclear explosives than certain people in Washington." She nodded toward their resident scientist. "But you wouldn't know about that, would you, Ludger?"

"*Nein?* You should try securing a reasonable appropriation from the EEC Committee on Space. Believe me, Brussels is as difficult to work with as Washington, plus you are expected to work in six languages. The only difference when scientific appropriations are involved is that Americans yell and scream at each other all the time, whereas Europeans only do so in public and then go out peacefully together to enjoy expensive gourmet meals at the public's expense. I've shared some of the best wine and food of my life with people who had just spent the entire day deriding my requests for a few extra pounds, guilders, deutsche marks or francs for additional research. If I was given half the money Brussels bureaucrats spend on meals and after-hours entertainment in one year, I could fund my own laboratory."

Miles chuckled sympathetically, then turned serious. "You really think this will work, Ludger? I know what all the experts have said." She nodded in the direction of the nearest port and its panorama of the rotating Earth. "But they're down there now and we're up here. How about an uncensored opinion?"

Brink replied with ducal gravity. "The calculations have been run thousands of times, the simulations hundreds of times. *They* insist this will work. There is no question in my mind that if the power of the explosives has been properly gauged and they are correctly emplaced, the orbit of the asteroid can be adjusted."

Miles nodded. "Me, I'll be glad when it's over and done with."

"We all will." Brink's smile was pleasant enough, she

thought, but lacking in something. Energy, perhaps, or enthusiasm. It had been adequate, however, to charm millions out of various government agencies in a dozen countries.

"What's wrong, Cora?" Borden glanced back from the copilot's chair. "Afraid that if something goes wrong, it'll cost you the election?"

"Actually, I should be, but I'm not. You know me, Ken. When we're out here, nothing else matters except the job."

"Yeah, sure," he deadpanned.

"This is not only exciting," announced Robbins, "it's fun. They don't tell you about that part." She continued to acclimate herself to the wonder of weightlessness, using the handholds to pull herself back and forth through the cabin, occasionally hanging upside down like a bat with her feet touching the ceiling. Everyone knew she didn't belong aboard, including Robbins herself, but her enthusiasm was infectious. It made it hard to take umbrage at her presence for very long.

Following Borden's little joke, she was careful not to touch anything, not even those controls whose function she knew for certain. With only five of them aboard, there was plenty of room for a novice to explore. The compact recorder she carried hummed incessantly.

Throughout the approach Borden continued to whistle obscure classical tunes, make jokes, compose limericks, and in general act as if he were embarked on a weekend excursion in the Adirondacks. It contributed to a work environment that was relaxed and short on stress in a way no official NASA program could duplicate.

At the same time, the copilot executed his official functions smoothly and efficiently. Low knew he didn't have to watch or otherwise check up on his colleague. If anything went wrong, he and the younger man would spot it simultaneously. Unbeknownst to either, they were fondly referred to by the rest of the mission team as the Boy Scout and the Undertaker.

At this point the shuttle was virtually flying itself. There was nothing to do now but wait until they caught up to the target when it swung back in close to Earth from the apogee of its orbit. Low leaned back in his straps, watching the heavens for the one point of light that would be moving faster than any of the others.

Even Borden went silent when it finally appeared on their screens. There had been several unmanned flybys of asteroids out in the Mars-Jupiter belt. Robotic spacecraft took excellent pictures but fared poorly when it came to expressing a sense of wonder. This was the first time in mankind's history that such an object had been seen close-up by the unaided eye.

Miles and Brink joined Robbins in hovering behind the pilots' seats so that they could share in the historic first sighting. When she finally broke the ensuing silence, the journalist's words did not exactly rank with those of Armstrong or Glenn.

"Doesn't look like much. Just another star."

"It's still a ways off." Miles jostled gently for a better view. "Don't worry. It'll resolve itself soon enough."

"We are blessed, my friends." Brink could not keep a certain Teutonic solemnity from his voice. "We will be the first humans to set foot on such an object."

"Right." Borden deliberately mimicked the scientist's tone. "And then we're gonna blow a couple of big holes in it. That's humans for you."

"So it is. But first we will learn what we can from this little piece of interplanetary pavement."

"Little?" Robbins twisted to eye the scientist.

"By cosmic standards our visitor is nothing more than a speck of dust, Maggie." Eyes shining, Brink turned to stare at the approaching dot of light. "Yet from that speck we may glean clues as to how the planets were formed, why their chemistry is what it is, and so much more. You must understand that I have devoted my life to the study of such bodies, forced to work only with photographs and the occasional small piece purchased from crazy adventurers like that Arizonan Haag, never dreaming that one day I would be able not only to touch the actual object of my obsession but to stroll upon its surface." For a while it was silent in the cabin.

"From a scientific standpoint, what we are going to do is

criminal. From a social standpoint, it is inevitable. But afterward, if all goes as planned, the object will remain in place for us to study. We will transform this visitor from the outer regions from a threat to a gift. It is a bequest from the void, unsolicited and astonishing. A package of wonders yet to be opened. We should all give thanks for its coming."

"We will," conceded Miles, "as soon as we've made sure the parcel doesn't go off in our faces. I don't think people would've been as grateful if instead of going into orbit it had come straight down into, say, France."

Brink's enigmatic grin returned. "That would depend on whom one asked." For just the briefest instant, Robbins wasn't sure if he was joking or not.

Their trajectories unimpeded by resistance of any kind, the distance between shuttle and visitor shrank with gratifying predictability. The dot became an oval, then a solid shape possessed of a visible outline. It acquired depth, and shadows. Low and Borden adjusted the shuttle's attitude, slowing it down and bringing them steadily closer to the silent, dark visitor.

Miniature peaks and valleys became visible on the surface, along with evidence of multiple meteorite impacts. None of the craters were very deep, none of the twisted crags very high. A shrunken version of the moon, it was still more than big enough to dwarf the rendezvousing shuttle.

Robbins wrestled with ancient terrestrial fears as the visitor loomed over them, striving to remember that it could not fall down and crush the shuttle because it was not truly "above" the shuttle, any more than they were drifting below it. Their positions were relative to each other and little else.

Having matched velocities, Low and Borden carefully brought the ship to within a prearranged distance of the tormented, stony surface. The asteroid's minimal gravity did not affect their maneuvers.

Low wasted no time savoring the historic moment. As soon as they'd reached the predetermined position, he began slipping out of his harness.

"Let's get going. Ken, she's all yours. Ludger . . . ?"

"I am way ahead of you, Commander." Brink was pulling himself toward the rear of the cabin.

With Miles's assistance, the two men began slipping into their suits. Low pushed his feet down into the integral boots. "Remember, Ludger, the sooner we finish what we came for, the more time you'll have to conduct studies. But that doesn't mean we're going to rush it."

"I have no inclination to do so, Commander." The scientist eyed Low unblinkingly. "I am perfectly willing to save the Earth before I begin my real work. Even France."

Low slipped his right hand into the glove end, wriggled his fingers experimentally. "If you see me doing something you think is wrong, don't hesitate to point it out."

"I am not shy about such things, Commander. I expect the same critical treatment from you. We cannot afford any errors." Miles was checking the readouts and connections on the back of his suit, making certain all seals were tight and that the redundant air supply system was fully operational.

"This will be very different from floating outside *Mir*," Brink commented. "We will be making for a destination."

"Not to mention a delivery," Low added tersely.

The scientist helped Miles position the helmet over his head and draw it down toward its seals. "There is that added spice. I hope you won't allow me to become distracted." His eyes were shining as he and Miles fitted the helmet in place. When he spoke again, Low heard him via the suit radio.

"This is, after all, the culmination of my life's work. Is it similar for you, Commander?"

"No. For me it's just another job."

"That is fine with me. I will be struck dumb with wonder, and you will be blasé. It is an apportioning I find agreeable. Each of us will achieve satisfaction in their own way."

They were ready. A final check of communicators, air and temperature settings, and then it was time to enter the compact airlock. Throughout the entire suiting-up procedure Robbins had hovered nearby, out of the way but within viewing range, her recorder humming relentlessly. Every hour she snapped it into a designated transmission port, where the contents were converted to digital signals and flashed groundward.

At least he wouldn't have to deal with her once he and Brink were outside, Low mused. No distractions could be permitted. They were about to take one hell of a shovel to an alien sandbox.

Once inside the airlock, he studied Brink closely. There was no indication that the scientist's excitement was affecting his actions. A better indication would come later, when it would be possible to see how much air he was using.

As soon as the lock had been cleared, they opened the outer door and moved out into the yawning payload bay. The Earth gleamed exquisitely below them, framed by the black of space.

Using the suit's attitude jets, he turned slowly, and there it was, hanging overhead. It was as if the moon had suddenly plunged toward him. For an instant he was shaken, but it passed quickly.

Brink was already unsealing the digger, the special device designed to plant the explosives, and Low moved to help. The unit was as compact as its official name was long. Upon hearing it, Borden had instantly shortened it to "digger", and so it was subsequently known to all involved in the project. In space there was no time to waste on protocol, whether human or mechanical.

Since Brink was more familiar with the device, he let the scientist do most of the work, helping when and where requested. It was not complicated. It couldn't be, given the limited time allotted to the task. They had to plant the explosives, retreat to a safe distance, and fire them before the bolide careened back out into space on its wild path.

Then they were heading up, toward the asteroid, the digger supported between them.

CHAPTER

5

They had no trouble securing it to the stony surface, once Brink had paused long enough to do a headstand and caress the rock with both hands. They waited while the machine did its job quickly and efficiently, excavating a sure slot for the explosive. Drifting down to a second preselected location on the surface, they repeated the sequence before starting back to the shuttle.

Once the unit had been restowed and locked down, they removed two remarkably small packets from a thickly padded container and retraced their path. Each package was roughly the size and shape of a scuba diver's tank. Working smoothly together, they emplaced the first in its waiting hole, then the second. Shaped charges, each was designed to thrust most of its energy away from the body of the asteroid, giving it a forceful shove without shattering the whole into dangerous fragments.

Despite the thousands of simulations, Low knew there was always the chance that the computers and their programmers had overlooked something, knew that disaster of varying magnitude was always a latent possibility. In which event he might as well stay in orbit and never return to the ground. No one had yet lynched an astronaut, he assured himself coolly, but there could always be a first time.

Am I the fatalist everyone claims, he found himself wondering? He shrugged it off. This was neither the time nor the place for personal introspection. He could do worse than reflect on the confidence everyone else seemed to have in him.

Brink worked confidently and efficiently, with nary a wasted move or gesture. Only in the scientist's eyes was there any indication that he was thinking about anything other than the task at hand. Low knew the other man was counting the minutes until he could return to the asteroid and commence his studies. He envied him his enthusiasm. That was a condition Low, too, had once suffered from, but had subsequently lost. He had to admit he wouldn't mind finding it again.

He doubted he'd locate it on the visitor, though. To Brink it was the culmination of all his dreams, a mile-wide Christmas present. To Low it was . . . a rock. No trees, no crabs, no seals, no crying gulls, no blue sky . . . he had to smile. Gray sky, anyway, this time of year. But better than black. He loved the fog. It shut out the night sky and kept the Earth close.

Here I am wondering if he's being diverted and I'm going on like a bad poet. Deliberately, he made himself focus on securing the last of their gear.

Then they were back in the airlock, holding while the shuttle breathed on them, waiting for pressure to equalize. It was a relief to reenter the main cabin. Miles was waiting to help them.

"You all right, Ludger?" he asked as soon as their helmets were off and they could once more speak without the aid of transmitters.

Despite the best efforts of his suit systems, the scientist was sweating heavily. "I'm fine, Commander, *danke*. I think we have done our work well." He glanced at a wall chronometer. "We are easily within the assigned time parameters." As he began to slip out of the suit, he added, "Did you know, Commander Low, that I have an unconscionable fear of heights?"

Low blinked. "No, I didn't know that."

"It stems from when I was six. My father dragged the family to the top of Köln cathedral. I was forced to 'enjoy' the view. It is a fear that has been with me ever since, but a simple one to defeat. You simply do not look down. Up here, of course, every way is down. Interestingly it confuses the fear as well as the mind."

"I wouldn't have guessed." Low stepped out of his suit and pushed off forward. "How're things on the ground?"

"Houston's running final checkout on your delivery." Borden was more subdued than usual. "Site-positioning lines up. You were off by less than half a meter on both locations."

"Naturally." Brink was mopping his face with a special absorbent towel.

"What happens now?" Robbins was hovering nearby.

"As soon as Houston gives us the all-clear," Borden told her, "we back off to a safe distance. Actually we'll be dropping down and moving forward to a safe distance."

"And then?"

"We wait. Houston will detonate the explosives. If everything goes as planned, the object's orbit will be stabilized and it will stay with us instead of flying back out into space. At that point we'll be able to rematch trajectories and hang with it for as many orbits as we're cleared to do."

She nodded wordlessly. A moment later the words "Well done" reached them from the ground, accompanied by the flutter of muted applause.

Low slid back into his seat. He knew he should be exhausted, but he was only anxious to finish the flight. "Everyone stabilize themselves, please. Ms. Rob . . . Maggie . . . I suggest you return to your seat and fasten your harness."

Miles assisted the journalist and then positioned herself. Borden initiated the shuttle's thrusters, and they dropped away from the asteroid. Soon it was once again no more than a dot in the distance, another unrecognizable point of light.

Technically it wasn't part of the flight program, but Low found himself unable to resist the temptation. Burning a little extra thruster fuel, he pivoted the shuttle on its axis so that they were racing backward around the planet. The attitude adjustment also left them facing the object of their recent attention.

Not even Borden was inclined to joke as the countdown crackled up to them from the ground. They had moved to what was considered a more than safe distance, but still . . . what they were about to witness had never been tried before.

There came a distant flash, disappointingly subdued. Low fancied he saw two distinct flares even though he knew both charges were designed to go off simultaneously. They faded rapidly. There was of course no noise.

"That's it?" Robbins strained for a better view.

"We're a long ways off," Low told her.

"A long ways," Miles added.

"What happens next?"

"We wait." Borden nudged a control. "We wait for several orbits until we find out if our little kick in the rockside did the trick. Find yourself something to do."

It was during the interminable period that followed that Maggie Robbins proved herself an asset to the flight instead of simply another piece of cargo. While the others strove not to speculate on whether or not the mission had been a success or failure, and largely failed, Robbins was everywhere: shooting video, asking questions, experimenting with her weightless condition, and generally doing her utmost to keep her companions occupied. In such a tense environment even silly questions had the value of diversion.

Her persistent intrusions into shipboard routine were welcomed. Anything to keep from contemplating the consequences of failure.

Suppose the explosives had been inadequate? Or improperly positioned? What if a critical calculation had been wrong just enough, and even now the asteroid was dropping dangerously low into the atmosphere? What if . . . ?

"Excuse me, Boston, but what does this do?"

He found himself trying to concentrate on her question, his depressing reverie broken. "That? There are multiple controls for operating the shuttle's thrusters, but it's still necessary for ground control to be able to override shipboard commands."

"Why?" she inquired innocently. And while he patiently explained, images of disaster could not form in his mind.

She wanted to know how everything worked, what everything was for. When she finished with the instrumentation, she started in on their personal histories. What was it like growing up? Did they always want to be astronauts? What did their parents think of their youthful aspirations? Their friends, their lovers, their spouses? On and on, hour after hour, orbit after orbit, the questions coming so swiftly and exuberantly that the recipients did not have time to think about anything else. Did not have time to contemplate catastrophe.

It was only much later that Low was able to reflect on the insistent interrogation and realize that many of the queries were nothing more than rephrasings of questions already asked. Only then did it dawn on him that she'd known exactly what she was doing, using her interviewing skills to keep them from dwelling on the consequences of possible failure. It wasn't journalism she had been practicing then; it was therapy.

The efficacy of a bug in the ear.

Borden was looking at him expectantly. "Houston calling, Commander." Ken Borden hadn't called Low "Commander" in years.

Low acknowledged. Within the cabin all was silence.

"Don't recognize the voice." He frowned, adjusted a control. "There's a lot of interference."

"Boston steps up to the plate," the voice announced excitedly from the speaker. "Here's the pitch . . . it's a curve down the middle. Boston swings . . . it's a hit! . . . a long drive, to deep left field! Kowalski's going back, back, to the wall. He jumps . . . it's over, it's over! A home run for Boston! The fans are going wild!"

Laughter could be heard in the background. By now everyone onboard was smiling. Some wit at ground control had prepared for this moment by lining up a tape of an old Red Sox broadcast, substituting the name of the team for the name of the anonymous batter. Low was forced to grin in spite of himself. The implication of ground control's little game was obvious enough.

Devoid of static, a more familiar voice came on-line. "Congratulations, Commander Low, Copilot Borden. Congratulations, all of you."

Low leaned toward the pickup. "What took you so long?"

"We decided to wait an extra orbit," the voice responded. "We didn't just want to be sure. Everyone wanted to be more than sure."

"Hell." Borden drifted lazily in harness. "I *thought* they were taking their time."

"According to the preliminaries, everything went exactly as planned." Even over the radio and the distances involved, the speaker succeeded in conveying his excitement. "All objectives attained and well within accepted parameters. The mission appears to be a complete success."

"Naturally," Brink murmured into the silence. "There was no reason for it to have gone otherwise."

Mission Control continued. "The Earth has a new moon. They're working on a name for it right now."

Miles kept her voice down. "Wanted to make sure it'd stay put before they named it. Politically expedient."

"Hey, what about us?" Borden groused at the pickup. "Don't we get any input, or what? As the first people to make contact with it, I think we're the ones who have the right to name it. Now, I propose—"

"Never mind, Borden," interrupted the voice from Houston. "There's no telling what *you'd* say." The quiet chuckle was clearly audible over the speaker. "Anyhow, you didn't make contact. That honor falls to Commander Low and Mission Specialist Brink.

"Which doesn't matter anyway. The final decision will be up to the President acting in consultation with the United Nations Council on Space."

"It does not matter." Brink shifted in his chair. "I would hope that my name would be remembered in a more constructive fashion."

Knowing that everything had gone as planned allowed Low to relax, insofar as he was capable of relaxing. He would not truly experience that condition again until he was back on the ground and back by his beloved bay.

The main objective of the mission had been accomplished. Now there was time, not much, but some, to carry out those subsidiary assignments on which the scientific community had insisted. Behind him, Robbins was scattering questions at Brink. The scientist did his best to answer, in simple sentences devoid of all but the most inescapable technical terms. Miles was uncharacteristically quiet, perhaps mentally tallying votes for the forthcoming congressional election, in which she expected to play a dominant part.

Then Robbins was in his face. Or rather, over it, hovering near the ceiling and clearly comfortable in zero-g. He raised his eyes to meet hers.

"Is there something I can do for you, Maggie?"

"Yeah. What is it with you, Boston? Doesn't anything rattle your cage? Don't you ever get excited? What you just accomplished was the equivalent of performing brain surgery with a forklift. You probably just saved millions of lives and you don't let out so much as a whoop. It's not natural."

He smiled thinly. "I never claimed to be natural. Only competent."

She refused to be put off so facilely. "Don't you feel anything? Don't you want to set off firecrackers, whistle like crazy, pop a bunch of balloons?"

"I'm not the crazy-whistling, balloon-popper type, Maggie. As for firecrackers, didn't we just do that?"

"Stop badgering the Commander, Maggie." Brink's admonishment surprised both interviewer and interviewee. "Those of us who stand in awe at the wonders of nature tend to celebrate our little triumphs internally. Not everyone feels the need to share his emotions with a worldwide television audience, no matter how many potential commercial endorsements may be at stake." Releasing himself from his harness, he pulled himself toward the nearest port.

"As for myself, I will celebrate when we return to our domesticated subject and I am able to study instead of coerce."

Robbins didn't miss a beat, switching her attention from Low to Brink. Nothing fazed her, Low had to admit admiringly.

"Are we sure that's safe?" she was asking. "I know a survey was in the overall mission plan, provided everything went well, but it seems awfully soon to be going back."

"The rock won't be hot, if that's what you're wondering." Miles looked over from her station. "The Russians insist their explosives are clean. Environmentally friendly, even. I don't know if I'd go *that* far, but if the charts I've seen are correct, the residual radiation shouldn't be anything our suits can't handle. Most of it will have been blasted out into space."

"In any event, we will not be lingering long in the vicinity. More's the pity, as the English say." Floating near Low's right shoulder, Brink pointed. "People are so paranoid about radiation. Out there is the biggest, dirtiest nuclear bomb imaginable. It's exploding all the time, right over everybody's head. Every time you step outside your house, you are being bathed in 'radiation.' " He shook his head sadly. "People grow frantic when discussing the output of cellular telephones and microwave ovens and big-screen television sets. Then they go outside and lie in the sun."

"Hey, no need to be sarcastic, Herr Professor Brink. I'm not ignorant."

"I did not mean to suggest that you were, Maggie. I merely chose to emphasize my point. A brief visit to the asteroid will place us in no danger."

"Well," she murmured, "so long as everybody's sure."

Low and Borden paid no attention to the discussion. They were too busy computing trajectories, velocities, orbits, and a thousand and one other necessities.

Low didn't even dwell on Robbins's planned participation in the EVA. When it had first been proposed to him, he'd naturally been dead set against it. But the agency had been adamant. The publicity was too promising to pass up. Besides, with Low and Brink to watch her every move, what could possibly go wrong? Spacewalking was old hat by now, the suits were idiot-proof and it wasn't as if they had to perform some complex engineering procedure during the EVA.

As it had been explained to him, it would be more in the nature of a stroll in the park. Brink would be carrying out the actual research. The Commander could spend most of his time keeping an eye on their resident journalist. If necessary, all of her suit functions could be operated remotely from the shuttle.

Nevertheless it was not an assignment that filled him with much glee.

Aware that he was arguing with a bureaucracy whose density approximated that of lead, Low had eventually given in. That did not mean that in the interim he had developed any enthusiasm for the proposal. If it had been left up to him, he would have voted for an immediate return to the Cape as soon as their main objective was accomplished. He did not propose the notion, knowing that Brink would sooner maroon himself on the object than surrender the opportunity to be the first scientist actually to do fieldwork on an asteroid. The scientist would freely have walked through the fires of any religion's hell for the chance.

Brink's urgency he could at least understand. For that matter, a small part of him he tried hard not to acknowledge was also looking forward to the encounter.

A compromise was reached. There would be an EVA, but it would be kept conservatively short. They would make one drop, do some basic surveying, take some surface samples, let Robbins gush breathlessly for the benefit of watching millions, and return to the shuttle.

"We have concluded the engineering stage of this mission," Brink was observing. "Now the work of science can begin."

"Not until we catch up to it again, Ludger." Borden glanced over at the hovering scientist. "Tell me, what did the biologist say when he saw something moving in the Black Forest?" When Brink did not reply, the copilot responded with a deliberately heavy accent, "Gee! Gnomes!"

Miles laughed, Low conceded a grin and a smiling Brink nodded approvingly. Robbins looked completely at a loss. Trying to puzzle it out, she drifted into the rear of Low's seat. One elbow nudged his arm.

"Give me some room, please, Maggie."

"Sorry." Using one finger, she pushed off the back of his flight chair. "Nobody's going to explain it to me, right? Right?"

"Hang on to something," Borden advised her cheerily.

Once more the shuttle's thrusters were fired, raising her orbit and slowing her down. Before long they were closing on their target for the second time.

"There it is!" Robbins pointed excitedly toward the one increasingly bright dot in the heavens, steadying herself with a handhold. "I can see it."

No one else commented. Low murmured a command to Borden, who executed the required function as fluidly and efficiently as a third hand. Complex operations continued to be carried out at the rate of approximately six per casual joke.

Soon the lambent disk they were closing on resolved itself into a crusted spheroid, becoming real instead of theoretical.

"I can see where one of the bombs went off," Robbins announced.

"Not bombs." Brink corrected her firmly. "Attitude-adjustment devices. All three space agencies involved will be most distressed if in your continuing reports you refer to the devices as bombs."

"Whatever," she snapped impatiently. "Look over there."

A deep gouge where none had been before was clearly visible in the surface of the asteroid. Since the rays of the sun struck the object at an angle, they were unable to see very far into the newly created chasm. A second, matching fissure lay somewhere farther to the relative west of the one they were hovering above.

Not only was Brink not displeased by this apparent desecration of the specimen, he was delighted. The cleft would provide access to the asteroid's interior, something never before examined. He fully intended to explore it as deeply as their suits would allow.

Low and Borden continued the delicate task of maneuvering the shuttle still closer to the object, until they were racing along in orbit no more than thirty meters apart.

"Looks clean." Miles played the shuttle's powerful external light over the heavily impacted surface. It illuminated a portion of the recently created crevasse, leaving the ultimate depths inviolate. "Not much debris floating around."

"The force of the explosions would have blown most fragments clear," Brink declared. "Pity."

"Compliments to the engineers who built the devices." Low turned toward the rear of the cockpit. "You ready for your stroll in the park, Ludger?" But the scientist was already pulling himself toward the rear of the cabin and the row of waiting suits.

"Level of residual radioactivity is high, but within acceptable limits." Miles eyed the Commander. "I wouldn't recommend more than the one EVA, though."

Low slid out of his chair. "That's all right, Cora. That's what we've scheduled, and that's all we're going to do."

"You're sure this is perfectly safe?" Robbins followed Low.

"A little late to be wondering, isn't it, Maggie?" He looked over at her. "You can back out anytime."

She flushed angrily. "I didn't say that. Did I say anything like that?"

"No, you didn't. And to answer your question, no, it's not perfectly safe. Very little in science is perfect. But it's pretty damn reasonably safe, or I wouldn't be going out there myself."

She nodded thoughtfully as she digested this. Behind her, Borden called out cheerfully. "See you guys in about an hour. If you happen to find a Circle-K down there, I'd like a cold six-pack and a giant bag of chips. Cajun-style."

"Anything else?" Low asked dryly as he helped Brink with the first suit.

"Nothing that I'd request in mixed company." Borden looked around the back of his chair and grinned. "I'll keep the motor running."

As expected, Robbins needed a lot of help donning her suit. How much instruction and practice had she been given groundside, Low wondered? This was crazy, taking a complete novice for an EVA. At least her suit controls could be overridden by commands from the shuttle. He reassured himself that once sealed inside, there was little she could do to hurt herself. Her suit purposely did not include a thruster pack, so she couldn't go shooting off toward the sun by accidentally hitting the wrong buttons.

Wickedly, he found himself speculating on what a spectacular final report that would make. On the other hand, it wouldn't exactly enhance his record. He would have preferred to spend the time inspecting the asteroid and assisting Brink instead of wet-nursing a talkative journalist.

While they suited up, Miles continued to call out the radiation readings and other stats pertinent to their incipient EVA. The levels continued to fall, albeit slowly, as helmets were donned. Checkout proceeded to intersuit communications.

He could hear Robbins breathing hard. If she kept using air at that rate, she'd shorten the excursion by twenty minutes.

"Take it easy, Maggie. Remember what they told you in Houston. Just breathe normally, as if you were on scuba. The suit's respiration system will supply as much air as you need. The more you hyperventilate, the faster you'll exhaust your supply."

She smiled back at him. Wanly, but gamely, he decided. Her breathing slowed.

"That's better. You'll be tethered to me at all times, so you won't have to worry about which way to go or how to get there. Just relax and enjoy the sights." A single nod and a slightly bigger smile this time. "Good. Don't touch anything unless you ask first. Try to act like a passenger."

"I'm good at that." Her voice arrived undistorted through his helmet speakers. "I'm not going to touch anything except my recorder, and it's pretty much automatic." She indicated the special camera that had been integrated into the left sleeve of her suit.

For the second time in a day he found himself Outside, hovering in the shuttle's gaping bay. It blocked most of the sunlight, which fell unimpeded on the asteroid's surface.

He could hear Robbins breathing hard again, but as they moved toward the rocky surface, it slowed. With Brink on his right, he adjusted his attitude so that they would make contact close to the crevice they had blasted in the surface.

"How are you doing, Maggie?"

Her voice breathed back at him. "Not so good . . . at first. Better now. I can't decide if I'm ascending or falling."

"Neither term has relevance up here. Don't worry about it. You're going *away* from the shuttle and *toward* the asteroid. That's all you need to think about." Even as he chatted with her, trying to be reassuring and comforting, he continued to check and recheck his own suit's status and instrumentation.

Sooner than seemed possible, they were down. "Don't let yourself be fooled by the solid surface underfoot," he told her. "Gravity's virtually nonexistent. You can't 'walk' anywhere here. We might as well be 'standing' on a ball of gauze."

"Such wonderful sights." Brink had oriented himself with his head facing the ground and was scraping samples into a carrying sack. The fragments were removed with difficulty. "Mostly nickel-iron with a smattering of rock," he informed his companions. "Not so very different from your usual bolide." Using his suit thrusters, he assumed a stance with his boots facing the ground. "Some olivine, and perhaps a few surprises. We will find out in the laboratory."

Robbins recorded Brink for a while, then turned her machine on the surrounding desolation. She asked few questions, and all were pertinent and well thought out. Low was pleased.

Time passed rapidly in space. He checked his chronometer. "Ludger? The fissure?"

"Ya, ya, I'm coming." The scientist added something under his breath in German. Low caught a few words, but too many were of the type commonly found in scientific German—half a meter or so long.

Low heard Robbins suck in her breath as they approached the rim of the abyss. He tried not to smile. "Easy, Maggie. Remember, you can't fall in. There's no gravity here. You're already falling constantly." He peered into the dark crevasse. Their suit lights illuminated only a portion of the upper reaches.

The two men discussed the proposed descent. The only danger would take the form of a sharp projection or overhang that could entrap them or possibly puncture their suits. They didn't expect to encounter any. The upper regions should be smooth as a result of the residual heat from the explosion. Indeed the surface in their immediate vicinity exhibited all the classic signs of having been turned molten and then rapidly cooled. It was a landscape as designed by Gaudi.

Brink was preparing to use a quick puff from his thrusters to drop down, when the unexpected happened. There shouldn't have been any unexpected. Everything had been worked out in advance, every possibility accounted for.

That was Nature for you, Low thought. Just when you were getting comfortable with the view, she up and smacked you in the face with something. Or in this case, with an entire extraterrestrial body.

Beneath them, the ground had begun to move.

CHAPTER

6

There was no sound, only a subtle vibration that communicated itself not to their ears so much as to their very bones. Around them the surface of the asteroid quivered visibly. Loosened chunks of surface material broke free and began to drift out into space. From within the fissure more material was jolted loose and came floating slowly toward them. Small nickel-iron boulders were easily nudged aside by gloved hands. Fortunately none of them had sharp edges.

Borden and Miles were trying to talk simultaneously, filling his ears with a confused babble. Ever the journalist, Robbins had aimed her arm-mounted camera downward. Close by, Brink reached out to snag one drifting scrap after another. Most he would fling aside, while a select few would find their way into one of his collection sacks.

The flurry of dislodged fragments had all but ceased when a brilliant shaft of light erupted from beneath their feet and bathed all three of them in its vivid glow.

Borden's exclamation of surprise overrode Miles's startled oath. "What the hell . . . ?" Low could envision him turning to shout back at the mission specialist. "Readings, dammit! Get some readings!" His voice contained not the slightest suggestion of humor.

The copilot shouted toward the pickup. "Boston! What's going on out there?" Miles dragged herself into Low's seat, her fingers fluttering over the instruments, half of which appeared to have gone mad.

"Something's happening," she muttered.

"Asteroid quake." Borden snapped a switch.

"Impossible. It's too small and too dead."

"Not as impossible as that light." Borden was staring at the beam that had inexplicably emerged from the depths of the crevasse.

"Whatever it is, it's not hot." She indicated a gauge.

"Hello, hello, *Atlantis*. Do you read?" It was the voice of Mission Control. Whoever was on duty sounded harried and anxious, Borden decided. And maybe just a little panicked. "What's going on up there? We've got nonorbital motion readings on the target."

"We've got more than motion, people." Borden stared in disbelief at a gauge that ought to be reading null. It was half lit. "There's a light of some kind coming from inside the object. Real bright, like a big searchlight. You ought to be able to see it from down there."

"You're over west-central Africa. We can't scope anything until you come within range of Mombasa. What are your readings?"

"No radiation," Miles reported. "Ken's right on when he describes it as searchlightlike. I don't think it's a residual ef-fect from the correction."

"Look, as soon as we know something more specific, we'll tell you," Borden declared. "It's a little weird up here just now."

"You'd better come up with something." Mission Control sounded peeved. " 'Weird' doesn't make it as far as scientific terminology is concerned. We need specifics."

"The asteroid's generating a bright light. Is that specific enough for you? Don't bother me. We've got three people down on the object." He looked grimly at Miles. "You got anything yet?"

"Nothing. If there's a source, it's either well buried or not hot. Doesn't show any signs of dimming." She checked another bank of readouts. "Limited motion is resuming throughout the target's entire length."

"Damn." Borden shifted his gaze from the instrumentation back to the object itself. "Boz? Talk to me, man."

Low's voice echoed over the cabin speakers. The Commander sounded slightly shaken, which in itself represented something of an unnatural phenomenon.

"We're fine. The vibration, or whatever it is, seems to be quieting down."

Borden glanced at Miles, who nodded confirmation. He leaned toward the pickup. "We see the light. It's not hot and it doesn't appear to be lasing, so I think you're safe in looking at it."

"A little late for that, isn't it, buddy?" Low's voice paused for a moment. "Put the spectroscope on it. The one we use for stellar analysis."

"Look," the copilot began, "if you think I'm going to leave you down there while I run recalibrations on the computer, you'd better check yourself for oxygen deprivation."

"No need to worry," Low responded. "The ground's stopped moving. There's just the light. Whoa, now there's not even that."

Peering through the ports, the two crew members saw that the beam had indeed vanished.

"Wonder what the hell that was all about?" Miles murmured aloud.

"Maybe it needs new batteries," Low replied. "Size double Z." He had to work for a smile.

Low was floating directly above the hole in the asteroid, staring downward. "There's still something glowing inside the crevasse. Ludger?"

"I have no more idea than you, Commander. Certain minerals can retain and then release heat. Others can do similar tricks with electrical charges. Perhaps we have just witnessed an entirely new natural mineralogical phenomenon." In his suit, he turned to face Low. "We would be remiss not to investigate farther."

"Reflection from a lingering pool of molten material?" the Commander suggested. "Smooth nickel-iron would make a mighty effective mirror."

"I do not think so. It was too bright, too coherent to be a reflection."

"Well, then, what?" the Commander pressed him. The scientist had no ready reply.

Something bumped into Low and he started, only to see Robbins drifting next to him. Using the tether, she had pulled herself close. "What was it, then? What happened?"

"We don't know."

"But we are going to find out," Brink added emphatically.

"I don't know." Hovering above the pit, Low considered the options. "We're not really equipped to deal with the unforeseen, Ludger. I don't like pushing our luck with the unpredictable."

"Nonsense, Commander. The phenomenon may not be repeated. We must pursue the cause while it remains fresh in experience. By the time the first formal scientific expedition arrives, the trail may have vanished." He returned his attention to the chasm beneath. "A body this small should not be capable of generating internal motion, much less ambient light. It has not flown apart, which attests to its internal stability. I do not think we have anything to fear."

"Spoken like a man for whom the unknown holds only answers, not questions." Low remained unmoved. "Your safety and Maggie's is my responsibility, Ludger."

"Hey, don't I have a voice in this?" Robbins tried to insinuate herself into the discussion.

She didn't much care for the result. "No, you don't," Low told her formally. "You're here to observe, not to insinuate. Don't forget that."

"We were going to enter anyway, Commander," Brink reminded him. At the very bottom of the crevice a faint efflorescence was still visible. "All the more reason now to proceed with our original intentions."

"No? What if we get down there and the shaking starts

again? What if this fissure decides to close up while we're in there?"

"Come now, Commander." Brink did his best not to sound like a lecturing professor, but without much luck. "The fissure is not going to 'close up.' This is not some soft, chalky sedimentary formation we are discussing. It is fused rock and nickel-iron. It is not easily malleable." He activated his suit thrusters. "I'm going in. You may remain behind if you choose."

"No," Low responded. "We stay together. Maggie, what's the reading on your tank?"

She read off a number from her helmet's heads-up display. Low grunted his satisfaction. "Twenty minutes, Ludger. No more."

"I accept your decision, Commander. Twenty minutes it is." He started down.

Low followed, keeping a wary eye on the walls of the fissure. There was no indication of movement, no hint of vibration. All was as still and quiet as when they had first arrived, except for the persistent, absurd glow from below. Robbins had her camera on continuous run.

"What about the structure?" he murmured aloud.

"I see nothing out of the ordinary, Commander." Brink continued to precede his companions downward. "Everything appears consistent with what is known or generally theorized. I don't know whether to be reassured or disappointed."

"Hey!" exclaimed a familiar voice via his headset. "How about an update, you guys?"

"The shaking or vibration has stopped completely, Cora. We are inside the fissure and descending. Ludger says that everything looks about as expected. There's some kind of faint illumination below us, which we're going to check out. We'll take a few samples and then start back. Keep my seat warm."

"Always." Miles's throaty laughter was greatly reassuring.

Robbins reached out to brush one wall with a gloved hand. "What are these glassy green deposits?"

"Olivine crystals," Brink explained. "Fused and smoothed by the heat of the detonation."

"You sure you're all right?" That was Borden, Low knew. The copilot was uncharacteristically serious.

"Fine, Ken. There's some loose debris, but it's easy to just push out of the way. Nothing sharp enough to threaten suit integrity. Not yet, anyway. Everything's normal."

"No, it is not," announced Brink as if on cue. Having reached the bottom of the chasm, the scientist had used a puff from his thrusters to halt his progress. Now he floated facedown in an effortless headstand a few inches above the rock.

"What is it, what's wrong?" Low immediately inquired.

"It is not so much that something is wrong, Commander. It is more that something is simply not right."

"I don't follow."

The scientist edged backward, using his fingertips to effect the motion. "Come and see for yourself."

Low adjusted himself, taking care to steady Robbins so that she would not go drifting past him to slam into the bottom of the crevasse. The gravity of Brink's appraisal was revealed in a single glance.

"Son of a bitch," a voice mumbled. His own, he determined.

"Say what, Boston? What was that again?" It was Borden, insistent and worried.

Low found he couldn't reply. He knew what he wanted to say, but the words wouldn't come. It was left to the ever-voluble Robbins to respond.

"We're okay, Ken. Everything's all right." She was staring past the two men, gaping at what lay between them. "It's just that we've . . . found something."

Below them and lodged in the bedrock of the asteroid was the source of the brilliant light that had for an instant so thoroughly and electrifyingly captured their attention. It flickered pallidly, no less wondrous for its present lack of intensity. The feeble light it was generating clearly came from somewhere within.

"Not quite the reflection you hypothesized, Commander." Brink had knelt by their discovery and was bracing himself against the nearest projecting rocks.

"It's metal, anyway." Low bent closer. "But not nickel-iron. And there are no olivine crystals embedded in it."

The source of their fascination and dumbfoundment was deeply scarred. That was part of the problem, for all of the "scars" were of uniform depth and breadth. Furthermore, they were arrayed in a pattern sufficiently uniform to suggest to even the most casual untrained observer that they were not the product of some natural force.

It was a plate of some kind; round and curved on top, unmistakably the product of sophisticated machining. It had not formed or condensed or precipitated out: it had been made.

"What's that? We didn't catch that last bit, Boston." Though less anxious, Borden was still not his usual jocular self.

Low turned his lips toward the helmet pickup. "I said that we've got some kind of metal plate here." He glanced at Brink, who nodded solemnly. "With what appear to be markings on it."

Robbins kept bumping up against him. "Am I hearing you two right? Are you saying that we've found some kind of artifact? An alien—"

"Just a minute, now, hold on just a minute." Low whirled on her with such force that he found himself sliding backward and had to reach out and reposition himself. "Nobody said anything about anything like that."

"Alien?" The catch in Miles's voice was comical. "Did somebody say alien? You've got a metal plate with alien engraving on it?"

"Nobody said anything of the kind," Low shot back.

"Commander Low." He turned to see Robbins eyeing him reprovingly. "You're shouting, Commander."

"I am not shouting," Low replied with careful deliberation. "Cora, Ken; we've found an anomaly here. It's far too soon to be rendering any formal determinations."

"Okay, Boz," Borden responded evenly. "So make a couple of informal ones. Just to keep us poor homefolks apprised."

Low exhaled slowly. "We've uncovered what looks like a machine-made metal plate that's inscribed with markings. It could possibly be—I say this reservedly—some kind of writing. But we don't know that yet."

"Writing." Miles's tone had changed to one normally used in church. "Then you are saying that you've found some kind of artifact, Boston."

Brink was running his gloved fingers over the indentations. "I do not think it can be doubted, Ms. Miles. It is clearly of artificial origin, as are the engravings or indentations that cover its surface. The source of the intermittent internal light remains a mystery. It seems to emanate from the metal itself."

"You'll both excuse me a moment." Robbins turned in nothingness so that her arm camera was focused on her and the scene at her back. "I think I have a story here." Clearing her throat, she began to recite.

"Notification Editing: Begin head. This is Maggie Robbins, reporting live from the now-stabilized and as-yet-unnamed asteroid." Pivoting anew, she aimed the lens at the yard-wide metal plate. "We have just found the first evidence of alien life beyond the Earth, a tablet or stella of some kind that—"

"Now, hold on a minute." Twisting, Low used his body to block the camera's view of their discovery. "We haven't exactly subjected this thing to detailed scrutiny, much less professional analysis. Right now everything, including possible source of origin, is pure speculation. It's not your place to go jumping to conclusions. You'll set all kinds of idiots to issuing unsupportable pronouncements."

She didn't back down. "And it's not your place, Commander, to tell me as an on-the-scene reporter what kind of conclusions I can and cannot draw. This is one instance where my experience exceeds yours. Are you trying to tell me that somebody from Earth managed to concoct this thing, sneak it up here, and bury it where we'd find it?"

"No, of course not," he replied impatiently, "but that doesn't mean—"

"It's an alien artifact, Boston. A solid metal plate that emits light. Give me another explanation and I'll gladly report it with equal enthusiasm."

He couldn't, of course. With grudging respect he allowed as how she wasn't afraid to make a case for herself. Behind them, Brink was scratching and digging at the area around the plate, using one of several special tools with which his suit was equipped.

"I wonder if perhaps there might not be something else here."

"There doesn't have to be." Robbins shoved the camera past an unresisting Low. "This plate alone is enough to make us famous the world over. Of course," she added with a hint of smugness, "*I'm* already famous the world over. So are you, Commander." She glanced meaningfully at Brink.

Looking up from his work, the scientist responded with that strange, enigmatic smile of his. "I am well known within a select small circle of individuals. That is enough for me."

"Better get used to the idea of being world famous, Ludger. It's inevitable now."

"It is the intrinsic scientific worth of what we have found that interests me, Maggie. Of course," he added gently, "I have no objection to being famous. Such intangibles are useful in raising funding."

She pushed still closer. "You think there might be more plates?"

"Perhaps." He dug carefully. "Or if we are lucky, something more."

Hanging back, Low checked his gauges. They still had some time. He wasn't sure if he was glad or not.

Using Brink's assortment of tools, they unearthed nothing else, but they were able to loosen the plate. The scientist slipped his gloved hands beneath the artifact.

"Careful," Low said warningly.

Brink smiled back at him. "No sharp edges, Commander. I checked. Will you give me a hand? It weighs nothing, of course, but I wouldn't want to accidentally jam it against a wall and break it in half."

With Robbins looking on and commenting excitedly, the two men easily raised the plate from its resting-place.

"Come on, Boston," exclaimed Miles into everyone's headset. "Don't start keeping secrets."

"We've freed the plate," Low informed her. "I see no problem in bringing it back to the ship. In an hour you can both be propounding your own theories."

"Dang, and me forgetting to bring my human-alien dictionary with me." Confident now that his companions were in no danger, Borden had returned to form.

"Hey." Robbins lowered her camera arm. "Hey, have either of you two looked *under* the plate yet?"

Carefully setting the artifact aside, Low and Brink turned back to face its original location. There was a hole where it had rested. A very deep hole.

A shaft.

It pitched downward; smooth-sided, cylindrical and nearly six feet in diameter. Low's first thought was that it was a natural extension of the fissure they had blown into the asteroid's surface and that the plate they had found had become dislodged and momentarily blocked it. Further inspection soon revealed that the passage was as artificial in nature as the plate they had removed. The walls were fashioned of or lined with a pale gray ceramic. No steps or indentations leading down were visible.

Robbins prodded him with words. "Well, Commander? You're the leader of this expedition. So lead."

Mesmerized, Low found himself staring down into the opening. It was clear now that the light they had been seeing emanated not from the plate itself but from somewhere beneath. It appeared, set aside against the rock of the cleft, to be solid and opaque. Yet there was no denying the steady, soft light that rose from somewhere below.

Robbins was less hesitant, jabbed a hand past him. "Over there, in the ground!" Her excitement broke his concentration.

She'd spotted another plate protruding from the fractured surface. No, not another plate, he saw on closer inspection. Three of them.

"You have excellent eyes, Maggie." Brink was already upending the first of their new discoveries. It came free easily and was identical in size and shape to the first. Only the inscriptions, or engravings, or whatever they were, differed.

How had they missed them, Low found himself wondering? A trick of the limited light? Or something more subtle and wondrous? Regardless, it took only moments to extract the additional plates and stack them off to one side.

That still left the mystery of the open shaft, which was not about to resolve itself. Using his thrusters and warning Robbins to keep some distance between them, he started down, following the light.

The shaft ran perfectly straight into the body of the asteroid. There were no side branches or offshoots, nothing to mar the smooth, satiny interior surface. As they descended, Low thought he felt weight returning. That was impossible, of course. As impossible as the shaft and the light and the plates. Which was to say it wasn't impossible at all.

"There's gravity here," Robbins announced with newfound authority. "I can feel it."

"Yes." Through the faceplate of his helmet Brink's expression was a mix of awe and puzzlement. "But there shouldn't be. Certainly not this much. It is very strange. I am starting to feel quite myself, yet we continue to descend at the same speed. If it is gravity returning, it is not gravity as we know it."

"There's more than one kind of gravity?" Low wondered aloud.

"It would seem so. Either that, or we are being affected by forces of which we have no knowledge and cannot yet identify."

"So long as we don't fall." Low kept his attention on the bottom of the shaft. His boots had now dropped below his waist and he was descending in a normal position, feet first. A glance to one side showed that Robbins and Brink were similarly aligned.

Tilting back his head, he saw the dark circlet that was the top of the shaft continuing to recede. If the unnatural condition could not be reversed, they were going to have trouble retracing their path.

He had no time to contemplate possible alternatives because at that moment the shaft opened out into a huge chamber. Clearly not a consequence of their explosive efforts, it boasted gently curving walls and a domed roof. In places the walls were covered with more of the distinctive inscriptions, in others they bulged with fluid, free-form shapes. The ceiling and floor were likewise decorated.

Gently their feet made contact with the floor.

"Not terrestrial gravity," Brink commented. "Barely Lunarian, and nowhere near as strong as Mars."

"I thought artificial gravity was a mathematical impossibility," Robbins commented innocently.

Low looked at her in surprise. She'd done some homework.

"Nothing that can be propagated as a wave is impossible to reproduce," Brink stated matter-of-factly, as if he were discussing something as simple as the pulley or the wheel instead of an effect beyond the ability of human science to duplicate.

"That's reassuring," observed Low dryly as he studied their surroundings. "I think I can safely say that we've found another artifact."

Brink studied the seamless floor. There was no sign of a seal, joint, rivet, screw, or other fastening or connection point. The entire floor might as well have been poured out whole and entire.

"I am wondering how much of the asteroid is asteroid and how much artifact? This chamber is large enough to hold several football fields. Has the bolidal material accumulated on its surface, or is the encrustation intentional? How does one ascribe motivation to creatures we cannot even envision?"

Bouncing like hurdlers, they took stock of their surroundings. Light came not from fixtures but from the building material itself. Low checked his gauges. All remained on null.

They were being illuminated by radiation that, according to his suit instrumentation, didn't radiate. As far as he was concerned, that was a phenomenon that ranked right up there with artificial gravity.

"I think we've done pretty well for a half hour's hunting." He turned to Brink. "We'd better try to figure out a way back. It'll be interesting to see if our suits can generate enough thrust to push us back up that shaft." With a wave of one arm he encompassed the expansive chamber. "There's too much here to try to inspect on one EVA anyway. This is a job for a properly equipped, long-term expedition. We came here as demolition specialists, remember?"

"Just another five minutes, Commander," Brink pleaded. The scientist's face was alight with the joy of discovery.

Robbins backed him up. "Come on, Boston. What's five minutes? We might find more plates, or something else not nailed down that we can take back with us."

Brink smiled at her. "Thank you, Maggie. As a representative of the international scientific community, I find your unconditional support refreshing."

"You're welcome." Her eyes were shining as she scrutinized their stunning surroundings. "This is just like the Yucatán all over again, only without the snakes and the bugs."

"Or air, water, and food," a reluctant Low felt compelled to add. He looked back over a shoulder. The location of the escape shaft was now well behind them.

"To think that someone built this." Brink was thinking aloud. "Look at these walls, with their folds and ripples. Are they the result of some alien aesthetic at work, or do they perform functions we cannot imagine. I see nothing resembling a switch, button or control as we would conceive of it."

"And the light," Robbins added. "It just comes right out of the metal."

Low indicated the floor over which they were bouncing. "I'm not sure this is metal, Maggie. It looks more like a high-grade ceramic, or plastic of some kind."

"I believe there is something of interest directly ahead." Brink continued to lead the way.

Low checked his suit gauge. They had ample air remaining—provided they could make it back up the shaft on the first try. He tried to contact Borden, but the material of which the chamber was composed effectively blocked his transmission. He tried to envision the scene on the shuttle, with Borden and Miles likewise unable to make contact with the EVA party. Ken was going to need all his vaunted sense of humor to cope with the temporary lapse in communications.

What must be happening down at Mission Control he didn't try to imagine.

All the rage and frustration would subside the instant the absent explorers reported their findings. Sheer bliss would replace fury as soon as they held up the first inscribed plate.

"Two minutes," he announced. "Come on, Ludger. There's more here than we could explore if we'd brought a year's worth of air with us. Remember, excitement makes the body use air faster."

"Then I am surprised to be still breathing." Brink's reply brought forth an appreciative laugh from Robbins. For some reason he couldn't explain, this had the effect of irritating Low.

"You can't breathe dreams, Ludger," he added curtly.

"I know, I know, Commander. Believe me, I have tried." He took another long leap toward the prominent stalagmite-like structure that lay directly ahead. "Let me examine this one prominence and then I promise you we can start back."

"All right." Low followed, moving more easily in his suit than either of his companions.

The metal swirl thrust up from the floor like a sharp dimple in the surface of a balloon. Stolid and featureless, it was as much an enigma as everything else they'd seen. Low leaped high for a look at the summit, while Brink and Robbins explored the base. As he drifted down from his jump, Robbins's ebullient squeal echoed in his ears.

"Commander! I mean, Boston . . . come and look at this!"

Low responded before he hit the floor. "What is it? More plates?"

"Not exactly, Commander." As usual, Brink remained in quiet control of his emotions. "You will know when you see for yourself."

The scientist was not lying.

One side of the pedestal, or column, was marred by multiple depressions. They were much deeper than the inscriptions that covered other parts of the chamber. All four were circular, shallow, and approximately a yard in diameter.

"The four plates." Robbins wore the expression of one who had just uncovered an alien Rosetta stone. "They'd fit these holes exactly."

"Maggie is correct." Brink smiled through his faceplate at Low. "What do you suppose might happen, Commander, if we were to place them in these empty receptacles?"

"Probably nothing." Low bent to study the depressions. Like the rest of the column, or for that matter the floor and ceiling, they were utterly featureless. "Maybe this is a giant alien dishwasher and they'll pop back out all nice and shiny. Or maybe they're the components of a giant bomb and we'll all be blown to Kingdom come." He shot a look at Brink. "I don't think it's a very good idea."

"Come, now, Commander," Brink chided him. "Doubtless this object has been drifting through interstellar space for eons. Whatever purpose its makers intended, I doubt that of a bomb was foremost in their minds. Besides, who would design a weapon that had to be armed from the inside out? I suspect you are correct in your evaluation. Most likely nothing will happen anyway."

"Let's try, Boston." Robbins was insistent. "If nothing happens, we can still take the plates back to the ship."

"Well, Commander?" Brink was staring expectantly. "Are you game?"

"Is that a scientific proposal?" Low considered. Using the plates meant returning to the top of the shaft where they'd been left. It would give him a chance to find out how effective their suit thrusters would be against the artificial gravity. The experiment would make things close, air wise, but if they moved fast, they could manage it.

"You get two," he told Brink decisively, "and I'll bring the others."

"What about me?" Robbins protested.

Low hesitated, then unhooked her. "You stay here and make sure the aliens don't run off with the holes."

"Oh, very funny, ha ha. No wonder they never ask any astronauts to host *Saturday Night Live*."

The two men started to retrace their long steps. "You can make a video of us bringing back the plates," Low told her. "That'll make for a nice, dramatic shot."

"Wide-angle to close-up, yeah. All right, I'll wait here. But don't be long."

"Afraid of ghosts?"

"Not hardly. I just miss your stimulating company, Boston."

With the task at hand foremost in their minds, Low and Brink chose to ignore the frantic flow of inquiries directed at them from the shuttle and, via the shuttle, from Houston. Answers could be provided when they had finished and when air time was no longer so precious a commodity.

The recovery and transference of the alien plates gave Low an opportunity to examine them at length. Save for the inscriptions, they were utterly featureless. Mindful of Brink's intentions, the Commander searched front, back and edges in vain for signs of prongs, plugs or anything resembling a means of affecting a connection with the mound rising from the chamber floor. There was nothing.

True to her word, Robbins had hardly stirred from the spot where they'd left her. She was happily filming away, turning slow circles and letting her arm camera document the interior of the artifact. Despite himself, Low felt self-conscious as he approached, knowing that the recording would probably appear later that day on televisions all over the world, no doubt accompanied by suitably breathless voice-over commentary and dramatic, wholly inappropriate music.

The inscriptions on each plate were unique. There was nothing on the mound to indicate where they might be expected to go, or if indeed they were designed to fit into the empty depressions on its flank.

"Would you like to do the honors, Commander?"

Low turned to the scientist. "I wouldn't think of it, Ludger. This was your idea, and it comes under the heading of archaeological exposition. You represent the science portion of this team. You do it."

"This hardly requires an advanced engineering degree." Brink took the topmost plate and carefully pushed it into one of the matching depressions on the side of the mound. As soon as they saw that it wouldn't fall out, Low started passing the remaining plates to his colleagues.

When Brink filled the last depression with the fourth and final plate, Robbins inhaled expectantly. Nothing happened to justify her mildly melodramatic reaction. The four plates occupied the four depressions with as much élan as they had the rocks surrounding the top of the shaft.

"Perhaps if we rotated them somehow," she suggested, making no effort to conceal her disappointment.

"They fit too snugly." Demonstrating by pushing on the edge of the nearest plate, Brink succeeded only in lifting himself sideways off the floor. "You can just put them in or out. See?" Hooking his gloved fingers into a deep inscription on the metal surface, he tugged gently. The plate came away easily in his hands. Having demonstrated the validity of his assertion, he reinserted it.

"Maybe they're nothing more than decorations." Low leaned forward to scrutinize the etched surfaces. "Pictures that have fallen off a wall. Maybe the explosives blew them loose and they drifted up to lodge in the loose scree near the top of the shaft. All except for the one that temporarily plugged it."

"They certainly do not appear to have any active function

that we can divine." Brink was not as disappointed as Robbins. Failure was common currency in his profession, to be accepted as such.

Low checked his chronometer. "I'm afraid I'm going to have to call an end to recess. It's time to get back to the ship."

"Yes, of course." Brink reached a second time for the plate he'd just removed and reinserted. "I think between the three of us we will have no trouble bringing these four along."

His fingertips never contacted the metal. "Did you see that, did you see it?" Robbins exclaimed as the scientist hastily withdrew his hand.

"I saw it." Low was backpedaling in the weak gravity. "Everybody get clear, move away."

The single bright blue spark that had jumped from the plate to Brink's suit had caused no evident damage, but it wasn't an event either the scientist or Low had any desire to see repeated. As the three of them retreated, more sparks flared, leaping from plate to plate. Others erupted and began to flash about the circumference of the mound like blue kraits overdosed on hormones. They jerked and twitched in an orgy of electric alien lust, occasionally burrowing into the vitreous substance of the mound itself, at other times singeing the vacuum around them.

Had Low allowed it, Brink and Robbins would have stayed and watched. But while admittedly hypnotic, the electrical display was not half as mesmerizing as the falling reading on the Commander's tank gauge.

In their wake the sparks intensified, miniature lightning bolts that began to explore floor and ceiling as well as the increasingly engulfed mound itself. Beams of light followed close upon the bolts, illuminated distant corners of the chamber with a seeming randomness that was anything but. Within the suit Low felt his hair beginning to stand on end.

Lights of different hue began to pulse within the mound, which had taken on the appearance of a tower of metallic glass. The opaque plates stood out starkly against the increasingly translucent structure. By now the metallic circles were wholly involved in dazzling bursts of intensely colored light, and it was impossible to look directly at them.

"How's that for an 'active function'?" Robbins was trying to run, float, and aim her camera backward at the same time. She would have fallen behind had not Low taken a firm grip on one of her suit straps and jerked her along. So bright had the light issuing from the plates and the mound become that his faceplate darkened automatically every time he glanced back over a shoulder. Nor did the incrementally intensifying display give any indication of slowing down.

Silent flowerings of light began to spew from the base of the mound and explode past the retreating humans. His suit gauges were going crazy, though the critical radiation meter remained well within tolerable limits. Around them the chamber was responding with flares and flashes and electrical eruptions of its own. Walls bulged and twisted, the ceiling rippled like beach sand, and the floor underfoot ran through a dizzying series of patterns, like a morphing squid gone berserk. Within the chamber only the three fleeing humans remained untouched.

Trapped within a psychotic rainbow, he thought tensely. Or an engineer's schematic of an exploding battery. Neither image was particularly reassuring.

All about them, the chamber was coming alive, and they were trapped in its heaving gut.

"The shaft! Use full power on your thrusters!" As he gave the order, he ran his own fingers over the relevant controls and felt himself beginning to rise. The suit propulsion unit possessed just enough thrust to counter the feeble artificial gravity. As they rose higher, the gravity weakened and the strain on the suit motor gradually decreased. Robbins performed admirably, letting Low tow her while she continued to operate her camera. He would have complimented her but didn't feel he could spare the time.

All of his attention was concentrated on the opening

above, the exit to fissure, surface, space, and shuttle. Four simple steps to security, four different landscapes to traverse.

A bolt of red lightning blew past him. It seemed to wink as it passed, a parade of semidomesticated charged particles.

"It's beautiful!" Robbins shouted over her communicator.

"You can describe it to me later."

"Damn, would you look at that." Eyes wide and unblinking, Borden leaned forward in his chair.

"Man oh man." Having left her station, Miles hung in the air between the two piloting stations.

There were no words for what they were seeing, no facile way to describe that which had never previously been witnessed, or even imagined.

Scintillating beams of light were erupting from the surface of the asteroid, or rather, from depths unseen. Their source was invisible, buried somewhere deep beneath the rocks. Though intensely bright, they did not lase. Depressions and small craters spat silent thunderbolts and fireballs, which raced off into space or arced back to smash afresh into the agitated surface.

"What's happening?" she found herself whispering. "What the hell's happening?"

"Maybe that's it. Maybe Hell's happening." A grim-faced Borden was trying to interpret readouts as fast as he could scan them. "More important is, why is it happening?" He shouted without looking up, knowing that the omnidirectional pickup would snatch his words out of the cabin's atmosphere. "Boston? Come back, Boz! What's going on down there? Where are you guys?"

". . . lights . . . ," a familiar and heavily distorted voice replied. "On our way out. Artifacts activated . . . device. We are—" Overpowering electrical interference stifled the rest of the words.

"Boston, Boston, say again!" With an effort, Borden fought down the urge to pound his fist against the speaker grid. Instead, he looked up at the mission payload specialist. "Did he say 'device'?"

She nodded. "Sounded like it to me."

"What kind of device, Boz? What did you *do,* dammit?"

"He said they were on their way out." Miles was icily calm, professional. "I imagine they're bringing explanations with them."

"Damn well better be." The copilot was angry, frustrated and afraid all at once.

Using handgrips, Miles turned on her axis. "We'd better be ready to pick them up."

"And to get out of here as soon as they're back aboard." Like Miles, Borden lapsed into silence as each of them attended to individual preparations. Neither bothered to acknowledge or respond to the increasingly strident calls that were being issued by ground control.

"Borden, Commander Low—what's going on up there?" The voice was by turns anxious and agitated. "We're getting all kinds of abnormal readings in your vicinity. Visual claims they're seeing flashes of light. *Bright* flashes."

"If this gets any brighter, viewers on the nightside will be able to see it with the naked eye." Miles was running post-EVA stats at three times the usual speed. "The spin-control boys are going to *love* that."

Borden was still railing at the pickup. "Boston, damn you, talk to me! Call me names, impugn my ancestry, but talk to me!"

Even if he'd been able to hear his friend imploring, Low was too busy to respond. They had another problem to deal with.

Gravity was increasing.

Despite the best efforts of their suit thrusters, they were drifting not up toward the entrance to the shaft but down, back toward the lambent, electrified floor.

"This is fascinating." Brink kept his hand on his suit thruster controls, to no avail. "Not only are we witness to a technology that can generate artificial gravity, it is also capable of varying it at will. One might call it cavorting gravity, in homage to a speculative predecessor."

"Let's hope the builders of this place didn't find Jovian conditions to their liking, or we'll have to call it something less whimsical." Low did his best to coax more thrust from his pack, to no avail. He was falling floorward as swiftly as his companions.

They came down not far from the tower, surrounded by anarchic bursts of light. Since they hadn't been fried, electrocuted, or microwaved by now, Low decided, it was possible they might live to contemplate future dilemmas. Whatever the cause and purpose of all the acrobatic energy dancing around them, it did not seem to be designed to kill.

The display had been sparked, as it were, by the insertion of the four plates into the tower. If even one of those plates could be removed, it was conceivable the circus of light would cease and conditions would return to what they had been earlier. Quiet would return and gravity would once more fall to a level they could escape.

Brink agreed readily with the Commander's analysis as they touched down. If the gravity continued to increase, they would be reduced to crawling about in their heavy suits. That made it imperative for them to disable the tower as quickly as possible.

Low got there first and reached for the nearest plate, trying not to think about the voltage of the sparks that by this time nearly obscured the inscribed surface. Remembering how Brink had done it, he hooked his fingers into the deepest inscription. Immediately the plate began to move.

Away from him.

Jerking his hands back in surprise, he watched as the plates sank *into* the solid matter of the tower, falling in and down as if they were sinking through gelatin. When he tentatively reached for the plate a second time, his fingers contacted what felt like solid material. With every passing moment, the plates sank deeper and deeper into the base of the mound.

Their descent halted about a yard above floor level, whereupon they began to move toward one another. As they touched, they began to change shape, flowing and melting to form a single, malleable non-Euclidian construct. To Low's astonished eyes the result resembled a child's toy jack more than anything else, except that the angles of the spikes were all wrong.

The conclusion of the process was marked by a burst of intense crimson light, which expanded outward from the tower's center like a ring of fire and which nearly defeated the lens-darkening response time of their faceplates. As it was, all three of them threw up their arms reflexively to shield their eyes. They felt nothing, no heat or shock wave.

When Low had at last blinked away enough lingering stars to see clearly once more, he saw that the spiked shape at the center of the mound had been replaced by a coldly burning ball no bigger than his fist.

"Well," he muttered tersely, "so much for removing the plates." He looked up and back, to where the bottom of the shaft now seemed impossibly far overhead. An experimental step turned into a respectable stride. Fluctuate the gravity might, but it was still less than Earth-normal. Maybe if he and Brink gave Robbins, who weighed less in proportion to her gear than anyone else, a running boost or shove, she might achieve escape velocity.

A murmured command into his helmet pickup returned nothing but static, hardly surprising in view of the amount of free energy that continued to crackle and flare around them. It had lessened somewhat since the melding of the four plates into the single ball but was still too intense and dominating to permit communication with the shuttle. For the same reason, Borden and Miles's frantic attempts to reach them were falling equally flat.

"*Atlantis,*" the desperate voice from Houston insisted, "something's *happening* up there."

"Now, there's an understatement." Having finished her preparations for EVA recovery, Miles had disengaged and drifted back to rejoin Borden. Both of them stared out the port.

The asteroid was changing. Before their eyes its shape and appearance were being altered by silent, unimaginable forces. It would have been easy to think of it as the work of a clever computer program, Borden mused silently, if not for the fact that three people were trapped somewhere within. Was the interior changing as well, and if so, what effect was it having on Low and the others? Were they being crushed, ignored, or treated to a fun-house ride the likes of which no human had ever experienced? With all channels of communication silent, there was no way of knowing.

It was absurd, preposterous, it made no sense. Mile-long asteroids did not surge and flow like modeling clay, did not trade in familiar, crater-pocked surfaces for sleek curves of glassy gray-white. A rock-collecting friend of the copilot's had once shown him a polished ovoid of rutilated quartz. Lit from within and turned semiopaque, it might be a twin to the object he now found himself gazing at in wonderment. The asteroid had now become something that, like many politicians, you could only see into a little ways before it defeated your best attempts at further perception.

Whatever the object really was, it was no asteroid.

Shafts of tinted lightning as broad in diameter as the shuttle coursed over and through its surface like skittish fish confined in a too-small aquarium. The shuttle's main instrument console began to vibrate discreetly beneath his fingers, and he jerked them back as if burnt.

"What now?" Miles grabbed for a hold with both hands.

"I don't—" Borden's reply was interrupted by the most dreaded sound in space: the hiss of escaping atmosphere. Twisting in midair, Miles located the source and shut it down. It was crazy, of course. In the absence of air, there was no reason for the shuttle to be subject to vibration, but vibrating it was.

Nor was it only the shuttle. Borden thought he could feel every cell in his body quivering, the corpuscles in his blood banging off the arterial walls. It was a sustained harmonic.

He would have clapped his hands to his ears if the vibration had taken the form of audible noise.

The explosions of light that now covered the surface of the object were intensifying. Soon they reached the point where they completely obscured the polished surface. Even as he found himself praying for the shuttle's hull to remain intact, he thought of calling out one more time to his absent friend and colleague.

Then it happened. Not *to* the alien object, but around it. The starfield in his line of sight seemed to twist like candy sprinkles cast into molten licorice. His brain tried to adjust, and failed. The object lurched ten yards to its right, blew off light like a bursting bulb and vanished.

Within the shuttle the steady and inexplicable vibration abruptly ceased. Not bothering to wipe away the sweat that was pouring off him, he barked back at Miles.

"Hull integrity!"

"The one small leak. I got it sealed." She was pouring over readouts, calling out numbers and names that would have been meaningless to anyone less highly skilled than the co-pilot. When she finished, it was apparent that by any standard the ship had remained mercifully intact.

The voices of ground control had gone from restive to anxious to desperate and now to imploring. "*Atlantis,* this is Houston. Do you read? *Atlantis,* this is Houston, do you read?" It was a mournful mantra that deserved to be acknowledged.

Borden's eyes hadn't left the place where the asteroid had been. A part of him continued to listen to the plaintive voices of Earth.

"*Atlantis,* we're registering an anomaly down here." A new voice, as curious as it was concerned. "Can you enlighten?"

"Sure," Borden heard himself replying. "We can explain. The asteroid is gone. Oh, and it wasn't an asteroid."

Silence from far below, from a place of reality and familiar surroundings, so different from the dark emptiness where the shuttle floated. Then, very tentatively, "*Atlantis,* say again?"

"I told you: It's gone. It changed shape, morphed, whatever you want to call it. It was an asteroid, and then it became . . . something else. And now it's gone."

A shorter silence this time. "That's what it shows here. But that's impossible. Asteroids don't suddenly pick up and move. Your position has remained constant."

"That's us humans for you." Miles took over from Borden. "Constant. Ken told you. It wasn't an asteroid. Whatever it was *did* move." She swallowed. "Real fast. As in instantaneous."

"Borden, can you confirm?"

He waited until the query was repeated. "Yeah. Yeah, I can confirm. It went poof. Just like the genie of the lamp."

More silence before, "Commander Low? Specialist Brink and Ms. Robbins?"

"I expect they went poof, too, since they were inside the object when it vanished." He exhaled slowly, suddenly very tired. "They found artifacts. Inscribed metal plates of some kind. Then they found a shaft, or tunnel, leading inside. So they went in. And now . . . they've gone away. That's the concise version. I'll try to be more illuminating later."

"Inside?" queried Mission Control. "Artifacts?"

"That's right. Nothing exceptional about finding artifacts on an artifact. Once they were inside, communications became intermittent. There was a lot of free energy running through the object and coming off it. Cold energy." He giggled, caught himself quickly. "Cold confusion. It skipped a little to one side, flashed a good-bye, and vanished."

"What you're telling us makes no sense, Mr. Borden."

The copilot responded without hesitation. "Thank you for confirming our hypothesis, Houston. We are awaiting orders." He could envision many very confused experts caucusing aimlessly.

"All right." A new, no-nonsense voice had wrested control

of the transmission. "If they are no longer there, then where did they go?"

Borden and Miles exchanged a glance before Cora Miles—daughter of a janitor, international chess champion, NCAA women's runner-up on the three-meter board, summa cum laude MIT, responded in her best congresswoman-to-be tone.

"Honey, don't ask us, but if you find out, we'd sure like to know. Because I'm telling you, they're not onboard, they're not in the lock, they're not within range of any of our instruments. They're *gone,* man."

Borden pushed back against his chair. "Wherever they've gone, I hope there are green trees, and morning fog, and the cry of gulls, or Boz is going to be pissed. But somehow I don't think there will be."

His eyes dropped to a gauge that monitored the shuttle's ground speed. Next to it was one that had been calibrated to do the same for the asteroid. It was frozen, showing only a long line of zeros.

Which happened to represent with unexpected scientific accuracy the sum total of their current knowledge as to the asteroid's makeup, purpose and present whereabouts.

CHAPTER

8

Adrift amid oceans of preternatural calm, there were continents. Each wore a reddish-pink halo of algal bloom in which fan-tailed sievers of bloated mien held court, arcing and diving like pale prima donnas in a perpetual alien pax de deux. Swifter of pace but lesser in bulk, other creatures inhabiting the sea frolicked around these masters of biomass conversion. The land held concourse with pacific denizens, while in the pale-blue sky thin-winged supplicants gesticulated alternately to clouds and mountaintop.

The three humans onboard the unasteroid saw none of this as their transport winked into the world at a predetermined boundary between soil and space. They were still confined to a tiny, circumscribed world of light and slippery surfaces, wondering what had happened to them but so surrounded by marvels that they had little time in which to bemoan possible fates.

The device circled thrice around the peaceful planet before commencing its descent. Those within felt no cessation of motion, just as they had felt none of the incredible acceleration. Robbins was preoccupied with the condition of her suit, into which she had, during an awkward moment, thrown up. She was as much embarrassed as she was discomfited.

No one knew what had happened to them or what was going on in the outside world. Nor did they have a clue that that same outside world no longer, to all intents and purposes, actively existed. They had known only intense light, subtle vibration, stomach-churning disorientation, and a complete lack of communication with their colleagues back aboard the *Atlantis*. Decision was on hold, life on automatic, thinking processes on maintenance. They would remain so until one of them succeeded in figuring out what the hell was going on.

In the south-central part of one rosy-tinged ocean, out of sight of the nearest continent, a rocky, bowl-shaped island surrounded by a handful of smaller islets thrust out of the sea from a stabilized volcanic bed. The unasteroid appeared above them, descending through a twilit sky. Slowing, it hovered for long moments while instruments within communicated with instruments situated below. Then and only then did it gently lower itself into a waiting, lined depression in the rock. Other instruments located on the outer islands observed silently without offering comment.

The stony flotilla lay anchored in an otherwise featureless sea. From each of the secondary islets a single shining spire shot skyward. Disturbed by the silent arrival in their midst of the mile-long mass, a few primitive island dwellers had taken fright. Reassured by the object's continued lack of motion, they soon returned huffily to their places of rest and nest.

It was Brink who first noticed that a gauge on his arm was signaling the presence of external atmosphere. When it had begun to infiltrate their formerly airless prison no one could say, but their suits pronounced it eminently inhalable. Despite Low's cautionary protestations, the scientist was quick to crack his helmet seal. The commander did not argue over much. All three of them were nearly out of air anyway.

The addition of a breathable atmosphere gave them something else to think about, not to mention a greater degree of comfort. They remained close to their suits, the shed skins laid out nearby lest invisible and unknown powers decide to withdraw the fresh air as capriciously as they had provided it. Robbins was understandably more eager than either of her companions to avail herself of the opportunity.

"What happens now?" Robbins was trying to unfasten the arm camera from the sleeve of her suit. She had managed to clean herself up reasonably well.

The last of the flaring illumination flickered and went out, as though someone had turned out the floor. Low considered the situation. "We try to get back in touch with the shuttle somehow. The manipulator arm won't reach very far down the fissure, but if it's still clear of debris, then Ken could lower a line to us. Drop us some refills for our suit tanks first, of course, and then—"

And then never came about, because one wall began to groan like an old Cyclops with a bad stomach, and an opening appeared in the side of the asteroid. There was no visible door. The wall simply separated and crinkled back in upon itself, like a torn sheet of aluminum foil.

Wan, yellow sunlight poured through the gap. Beyond, they could see peculiar-shaped trees and bushes; short, scruffy grasslike vegetation; rocks, clouds and sky.

Low took a cautious step toward the portal. "You know what? I don't think we're in geosynchronous orbit above Kansas anymore."

"Should've listened to the dog," Robbins remarked uneasily. "The dog always had more sense than any of them."

"Tell it to the wizard." Low was striding purposefully toward the light. "At this point, I'm willing to believe he just might be hanging around."

"Different milieu, if I am interpreting the reference correctly." Brink followed closely. "I see no Emerald City, Commander."

Low reached the opening. Sure enough, it went all the way through the outer wall of the asteroid. "Given where we were just a few hours ago, Ludger, I personally find the presence of trees even more remarkable."

They exited simultaneously, and even the redoubtably loquacious Robbins was at a loss for words.

The gleaming outer surface of what had once looked like an asteroid was mirror-smooth and nonreflective. The object now rested in a hollow that it had gouged in the ground . . . or that had been prepared to receive it. Beyond and around there was only air, sea, sky and plant life. The appearance of the few clouds hovering overhead was achingly normal. Low estimated the temperature to be between seventy and seventy-five degrees, with the ambient humidity appropriately reflective of their coastal locale. Except for the lapping of small waves on the nearby shore, it was silent, though Low had experienced greater silence elsewhere. Northwest Australia, for example.

As if further proof was needed, the silhouettes of two moons hung conveniently in the sky, proclaiming with lunar finality the alienness of their location.

That did not prevent them from seeking signs of familiarity. As to the atmosphere, if it contained anything poisonous or otherwise lethal, they would discover it soon enough. Their nearly airless suits offered a poor second choice. Besides, it smelled good; fresh, sweet and unpolluted, with a faint mix of natural fragrances Low was unable to identify.

Each of them wore a service belt equipped with a number of efficient, miniaturized devices, for use both onboard the shuttle and outside it in the event any of their suit units should malfunction. Removing the small subsidiary communicator, he switched it on. It was encouraging to see the tiny green indicator light respond, though when he spoke into the pickup, he was lacking both hope and enthusiasm in equal measure.

"Borden, this is Low. Come in, please. Ken, do you read?"

There was no response, not even static. Not that he had expected any. The unit emitted a faint, mournful echo of a whisper, barely enough to confirm that it was functioning normally. Alien sunlight filtered languidly through high, greasy clouds and warmed his neck and shoulders.

Just to be sure, he had Brink try on his own communicator. Requesting a response in English, German and Russian, the scientist received none. A tepid breeze rose from the silent sea to ruffle their hair.

At least they were out of the damn suits, Low thought. It was a great relief, after the strain and tension of the last few hours. It would have been nicer to have been out of their suits and onboard the *Atlantis,* or better still, striding down the landing ramp at the Cape.

Squinting skyward, he saw that the two visible moons differed in outline and mass. As he stared upward, a trio of narrow gliding shapes passed silently between his view and the moons. They had yard-long, membranous wings through which the sun shone brown, and angular, pointed skulls.

The spires that dominated the surrounding islets hinted at the presence of additional otherworldly revelations. Smooth of side, they pierced the silent alien sky like needles, mysterious messengers removed from their bottles. At this distance he could not tell whether they were solid or hollow. If hollow, he found himself wondering, what might they contain? Were they identical inside as well as out? He wondered if they might somehow be connected to one another, or even to the island on which they presently found themselves.

Behind him, the enormous metamorphosed mass of the unasteroid rested unassuming in its crater, or landing platform, or whatever the depression in the ground constituted. It was a gateway, a link, transportation to this world for whoever had the brains, wherewithal and misfortune to deduce that inserting the four metal plates into four empty receptacles might produce interesting consequences.

Couldn't deny that what had happened to them was interesting, he decided. Now, if only there had been some way to control the process. He felt like a five-year-old who knew how to start his parents' car but didn't have a clue as to how to steer it. They'd turned the ignition key on the asteroid-ship and accelerated on down the road, only to fetch up here, unable to restart the vehicle or turn it around.

He doubted the alien version of an auto club was to be found anywhere in the immediate vicinity.

On another plane of existence, which occupied a region

indescribable in human terms, the warm breeze and the meteorological mechanics that had generated it remained imperceptible. It was the same with the diffused sunlight and the sweet-smelling air. In their place, other realities, other perceptions held sway. Time and space fraternized in a flurry of vulgar mathematics, with the result that both became bastardized.

Amid this confusion of totality, a multiplicity of intelligences were present, riding the currents of a deformed actuality like so many moon doggies surfing a succession of predictable curls. This they did effortlessly, pushing themselves along with earnest thought-waves, interconnecting with lazy notions, rising and falling on the back of abstruse speculations.

They were not ignorant of real-time or real-space. It was visible to them as a parade of images viewed through thick glass. Much of the time they did not look. The memories had become too painful, and it was easier to ignore the falling of a leaf, the splash of a leaping fish on the surface of a real sea, than to deal with what might have been.

Within themselves, they were omnipotent. But they were not happy.

"Others have come," declared the presence nearest the unexpected new disturbance. Initially perceived as a ripple in reality, on closer inspection the intrusion had resolved itself into a trio of intelligent physicalities. It was a surprise that engendered casual inspection but no hope.

"Again?" The response took the form of a voiceless chorus, a coordinated disturbance of subatomic particles that came together with the usual perfect, dreary unity.

"So it would seem." Without eyes, the discoverer gazed speculatively upon the bipeds as they moved hesitantly through the tumid slipstream that was the real universe. "These are different from any who have come before."

"As those who preceded them differed from their predecessors." The new presence stank of the same resigned ennui that afflicted them all. "It is ever the same. They will be no more successful than any of the others."

On this point there was universal agreement. It was not voiced, or felt. It simply was, and by virtue of being, became simultaneously known to any who had an interest. Of these there were few, boredom having largely obliterated all but the last traces of curiosity among those who were present.

The equivalent of thought-ideograms passed between individuals, the shape and style of each serving to identify those who generated them more accurately than any name. It was the mental equivalent of thinking in fully formed pictures, complete to coloristic shadings and fine detail. Communication as art, art as communication. It was very nearly the only aesthetic left to those who propounded it. As such, they clung to it, molded it, and refined it with care. They had forsaken all other forms of art, much to their eventual regret.

Realization had become tainted by despair, which had given way finally to resignation. All that remained to them of existence was overtones, shadings, smoke and suggestion. Rather than being prized, the bipedal interruption served only to remind them of what had been lost. It was painful to perceive.

Nevertheless, several persisted. Stubbornness, too, was a means for combating boredom.

"They don't look like much," remarked another presence as it hovered directly above the new arrivals.

Robbins frowned at Low. "Did you feel that?"

Low was eyeing the interior of the island. The plateau on which they were standing gave way to low but rugged peaks. Twisted vegetation clung to hollows and small canyons. Some of the growths were yellow and purple rather than green, while one spotted a multiple trunk that formed a single stem, as if it had been planted in reverse. Tiny, brightly colored arthropods skittered from rock to bush, crevice to tree, minimizing their exposure to the open sky. He remembered the flying creatures they had seen earlier.

"Feel what?"

"I don't know," she replied impatiently. "If I knew, I wouldn't be asking you."

"And if I'd felt anything, I'd have given you an answer." He took a step forward. "Probably just a little wind. Looks like that little arroyo might be passable."

The reporter blinked, then whirled sharply. There was nothing behind her, nothing close, not even an alien gnat. Yet the feeling of something watching her was one she had encountered and acted upon many times in the past.

Absurd, of course. There was nothing here to do the watching. If she persisted, she'd only end up irritating and probably amusing both of her companions. Was the sea watching her? The rocks, the sun? She couldn't shake the feeling, but as she turned back to follow Low, she did her best to ignore it.

"They have awareness," proclaimed another presence.

"No more so than many who have come before," argued another.

"That is so." This from the one who had made first notice. "But it behooves one to be optimistic."

"To be foolish, you mean." Thought-forms swirled about one another in a realm outside experience. "Optimism is an outmoded concept with no validity in the present. I ceased practicing it, even as a theory, about a thousand years ago."

"More or less," agreed another.

They were exempt from the ravages of senility, the organized thought-forms that composed their minds and their selves unthreatened by the slow disintegration that reduced to rubble creatures of flesh and blood. But they were not immune to argument, which they relished as one of the last vestiges of a fading commitment to reality.

"Problem solvers. They must be problem solvers, or they would not be here." Curious, several new individuals joined the convocation of thought-forms.

"As were those who preceded them." The loudest font of

negativity sounded tired. "It will make no difference. A diversion only. Remembrance brings pain."

"Pain can be tolerated and is a concept only," insisted the discoverer. "Even pain is variety, and that is something I still value."

"Then you are a fool," insisted the other. Together it drifted away with its companions of like perception, leaving only a few behind to maintain the discussion.

These continued to observe the newcomers: from above, from the sides, from below, from inside their bodies, the detailed examination taking place without the examined aware they were being probed. No great revelations were forthcoming. Structurally the bipeds were unexceptional.

Maggie Robbins put a hand to her stomach. "Didn't you feel something just now?"

Preoccupied with his inspection of the terrain, Low replied absently. "What? No, nothing." If this world was inhabited, he thought, the locals were keeping to themselves. Their works were self-evident—those spires towering above the other islands—but of the builders themselves there was no sign. Had they died out, leaving only their buildings and machines behind? If so, how long ago had it happened? Perhaps they might find something useful.

They damned well better, he told himself. Any hope of returning home lay locked within alien structures and alien artifacts. He wasn't even sure how to start looking. An experienced archaeologist would have known where to look, where to dig. Would have known which building to start with and which to avoid. He'd been exposed to very little archaeology while in school. Did you dig up or down, plan a search grid first or just start in on the most likely structure? With no convenient text to refer to, they were going to have to improvise as they went along. Improvise, and hope they didn't make too many mistakes as they learned.

Especially of the fatal kind, he thought. While some alien relics might prove useful, others could as easily possess less benign functions. How to tell which from what? He'd always been a supporter of hands-on learning, but right now he wished fervently for some simple visual aids.

One thing he was certain of: This was no dream. The ocean smelled too strongly of salt, the air too pungently of growing things. His companions were real enough, as was the pain he felt when he bit his lower lip.

So much, he mused, for the easy way out.

He sucked oxygen-rich air into his lungs, grateful for small favors. The world on which they had been dumped might have differed only slightly if they'd been unlucky. Same rock, same ocean, same sights, but an atmosphere of methane. Or an ambient temperature of a hundred below. Things could be worse.

They had air. Potable water next, then edibles. Only then would he devote his energies to finding a way home. The water and liquid nutrients in their suit systems, even if carefully husbanded, wouldn't last more than a day or two. They were intended for day use, not long-term camping. In crude confirmation of higher thoughts, his stomach growled.

Brink sidled over to the journalist. "Spirits, Maggie? Ghosts? *Ubermenschen?*"

"What? I don't know any German, Ludger. You know that." She turned away. "I just thought I felt something, that's all."

"Gas," he suggested pithily. "Wind on your cheeks within and without." His gaze roved the landscape. "We are blessed beyond all scientists since the world began. You wanted an alien artifact, Maggie Robbins. You have been given an entire world."

"Right now I'd trade it all for a cheeseburger and a lift home." She sniffed a strange odor, like burnt cinnamon.

"Stick out your thumb." Brink chuckled. "You never know."

"Very funny." But when he'd turned away and when she was sure Low wasn't watching, she did exactly that, feeling

foolish as she did so. She only did it once, and then not for
very long.

"It is clear that the object we believed to be an asteroid is
in reality some kind of automatic transport. When activated,
it returns automatically to this place. We found the key and
unwittingly engaged its systems." Brink knelt to examine a
white rock full of tiny clear crystals. "It brought us here."

"Fine. So we're the greatest explorers since Columbus. I'd
still like to know where 'here' is." She tried not to think of
food.

"Columbus?" Brink looked up from the crystals. "Columbus was a neighborhood layabout compared with us. This is
the find of the ages. What we have done ranks with the discovery of the wheel, of fire."

The journalist eyed a tree that was short on leaves and
long on spray-tipped needles. "I'd rather discover a cheeseburger."

"We may need wheels and fire before we're through
here." Low leaned back to study the cliffs before them. None
appeared insurmountable, but it would be easier and smarter
to find a way through or around instead of trying to go over.
He had no idea what he hoped to find, only knew that it was
better to be searching than to stand around waiting for fate to
intervene.

"Patience, Commander." Brink held the cluster of crystals
up to the light. "I share your anxieties, but can you not take a
moment to contemplate the wonder of what has happened to
us? We have accomplished a marvel."

"Have we? I'm not so sure we've done that much. Given
enough time, rats in a maze eventually find the bait, but it
still doesn't make them anything more then clever rats. It's
not like we found plans and built a space drive."

Brink was not discouraged. "Then let us at least explore
the maze." He smiled thinly. "Perhaps we may find the bait."

"That's what I had in mind." So saying, the Commander
turned and started off toward the cleft in the rocks.

Robbins lengthened her stride to catch up to him. "We're

stranded here, God knows how far from home. Doesn't Brink care?"

"Sure he cares, but I know scientists. There's something that kicks in when they've made a new discovery." He nodded back at their companion. "Some gene or something. Give them a new discovery to study and they'll walk till they drop of dehydration or starvation, a precious weed or bug clutched in their dying fingers. Not only that, they'll die happy."

"Sorry. To me that's a contradiction in terms. First thing *I'd* like to find is some water. You sure we can't drink what's left in our suits?"

Low shook his head. "Not yet. That's our last option. You're not really thirsty yet. Your mind's just trying to fool your body."

"Well, it's doing a damn good job of it." Robbins licked dry lips. "Won't it just evaporate if we don't drink it?"

"Suit supplies are sealed against evaporation. When you start staggering, we'll discuss making use of the last of our known supplies. Meanwhile, I wouldn't panic. The plant life hereabouts looks pretty lush. We're sure to find drinkable water nearby."

She stared back at him. "You really believe that?"

"I could lie, but actually, I do. Might as well, because we *have* to find water."

She acknowledged the truth of this, glanced skyward. "I wonder how far we are from Earth? A light-year? Two or three? A thousand?"

He considered. "Maybe at night there'll be some constellations we can recognize, but I wouldn't count on it. A thousand's more likely than two or three. Might be ten thousand. Does it matter?"

"I suppose not."

"Better keep your eyes open. If I have Brink pegged correctly, he'll be spending his time staring at the ground instead of looking for food and water." He glanced significantly at her left arm. "You didn't bring your camera."

"It's a lot heavier down here than it was in space. After we've found water, I'll come back for it." She pointed to her eyes, then the side of her head. "Until then I'll use these cameras and this recorder. They've worked well enough for me in the past."

He smiled condescendingly. "I hope they find what we're looking for. Four loose plates would be nice."

She nodded agreement. "How about a pair of ruby slippers?"

"Hey, right now I'd try anything." He took a deep breath. "At least it doesn't smell bad."

"You sure it isn't poisonous?"

He shrugged. "I checked your gauges. You had four minutes of air left in your suit when we cracked our helmets. It's not like we have any choice. If there are dangerous trace elements in the atmosphere, they'll save us the trouble of trying to find a way home. Meanwhile, you might as well relax and inhale."

She sniffed. "Cloves?"

"That'd be about right. We'll find a hundred different kinds of spice, and nothing to put it on. I've always felt that irony was one of Nature's specialties."

"Man, you *are* a congenital pessimist!"

"Goes with commanding shuttle missions. Watch that crevice." He lengthened his stride as he stepped over the crack in the surface.

CHAPTER

9

"See? No exaggerated out-pourings of misplaced emotion, no standing about aimlessly, no collapsing into fetal positions. They have already set them-selves to problem solving."

"Simplistic and basal reactions, hardly indicative of ad-vanced cognition." The other presence was dubious. "Com-mon survival traits. Any ignorant animal would react similarly."

"What needs to be seen," declared a third of their number, "is how they proceed, if it is done with forethought and plan-ning or simply haphazardly. If the latter, then they will rapidly descend into panic."

"I concur." The first presence was more hopeful than its companions, but it was also realistic. After all, precedence was hardly encouraging. "Let us at least monitor them with-out condemnation. Is there anything else to do?"

"A diversion." The others who had gathered and remained chorused simultaneously. "A diversion."

"One wing-beat." The disdainful disappeared in a swirl of departing disenchantment. They knew that time was not on their side.

By the following morning the three travelers had made several important discoveries, the most welcome of which was fresh water. Collected in hollows eroded from the rocks, it had the appearance, smell, and taste of pooled rainfall. No one mentioned the possible presence of inimical microorganisms. Thirst will conquer prudence every time.

In any event, no one became ill as a result of drinking deeply. Whether they were simply lucky, whether local protozoans had no liking for the human gut or because Brink thoughtfully filtered each cupful through the cotton mesh of his undershirt they could not say. Regardless, it was clear that from now on, water would not be a problem. The pools were many, and several were deep.

In addition, Robbins pointed out, industrial pollution was not a factor.

Low was more concerned about dissolved minerals than microscopic bugs. "If there are any toxic salts in the water, signs should appear by tonight."

A playful Robbins tried to splash him. "C'mon, Commander, lighten up! It tastes good and it looks good. Besides, there are better things to die of than thirst. Honestly, you worry about everything. The water, the rocks, the air, whether the ground's going to open up under your feet. How'd a pessimist like you get into the space program, anyway?"

He replied softly. "That's one reason I did. It's my nature to question everything. For example, while we've been drinking, I've been wondering if any of this vegetation might be edible."

Unlike the water, the trees, bushes and lichens didn't look very inviting. "I'm no bovine," Robbins pointed out. "Just got the one stomach to work with. Let's try to find something softer than twigs."

"Hey, I'm no vegetarian myself." Low was leaning over to inspect a fist-sized hole in the cliff face. If it was occupied, the owner was disinclined to receive visitors. Wariness suggested predation. Low hoped they wouldn't find any holes too much larger. Bear-sized, for example.

It was wonderful to learn that life existed beyond Earth. It would be less wonderful to discover that it, too, was home to participants in the game of predator and prey.

He kicked aside an orange-tinged log that would have been priceless on Earth. The collecting of specimens would have to wait until their immediate continued survival was assured. At least if the climate turned cold, there was no want of firewood.

Besides the native rock, they passed ruined walls of strange plastic-metal, collapsed arches of some unidentifiable ceramic material, and another ship that resembled theirs only superficially. It was clearly a vessel of some kind, though whether older or newer than the unasteroid they had no way of telling. Its gaping interior proved dark and uninviting. There was no sign of occupants, living or otherwise. Only a musty smell that might have had organic origins, or might simply indicate great age. Low wasn't encouraged.

Brink had given up his study of the geology and vegetation in favor of scrutinizing the profusion of ruins. Certainly any hope of finding a way home lay within alien walls and not with the indigenous flora and fauna.

"Since we are now embarked on what might better be described as an archaeological dig," he ventured unexpectedly, "perhaps it would be best if I were to take charge."

More amused than bemused, Low stopped and pondered a moment. "There's only three of us. What kind of charge did you have in mind? Just for the record, we're engaged in survival, not a scientific expedition. Want to bet which one of us has more experience in that area?"

"Under different circumstances I would take that bet, Commander. I have led several expeditions to the south-central Sahara, to Mongolia and to the South Pacific. The latter resulted in all parties suffering through a situation not unlike the one that confronts us now. However," he added with a conciliatory smile, "the number of moons that shone down on that unhappy group was only one."

"None of that has any bearing on our present situation. We're dealing with alien conditions, and an alien world. If nothing else, I'll wager that I've read more science fiction than you. That's as valid a preparation for dealing with our present situation as anything else."

"Excuse me a minute?" Turning, they saw an impatient and obviously irritated Robbins gazing back at them. "If you *men* don't mind, I was wondering if I had a say in this, or if I'm just supposed to tag along the traditional ten paces behind, then plow the fields, shuck the corn and do the cooking?"

Low was taken aback. "I didn't mean to imply—"

Again she interrupted. "Of course not. It's been my experience that men don't. Which doesn't prevent them from doing so."

At a loss how to proceed, he assured her that her vote counted for as much as either his or Brink's. "Maybe you'd like to take charge?"

"I didn't say that. Though I'm not short on survival experience, I can't match stories with either of you. All I'm saying is that I know how to get by in a tight spot and I think that my input should count for something."

Both men exchanged a glance, then looked back at her. "So input," Low proposed crisply.

"I will. I think Commander Low should remain in charge. Technically we're still on a NASA mission. Even if it's been"—she hesitated—"somewhat extended and modified in scope. On the other hand, if we start prowling inside alien ruins in search of metal ignition plates or anything similar, then I think we should defer to you, Ludger."

The scientist nodded once. If the small personal defeat troubled him, he didn't show it.

Low was gracious in turn. "Look, Ludger, I don't think of anybody as being 'in charge' here. We're all in the same boat and we're too small a group to worry about formalities. If anyone comes up with any good ideas, they need to broach them. We'll analyze and decide together."

"Naturally. Well, if nothing else, I can at least name this place."

"Me, I'd just call it 'Island,' " Robbins quipped.

"I've no objection to that." Low's response caused her to eye him quizzically. Any hidden meanings in his acquiescence remained hidden.

"I am sorry, but I must disagree. So lofty a discovery deserves grander nomenclature. "I would prefer to call it Cocytus."

Robbins frowned. "Is that a Germanic name?"

The scientist smiled slightly. "Not exactly. In Dante's *Inferno,* Cocytus was the name of the Ninth Circle of Hell. Intimidating it may sound, but it was also the way back to the outer world."

"Charming. Oh well, if you insist. I suppose it carries a greater cachet than 'Island.' " To her credit Robbins didn't sulk.

"Not a particularly hellish place," Low demurred. "You said you've been to the Sahara and the Gobi. Except for better communications, I'd rank both worse than this. Cocytus it is, then." He resumed his climb, and the others followed, Brink discoursing on the nature of the ruined walls and half-buried structures between which they were passing.

"See how they argue and debate." The presence that made the observation drifted high above the trio as they left the asteroid transport behind and made their way toward the center of the island. "High above" was only a relative spatial designation. "Elsewhere proximate" would have been a more accurate description.

"To what end?" declared another. "They amble about. Perhaps not aimlessly, but with no real end in mind. They have solved nothing, done nothing. They stare and do not see. They listen and do not hear."

"Their senses are circumscribed." The first refused to be discouraged.

"See how they walk? So narrow and thin. It would seem they would unbalance and fall over. They have only the slim upper limbs to balance with. No tail, no wings, no cape, nothing. Yet they stride along, clumsy but erect. Their sense of balance must be well tuned."

"But not their sense of position relative to the rest of reality. That is easy to see," insisted twelve forms nearby. While observing, they amused themselves by inventing a series of intricately evolved dynamic fractal patterns composed of long sequences of related thoughts.

"Why should they worry about it? They are reality based. If you will remember, that is enough." There followed many thought-exhalations that elsewhere and under different conditions could have been interpreted as sighs.

"Tactility." Five others temporarily existed as an integrated pentagram of contemplation. "Smell. What would not be traded for the scent of a decomposing flower, or the feel of wind on a face."

"Enough of that," swore eight nearby. "What use in teasing up old memories? It has been hundreds of years."

"No, thousands," insisted fifteen others. And they fell to arguing the specifics of memory.

The scent of a flower. The one who had first encountered the new arrivals drifted and watched. Smell. Touch. For any of those it would have traded immortality in an instant.

There is a difference between living forever and existing forever.

They could not impinge on reality except in the most peripheral, transitory fashion. They had rejected it, and it in turn had disavowed them. They could have no more effect on the three travelers than a falling leaf.

But sometimes, the watcher recalled, a falling leaf could set in motion great events—if circumstances were exactly right.

"What do you think of the name they have given to our world, and by implication, to us?" Six new arrivals found within the situation something new to discuss. It was eagerly taken up, as was anything new.

"Their thoughts are crude, but clear enough when verbally

enunciated. They are images etched not in stone but in air."
Seven joined three to make ten.

"Two of them seem conflicted. We sense desire, admiration, fear, and hate all beaten together. Very typical of immature species."

"Remember," remarked the first, who remained a solitary point of cognition amid all the melding, "once we, too, were subject to such surges of emotion. Sometimes I miss them."

"Everything is missed," avowed thirty or more, who came together out of concurrence.

Watching those who were watching the bipeds was the entire population of that world, who in deference to the new arrivals' whim would henceforth refer to themselves as Cocytans. It was a lark and, as something new, much appreciated. It would last as long as the bipeds themselves lasted, which, given their aimless meandering and obviously brief life span, would doubtless not be long.

"Help them," whispered five of the presences.

"Help them," concurred the rest of the populace.

There was a caucusing, whereupon it was given to the discoverer as one of the most determined among them to make the effort.

"It will be of no value," declared the pessimists. "It never is."

"We can but try," insisted the more positive among those present. "We have nothing if not time."

The narrow canyon up which they were advancing was lined with low scrub whose needles seemed to flex in their direction. Low considered pinching off a twig or two to test their consistency but thought better of it. From the looks of the twitching greenery, it might decide to pinch back. A narrow trickle of dirty water ran down the middle of the crevasse, encouraging but probably not potable. A large orange shape popped out of a hole high up on their left and inspected them briefly before vanishing back within. It hadn't lingered long enough for him to get a good look at it, but he was sure it had more than two eyes.

Robbins put a hand on his arm. "Wait a minute. I thought I saw something."

The pilot looked over at her. "First you hear something, then you feel something. Now you're seeing somethings."

"No, really." She moved up alongside him, staring.

"Aerial?"

"Terrestrial. No, I'm not sure."

"How many legs?"

"Look for yourself." She pointed sharply.

A wisp of color flashed in the air before them. Not a flame, but the ghost of one. It flickered, never more than a suggestion of shape, never more than an indistinct outline. As manifestations went, it was disappointingly insubstantial.

As they stared speculatively, it circled, forcing them to turn slowly to follow its progress. The outline it formed varied in size but never in density. Low had seen far thicker fog.

After circling them twice, it appeared to shoot up the canyon and off to their left, each time attenuating to nothingness. Returning, it repeated the sequence. Was there a face buried in that color and mist? Robbins fancied she saw one, but it never lingered or held its shape long enough for her to be certain.

A daylight dream, it vanished completely after executing the second run up the canyon. Silent as a zephyr, it was a transitory phenomenon whose passage excited considerable discussion among the travelers.

No one said, "Did you see that?" because all of them had tracked its passage with their eyes.

"No heat," noted Brink. "At least, none that I could feel."

"No, it was a cold light. Didn't give off anything, near as I could tell." Low was equally baffled.

"So, what was it?" Robbins waited.

Brink was noncommittal but willing to speculate. "Swamp gas. Will-o'-the-wisp. I won't torment you with the German name. A local atmospheric phenomenon, apparently harmless."

"I thought it was suggesting that we should bear to the left," she insisted.

Low was patient with her. "Come on, Maggie. We can't start relying on lights in the sky for direction."

"Why not?" She eyed him challengingly. "Given our knowledge of this place, which is to say none, it seems to me as good an indicator as anything else."

Low looked at Brink, who shrugged as if to say, "She wants you to be in charge, remember?" The Commander considered the canyon ahead. Might as well go left as right anyway.

"All right. We'll take a hint from your light, Maggie. And if it leads to a vertical cliff, you can be the first one to jump off."

"Fine." She strode past him and took the lead. He followed silently. There were times when he'd acted on the result of a coin flip, so why not on the vagaries of an inexplicable light? If nothing else, its appearance had been worthwhile because it had energized the journalist and at least momentarily taken her mind off their unfortunate circumstances.

"Probably airborne particles reacting with the sunlight," Brink hypothesized, "or some piezoelectric reaction in the substance of the old walls. Although I suppose it could have been something else. A visual street sign, perhaps, lingering from ancient times."

"Yeah," muttered Low. " 'This Way to the Garbage Dump.' "

Brink was not displeased. "I would not mind finding that. Dumps are always full of useful things."

"You know, Ludger, you're an incorrigible. An incorrigible what, I don't know, but an incorrigible."

"I accept the designation with honor, Commander."

"I think you're both wrong." Robbins stepped over a collapsed section of wall. "That was no natural phenomenon. It was trying to show us something."

"Anything is possible, Maggie." Brink worked at not sounding condescending. He didn't always manage it. "This is an entirely new world. Who is to say what natural laws may or may not be obeyed here? Perhaps even flickering lights that give directions."

"There was a face," she insisted. "Just for an instant, but I saw it."

"You are anthropomorphizing. Just as one sees faces in the clouds, or silhouettes in the stars."

"It was a face. Not human, but distinct. My observation's as valid as yours."

Low tried to calm her. "It could have been a face. It wasn't around for very long, so it's hard to say. Remember, Maggie, the first rule of science is to disbelieve everything you see, not to accept it. Extraordinary events require extraordinary proof."

"Maybe it'll come back," she decided. "Watch out. There's a hole here."

"I see it," he replied testily, and was immediately sorry. She was only trying to be helpful.

"See!" Having exhausted itself with the effort, the first discoverer addressed the others. "They are not entirely bereft of perceptual ability. Excuse my dissipation. That was quite a strain." Despite maximal exertion, a brief flicker was as much as any of them could impinge anymore on the real world.

"An admirable effort, but to limited effect." A dozen decriers swirled nearby. "They are reluctant to accept the evidence of their senses."

"That is natural enough," insisted those who supported the first.

"Questioning is a sign of mental strength, not weakness," avowed several who had remained neutral. "They proceed in the direction that was suggested."

"Not a sign of acceptance," the naysayers declared. "Their options were limited in any case."

"Possibly if you tried again." Avid supporters gathered around the first.

"I cannot. The attempt has left me spent. Perhaps later." Any noncorporeal being would be weakened by the effort of trying to impact on the physical world. "They must proceed now on their own. But if another wishes to try . . ."

None did. Among those so inclined, none had the strength or talent. They could only flow and observe, drifting as easily through the rock beneath the travelers' feet as through the air above their heads.

Low was tiring of ruined walls and crumbling structures. "Look, we're not going to find anything up here. We should've gone the other way."

At which point Robbins halted and pointed. "Is that so? Isn't that another one of those metal plates? The kind that we used on the asteroid?"

The scientist shaded his eyes. "I believe you are right, Maggie." He hurried forward, the others following.

It might have been a little larger than the four plates they had used to activate the asteroid-ship, but there was no mistaking the shape, the way the inscriptions were laid out, or that soft charcoal-gray sheen.

"Let's take it back to the asteroid and see if it fits the dome," Low suggested. "Maybe it'll kick the thing into reverse. Maybe it'll do *something*."

"It's certainly worth a try," Brink agreed.

Spreading out, they dug at the loose dirt and gravel until they could slide their fingers under the plate's curving edge. Despite their best efforts, it would not come free.

Lying prone and squinting, Low continued to scratch dirt from beneath the metal. "It's set in a groove of some kind. Maybe we ought to leave this one alone."

"Nonsense!" Brink moved forward. "Here, let me."

Additional work reduced the height of the surrounding soil

until they had room to shove the disk to one side. It shifted reluctantly to its right, sliding on ancient bearings.

They probably shouldn't have been surprised, but were, when a shaft was revealed beneath. It was wider and not as deep as the one that had led them to the asteroid's interior.

"I can see the bottom." Robbins leaned over to peer cautiously downward. "There's a smooth floor and some loose rock." She took a step back from the opening. "It looks like debris that's fallen in."

"The result of natural weathering processes," Brink explained. "There is no vacuum here to preserve structural integrity." He glanced over at Low. "If you would like to be the first to enter, Commander, I will gladly defer."

Low considered. He'd been watching and studying Brink as well as Maggie ever since they'd left the asteroid. The scientist seemed as competent on the ground as he'd been in space, if a touch overly eager to leap ahead where Low would have acted cautiously. It was going to be impossible to restrain his enthusiasm forever. Maybe now was the time to let him take the lead for a while. It would be useful to see how he would act when allowed to choose the direction of their advance.

"Ludger, I think archaeology's probably more your line. I'm liable to disturb something when I don't even know what I'm looking at. You go first."

The scientist considered the drop. "It is not that far. Getting out again may pose a problem, however."

"We'll just use the escalator." Low grinned. "Can't find anything useful if we don't look."

Brink nodded. Slipping his legs into the gap, he started to turn, intending to grip the inner edge of the shaft and then lower himself as far as possible by his hands before dropping free.

"It's not bad," he informed them. "If I can just reach—"

There was the sound of rock giving way, and Robbins screamed, "Look out!" as she stumbled backward. Low dove forward, grabbing for the scientist's wrists, but he was too late. Brink lost his grip and fell.

Instead of quieting, the rumbling and grinding grew more intense. "Get back!" Low yelled at Robbins as he scrambled backward. The warning was unnecessary. She was already retreating.

The entire section of ground in which the shaft opening was embedded promptly gave way, collapsing into the chamber below. Dust and echoes rose from the cave-in, accompanied by a single muted curse in German. Then there was silence, broken only by the plastic *click* of broken rock settling into place.

Low rose and brushed at his coveralls. The opening at his feet was now some twenty feet across. "Maggie, you all right?"

She was standing on the far side of the hole that had opened in the ground, cautiously peering down and waving at the dust, which continued to drift upward.

"Ludger? Ludger!" There was no response.

Treading carefully and testing his footing before putting down his weight, Low walked around the opening to rejoin her. The ceiling collapse had left a pile of rubble that reached nearly to ground level, offering a comparatively easy way down. Of their companion there was no sign.

"Ludger!" Cupping his hands to his mouth, Low leaned over and bellowed into the depths. A couple of eerie echoes were all that responded. He turned to Robbins. "We've got to go down and find him." She nodded assent, her expression stricken.

They searched until they found the point where the pile of collapsed material came closest to ground level. Gritting his teeth, Low took a running start and leaped for the crest of the pile. He landed solidly, slipped backward and found himself tumbling out of control.

The floor was featureless and unmarred by the collapse. Robbins was at his side in seconds as he struggled to sit up.

"You okay?"

He brushed gravel from his sleeves. "Yeah. Lost my balance. Looks like you didn't have any trouble."

She smiled apologetically. "Three years' varsity gymnastics. My mother thought I was wasting my time." She helped him to his feet.

"Stay close," he told her.

She eyed him sardonically. "Why? So I can give you a hand, or so you can give me a hand?"

"Whatever," he snapped. Together they began to circle the base of the collapse. Ancient building material and natural rock and earth mixed to form the high mound.

As they searched, they spared an occasional glance for the underground chamber in which they found themselves. It was enormous, much larger than the interior of the asteroid. As with that vehicle, pale illumination emanated directly from the walls and floor. The ceiling, however, gave off no light. Either that part of the system had failed or this chamber was differently designed. As a result, the illumination was dimmer than it had been aboard the transport.

Low's examination of their new surroundings was interrupted by a cry from Robbins. "Oh my God!" Darting forward, she knelt and began pulling at something sticking out of the pile of detritus. An arm.

The only visible part of the scientist, it was still attached to the rest of him. "Careful." Working frantically, Low moved the larger rocks while Robbins dug away the smaller debris. "We don't want to bring any more of this down on him."

It seemed to take forever before they had enough of the rock shifted to be able to drag Brink's body from the heap. The scientist's eyes were shut, rock dust covered him from head to foot, and he was badly bruised and scraped. The multitude of small cuts, however, paled beside the deep bruise above his temple.

"Concussion," Low announced curtly as he studied the wound. "Maybe contusions. Could be internal bleeding.

Damn." Removing his shirt, he made a crude pillow for the scientist's head, resting it gently on the compacted garment.

They alternated performing mouth-to-mouth and CPR. Low tried everything he knew, and Robbins added a few first-aid tricks she'd picked up in her travels, but nothing worked. Angry and frustrated, the Commander finally leaned back against the small mountain of debris, running a hand through his dust-speckled hair.

"Well, that's it."

"What do you mean, that's it?" Robbins's professional demeanor was badly shaken. "It can't be! We haven't been here half a day."

"Doesn't matter how long we've been here." Low spoke quietly, evenly. "If we'd been here a week, he'd still be just as dead." It sounded harsher than he intended. He looked away from her. "There's nothing we can do."

Robbins knelt by the scientist's side. She'd seen a great deal of death, altogether more than was reasonable for someone her age. It had been by choice, an unavoidable corollary to several of the dangerous stories she had volunteered to cover. It was the suddenness of Brink's passing that hit her so hard now. The suddenness, and its matter-of-factness. They were not in a war zone, not trying to avoid terrorist fanatics, not dealing with the deadly vacuum of space. The scientist had been doing his job, was all. And now he was dead, victim of the dispassionate collapse of the entrance to still another alien construct. It was so damned impersonal. A lousy rockfall, something that could just as easily have happened back home in Germany.

Here, on the verge of great despair and equally great discovery, it struck her as obscene. She did not cry. It would have been unprofessional, and besides, she was too furious at an indifferent Fate.

"They do not grieve over-much," postulated a trio of Cocytans hovering in the vicinity of Robbins's hair. Their presence did not disturb a follicle, did not brush suggestively against her skin. But the temperature in the vicinity of her neck rose one-quarter of a degree, too slight to be noticed.

"If anything is to happen, it will take time," declared a hundred others, watching. "Each species has its own time frame."

"If they do not grieve for their dead, then they cannot be counted very intelligent." The trio was confident.

"If only they knew that there was much they could do," remarked a small dozen thought-forms. "So much at their fingertips, so much for them to discover. It is better they do not linger."

"Indeed it is," murmured a cooperative pair, "for they have lost a third of their complement already. We see no hope in these, just as we saw no hope in those who came before them. They are an entertaining diversion, no more."

"Did any think it would be otherwise?" queried the hundred.

The one who had exerted a mighty effort, only to see its presence in the real world disparaged as a ghost of an illusion, remained defiant.

"They will grieve, and then resume looking. I think it is in their nature. They will not give up."

"They will give up, after a while. The isolation and the

hopelessness in which they see themselves beats the best of them down." The dozen were merciless. "Another day or two of their time will see them start to go mad. The precedent is there."

"These are different," insisted the first. "They have to be more determined than those who preceded them. They are physically weak and unimposing. Therefore their development must have tended to the mental."

"Intelligence is useless without drive." The dozen split and split again, but their thoughts remained cohesive.

"Have they drive? We will see. A diversion." The hundred were joined by nine, and became a thousand.

"Wasteful expenditure of energy." They became silent, waiting and watching.

Maggie Robbins had flung herself against Low and was pounding her fists into his chest. The startled commander tried to grab her wrists, but she was much stronger than she looked. At least, he reflected, she wasn't hitting him in the face. How much of her anger was directed at him and how much at their latest misfortune he was unable to tell.

She quickly enlightened him. "You son of a bitch! You told him to try that entrance!"

"Now, just a minute, Maggie." He finally succeeded in getting a grip on her forearms and held her off. She had been so completely in control of herself, so utterly professional up till now, that the sudden emotional flare-up had caught him completely by surprise.

"In case you've forgotten," he reminded her coldly, "you voted for me to stay in command. Being in command means telling others what to do." He nodded curtly at the crumpled body of their companion. "Would you feel better if it was me lying over there instead of Brink?"

She hesitated, took one last futile swing at him, and then yanked her arms away. Wiping at her eyes, she discovered that she was annoyed at herself more than at Low. Not only for losing control, but for making an insupportable accusation. She realized suddenly that she'd been putting off the enormity of what had happened to them. Brink's death had shattered the wall she'd erected between her emotions and this strange new reality. She'd allowed one wonder after another to mask an unpleasant inevitability.

Now it had all come crashing down on her at once, clear and sharp in her mind. Brink was dead, they weren't going home, and she'd never see her friends or family again. And in a few days, or if they were lucky, a few weeks, she and Low would be dead too.

"Would you prefer it was me?" she shot back. "I know you think I'm pretty useless. You'd probably trade my life for Brink's in a minute."

"No," he said quietly and without hesitation. "No, I wouldn't. I don't think like that." Again he looked past her. "I'm as sorry as sorry can be for what's happened. I liked Ludger . . . well, I can't say that I *liked* him, but I respected the hell out of him. He was the best at what he did. If he was a little too devoted to himself, well, I've been accused of being something of a cold fish myself." He raised his gaze.

"No one could have foreseen that the whole ceiling around the portal was ready to collapse. It looked solid enough to me. It must've looked solid to Ludger too. Remember, he was the one with the degree in geology. If he'd thought it was unstable, I'm sure he would've said something."

She shook her head, wiped the back of her hand across her nose. "Naw, not Ludger. He would've gone ahead anyway. His curiosity would've overridden his common sense. I got to know him well enough to know that, anyway."

"It doesn't matter. At least he went quickly. We're probably both going to end up like him anyway."

She stopped daubing at her eyes. "You really believe that?"

He shrugged. "I'm a realist, Maggie. We'll keep trying, keep looking, but I'm not sanguine." He swept an arm in a broad circle to encompass the gigantic chamber in which they found themselves. "I don't know what any of this does, and I don't know how to find out. That's assuming any of it is still functional. Maybe Ludger could've done better."

"There has to be a way to reactivate the asteroid-ship, a way to make it take us back to Earth."

He smiled tolerantly. "Does there? Why should it be anything but a one-way trip? Even if the asteroid is capable of making a return journey, what makes you think it carries enough fuel, or whatever it utilizes for propulsion? We could figure out a way to start it back up and *still* go nowhere."

"Then why did you push to come up this canyon?" Her tone was bitter. "If it's so hopeless, why are we even trying?"

"It's like Ludger said. The first rule of science is to disbelieve everything. So even though I'm convinced we're not going anywhere, least of all home, I can't let it stop me from searching. Science is always frustrating."

"Well, if that's the way science works," she muttered, "then science sucks!"

All he could do was smile. "Only if you're talking hydraulics. Wish I'd had some archaeology, but it wasn't exactly a prerequisite for flight school." He turned to examine their surroundings. "Might as well get started. Which way, Maggie?"

"You expect me to come with you?" She stared at him in disbelief. "So you can tell me to dive into the next hole or stick my head in the guillotine? No thanks, no thank you, *Commander.*" She made it sound like a curse. "If I'm going to die here, then I'm gonna spend my last few hours going my own way. Try acting on your own orders for a change."

With that she whirled and stomped off in the opposite direction, no particular destination in mind, knowing only that she wanted to get away from *him.* She was thoroughly incensed . . . and thoroughly confused.

Low started after her, then halted. She was upset, frustrated, and badly frightened. She had every right to be. There was nothing he could do about it. The boundless energy that had served her so well on this journey as well as on innumerable foreign assignments only compounded her distress. Arguing would do no good, would only waste resources better conserved. In the coming days they were going to need whatever strength remained to them, mental as well as physical. Better to let her go her own way for a while and burn off some of the tension.

He didn't think she'd go very far. The chamber was large but not excessively so, and he didn't see her wandering about on the surface by herself for very long without checking back with him. Meanwhile, aloneness and isolation would calm her down faster than he could. They'd just listen, and wouldn't shout back. When she got tired of railing at invisible demons, she'd come looking for him. She was a rational, reasonable individual and he doubted it would permanently strain their relationship.

Did they have a relationship? Whatever it was, he would deal with it as circumstances required.

Turning, he resumed his inspection of the grand chamber. Though still vast, it wasn't as enormous as it had appeared at first glance. Except for the area immediately around the edges of the initial collapse, the ceiling seemed structurally sound. He couldn't see any additional cracks or stress fractures. The rest of the roof wouldn't have been subjected to the same forces as the more sensitive portion near the opening.

He decided to walk a complete circuit of the chamber, during which time he identified five high arches set into the meandering wall. They might have been works of art, or simple designs intended to break the monotony of the interior, but to his eye they more closely resembled doorways that had been tightly sealed. All five were uniform in appearance and construction.

The small tunnel he found was not blocked, and this he was able to explore. Pulling the compact flashlight from his utility belt, he gave the interior a quick once-over before returning to the main chamber. The darkness of space didn't bother him, but tunnels and unexplored caves did.

On his way back out he stumbled. Catching himself, he looked down to see that he'd lost his balance because of a depression in the floor. Did it indicate the presence of another shaft going deeper still? A metal plate lay nearby, apparently designed to fit the depression. It's discovery ought to have excited him. Instead, he felt only a mild elation. It was frustrating to know that you had tools in your hand in the form of the plates but not know how to use them.

Nevertheless, he carefully picked it up and snugged it under an arm. Four similar plates had activated the asteroid-ship. Whether four more would reactivate it and send it speeding back to Earth he had no way of knowing. But first he needed to find three more. At least now he had a goal, and it gave him something to do besides stumble about blindly in the hope that Providence would intervene on his behalf. If nothing else, the plate was heavy, solid and comfortingly real.

He intended to leave it near the base of the rubble pile, that being as convenient a rendezvous as any, but as he was starting back, he noticed a depression in one of the many consolelike bulges in the wall. Like the others he'd seen, it was also studded with slots and strange gouges. Its proximity to the plate, which had been lying loose on the tunnel floor, was too much of a coincidence to ignore.

"Truly problem solving they are," avowed the first presence.

"I was certain the creature was going to continue past." Though many of the others remained dubious, sparks of reluctant optimism began to evince themselves.

"Will it take the correct action?" wondered a dozen others. "Oftentimes the primitive will perform the unexpected."

"But if it does the *wrong* thing . . ." The fifty who had spoken left the thought unfinished.

"Manifest yourself," several urged the first. "Show the creature the way. Give it a sign."

The first strained briefly before giving up. "I cannot. Not

enough time has passed. The regeneration of personal energy takes time."

Every presence paused to observe the biped's actions. "If it acts wrongly, it will die like its companion. As have so many who have come before."

The first presence might not have had enough strength left to manifest, but it was quite capable of continued argument. "Do not blame the creatures for the one death they have suffered thus far. There was no correct way to enter the chamber. Time has finally begun to destroy what we left behind. The opening would have crumbled no matter what approach the bipeds had taken. They could not have known that. If blame for their failure needs to be apportioned, then part of it lies with us as the builders."

"If only it were possible to manifest more strongly," several lamented. "We could save these creatures, and they in turn could help us."

"If we could do that," reminded a thousand others, "we would not need the assistance of stranded primitives. We could save ourselves. Alas, for all that we have accomplished, for all that we have learned, we cannot."

All they could do, in fact, in their tens of thousands, was watch . . . and hope.

Loath to give up the plate, Low hesitated before the depression. What if it sank out of sight, absorbed by the substance that composed the wall? That's what had happened to the plates onboard the asteroid-ship. He held his prize up to the depression. It would fit perfectly.

He would have consulted Maggie, but she had taken herself elsewhere, and Brink was no longer around to offer counsel. Reaching a decision, he slipped the plate into the concave receptacle. It fit flush with the wall.

A soft humming became audible, only occasionally interrupted by the grind of centuries passing. Or perhaps it was merely dust being blown in through the opening in the roof. Wary, he retreated a few steps.

His heart sank along with the plate as it melted into the material of the wall. From previous experience he knew it was now unrecoverable. Well, it had been worth the experiment, he decided, refusing to be discouraged. Any additional plates he found would go straight to the base of the rubble heap, to wait there until they could be carried back to the asteroid-ship.

The consolelike bulge into which the plate had vanished began to pulse with a glow unlike the light that emanated from the walls and floor. The grinding sound came not from the sinking of the plate into the depression nor from the presence of blowing sand but from a nearby section of floor. Low kept his distance until the passageway was completely revealed.

Approaching cautiously, he peered over and down. The same soft, pleasing refulgence that illuminated the big chamber also allowed him to see into the room below. Instead of arcane bulges and mysterious swellings, it was filled with an assortment of devices and artifacts, all in varying states of preservation or decrepitude.

Lifting his head, he turned and shouted. "Maggie! Hey, Robbins, get yourself over here! I've found something." There was no reply. Where had she gone?

Well, he couldn't wait on her, he decided anxiously.

There was a ladder, of sorts. A bizarre arrangement of bars and steps that resembled something lifted from a bombed-out school playground. Clambering down as best he could, he found himself standing in what reminded him more than anything else of an old janitorial storeroom. Nothing was stored carefully. The jumble of devices had the appearance of an afterthought, as though they had been dumped here at the last minute.

The last minute before what, he found himself wondering?

Careful to disturb nothing, he moved from one artifact to the next, inspecting but not touching. Was any of this alien junk still functional? And if so, how could he divine individual functions?

He halted before one that caught his attention. Not because it was unique of design or remarkable of appearance but because it seemed better preserved than anything else in the room. Dust and grime did not coat its every exposed surface, and there were faint suggestions of recent automatic lubrication. Had it been somehow employed by the vanished occupants of the other vessel they had found here? Or was it some kind of maintenance device, forgotten by its makers, left to perform whatever task it had been designed for until it collapsed or its power source finally ran down.

He let his fingers trail along the smooth, machined flanks. No circular metal plate bulged from the artifact's middle or protruded from within. Therefore he was more than a little startled when a soft *click* sounded. He retreated hurriedly, ready to scramble up the alien ladder should the device exhibit hostile tendencies.

It did nothing of the sort. Instead, it continued to squat in the shadows and hum softly to itself.

"If you're waiting for instructions," the Commander announced, "you've got the wrong programmer."

Or maybe not. In response to his words the device pivoted to face him, attentive and waiting. When Low took a step forward, the machine matched the movement.

He studied it closely. The front was studded with multiple projections that might have been tools. But tools for what? The squat device might be anything from floor cleaner to portable dentist. One thing was fairly evident: it had reacted to his presence and was continuing to do so.

It had been stored here, in this room below the grand chamber. That suggested its functions were tied to the chamber itself. Low had no special desire to see the floor polished, or have his teeth worked on, but might not the gizmo be able to serve more prosaic functions?

For example, could it open a sealed door?

Tilting back his head, he studied the ladder that led upward. "How am I going to get you up there?" he muttered aloud. The machine did not reply, merely continued to stand on its feet and wait patiently.

"The machine lives."

A mental sigh passed through a hundred thousand watching Cocytans.

"See what one of them has accomplished already." Supporters of the first were much encouraged.

But hardly convincing. "It means nothing," declared a sizable concatenation of skeptics. "It stumbles about blindly. Luck favors the ignorant."

It was left to a supporter of the first to respond. "Luck is nothing more than a skillful realignment of pertinent values the final positioning of which is never left to chance. The biped made this happen."

"Made what happen?" responded the others. "See what it does now? Nothing! Its primitive thought processes are at an impasse and it waits for fate to intervene. That is hardly proof of appropriate motivation." Many could not be convinced to allow themselves a glimmer of optimism. Down through the centuries too many hopes had been dashed.

"Patience. It is true that the creature's reaction times are slow, but they are in keeping with its progress thus far. See, it is thinking. Considering alternatives. Criticize not its sluggishness but the results."

"What results?" sniffed the naysayers through the ether. But despite all their bemoaning, they, too, continued to watch.

Low walked carefully around the device, never taking his eyes from it. As he circled, the machine pivoted patiently to face him. Defensive posture, he wondered? Or simply a standard programmed reaction to movement? He could always give it a swift kick and observe the reaction. Of course, if it was equipped to defend itself, that wouldn't be a very bright idea. Besides, he doubted it was the accepted way to activate any useful functions.

The multiplicity of devices bristling on its front side continued to intrigue him. Would any operate the console-mound in the asteroid? He discarded that thought quickly. Despite its armory of instruments, the machine boasted nothing resembling the large metal plates that had set the asteroid-ship in motion. Furthermore it was unreasonable to assume that something locked away beneath the floor of the big chamber was incidentally designed to operate interstellar transport. No, he decided: the little machine might be capable of many things, but flying them back to Earth probably wasn't one of them.

It was self-evidently too heavy to carry, even assuming it would allow the attempt. Could it climb? It certainly had limbs enough. There was one way to find out.

Turning toward the ladder, he looked back and beckoned. "Come on, then." The words sounded foolish and misplaced in his own ear, even though there was no one around to hear him. "Let's see if you can make it to the top."

He started up the ladder. After a moment's hesitation, the machine followed. Despite the absence of anything that could reasonably be called an arm, or a hand, it displayed surprising agility while following in his wake. It slipped once but did not fall.

There was nothing endearing about it; no eyes, or other recognizable facial features, but Low found himself admiring the device's persistence. Despite a hiatus of indeterminate length, it had responded to his presence and now seemed content to follow him about like a dog. He would have preferred the companionship of Robbins, but in her absence it was somehow reassuring to once more have something ambulatory for company.

He bellowed her name again as soon as he emerged back onto the main floor, and once again received no response. A search was no doubt in order, he knew, but if he found her, she'd probably resent the intrusion, regarding it as an affront to her self-reliance. He'd give her more time, he decided. The alien fauna they'd encountered thus far had been decidedly nonthreatening, and she was doubtless doing just fine on her own. When she was ready, she could just as easily find him.

Turning to the device, he said without much hope, "All right, let's see what you can do."

Approaching the nearest arch, he scrutinized the inscriptions and indentations etched into one side. They might be control surfaces, loud warnings, elegant hieroglyphics, or nothing more than some kind of elaborate alien graffiti. Nothing to lose by trying, he told himself.

Running his fingers over and through the sinuous engraving provoked no response. Perhaps a more specific touch was required. Turning, he gestured broadly at the machine.

"Can you do anything with this? Is there anything that can be done with this, other than to admire the workmanship?"

The device squatted on its legs, indifferent to his entreaty. It was attendant upon him, but otherwise nonreactive.

Stymied, he walked slowly around the machine, watching as it once again turned to face him. At the completion of the circuit he found an idea waiting for him. Another half circle placed the device between him and the arch. Now he started deliberately forward. Responding, the little machine retreated proportionately. What would it do when it ran out of room? Skitter off to one side, or jump him, alien instruments whirring and clanking?

He was taking a chance, he knew, but it was time for that. Besides, this was a machine he was dealing with, not an animal. He knew how an animal would have reacted. Would the device also see him as a threat?

With the wall at its back the machine pivoted abruptly and rammed itself into the unyielding obstacle. For a crazy moment Low found himself wondering if it intended to commit some kind of outlandish mechanical hara-kiri. Edging forward, he saw that several of the instruments located on the machine's front end were moving; sliding into slots, filling holes, and caressing grooves. Though he watched carefully, he knew it was a pattern he could not duplicate. For one thing, he did not possess the requisite number of limbs.

A deep hum sprang from within the arch, and Low tensed. Something whirred like a giant gyroscope. The machine withdrew its tools and trundled backward.

Together, they watched as the barrier seemed to melt in on itself, to reveal a high, imposing portal beneath the arch. Low marked the phenomenon with something approaching awe, while the device gazed upon its handiwork with the same unvarying, phlegmatic mechanical stare.

He searched in vain for signs of the missing barrier, finally gave up and attributed its remarkable disappearance to an alien engineering he could not understand. Of much more interest was what lay beyond the now-vanished doorway.

A large tunnel stretched off into the distance. No circle of light gleamed at its end, no comforting gleam of sunshine. To his right stood a raised platform. Alongside it was a transparent sphere that might have been fashioned from pure quartz, flawless glass or more likely some completely unknown material. For all Low knew, it was an artificial diamond, though it more closely resembled a hollow pearl.

He started forward. Aware that the little robot wasn't following, he turned and beckoned as he'd done down in the storage room. It didn't budge. Not all his shouts or urgings could induce it to advance. When he tried the trick of circling around behind and backing it toward the tunnel, it simply darted out of his path. No matter how strenuous an effort he mounted, he could not get it to step through the archway.

"Fine," he finally snapped, exasperated. "Stay here. I'll open the next door myself." He had to smile. "Stay, boy, stay!"

The machine did not reply, nor did he expect it to. It simply remained in place, motionless, and would presumably be there when he returned. Yet had it sat back on its distorted mechanical legs and put its fore instruments into the air, he would not have been surprised. He had long since lost his capacity for astonishment.

Or so he thought.

Entering the tunnel, he ascended the platform and cautiously rested one hand against the beautiful clear material. Inside he saw a peculiar bench, or bed, or storage rack. Having no knowledge of Cocytan anatomy, he had no way of identifying its proper function. The interior was large enough to hold several people. Or one alien, he wondered?

For an instant he thought he saw a flicker of orange light behind him, not unlike the one that had manifested itself during their march up the canyon. It wasn't repeated, leaving him to contemplate its source and meaning. It might, he realized, have been nothing more than a reflection induced by his movements.

The entrance to the sphere was round and doorless. Once inside, he searched in vain for anything resembling a switch, button or lever. There was nothing. No console, no floor controls, not even a light panel. Only the peculiar flowing bench and the dark tunnel ahead.

Leaning forward, he saw that the floor of the tunnel was deeply grooved right up to the base of the sphere. The inference was obvious, but not the mechanism. The presence of a track indicated that the sphere was intended to travel along it, though by what means of propulsion he couldn't imagine. There was no sign of an engine, exhaust, rocket ports, or wheels. It suggested that motive power was supplied not by the sphere but by the groove, or perhaps the tunnel itself.

Of one thing he was certain. The sphere was intended for local transport only. It would not get them a thousandth of a light-year closer to Earth.

Which left open the question of just where it did go. To another asteroid-ship launching pad? Too much to hope for. To a room full of ship-activating plates? A more reasonable possibility.

The circular opening displayed no inclination to close behind him, and nothing he could do would persuade the system to activate. If, he reminded himself, it was still functional.

Once again he debated whether to go looking for his sole remaining companion, and once again he determined to give her the space she evidently desired. Low could repair and fix a great many things, but a blue funk wasn't one of them.

Climbing onto the platform, he found himself marveling at the material. It looked like polished wood, until he bent close and discovered that he could see partway into its brown depths. Nothing here was completely solid. He found himself wondering if the effect was intentional or simply a by-product of Cocytan manufacturing techniques.

Maybe staring hard at the bench was the accepted method of activation, or perhaps his weight tripped some concealed mechanism within the bench. Or possibly the weight of ages had resulted in a longer-than-normal delay in departure. Whatever the cause, the opening behind him irised shut, encasing him within the sphere. The door had materialized out of nothingness in much the same fashion as the archway to the grand chamber had disappeared before him.

He hammered on the barrier, to no avail. It was sealed tight. How tight? He found himself wondering if the Cocytans had perhaps traveled in the sphere in a state of suspended animation, or naturally induced estivation. If so, the device's occupants would not have been burdened with the need to breathe.

Unfortunately, he was.

Light bloomed on the surface of the sphere, both within and without. What had he gotten himself into? The air remained fresh and plentiful—for now. Had he misinterpreted the machine's function? Was it indeed part of some local transportation system—or the Cocytan version of a high-end mousetrap?

The sphere rocked as if jolted by something unseen. He closed his eyes, waiting for the bolt of electricity or hiss of poison gas. When neither materialized, he opened his eyes . . . and found himself staring down the long black line of the tunnel.

The sphere was moving forward. Looking back, he could clearly see the platform and the open archway that led to the big chamber receding behind him. Reflections proved that the sphere was rotating within the groove like a billiard ball speeding back down its loading chute, but within the sphere all was stable. The bench did not even vibrate, remaining level and steady as the vehicle continued to accelerate.

There were no landmarks within the featureless tunnel, no running lights or glowing signposts. This made it difficult to estimate his speed, but calculating comparative velocity was something Low was particularly good at. He determined that the sphere was racing along at well over a hundred miles an hour. How far over he couldn't tell.

He tried to recall what little they knew of the terrain they'd crossed. Brink had alluded to the possibility that they might have come down on an island, but without circumnavigating it they had no proof it was not part of a larger body of land. Based on what they'd seen, Low doubted they'd landed on part of a continent. A peninsula perhaps, if not an island.

If that was the case, then there was a good chance he was now traveling beneath a Cocytan ocean. Sitting back on the bench, he could only hope that the tunnel would terminate somewhere above the surface.

Others recorded his progress, effortlessly pacing the sphere. Though once they had been conscious of such things, they no longer had any need to calculate its speed. In their present state, intangibles such as relative velocity meant nothing to them.

Several hovered high above the ocean, tracking the sphere's forward motion as though sea, sky and stone did not exist. Which for them, it no longer did. Others followed down the tunnel, while a hundred companions passed effortlessly through the same solid rock. Density was a concept that for them held only philosophical meaning, and they traveled as easily through iron as through air.

They were indifferent to solid matter, but passing through the trees as effortlessly as through the forest no longer held any thrill for them. There is no challenge in that which is simple, and where there is no challenge, life is but a poor thing. The thousandth time one does something, it stinks of repetition rather than discovery.

Gladly would they have given up their ease of passage to feel the rock, smell the air or taste the water. None of these were options open to them. They had voluntarily abandoned the real world and could not find the way back. At first, pure thought had been a new sensation. It had grown dry and tasteless with remarkable speed.

The pleasure of anticipation was one of the few that still remained to them.

"See what they have accomplished already," declared a rotating polygon of presences.

"It stumbles about. Only natural that it should occasionally stumble into good fortune." The doyens of depression were still as active as ever.

"They are not animals. The intellectually inhibited would have run from the door-opener instead of making use of it."

"Very well. That which is supported by proof must be conceded. The bipeds possess a low-level intelligence and some problem-solving ability. That makes them little different from those who have come before . . . and failed. Others have succeeded in opening doors. Where they fail is in what they do with what they find."

"Be not impatient for failure," chided one-and-forty on the verge of auspiciousness.

"Not we," came the response. "We only observe and extrapolate."

"Then do not extrapolate failure. We swim in a sea of it already. There is no need to add to the volume." Even argument about arguing provided respite from the all-encompassing tedium. In that respect the arrival of the three humans had already proven beneficial to the displaced masters of the fourth planet.

There was so much they could have told the travelers had they only been able to make contact. A whisper in the mind, a few carefully planted thoughts, would have prevented Brink's death and smoothed the way. It was not possible. Despite their mastery of time and space, the Cocytans could only wait and watch, as frustrated as any snail seeking to circumnavigate a sequoia.

They could, however, still feel.

So gradual was the tunnel's descent, so perfectly fabricated its walls, that even Low, who had a better sense of up and down than most humans, could not tell how deep he had traveled nor how far. There was no mistaking when the sphere began to lose speed, though.

Light appeared up ahead, and the remarkable transport

mechanism deposited him gently in a docking chamber that was identical to the one he had just left. Only the fact that the ceiling was slightly lower indicated that he had not traveled in an aimless circle. He had definitely arrived somewhere.

Rising from the bench, he began carefully to feel that portion of the sphere's interior that had originally contained the entrance. It remained solid to the touch.

Careful, he told himself. *Don't lose it here.*

Maybe he brushed over a switch as transparent as the wall itself, or perhaps the entrance simply took time to cycle. Whatever the cause, it irised open and allowed him to disembark.

There was an arch off to his left and he walked toward it. A glance back showed that the sphere remained where he'd left it. As it displayed no inclination to return on its own, he felt safe in assuming it would wait for his return.

The sealed door presented a greater problem. There was no versatile robot here to activate concealed mechanisms and no suggestion in the floor of subterranean storerooms where one might be found. Enigmatic glyphs and engravings reflected back at him, teasingly obvious. Not knowing what else to do, he reached for one.

The barrier melted aside.

Interesting, he mused as he passed cautiously through the gaping portal. The activation of certain ancient mechanisms required special tools, whereas others apparently responded to one's mere presence. Apparently there was no predicting which were going to be cooperative and which obstinate. The door stayed open behind him.

He found himself in a vaulted room much smaller than the one he'd left behind. It was filled with the usual flowing bulges and distortions in the walls and floor. More inscrutable alien devices. An open portal led outside. That, at least, he knew how to make use of.

A gentle, warm breeze greeted him as he stepped through. He found himself on a rocky bluff overlooking the sea. It was steep and sheer enough to tease an experienced diver, which didn't matter. A recreational swim was not high on his current list of priorities.

In the distance rose the mass of the central island. From his new perspective he could see that it was truly an island, and that if this world boasted any major landmasses, none lay within range of the naked eye. The bulbous outline of the asteroid-ship was just visible off to the right of the central peak. In opposite directions, other islands thrust up from the seabed. Their mysterious spires glistened in the diffuse sunlight.

An impressive body of ocean lay between the main island and his present position. He hoped fervently that the spherical transport system would respond a second time to his presence, and that he would not be required to swim back. While the water might be warm, he had no way of predicting the strength of local currents, and it was unlikely that so placid and nurturing a sea would be devoid of highly evolved predators. They might find his taste strange and his flesh unpalatable, but by the time they figured that out, it wouldn't matter to him.

No, the sphere offered a much more reasonable means of return.

I'm getting old, he thought, *but I wouldn't mind getting a little older.* With that in mind he turned to study the spire that dominated this island as it did its companions. It thrust sharply skyward, defying the elements, a wonderfully organic testament to the aesthetic as well as the engineering talents of its builders. Not some hollow monument but a fully functional structure, it tapered to a point several hundred feet above the ground. The wondrous alloy of metal and glass shimmered in the sunlight, in color a pale gold. *Champagne,* Low thought. As a scion of the House of NASA he'd had to deal with plenty of advertising and PR people.

A few swirls of color, rose and pink, blushed the lower levels. In bright sunlight it would be almost too harsh to look at. Native vegetation grew right up against the sleek walls. One bush boasted tiny blue pustules that throbbed in and out.

He decided to give it plenty of clearance. Dangerous plants as well as dangerous animals often flaunted an innocent appearance designed to lull potential prey into too-close examination of their false beauty.

In response to his approach the distinctive reddish ground-cover seemed to contract in upon itself to avoid being stepped on. Motion-responsive elastic stems, he wondered, or some other as yet unknown alien phenomenon? Alongside archaeology he added botany to the list of subjects he wished he'd studied more deeply in college.

Back inside the spire, he began to examine more closely the bulges in the walls and, in particular, various alien devices that rested inanimate in corners or clustered together on the bare floor. Some were encased in flowing transparent cocoons fashioned of material like spun sugar. These proved impervious to his touch.

Glowing labels hovered above or in front of many displays like convocations of fireflies participating in some lampyridaecous military tattoo. They shifted and turned with him so that they were always visible no matter where he happened to be in the room. In addition to the ambient light that emanated from the walls and floor, the cases generated their own internal, slightly more intense variety of illumination.

Low speculated on the possible functions of their contents. Some resembled household utensils, others peculiar weapons. There were cases that featured educational displays and others battered equipment that might represent the local equivalent of historical preservation. None took the shape of something that might have been designed by human hands. Even the smallest object displayed in its design a marked aversion to sharp angles.

There was very little duplication, and everything was clearly intended to fulfill a specific purpose. *Now, if only,* he mused, *I could find a label that reads, "Interstellar Transport, Key, for the Activation Of."*

While nothing so obvious presented itself to his searching eyes, he did come across several entrancing examples of alien design. Most notable was an egg-shaped lump of green crystal. On Earth he would have suspected tsavorite, emerald or chrome tourmaline, in that order. For all he knew, here it might well be composed of petrified alien blood.

It wasn't very big, about the size of a paperback book. More impressive was the method of display. Instead of lying on a shelf or standing in the grasp of a special mount like so many of the other exhibits, the crystal floated in suspension within a glassy, transparent sheath. Furthermore, it glowed softly from some internal source.

As he walked around the display, the crystal pivoted slowly to follow him, as if possessed of some curious inanimate life of its own. More than its sheer physical beauty, the mechanics of its suspension attracted him.

It probably would have gone no farther than that: a few moments of casual admiration for still another marvel of Cocytan engineering. Except that instead of walking away he leaned forward, resting his hands on the transparent case while he sought a slightly better look.

Images materialized in front of his eyes, sharper and clearer than any holographic projection he'd ever experienced. He stepped back sharply, then lingered to watch. In addition to the visuals, there was an accompanying narration or musical score (he couldn't tell which). It filled his portion of the chamber with a fluid, tenorous singsong. It was soothing to the ears, and he wondered if it was language or music. Not that it mattered. If the former, it remained utterly incomprehensible.

Of more interest was the succession of images, which showed the green crystals employed in various tasks. Apparently they were some sort of general repair-and-relief device. He never saw any Cocytans themselves, only crystals and their applications.

He watched as crystals repaired broken machinery, renewed faded artworks, purified water, fulfilled a dozen other unrelated functions and, most significantly, were shown reviving or treating the wounds and diseases of several alien life-forms. When the demonstration, or instruction manual, had run its course, the last image faded.

He'd obviously activated the performance when he'd leaned against the case. Perhaps repeating the gesture and contact would trigger similar displays in other cases.

That could come later. Right now he was interested only in the incandescent crystal and what he'd learned about it. If it could invigorate crops and revive alien animals, what might it do for an injured friend? Well, more than injured, but still. . . .

How could he gain possession? He walked completely around the freestanding case, searching for signs of alarms, booby traps or hidden connections. Seeing none, finding none, he steeled himself and reached out a second time, intending to test the solidity of the case directly in front of the crystal.

His hand passed through what felt like silver gelatin. Fingers contracted around the crystal's sheath. It was warm to the touch, but not unpleasantly so. When the case did not react, either by slicing off his arm in midreach or through some other equally dramatic rejection, he exhaled with relief and withdrew his prize.

It lay in his palm, glowing softly. No alarms echoed through the spire, no lights flashed, no armored doors slammed shut to imprison him within. One moment the crystal had floated before him, beckoning from within its container, and the next it lay inoffensively in his hand. His skin tingled with the contact. He could only hope any side effects were noncarcinogenic.

But then, he thought to himself as he retraced the route he had used to enter the spire, it was unlikely that anything that had such demonstrably salutary effects would also harm its holder. Of course, human body chemistry doubtless differed from that of this world, but the versatility of the crystal allowed him to hope. He had already seen how effectively it worked on a multitude of forms and devices.

Might it also not work on a human?

As near as he could tell, the sphere hadn't moved. The unique circular portal remained open. It allowed him ingress until he resumed his seat on the bench, whereupon it sealed shut behind him as before. A gentle jolt, and then he was moving again.

What if it was not merely some kind of highly efficient shuttle but rather a much more elaborate transportation system preprogrammed to convey its passengers to far-distant locations all over the planet? It was difficult to guess direction, but as nearly as he could tell, it was rolling back along the same route he had originally taken. Alert for any sudden shifts or changes of direction, he remained tense until it came to a halt in a docking chamber very much like the one he had recently departed.

It was in fact the same. There was the impressive entrance to the vast central chamber, which he now knew for certain was located on another island. Additional confirmation took the form of the scree pile in the chamber's center and the unmoving little robot, which remained exactly where, and as, he had left it.

Breaking into a jog as he headed toward the rubble pile, he began shouting for Robbins. To his exasperation, the wandering journalist remained out of earshot.

He slowed as he neared the rock heap. Brink lay as they had left him, lying on his back with his hands placed across his chest. Surely there must be scavengers among the local fauna, Low knew, but thus far they had been gratifyingly reluctant to enter the huge chamber through the breach in its roof. The body was undisturbed.

He'd been gone less than an hour and wondered how much brain cell function had been retained. The study of human memory was an ongoing one, and many unknowns remained. He was about to put contemporary research to the test.

What he was about to attempt was impossible. Of course, so was interstellar travel. Since they'd already put one impossibility to rest, why not another? Instead of questioning alien technology, he intended to make use of it.

But what was he expected to do with the crystal? How was he supposed to apply it? Was there only one right way and many wrong ones? What if he did the wrong thing? Of course, with Brink already dead that ought not to be a real concern.

He tried to remember every detail of the demonstration projection he'd viewed back in the museum spire (for that was how he'd come to think of it). Was the crystal still even functional? The green glow might be nothing more than some ancillary residual effect. It shone softly in his palm, exactly as it had appeared in the projection.

Not knowing what else to do, he simply laid it on the scientist's chest, stepped back and waited.

For a long moment nothing happened. Then the green glow intensified, as if the crystal were reacting to unknown programming, or perhaps to contact with a damaged lifeform. Had he done the right thing? He reassured himself with the knowledge that he couldn't make Brink any deader than he already was.

What happened next made his lower jaw drop, and Boston Low was not noted as a jaw-dropper. The crystal disappeared, not by evaporating into empty air but by sinking into the scientist's chest. Hurrying forward, Low knelt at the other man's side and ran his fingers over the place where the crystal had been. It had not turned invisible. It was most definitely gone. Into the scientist, melting through clothing and skin like green ice on a hot plate. A faint greenish aura spread over Brink's torso, lingered a moment and then was gone. It was like nothing Low had seen in the museum.

Greater miracles were to follow.

Brink coughed.

As the scientist's body began to twitch, Low stepped back, wondering if there was anything he could do to help, to expedite whatever remarkable process was taking place. Lack-

ing specific knowledge, he could do nothing but watch helplessly . . . and hope.

As astonishing as the efficacy of the process was the speed
with which it worked. Hardly a few minutes had passed
when Brink sat up, rubbed his eyes and took several energetic swipes at something unseen in front of his face. Turning slowly, he focused on Low as he struggled to his knees.

"Want a hand?" Low watched intently.

"Not . . . just yet, thank you." The scientist blinked, and
shook his head as if trying to remember something important. "What happened, Commander?" His gaze finally settled
not on Low but on the massive pile of broken rock and other
material that towered behind him.

"You fell." Low was observing him carefully for any signs
of lingering trauma, but Brink acted like anyone who'd unexpectedly been roused from a deep sleep.

"Yes. I fell." The scientist tilted his head back to stare at
the greatly enlarged opening in the roof of the chamber. "I
remember falling. There was pain. . . ." One hand went to the
back of his neck. "Then . . . nothing. I must have lost consciousness."

"That's not all you lost," Low informed him grimly. "You
broke your neck."

"Broke . . . ?" At a loss for words, Brink looked blank.

"How're you feeling?"

"Why are you looking at me like that? I'm a little light-
headed, I suppose, but that's all. You know how you start to
feel when you've had enough good wine? There is no pain.
Surely I could not have broken my neck." As if to demon-
strate the state of his health, he climbed easily to his feet.
"Could a man with a broken neck do this?"

"No. No, he couldn't. Excuse me." Approaching, Low put
one hand on the back of the scientist's neck and pressed. A bemused Brink allowed the exploration. Low stepped back. "The
last time I did that, your head moved around like one of those
spring-loaded dolls you sometimes see bobbing in the back of
people's cars. It was broken, Ludger. Now it feels as if there

was never anything wrong. There's not even a bruise." He indicated the rubble.

"You were buried in that when this section of ceiling collapsed. Nothing but one arm was showing. Maggie and I pulled you out." His voice was flat. "You were dead, Ludger. Stone-cold dead. You've been dead for over an hour."

"Really now, Commander!" The scientist pinwheeled his arms. "I assure you I have never felt better in my life. Assuming for a moment that I accept your evaluation of my previous condition, to what do you attribute my apparent resurrection?"

"I can't show you," Low replied promptly.

"Ah!" Brink looked smug.

"I can't show you because it's inside you, whether intact or dissolved I don't know. I found an interisland transportation system. If you remember, we speculated on that possibility soon after our arrival. I can now confirm it. Within view there is only this island and several surrounding smaller islets. I traveled to one of the lesser islands and found what looks like a museum of some kind, though it might just as easily be an old warehouse. There's a lot of stuff there. Some of it might prove useful.

"One thing that caught my attention was a kind of green crystal. When I touched the case that held it, I got a three-dimensional projected treatise on some of its uses. Among them was the utilization of the crystal to cure badly injured animals." He shrugged. "I didn't see any harm in trying it out on you. Pretty hard to make a corpse worse off." His eyes locked on the other man's.

"I extracted it from its case, brought it back here, and put it on your chest. It sank or melted into you, made your upper body glow for a minute, and then you started coughing. Tell me, what's it like being dead?"

Brink didn't reply right away as he pondered Low's words. Finally he murmured, "Like sleeping, Commander. Just like sleeping. I have no memory of being seriously injured, of dying, or of coming back to life. I know only that one moment I was unconscious, and the next I was looking around curiously. Believe me, I am sorry I cannot better analyze what happened to me in the interim. I see that I must believe your story."

"I wouldn't make something like that up," Low assured him. "Wouldn't know where to start. Maggie would, but she'll confirm that you were dead too."

Brink looked around thoughtfully. "And where is the inquisitive and vivacious Ms. Robbins?"

Low made a face. "Your death set her off. I think everything hit her all at once. She stomped off, she said to get away from me, but I think to be alone with her own thoughts. She's more angry at the situation than she is at me, but she needs time to figure that out." He peered past the scientist. "Thought she'd be back by now. I'll leave her be awhile longer yet." He manufactured a smile.

"You need to see this museum, or storehouse. You'd be like a kid turned loose in a candy store, Ludger. I suspect that if touched, many of the other storage cases will also project explanations of their contents. It'll be a show. We ought to learn a lot."

"Such as how to reactivate quiescent starships?" Brink was quietly amused. "One can but hope. You had no difficulty in removing this crystal from its container?"

Low shook his head. "If there was ever any kind of alarm system, it's dead now. Or maybe it went off in some distant, empty office. An alarm system's not much use if there's no one left alive to respond to it."

"You said that you found a transportation system?"

"One-way, but wait until you see it. It goes around and around, and you come out there." He grinned anew. "Noiseless and vibrationless, just like the crystal. It's quite a discovery, Ludger. I've seen people take longer to recover from a bad headache."

"You're absolutely certain I was dead, Commander?"

"Indisputably. As dead as that rock." He indicated a basketball-sized boulder that had rolled clear of the rest of the mound. Both men stared at it for a moment. Then their eyes met, and they shared a knowing laugh.

"Take nothing for granted," Brink declared.

"I know. We really should find Maggie and let her know that you're all right."

"As you say, she will return in her own time."

"I know, but I'm starting to get worried. I don't see her surviving very long on her own."

"She will come to her senses and rejoin us." Brink spoke with assurance. "Or she will remain by herself and die."

A startled Low thought the statement callous, then decided that the other man was simply stating the obvious. Besides, he'd just been dead. He was entitled to some leeway. Low returned to what would necessarily remain for them the principal topic of conversation.

"You and I need to do some exploring and see if we can find anything that will help us get back home."

"Agreed. I am more optimistic than I was before. If there exist here devices that can raise the dead, then who is to say what might be possible? You say there are many mechanisms in this museum of yours?"

"Hundreds, maybe thousands."

Brink nodded. "Among many thousands we need find only one that will reactivate the asteroid-ship. We have much work ahead of us."

"Don't I know it." Low let his gaze rove around the great chamber. "The people who built this place may have died out or moved on, but they left a potent legacy behind them." He turned. "Come on, and I'll show you the museum. Admission's free today. Also tomorrow, and the day after that, and on into the next millennium."

"I should hope," remarked Brink easily, "that we will have sorted out its treasures before then."

"What do you think of that?" The septet of supporters put the challenge to the caustic. The great majority of the undecided confessed themselves favorably swayed, though far from convinced. "The creature not only discovered the crystal but divined its most important use and applied it correctly!"

The serious decriers were not moved. "It takes very little initiative and intelligence to determine how to utilize a crystal for organic repair when one is provided with visual instruction in the process."

"Yes. We thousand will be better convinced when the ability to reason more abstractly has been demonstrated. The creatures must show they can deduce without assistance."

"You cannot deny what they have already accomplished," asserted the first hundred. "They have found and made use of a crystal, the island transportation system, a door lock and more. The auguries are better than they have been in centuries!"

"The auguries were good for us as well before we stepped over," reminded a cluster of aged thought-forms, "and see to what state we have been brought."

A hundred and twenty thousand neutral perceptions brought forth a conclusion. "Progress has been demonstrated. Much remains to be done, and it is uncertain if these creatures are up to the challenge, but we see reason for hope."

"Hope?" Two hundred thousand negative rejoinders coalesced simultaneously. "This is nothing more than another diversion. More entertaining than most, but no more conclusive."

"Hopeful, yes!" shouted their opponents across the ether, which was as much as a light-minute wide and as short as the length of the average peptide chain. "Will you not concede the point?"

The argument continued unabated. As one of the only forms of viable recreation left to them in the Nirvana in which they had been imprisoned, the Cocytans pursued it with vigor.

Brink gave no sign of being awed by the remarkable undersea transportation system. Low had learned that the scientist was not easily impressed. After having already experienced the reality of interstellar travel, not to mention resurrection from the dead, this was understandable.

As the sphere raced a second time down the dark tunnel, he kept a careful eye on his companion, watching for any signs of abnormal behavior. So far, Brink was the same old Brink. His skin hadn't begun to slough away, he wasn't rolling his eyes madly, and if anything he seemed more composed than usual. Maybe because he had just enjoyed, as he so tactfully put it, a nice nap.

The scientist was indeed impressed by the variety of devices on display in the museum spire. He went from one to the other, lingering over some, passing quickly by others.

When they had concluded their cursory inspection, they stood together framed in the open portal that led outside, studying the alien sea and sky.

"What I would really like to find are some more of those green crystals." Brink shielded his eyes, which were more light-sensitive than the Commander's, from the sun. "Can you imagine their scientific and commercial worth? I cannot. Such values are beyond me. And according to the display you say you witnessed, they are capable of many other functions as well?"

Low nodded. "Some of them I couldn't even give a name
to. Don't have the necessary cultural referents."

"If they can bring back the deceased and heal a broken
spine, perhaps they can cure anything. Cancer, AIDS, Chagas'
disease, malaria, dengue fever . . . take one crystal and call me
in the morning."

"I don't know." They turned and walked back into the
chamber. "I can't imagine how it could analyze what was
wrong with your alien system, recognize the problem, fix it
and then resurrect you."

"I cannot imagine traveling faster than light, either, but we
did it." Brink was thinking hard. "You say you placed it on my
chest and it 'melted' into my body?"

"That's the best description I can give you."

Brink nodded. "I wonder if it remains intact somehow inside me, or if its substance has disintegrated and spread
throughout my bloodstream, or perhaps my entire cellular
structure?"

"Wish I could help you, Ludger, but I'm running a little
short on medical imaging equipment at the moment."

The scientist put a comradely arm around the other man's
shoulders. "Fortitude and persistence, my friend. We will find
the answers to these mysteries. For example, have you not
wondered if the curative effect is permanent, or only temporary?"

Low started. "I hadn't gotten around to that one."

Brink grinned. "I assure you that it occurred to me soon
after your explanation of what took place. Therefore, if I
should fall over dead in the middle of a sentence, you will
know the cause."

"I'd rather not consider that a possibility." Brink's sense of
humor could be quietly ghoulish. "Let's just assume it's permanent. Do you expect your spine to rebreak?"

"It certainly seems unlikely, but we have no way of knowing. There may also be side effects that have yet to manifest
themselves."

"I'll keep a lookout." Low sought to change the subject. "If you start glowing green, I'll let you know right away."

"I've always considered green one of the more attractive colors." The scientist smiled.

Despite their best efforts they could locate no more of the crystals. In fact, they found nothing of immediate usefulness. None of the alien devices responded to their ministrations, either manual or verbal.

They did, however, find several more of the small robotic door-openers. These followed them willingly back to the sphere. While they might do nothing for the asteroid-ship, there were several large doorways within the central chamber that remained closed.

"Watch." Back on the main island, Low had coaxed one of the devices over to another arch. "When trapped between one of us and a door, they'll turn and open it." He proceeded to crowd the robot.

It backed up against the section of wall next to the arch and stopped. Low advanced until he was pressing against it with his legs. It ignored both proximity and pressure with equanimity.

"Well?" Brink stood nearby, waiting.

Perplexed, Low backed up to give the robot some space. "I don't understand. When I crowded the other one, it turned and opened the entrance leading to the transportation chamber. The barrier just melted away."

The scientist inspected the solid wall beneath the arch. "Well, it does not appear to be melting to me. Perhaps we should try another portal?"

Following the curving wall, they reached a third arch, where Low repeated the procedure that had been so successful earlier. When that failed, they returned to the second and tried another of the little robots. the result was the same: Nothing happened. When Low coaxed the original robot over to the second door, it proved as passive as its newly discovered brethren.

"Do not be discouraged, Commander."

Swell, Low groused silently. *I'm being consoled by a dead man.* "Okay, I'm all out of bright ideas, Ludger. Your turn."

The scientist's gaze roved the chamber. "There are several much smaller doorways. Perhaps one of these devices will open one of them?"

Low looked doubtful. "Why bother with the small doors?"

To his surprise, one of the newly acquired robots did indeed cause one of the smaller barriers to melt out of the way. The modest storeroom thus revealed contained nothing as impressive as the sphere transportation system. Instead, it was filled with piles of reflective straps and plates that were clearly designed to be worn by something nonhuman. There were long tubular instruments that might as easily have been agricultural tools as weapons, or perhaps simply ceremonial staffs. Unable to induce them to do anything besides ring hollowly on the floor, Low had no way of identifying their intended function.

Probably a lousy clothes closet, Low found himself thinking. *Raincoats and umbrellas.* That'll *get us back home.*

Brink called out from the far end of the room. The scientist's voice was trembling. "Commander Low! Come quick."

"What is it, what's wrong?" Low hurried forward, past mounds of inexplicable gear.

Nothing was wrong. Brink was standing before a transparent case not unlike those that dominated the display in the museum spire. It was a little larger than most and hung by invisible means to the back wall of the room. Glowing green crystals floated within.

Lots of glowing green crystals, glistening in their transparent sheaths.

Except in quantity, they were identical to the one Low had found in the museum spire and had used to revive Brink. A glance at the scientist showed him staring unblinkingly at the trove, eyes focused and glistening.

"We must get them out!" There was an uncharacteristic quaver in his voice.

"Hold on a minute." Low frowned at his companion. "Sure we'll get them out. They're potentially useful, and valuable, and we're not going to just leave them sitting here. Never can tell when we might need one. But why *must* we get them out?"

His words seemed to penetrate the scientist's mind slowly, as if they had been delivered one at a time over a long interval. He blinked. "Why . . . I should think that would be obvious. If my revived condition is temporary, a possibility we discussed, then application of a second crystal may extend my life."

"Fair enough," Low replied guardedly, "although you look perfectly healthy to me. Better than you did when we arrived here, as a matter of fact."

"I am pleased to hear it." Was he starting to sweat? Low couldn't be sure. "We need to extract these." He moved to go around the pilot, who was standing between him and the case.

Low edged sideways to block the other man's path. "Just a minute, Ludger. Just because these look like the crystal I used on you doesn't mean they have the same function. Shouldn't we proceed with some caution? Maybe one or two of them have other functions. Dangerous ones. What's the rush? It's not good research to be in such a hurry."

But Brink wasn't looking at him anymore. He was staring past him, back in the direction of the entrance. "Perhaps someone else feels similarly."

Low turned. Flashes and sparks filled the center of the storeroom. They were echoes of the ghost-light that they had encountered briefly soon after stepping out of the asteroid-ship. Once more they appeared to be trying to form some sort of solid outline, and once more they remained nothing more than fireflylike glitterings in the air. Low thought he detected urgency in their motion, but decided he was being foolish.

"What are those things, anyway?" he heard himself murmuring.

"A natural phenomenon of some interest." As the lights drifted forward, Brink edged closer to the case.

Low held his ground as they swarmed around him. "I wonder if they carry a charge. Some of them look almost solid."

"I would doubt it." Brink waved at the nearest cluster. His fingers passed easily through them. "I feel nothing. A slight tingling sensation, perhaps. They are lights, that is all. A harmless local atmospheric phenomenon."

Low held out a hand palm upward. Several of the lights settled onto his skin, and he felt the tingling to which the scientist had alluded. It was not painful, more of a persistent tickling. As he stared, the sparks vanished one by one.

"I guess you're right, Ludger. It's an interesting phenomenon, but that's all." Feeling oddly disappointed, he turned back toward the rear of the room.

"A thousand years' frustration!" A dozen thought-forms whirled precisely about a predetermined axis. "Can we do nothing to stop them, warn them, help them?"

"Why should it be any different with these than with their predecessors?" declared a hundred others, who had clustered together in a unique geometric form that nine out of ten human mathematicians would have said was a theoretical impossibility.

"No matter how hard we try, we cannot affect the physical dimension in any meaningful way." Half a million caucused resignedly. "That was the choice we made."

None present, which meant all, needed to be reminded of that sorrowful fact. Sadly, restatement of the unpleasant obvious was a catechism to which they had long been addicted. Paradise was rife with discontent, and few had the energy to dispute it. They had achieved a most unhappy perfection. All they could do was exist, and observe.

"Beautiful! *Wunderbar*!" Brink reached for the case, his fingers penetrating with the same ease Low had experienced in the museum spire. His fingertips began to tingle as they neared the cluster of crystals.

"What about possible dangers?" Low hesitated, uncertain how to react.

"Nonsense! Who would make a deadly analogue of something designed to restore life? You are overcautious, Commander. Besides, having no resources for detailed analysis, we must content ourselves with empirical demonstration."

It wasn't as if the scientist had been hypnotized, Low decided. Simply that he was preoccupied with the crystals to the exclusion of nearly everything else, including potential danger. His attitude might border on the irrational, but he had a ways to go before he could be accused of having stepped over. Low determined to keep a close watch on him.

"I admit we don't have the means to do a proper study. What did you have in mind?"

Brink smiled at him. "We cannot imagine the full capabilities of these crystals, but we have proof of their partial potential. I am it. I wish I could have observed the actual action of the crystal on my body." His smile widened and Brink relaxed a little. "Being dead certainly inhibits one's studies." His fingers closed around the nearest sheath and he inhaled sharply at the contact.

"We must take at least a few of these with us."

"Why? The door's open now and we know where they are. We can come back for them whenever we need one."

"We cannot take that chance!" Struck by the sudden vehemence of his own response, Brink took care to moderate the remainder of his words. "Be reasonable, Commander. We have no way of knowing what devices and mechanisms may return to life in this place at any given time. In our absence, however brief, this room may choose to reseal itself, barring us permanently from its treasures. Additionally, should we encounter future difficulties, it would be useful to have crystals on hand for medicinal purposes."

Low agreed reluctantly. "You argue persuasively, Ludger. All right, I concede your points. Take the crystals. But I'm not going to lug them around. You carry most of them."

"With delight." As Low looked on, the scientist eagerly removed one crystal after another, stuffing them into every available shirt and pants pocket until he resembled someone who'd swallowed a green searchlight. As a precaution, Low pocketed a couple of the crystals himself. Their gentle warmth could be felt through the material of his pants.

"See, Commander." Brink fingered the last crystal, rolling it sensuously back and forth between the palms of both hands. "I am neither dead nor injured, so it does not sink into my fingers."

"Maybe it only operates at specific entry points," Low suggested. "Maybe fingers don't qualify."

His lower lip pushed out, Brink responded approvingly and with only the faintest hint of condescension. "Very good, Commander! A valid observational deduction." His gaze dropped to the crystal. "I hold in my hands the key to the resurrection of the dead. Perhaps I hold also the answer to everything mankind has ever dreamed of."

"Kind of a blanket inference, don't you think?" remarked Low sourly. After the spaciousness of the main chamber and the museum spire, the storeroom was beginning to feel cramped. Also, he was mindful of Brink's comment about doors being permanently and unexpectedly sealed.

"Let's get out of here."

"Nervous, Commander?" Brink followed Low as the other turned and started for the portal.

"Just thinking about what you said earlier. If doors can open here, they can also close." He breathed easier when they stepped back out into the high-domed chamber. It was brighter outside the storeroom. A man could see. And think.

He turned on Brink sharply enough to startle him. "You know, if these crystals are some kind of all-purpose tool, maybe they can open doors?"

The scientist grimaced, then considered, and finally found himself nodding in agreement. "A combination universal health clinic and door-opener? I would think such a thing not only impossible but absurd. However, that would be thinking like a human. We are on an alien world and should strive to employ nontraditional ways of thinking. Nonhuman, one might almost wish. As to your proposal, however, why not? What harm can it do to try?"

The crystals did nothing for the second sealed archway. Low touched one to the barrier, ran it along the line between door and floor, used it to trace the glyphs etched into the wall nearby. Beyond leaving him feeling really stupid, the exercise had no effect.

"What about your little robots?" Brink made the suggestion when Low had finally conceded defeat.

"We tried them, remember? They didn't work."

"You tried one at a time. What if you were to utilize several simultaneously?"

Low was skeptical. "Why should that work? The first time it took one robot to open one door. Why should the second door be any different?"

"Perhaps because it is different." Brink was persistent. "You are thinking like a human."

Low eyed the scientist uncertainly. "That's because I happen to be a human, Ludger. So are you. Don't start forgetting that."

Brink smiled enigmatically. "I am merely trying to emphasize the fact that the Cocytans may have thought dissimilarly. What strikes us as irrational or even capricious may have made perfect sense to a Cocytan." He put a hand on the pilot's arm. "Come, let us try. Are you now in the business of conserving robotic energy?"

When the second door melted open, Low was too delighted to take umbrage at the scientist's smug smile. As Brink had hypothesized, using different combinations of robots allowed them to open all the remaining archways save one. No combination of imprecations and robots would force the fifth barrier. Perhaps it was broken, Brink thought.

He soon forgot about the stubborn fifth door. They had four other destinations to explore. Beyond each lay another familiar sphere-and-tunnel transport station.

"I wonder if absorbing that crystal did anything to your brain," Low remarked.

"Boost it, for example?" Brink demurred. "I feel no different, Commander. I have no doubt you would have figured out this solution on your own. Later, perhaps, but eventually for certain." He was gazing through the high portal of the last archway, contemplating the resting, waiting sphere. "We could do worse than explore farther."

"I agree." Low moved forward. "Might as well start with this one."

Brink followed, green light comically radiating from his overstuffed shirt and pants. "Five archways, five outlying islands. No surprises there."

Low entered the sphere. "I wonder if they'll all be like the first? Storerooms or museums."

The transparent door irised shut behind them, and once again Brink marveled at the mechanism. There was nothing so primitive as a bolt or hinge visible.

With a slight jerk the sphere started forward, rolling faster and faster down the tunnel while the passengers within remained level and stable on their bench.

"I have this feeling," Brink commented as he stared at the black tube ahead, "that each island will be different."

"Intuition?" Low was fascinated by the featureless tunnel.

"No. Merely common sense. If I wished to leave behind a museum, I would concentrate it all in one place."

"Sure, but now you're thinking like a human."

Brink chuckled. "Ah, Commander. We may yet find a way off this silent, dead world."

It was neither silent nor dead, of course. Cocytus was in fact occupied by a population of immortal mutes. All-powerful, they were helpless. All-seeing, they could not share their visions. All-knowing, they could not impart knowledge. Dysfunctional angels, they could only observe, debate and hope.

It was Low's turn to smile sagely when they arrived at the second island and entered the welcoming spire. It was filled not with mounds of artifacts or cases of mysterious devices but a grand procession of softly glowing, artfully projected maps, globes and starfields. The second spire was a shrine to topography both terrestrial and galactic.

Many of the diagrams and schematics were unrecognizable. As with many of the artifacts they had encountered, the two humans simply did not possess the necessary referents to facil-

itate comprehension. They marveled at the confluxes of lines
and dots and images, walking not only around but through
them, and wondered at their meaning.

"Perhaps these represent the planet's internal landscape,
represented in ways we cannot fathom." As he spoke, Low noticed that the scientist was idly caressing a crystal protruding
from one shirt pocket. "How do you map the troposphere?
This is science beyond ours, my friend."

"Not all of it." Low pointed to an exhibit off to their left.

There was nothing arcane about the softly lambent three-dimensional representation he had pointed out. It showed the
central island surrounded by its five smaller neighbors. The
shapes of the outlying spires that dominated each individual
islet were unmistakable. A few small subsidiary rocks poked
their heads above sea level, but they were clearly too insignifi-
cant to contain any ruins of significance.

"It's almost as if this archipelago was chosen for its isolation." Low studied the map, which he could walk through at
will.

"This appears to be some sort of console or control board."
Brink passed one hand experimentally over a smooth-sided
mound projecting from the floor directly alongside the map.
Instantly the projection expanded to include undersea features,
none of which were as remarkable as the system from which
they sprang.

"You take charge of this, Commander." The scientist
stepped aside. "I am a reasonably skilled map reader, but not
as good as you, I am certain."

Low wasn't quite sure if Brink was being straightforward or
condescending again. Shrugging it off, he stepped forward and
began experimenting with the control mound. Assorted hand
movements called up various functions, from a depiction of
the islands' internal structure to overlays showing vegetation
and animal populations, both above and below the water.

A certain twist of the hand, no more radical than any other,
and the entire projection disappeared.

"It's gone." Low gaped at where the projection had been floating.

"No, not quite." Kneeling, Brink picked something off the floor. It was a miniature version of the control mound. "Try this. Go on." He handed it to Low.

Assorted hand passes allowed one to expand or contract the map, to move around within it, and to access all of the device's numerous functions at whatever scale the operator required. When shut down it rested slick, cool and alien in his palm.

"That's handy." He slipped it into an empty pocket, feeling it nestle against his thigh. "Let's see what else we can find."

Everything they encountered was interesting, especially the maps showing Cocytus's major continents. One placed them a considerable distance from the nearest shore. None hinted at the presence of a viable population. Only the map of the islands, however, was portable.

When they turned to depart, they had a nasty shock. One of Brink's principal fears had been realized.

While they had been deeply engrossed in the contents of the map spire, the door leading back to the transport tunnel had closed silently behind them.

"And me without a door-opening robot in my pocket." A worried Low ran his fingers over the barrier. It was as solid as the floor. "Now we do have a problem."

"Perhaps we can find another robot."

Not knowing what else to do, they performed another circuit of the map chamber. While they encountered wonders aplenty, they found none of the compact door-openers.

This time it was Brink who was ready to give up, but after all they had accomplished, Low wasn't about to be condemned to death by a recalcitrant door. Further searching revealed a small service panel set flush with the floor not far from the side of the door where a robot would normally stand. The line that set it off was so fine that they had walked over it a dozen times without seeing it. Fortunately, Low had exceptionally sharp eyesight.

When they finally succeeded in prying up the cover, a nest of lines and conduits was revealed. In their normalcy of appearance and unambiguousness of function they were almost heartbreakingly familiar.

"Cables," Low muttered. "Plain old ordinary cables."

"Plain perhaps," remarked Brink. "Old certainly. Ordinary? I would not wager so."

"They're cables, that's all. We need to instigate an engineering procedure known as 'messing with.' Give me a hand here, Ludger."

Brink was reluctant. "We could blow ourselves up."

Low grinned at his companion. "That shouldn't worry you. You're packed with crystals. If you blow up, I'll bring you back. You can return the favor. Grab this." He indicated an inch-thick cable.

Together the two men pulled until the cable snapped from its braces. The interior was not metal but some white, waxy material. It did throw off a satisfying shower of sparks, however, substantial enough to knock both men off their feet.

"Ludger!" Low sat up and tried to clear his eyes. "Where are you?"

"Over here, Commander." Brink was rising shakily to his feet. "A shocking experience."

Low winced. "If you're going to pun, stick to German, will you? That way I won't be able to understand you." After a quick glance he added nonchalantly, "Door's open."

Indeed, the barrier had vanished. Access to the tunnel was once more available, and the sphere rested motionless on its track.

Not waiting to see if the effect was permanent, or if some backup system was even then working to override the interrupt, the two men hurried through the gap. It remained open as they climbed back into the sphere.

"Now, that's what I call a worthwhile experiment." Low sat down on the bench. "Even the most advanced technology is susceptible to the application of brute force."

"The selective application, Commander," Brink corrected

him. "I admit I'm gratified by the results. It's nice to know that there are situations where our primitive muscles may actually function to our benefit." The sphere swayed and began to accelerate. "Hopefully there will be no secondary side effects. We forced a door. With luck that will not lead to, say, a clean-out portal opening in the roof of the tunnel to admit the ocean."

Low glanced involuntarily upward, at the curved black ceiling. "Hopefully. I was afraid the sphere might be deactivated and we'd have to walk all the way back to the central island."

"I think our efforts were facilitated by the age of this complex. Any of it could cease working at any moment. We have been lucky thus far."

"If this is luck," Low grumbled, "I'll take vanilla."

"I do not understand," Brink replied. "My mastery of colloquial English is not perfect."

"You do fine, Ludger, just fine."

"In any event, we still have these." The scientist indicated his crystal-filled pockets. "They can help us through any difficulty."

"Is that a fact?" Low stared curiously at his companion as the sphere began to slow, pursuant to its arrival back at the main island. "How do you know that? Have you read something I haven't read, seen something I haven't seen?"

"Not at all." For a moment Brink was self-confused. "I seem simply to feel it."

Brighter light flooded the sphere as it rolled to a halt at the arrival station. "Whoa! I didn't think scientists 'felt' conclusions. I thought they required substantiative proof."

"I cannot explain it." Brink rose from the bench. "I just know."

"Suit yourself." Low followed him through the exit. "Next maybe you can 'feel' a way to reactivate the asteroid. I just 'know' you can."

An uncertain Brink did not return the Commander's smile.

CHAPTER

13

"They continue to make progress." The thousand and one perceptions projected positive assurance. "The life crystals have given them no trouble. They have not misused them nor attempted to make invalid applications."

"Common sense does not equal true intelligence." Five hundred and two dissenters dismissed doubtful assertion. "An animal that walks into an electric barrier learns not to repeat the experience. This constitutes learning, but in the absence of real intelligence."

A couple considered. "In addition to the life crystals, they have discovered and made use of the map spire as well as the interisland transportation system. We will bet the scent of a flowering fungus that they will now move on to explore the other towers."

The doubters were disdainful. "Anyone can bet freely with that which they do not possess, cannot obtain and can hardly remember." There was a distinct note of wistfulness in the rejoinder. "Would that it were otherwise."

"Unmoderated curiosity can be detrimental." The great majority of observers remained noncommittal, genuine emotion being too precious a commodity to waste on misplaced hopes.

"Doing nothing would be more detrimental still." This exclamation came from a platoon of the purely prosaic. "They must move on in spite of risks they cannot envision, for to stand still is to begin to die."

"Except for us," remarked several others. "More's the pity."

"How can we die?" They were all philosophers, out of necessity if not desire. "Is this existence we enjoy a kind of life or of death?" It was a question that had been debated for hundreds of years, and for which they had yet to concoct a satisfactory answer.

"Observe. Already they advance toward the next tunnel."

"Another obstinate door might be enough to defeat them," theorized three-and-thirty.

"Not these." It was the first who spoke now, the one who had made the original desperate attempt at contact. Its failure had only inspired fresh thinking. "They are resourceful beyond the bounds of prediction. Did you not see how they dealt with the barrier?"

"Unsophisticated," remarked an arc of mind-thoughts. "Inelegant."

"But in the final analysis, effective," argued the first. "And that is all that matters." Drifting low, it hovered somewhere between the crest of the central island and Brink's eyebrows. "If only we could break through and warn them! If only we could provide assistance instead of mild bemusement. Who did not see during the last attempt? Exerting to the utmost, those who strove achieved only futility."

"Perhaps the occasion will arise in which to try again." A number of the first's supporters gathered close. One moment there were three or four of them, and the next, half a million. "Perhaps circumstances we cannot foresee will prove more fortuitous."

For all their accomplishments and all their learning, for all the time that they had existed in first one dimension and then another, one thing the Cocytans could not do was see into the future. Had they been able to do so, they would not have been in the stultified state in which they found themselves now. For as surely as Cocytus rotated on its axis, they would have chosen a different path into the future. One that would have allowed them to show all that they had left behind to their latest visitors. One that would have allowed them to *explain.*

For the second time that day the two men spent time calling out to Maggie Robbins, and for the second time there was no response to their shouts.

"Something's happened to her," Low muttered uneasily. He started to reach for his pen communicator.

"Not necessarily." Brink considered the possibilities. "Perhaps she has climbed up the rubble pile and is exploring outside. Seeking familiarity among the unfamiliar, she may have returned to the asteroid. Or possibly she is bathing in the waters of this ocean, seeking temporarily to distance herself from the overwhelming difficulties that face us. If the latter, then I envy her her sense of proportion. I could do with a swim myself."

"Later," snapped Low. "We have spires to explore."

"There, you see?" Brink gently chided his companion. "That is exactly the kind of attitude I mean. If we are not careful, the stress and strain will do us more damage than any uncooperative alien device."

Low whirled on him. "You want to go swimming?"

The scientist glanced away. "Well, not just now. As you say, there are two other spires to inspect."

Low grunted his satisfaction. "Thought so. You're as driven as I am."

"I regret to say that you are right. But let us not condemn the resourceful Ms. Robbins for possibly believing and acting otherwise. If she is indeed taking time to relax and mentally recuperate, then she is behaving in a more sensible fashion than you or I. Anyone who can survive and thrive in the inhospitable universe of international media can surely keep her wits about her on a mere alien planet."

Low had to smile. "Glad to see that your sense of humor survived too."

"I am pleased you find it so. I have, on occasion, been accused of not having one. Perhaps the application of the crystal, which, by the way, I should like to call a life crystal, improved upon it. Nothing like dying to enrich one's sense of the comic."

"I'll take your word for it." Low gestured. "But I still think it's time we checked in." So saying, he pulled the pen communicator from his belt and switched it on. The corresponding LED for Brink's unit glowed brightly, but the third remained blank.

"Doesn't matter," he grunted. "She's switched her unit off. I can't contact her until she turns it back on." Frustration was evident in his tone. "Dammit, she knows she's supposed to keep her unit activated at all times."

"You see, Commander? She wishes to preserve her solitude."

"Fine," he snapped. "I can't order her to turn her unit back on until she turns it back on. So for right now it looks like we've no choice but to let her be for a while longer yet. Let's get going. I don't fancy getting caught out on one of the smaller islands after dark. Maybe the transport system shuts down at midnight."

"Or if we do not return here in time, we both turn into pumpkins, perhaps?" Brink chuckled softly. It didn't sound quite normal, somehow, but Low had other things on his mind besides the nature of the scientist's laugh.

As they walked toward the third beckoning archway, they continued to call to the absent Maggie. Despite Brink's sensible reassurances, Low remained concerned.

"Even if she was off resting somewhere, she ought have come back by now, if only to check up on me."

"Perhaps she has been trying to do just that." Brink had to break into an occasional jog to keep up with his companion. "She may have circled this chamber a dozen times while you were sifting through the contents of the museum island or the two of us were learning the secrets of the map spire. Not finding you, she may have gone searching elsewhere. Maybe we will find her on the third island, or the fourth, awaiting us with characteristic impatience.

"I would not worry about her overmuch, my friend. I suspect she has survived worse than this."

"How would you know?"

Brink eyed him uncertainly. "I am not sure that I follow your meaning."

"Never mind, it's nothing. You're probably right, Ludger. I'm driving myself nuts worrying about her while she's probably off somewhere divining alien secrets and wondering where the hell I've been. We'll find her soon enough."

As on previous occasions, the door to the sphere cycled silently shut behind them as soon as both were properly seated on the passenger bench. For the second time, Low found himself wondering how many Cocytans the transport was designed to hold. A dozen, or one unimaginably large one? His contemplation was cut short as the sphere began to roll.

"I've been wondering about these tunnels." Low spoke as the two men sat side by side, staring ahead, waiting for the inevitable light. "Been wondering about them since the first time I saw one. Wondering about them now."

Brink replied tolerantly, since it was obviously expected of him. "And what have you been wondering, Commander?"

"If they're all intact. If any of them happen to have ceilings as weak as the one doming the big chamber we just left. It collapsed and killed you." He glanced significantly upward. "A breakdown here would kill both of us, and even if Robbins figured out how to use the crystals, it wouldn't do any good. I don't think the crystals are capable of resurrecting pulp."

"For a supposedly phlegmatic type, your images are very vivid, Commander." Brink considered the possibility. "I would think that the engineers of this world would have ensured that any type of undersea excavation would be built to far more exacting standards than simple land-based edifices. In my opinion, these tunnels are probably the sturdiest structures we are likely to encounter. In addition, they are doubtless equipped with any number of fail-safe and backup systems designed to deal with the first sign of structural failure.

"For example, at the first hint of flooding I would expect these spherical transports to be shut down. Therefore we may assume that so long as we are moving, there is no structural danger." Low was about to comment, but Brink forestalled him.

"Nor do I believe that conclusion means that I am 'thinking like a human.' I would expect sensible engineering to transcend species."

"Sounds good to me." The seat quivered ever so slightly beneath Low's backside. "Unless the fail-safe mechanisms have failed first. Then there'd be no warning."

"I can see why they made you a shuttle commander, Boston Low. You worry not only about the obvious but about the invisible. I suspect that if you were sitting motionless in a completely empty dark closet, you'd find time to worry about the makeup of the atmosphere within."

"Shoot, I do that all the time. Comes from spending so much of my professional life carrying my own air around with me. Your nose gets real sensitive and you find yourself starting to question individual molecules." He lapsed into silence, staring down the tunnel.

Having completed two successful journeys via the spherical transport system, they felt comparatively confident when they stepped out for the third time. As expected, there were no surprises waiting for them. The transport station was a duplicate of those at the map spire and museum spire, and the large portal on their left stood open and inviting.

The interior of the new spire was considerably different, however. Careful inspection revealed it to be absolutely empty, a vaulted cylinder harboring smooth, bare walls and nothing else. There weren't even any of the distinctive protrusions that commonly bulged from floor and siding. Not an artifact, not a console, not a pile of sealed containers: nothing whatsoever. The spire of the third island was barren.

Low studied the floor. Like all Cocytan paving, it was subtlely reflective. You couldn't see your face in it, only vague outlines. Most certainly it was composed of the same material he and Brink had encountered everywhere else.

"Looks like a dry hole, as they say in Texas." A disappointed Low started forward. "Might as well make sure."

As they entered, their booted feet made soft padding sounds on the polished surface. By what mechanism these ancient monuments remained free of dust and dirt they couldn't imagine. Low hypothesized tiny cleaning robots that emerged from concealment only when necessary, while Brink opted for some kind of inbuilt electrostatic repulsion system. They argued as they strolled bemusedly toward the center of the room.

"I don't get it." Low didn't know what to expect, only that he'd expected to find *something*. Especially given the profusion of wonders they had encountered in the other two spires. "What was this place?"

"Who can say? Possibly it was never utilized, or perhaps the Cocytans emptied it out before their unknown fate befell them. It could have been intended for use as a storeroom that was never needed. We might as well return to the central island and try the last spire."

"In a minute. There's something wrong here." Something about the meticulously maintained emptiness continued to bother him. "It's *too* clean, too spotless. Maybe the Cocytans were cleanliness fanatics, but we've found debris elsewhere. Why would they devote so much energy and engineering to maintaining an unused building in immaculate condition when both of the other two spires show routine signs of neglect? Look at this floor." He scuffed the glossy surface with his boot. "Can't even raise a whiff of dust. It doesn't make sense." His gaze roved the walls and ceiling.

"This place still has a purpose."

Brink was unconvinced. "Yes. To mystify curious visitors, for one thing. I see nothing unnatural in a fetish for hygiene.

In Hamburg and Kiel there are unused shipping warehouses that are maintained spotlessly."

"I don't doubt it." They had almost reached the center of the spire. "But those are kept clean in expectation of eventually receiving sensitive cargo. If that's the case here, then why keep the sphere transport system running to this island? Why not shut it down until needed?"

The scientist shrugged. "Perhaps the Cocytans were profligate with their resources. It is possible that . . ."

The room vanished.

Though he was among the handful of his kind trained and mentally equipped to deal with such a dislocation, such as when an orbiting shuttle might lose all power and light, Low still swallowed hard when the spire's primary function engaged. There had been no warning. But then, none would have been necessary for the Cocytans, who came to this island familiar with its function. They would have known what to expect, would have known that standing in the exact center of the room was all that was required to activate the concealed equipment.

The abrupt transformation was much harder on Brink. Gasping involuntarily at the sight that now confronted them, the scientist mumbled something in German and stumbled into Low. Reaching out, the Commander got a firm grip on his companion's arms and managed to steady him.

"Take it easy, Ludger. It's just an illusion, a projection of some kind. You can still breathe, can't you? Gravity's still at work. We're not falling. It only looks that way."

"An illusion." Brink found in the Commander's calm expression an island of stability amid utter distortion. His gaze kept returning for reassurance to that composed visage. "I am used to witnessing illusions, not to being a part of them."

"It's a complete experience," Low agreed. "Nothing left out." He turned a slow circle. "All-encompassing. It doesn't move with you. I know a couple of astronomers who'd give up five years of their lives for the chance to spend a week in here."

They were floating in space. Stars, nebulae and other stellar features surrounded them. Some types were utterly unfamiliar, each representing a new astronomical discovery hitherto unknown on Earth but presented within the spire with the assurance of long familiarity.

Close to Low's face hovered a star and four planets. The sun blazed in spectacular miniature, periodically casting off minuscule prominences, while the planets slowly rotated in their orbits. Low wondered if the star would be warm to the touch. Squinting and leaning close, he could see individual cloud formations moving within a pair of tiny atmospheres. As he stared, a typhoon the size of a pinhead slowly rotated into view.

He reached toward the diminutive globe and saw it expand in response. Now it was the size of a tennis ball, individual landmasses and seas standing out clearly. The nearer he moved his hand, the larger it became, until the globular projection had expanded to where its diameter was twice his height. One region in the eastern ocean particularly attracted his attention.

"See there, Ludger. There's the main island and the surrounding islets. It's Cocytus."

Overwhelmed by the simplicity of the planetarium's design as well as by the technology that made it possible, Brink could only murmur in amazement.

"I wonder, my friend. If we were to continue to expand magnification, continue to refine the resolution, could we focus down on this single island, enter this spire, and end up gazing at representations of ourselves staring back at us?"

"Don't know." Low drew back his hand and watched as the globe of Cocytus shrank back down to the size of a marble. "Don't need to know. If I want to look at myself, I'll use a mirror."

Turning, he gestured in the direction of a cluster of dense red stars. Instantly they swelled and rushed toward him. He had to steady himself to avoid flinching away from the onrushing fiery spheres. Concentrating on the largest, he caused it to expand while dismissing its companions as effortlessly as one would push aside soap bubbles in a bath.

Two planets circled the red giant, which also wore a tiara of comets and asteroids. Cursory inspection revealed both worlds to be charred and lifeless. With a gesture, he flung the stars aside, casting them back to their rightful places in the firmament with a casual wave of his hand.

"A planetarium." Brink spoke as if in a cathedral. In a sense, it was—a place to worship astronomy. "But *what* a planetarium. I do not recognize a single constellation."

"Neither do I. Look beneath your feet."

Brink complied. There was no floor. They were standing on nothingness, contemplating depths that extended forever. Stars swirled beneath his toes. The miniature of a grand nebula, remnant of an ancient supernova, illuminated one heel with crimson and yellow highlights.

Experimentally, Low took a step forward. The illusion lost none of its perfection. He felt but could not see the solid surface underfoot. They weren't about to fall off, to go tumbling forever through an inveighed against cosmos. The planetarium was marvelous, but no place for anyone with vertigo.

"Nothing's changed," he assured Brink. "The floor's still there in every sense except the visual. Come on, you try it."

"I will remain here, thank you."

"Suit yourself." Taking several steps into the spangled void, Low amused himself by enlarging and then shrinking an assortment of stellar objects. "Pick a world, Ludger. Any world. Just use your hand."

The scientist nodded. At his behest, the supernova nebula rose from his feet, expanding until they were both standing within it. The colors and light were mind-numbing. Embedded within the fluorescent gas were innumerable individual fragments, the detailed study of any one of which would have settled questions of a hundred years' standing among the astronomical community. Behind the nebula lay stars unknown on Earth, whole constellations unsuspected.

"Small gestures, that's the ticket." Low demonstrated,

calling up features as tiny as craters on individual moons. Though he never gave up on the hope, nowhere did he find signs of intelligent life. But then, the galaxy was vast, he had no idea which direction to go or where to look, and they'd only been playing with the system for a few minutes. Given time to learn how to operate the remarkable mechanism more efficiently, there was no telling what they might find.

"Fascinating." Brink was toying with a system that contained no less than three asteroid belts and fifteen planets. "It responds to limbs of any size and shape. No actual contact is necessary, so we can operate it as easily as a Cocytan, or any other intelligent being. Apparently mere presence is sufficient for activation."

"Can you imagine what a teaching tool this would make?" Low flung a handful of deep-space comets back into their orbits. "The sense of empowerment it would give a child? You'd never get a group of ten-year-olds out of here."

"I am most reluctant to leave myself," Brink admitted. "If we only knew what direction to probe, how far to go, I suspect we could call up a perfect representation of the solar system. Assuming that their observations extended that far, of course. The Sun and Earth may lie outside the boundaries of this highly detailed map. Our solar system might not be discernible in detail from Cocytus."

"There has to be a key somewhere. A galographic index," Low surmised.

Brink agreed. "I suspect there is, but finding it is another matter. And if found, how are we to read it?" He waved at the enveloping artificial firmament. "Without knowing even in which direction to begin, it would take years to examine every individual system contained within this projection."

"I've been looking. Concentrating on the brightest stars." Low's expression was glum. "I still don't recognize so much as a single sun."

"There is no imagining the distance we have traveled. We must be far from home indeed."

They immersed themselves in the delights and marvels of

the planetarium, until Low reluctantly reminded his companion that they still needed to check out at least one more spire.

"This is fun, and enlightening, but it's not getting us any closer to home. I'd like to find Maggie, too, and introduce her to our discoveries."

"I confess you have me wondering about her condition." Brink stood surrounded by stars, his head tilted as he surveyed a sky like no other. "How do we turn it off, I wonder?"

"By doing the opposite of what's needed to turn it on, I guess." Low studied the darkness. There was nothing to indicate a way out—no illuminated arrows, no distant light demarcating the location of the arch, nothing. "I *think* the door was back this way." He headed off through the stars, Brink following him closely. The scientist had a good sense of direction, but knew it would be no match for an astronaut's.

They'd walked for what seemed like half a mile but in reality was much less, when the universe twisted around them. The incredible artificial cosmos vanished. Once again they found themselves in a high, featureless, empty domed chamber. The exit loomed just ahead, and beyond, the transport sphere waiting silently on its track bed.

"Incredible." Brink turned a slow circle. There was nothing to indicate that the room held so much as a dim light bulb. The only remaining glow came from the life crystals that filled the scientist's pockets. "We must come back to this place!"

"Yes." Low was in complete agreement. "After we've found something we can eat."

"I wonder what marvels remain to us."

"I'd settle for a return ticket."

As it developed, further exploration was to be delayed.

Brink pulled up suddenly and pointed. "Commander, I thought I saw something move over there."

Low whirled. "What? Where?"

The scientist pointed. "That way, near the back of the tunnel. The sphere loomed before them, beckoning. Brink cupped his hands to his mouth. "Maggie? Maggie Robbins!" There was no reply. "Could she have followed us here?"

"Not unless the sphere went back for her, or there are two running on this same track. You've been squinting at too many nebulae, Ludger."

"*Verdampt!* I was sure I saw something." He started forward . . . and found his progress blocked.

The creature had no legs. That in itself was not surprising. Legless life-forms were common enough on Earth. But as a general rule they did not run to size. This Cocytan counterpart was *big*. As massive as Low, it boasted a bony exoskeleton that was dominated by a swelling rib cage. The equally gaunt skull swayed back and forth on the end of a long, flexible neck, while the tail terminated in a spatulate, diamond-shaped flange. Two thin but strong structures that might equally well have been arms, legs or wings protruded from the upper third of the emaciated body.

As to the function of one visible structure the two men shared no doubts: The double jaws were filled with sharp white teeth. In addition to teeth, the creature also had company.

"Easy." Low's voice dropped to a whisper. "We're an alien form. Maybe they won't know what to make of us."

Responding to the pilot's voice, the creatures raised themselves up and began to hump across the floor toward them. They resembled an ambulating boneyard, a brace of pythons turned inside out. Convinced the creatures had no intention of presenting him with a bouquet of posies, Low began to backpedal toward the archway.

"Eellike motions." Brink kept pace with his companion. "They could belong to any phylum, any family."

"Look at those teeth," Low exclaimed. "Those didn't evolve to crop grass." He halted, and Brink bumped into him.

"Really, Commander. I think we should continue our retreat. Perhaps activating the planetarium will disorient them."

"Too late, Ludger."

Three more of the monstrosities had materialized behind them, leaving the two men to wonder how the beasts had gained access to the doorless, windowless, featureless planetarium chamber. It was a mystery whose solution would have to wait. The active, inimical creatures posed a more immediate problem.

Cut off from the planetarium and the transport sphere, they turned and ran toward the back of the boarding platform.

"Somehow we've got to get around them and into the sphere!" Low exclaimed as he ran. "And we've got to do it before one of those things accidentally flops inside and sends it racing away, or we'll be stuck here. I don't know about you, but I don't want to have to try to walk that tunnel. Not only aren't there any lights, it would be a real awkward place to get caught if a sphere came rolling toward you."

"They appear capable of rapid movement," Brink declared, "yet they are reluctant to attack. They pursue us, but remain wary."

"We may look like food," Low panted, "but maybe we don't smell right or something. Assuming they have a sense of smell, or any other senses that we'd recognize."

Brink looked back over his shoulder. The creatures were continuing their horrible, humping pursuit. "Whatever they are employing, it is enough. They know we are here."

"Throw 'em a life crystal," Low suggested.

"Don't be absurd, Commander! Not only are the crystals priceless and the supply finite, it would probably only give them strength."

"You might be right there." The vehemence of the scientist's response caused Low's gaze to narrow. "But we've got to try *something*." He found himself wishing for a nice, freshly lubricated, unscientific .30-.30. No doubt a number of exotic weapons sat in display cases in the museum spire, appropriately labeled and ready for use. Trouble was, they didn't know what was a weapon and what a kitchen blender. Besides, they were on the wrong island.

"I see several doors ahead." Brink was having trouble breathing. "Which one?"

"Any one that opens," Low shot back. Behind him, the eels were closing ground. As their bony bodies smacked rhythmically against the floor, they emitted nasty hissing sounds that seemed inadequate for their mass. Occasionally one would lift the upper third of its bulk off the floor, the better to locate the retreating humans before resuming pursuit.

Low reached the middle door. There was no handle, but deep grooves were etched into both sides of the barrier. Hooking his fingers into first one series of slots, then the next, he tried tugging hard.

Brink stood nearby, watching. "Hurry, Commander!"

"What do you think I'm doing? This doesn't require any special scientific expertise, you know."

Taking the hint, Brink started prying with his own fingers. He had no more success than his companion. The door remained resolutely shut.

Fumbling in his pockets and at his service belt, Low tried every compact tool he had. Nothing worked, and the eels were very close now.

"I'm all out of bright ideas," he growled.

Brink had his back against the smooth wall. "We will have to try to fight them."

"Maybe your teeth are sharper than mine. There's one thing we haven't tried yet."

So saying, he retraced their steps until he was almost within biting distance of the nearest eel. Then he turned, lowered his shoulder, and charged.

Under the impact, the door gave way with a satisfying crash.

Both men found themselves in a small, narrow hallway whose damp confines were anything but encouraging. It stank like a charnel pit. Piles of bones and other organic debris littered the floor.

With the eels pressing close on their heels, they retreated into the room. Low momentarily lost his balance, cursed, and didn't look down to see what had caused him to slip.

"Feeding time at the zoo and we've holed up in the food locker. Great!"

"I have no desire to become a lunch myself," muttered Brink. "I cannot imagine what these creatures normally eat, but it is evident that their intentions toward us are anything but benign. Their aggressiveness suggests that they are more than simply scavengers." The eels were inside the doorway now, their warped skulls weaving slowly back and forth as they took stock of their surroundings.

Low sniffed. "Hey, maybe they don't like German food." It was a comment more worthy of the long-absent Borden. Brink looked at his companion in surprise, and Low took note of it. "I always said that I'd try to be upbeat before I died." New concern brought an unpleasant vision to the forefront of his thoughts.

"I hope Maggie hasn't run into anything like these and that's why we haven't heard from her." Something caught his eye before the scientist could comment, and he gripped the other man by his shirt. "Over here! Get out of the way!"

"There is no 'out of the way,' " Brink replied morosely. "We are trapped here and . . . *vas ist mit ihnen los?* What's the matter with you?"

Low had grabbed him and bodily heaved him to one side. A moment later the first eels dug in with their primitive limbs and threw themselves forward. Brink shut his eyes, but it was other quarry the creatures had in mind. Less mobile quarry.

Landing with a great squishing sound they splashed into the nearest of the organic mounds. They were followed in short order by the remaining three. Soon all five were slithering and crawling through the slimy sweepings. The sounds of swallowing, gulping and bones breaking filled the room. Decaying compost was ripped apart.

Low waited, concealing himself and Brink behind another refuse pile until he was certain the creatures were fully occupied. "See? They weren't after us, per se. They wanted in *here*. We just happened to get ourselves caught in the wrong place at the wrong time."

"Astute observation, Commander. My congratulations. And now, not to put too fine a scientific point on it, I think it would behoove us to get the hell out of here, *nicht wahr?*"

Moving slowly so as not to attract undue attention in the event that one or more of the eels might be tempted to try a change in its diet, they slipped out from behind the mess and tiptoed toward the open doorway.

"It doesn't make any sense," Low educed when they were finally back on the transport platform. "Why should those creatures be roaming freely around here? What purpose do they serve?"

"Ask a Cocytan." Acutely conscious of their narrow escape, Brink was in no mood to entertain irrelevant theories. "Come, Commander. As you so accurately put it before our path was crossed, we have another spire to inspect."

Though unable to put the incident aside, Low did not let it affect his feet. Climbing into the sphere, he sat down next to Brink. The familiar, unupholstered bench felt as comfortable as the plushest couch. A moment later the entrance irised shut and the orb began to roll.

Only then did the two men allow themselves to relax. It had been brought home to them in unmistakable fashion that not everything they were likely to encounter on this world was guaranteed to be benign or inanimate.

"Local vermin." Brink had leaned back and crossed his arms over his chest.

Low's brows pulled together. "I beg your pardon?"

"That's the explanation. Those eel-creatures *had* no special purpose. After this place was abandoned by its makers, they somehow found their way in. They are simply scavengers, like rats or roaches."

"The room full of organic debris?"

Brink had an answer for that too. "An ancient repository. Or one that continues to function on automatic. As to the source of the organic material, devoid of information I do not feel justified in speculating further. I can say only that I think it would be best if we continue to watch our step."

"Amen to that."

"As we roam deeper into these complexes, we may encounter more such creatures, or even worse."

"I've thought of that." Low's fingers itched. "Wish I had a gun."

"Its usefulness would be debatable. I feel that possession of a gun in dangerous surroundings carries with it a corresponding increase in overconfidence."

"Fine," Low swore. "Give me a Mossburg street sweeper and I'll deal with the overconfidence. Sorry if that's not showing the proper scientific spirit."

"Under the circumstances, Commander, I forgive you." The scientist sighed. "Ever since we stepped outside the asteroid and I saw the first small invertebrate scuttle under a rock, I felt there must be larger, more menacing creatures living here. What could be more natural for them than to take shelter in these numerous chambers?"

"If we find one that can activate the asteroid," Low murmured, "I'll gladly feed it a finger or two." The sphere was picking up speed now, accelerating smoothly along its unsullied track.

"I thought the bipeds handled that rather well."

The Cocytans had gathered in a cluster above the main island. So dense was the distortion induced by their concentrated presence that no other thought was possible in their immediate vicinity. Confused fliers sank to the ground or flapped dizzily toward the distant mainland, while within the confines of rock and earth, creatures simpler still shuddered and settled deep into their burrows. Only those that were relatively mindless, such as the scavenger-eels, were not affected. Those, and any capable of higher thought, which automatically acted as a shield against the monumental mental presence.

Among the latter could be counted only three, and they had trouble enough to deal with.

Most of the imperceptible visitors were not directly perceiving the bipeds. They were content to allow those who had been involved from the beginning to debate meanings and actions, satisfied to let them interpret and promulgate. There was else to observe, other to contemplate. They paid attention with only a portion of themselves, yet understood with lucid simultaneity. The system was perfectly efficient and historically unfulfilling.

Paradise, they had quickly learned, was paved with ruts from which none could escape.

"With the full resources of the planetarium at their disposal they could not even locate their home system!" The four-and-twenty who commented did not try to hide their contempt. Their forcefulness was such that it bestirred a fragment of leaf to take flight. No one noticed because there were none present to notice. There were only the marooned bipeds, who were wholly immersed in transitory moments of their own.

" 'Eels', they called the scavengers. A short name for a lengthy entity. They avoided them neatly."

"Pure accident, fortuitous coincidence," insisted thirty-three others as they sought sixty-six of like mind to make three-thirds that would be less than a hundred. "They fled and hid and stumbled blindly out of the way. No credit attaches to such action. They did not try to understand, or resist, or meld."

"They survived," vouchsafed the supporters of the first. "They cannot be criticized for inelegance of solution. What matters are results."

"They are favored by the grand intangibles. They alter variables in their favor." The great mass of undecided declaimed emotionlessly. "We have seen so many come and go. They fleetingly amuse before their bones energize the landscape. These may yet join their predecessors. Meanwhile, it cannot be denied that they have advanced. Meanly, poorly, but advanced nonetheless. They deserve reflection."

"I maintain that luck can be quantified as effectively as any natural law." Doubters in their many descended on the individual who had thus postulated. Supporters lined up in their hundreds to argue on its behalf. And so it went, one of innumerable such discussions that raged above the islands. Below, the bipeds continued to amble ignorantly from place to place as storms in heaven went unperceived.

The sphere began to slow, eventually rolling to a stop at the end of the planetarium line. After lingering to assure themselves that the tunnel was otherwise deserted, Brink and Low exited and walked quickly back into the main chamber. Nothing had changed since their previous visit. The heap of collapsed ceiling still dominated the sleek floor. As before, there was no sign of the third member of their party. A check of his own unit showed Low that she had yet to reactivate her pen communicator.

"That's it," rumbled Low with finality. "She's done enough exploring. I think it's time we all got back together and discussed what we're going to do next. She may have acquired information we can use."

"You go and discuss it with her, Commander. There is something that I must do first."

Low eyed his companion uncertainly. "Something you *must* do? I don't follow, Ludger. There's nothing here that 'must' be done. Come and help me find Maggie. If she won't turn her communicator back on, we're just going to have to track her down without them."

Brink took a step backward. "Later." A faint glaze had come over his eyes. "As I told you, there is something I must attend to first." So saying, he turned to leave.

"Wait a minute." Low hurried to block the scientist's path. "What's so important that it has to be done now, all of a sudden? What's more important than finding out what's happened to Maggie?"

The other eyed him in disbelief. "Why, the life crystals, of course. They need to be examined closely, studied in depth. They are the key."

"The key to what?" Low had grown tense. "The key to finding food? The key to returning home? If it doesn't include either of those, it's not a key I'm interested in and it's not a key we have to worry about right now."

"Why I . . . I'm not sure, exactly." Honest bemusement was writ large across the scientist's face. "I just have this feeling that they're the solution to everything."

"I thought you never acted on 'feelings.' I had the impression you were a strict empiricist."

"Which is why it is vital that we study these crystals now, in depth." Brink turned to pleading. "Come with me, Commander. Even though you are a generalist, your input is valuable. You have insight, along with other abilities."

"I'll be glad to help you study the crystals," Low agreed, "*after* we've found Maggie and discussed what we're going to do next. What do you intend to study the crystals with? We have no equipment, no appropriate instruments."

The scientist's confusion visibly deepened, further adding to his unease. "I don't know," he replied crossly. "I will make do with whatever is available."

Low was watching him carefully. It was an illogical response, uncharacteristic of the methodical, rational Brink that he'd come to know. Something was definitely wrong.

"Will you, now?"

"*Ya!*" Brink's befuddlement had turned to defiance. "I will." He peered down at his pockets, overflowing with softly lambent life crystals. "They need to be attended to."

"Attended to?" Stepping out of the scientist's path, Low followed alongside, trying to find in the other man's expression some clue as to the source of his irrational behavior. Physically Brink seemed fine, undamaged by his recent brush with death. Were the crystals somehow affecting him adversely? Or was it something else?

"Where are you going?"

"Back to the storeroom." Brink's eyes were set resolutely forward.

"Why? You're carrying around a whole suitcase full of the stuff. What do you need to go back there for?"

"To ensure those we left behind have not been disturbed. It would be terrible if they disappeared."

Low skipped forward so that he was a little ahead of his companion and could look back at him. "Ludger, listen to me. They're not going to get up and walk away, and there's nobody else here. Nothing's going to mess with any we might have overlooked. Why this sudden concern? And I still don't know what you're talking about when you say they need to be attended to."

"I may have put that wrongly," Brink replied slowly. "*I*

need to attend to them. They emit a . . . I am not sure how to say it in English . . . a resonance, an all-pervasive warmth."

"Don't the ones you're carrying warm you enough?"

"You don't understand."

"That's what I've been saying," replied Low carefully.

"I need to attend to them."

"Okay, fine!" Low'd had enough of the scientist and his nascent peculiarities. "You go and attend to your precious crystals. I'll come back for you after I've found Maggie. Suffocate yourself in them if you want. Stick a couple up your nose. You're forgetting what's important here, Ludger."

Brink turned to look back at him, his eyes misty. "No, Commander. It is you who does not understand what is important here."

"Is that so? Funny, I thought it was finding Maggie, food and water, and then searching for a way back home. Silly me."

For a moment Brink seemed himself again. "All laudable ends, Commander. Each will happen in its own good time. But the crystals must be attended to first."

"I wish time meant as little to me as it does to you, Ludger. The life crystal revived you. It didn't make you immortal."

"I know that." Brink was walking rapidly backward now. "Though it is an interesting notion to ponder."

"Swell. You go play with your crystals and ponder. I'm going to find Maggie." With that he spun on his heel and stalked off in the opposite direction, leaving the scientist to his inexplicable obsession.

He sought but did not find. There was no sign of the errant journalist anywhere in the grand chamber. A few small side doors yielded to his entreaties. They revealed storerooms in varying degrees of disarray, but no Maggie.

His next thought was to ascend the rubble pile and return to the surface. As he debated whether to follow through on the idea, he couldn't help but notice that he was standing before the last of the open four portals. One more island to visit, he told himself. One more spire to check out. Could Maggie have discovered how to use the simple interisland transport system on her own, and gone exploring? If she was somewhere on the fourth islet, it would certainly explain why they hadn't encountered her, and why she had failed to respond to his repeated shouts and calls.

He considered. Brink was preoccupied with his crystals. Why not make a quick visit to the last spire while daylight remained?

By now he was as comfortable with the transport system as with the BART trains back home. Except, he thought as he mounted the platform and hurriedly entered the sphere, back home hideous unnamed creatures didn't come lurching and listing their way in your direction in search of food and sustenance, intent upon indifferent mayhem and worse.

Of course that did depend, he mused as the sphere began to roll down its dark track, on which San Francisco or Oakland station you happened to be in at the time.

At first sight the interior of the fourth tower was no different from the first. It was filled with alien artifacts, many preserved in cases that reminded him strongly of the museum. But this was clearly no archive. Too many containers were stacked high atop one another or crowded too close to their neighbors to pass between. None were equipped with incomprehensible labels or responded with explanatory projections to his questioning touch. There was about the entire vast assemblage an air of long disuse, of a warehouse where last-minute items and forgotten inventory had been haphazardly stowed.

He recognized nothing. If any of the museum exhibits were duplicated here, they lay buried beyond his range of vision. There were corners and corridors he was hesitant to visit, where the light from the walls and floor hardly penetrated. A number of particularly impressive containers were large enough to hold objects the size of the *Atlantis*. If only he cold find a way of deciphering the glyphs etched into their flanks, he might be able to descry their contents. Failing that, he could only guess and imagine.

Directly beneath the cusp of the spire and dominating the room was a massive triangular edifice. There were enough elusive twists to the walls, sufficient bends in the angles, to prove it had been designed by other than human hands. Low searched his memory for a terrestrial reference, gave up in disgust. It was a pyramid, and it wasn't; an obelisk, yet not.

Erected of the wonderful metallic glass that seemed to have been a favorite building material of the Cocytans, it cast a golden glow over its surroundings. Tiffany had once made glass like that, Low mused. He'd seen examples of it at the Met, of glistening vases and bowls fashioned of what appeared to be spun gold shot through with the most delicate reds and greens, pinks and blues. Except that he knew this stuff would support a train.

Curious to know what precious artifacts it had been built to hold, he methodically walked around the entire edifice. His hike took less time than he'd expected and left him midway between the singular structure and the archway that opened onto the tunnel station.

While circling the structure, he'd kept an eye out for and found not a single window or door. More puzzling was the complete absence on the sloping walls of the familiar glyphs and engravings. Everything else he'd encountered, from the walls in the main chamber to the containers that filled the rest of the spire, was covered with them. Their total omission here posed a conundrum.

He considered possible explanations. Perhaps it was a solid block of material that the Cocytans considered valuable for some unknown reason. Maybe it was a sculpture, albeit on a vast scale. Or it might be a place of worship, which engravings would only defile, a sort of interstellar menhir or altar.

He was on his way out when a weight in his pocket gave him pause. His fingers curled around the portable alien mapping device he had borrowed from the second spire. Why not give it a try and see what it could really do?

Removing it from his pants, he passed his fingers over the engravings as he had done before. A projected globe of Cocytus promptly appeared in front of him. Increasing the magnification and reducing the scale shrank the image until only the six islands and their portion of sea floated in front of him.

With careful adjustment he was able to eliminate the other islands to focus on the islet on which he stood. As he'd hoped, the incredible map reduced his point of view still farther until he found himself looking at a projection of the pyramidal structure in front of him. The double view was mildly disconcerting. At least, he mused, the device didn't show him looking at himself. It was a map, not a real-time imager.

Despite his best efforts he could not realize a view of the pyramid's deep interior. That was apparently asking too much of the marvelous device's powers of resolution. But careful manipulation did reveal a tunnel leading inward. He was pleased both with his intuition and with the mechanism's performance.

Moving around to one side of the structure, he paused before the tunnel's location. The sloping, gleaming piece of wall before him looked exactly like every other section of wall. There was nothing to indicate it concealed an entrance. Of one thing he was certain: He would never have found it without the mapping device.

He searched in vain for a door-opening robot similar to those he had utilized so successfully on the main island. In lieu of robots, he found a number of other devices sitting near the concealed entryway. Time passed while he struggled to find the right combination of devices to employ. He was about to give up when his last effort caused a portion of the wall to shimmer as if it had suddenly been doused in running water, and an opening appeared in the surface.

It was several times his width and about twice his height. Whether that reflected ceremonial proportions or a tight squeeze for the builders he had no way of knowing. He still had no idea what the founders of this lost civilization had looked like. Taking a deep breath, he entered.

Several paces in he paused to look back and was gratified to see that the portal remained open. He could clearly see out into the spire's main chamber. Thus reassured, he continued on, moving deeper into the heart of the pyramid. As he advanced, light flowed from the floor, ceiling and walls around him, illuminating the way forward even as it dimmed behind him. What hidden automatic implement tracked his progress he didn't know, but he resolved to try to find out.

Unless they found a way home, he was going to have plenty of time for such diversions.

The floor of the passageway led down at a slight angle, eventually depositing him in a small chamber filled with other devices. He had to spend more time analyzing their possible purpose, until he recognized several from previous encounters. Combining these opened a second door, allowing him to proceed farther.

Unlike the exterior of the pyramid, the chamber and doorway were magnificently ornamented with inlaid etchings and glyph work. While they appeared at first glance to be abstract in tone, closer inspection revealed plants and animals, minerals and stars: a splendid panoply of life on Cocytus. A few of the lowlier creatures he recognized from their brief sojourn on the surface of the central island.

Nowhere in the elaborate renderings, however, did he find anything that might have been a Cocytan.

"He looks directly at us and does not recognize," declaimed a hundred critics.

"How is he to distinguish us from the other life-forms?" The first was not at all discouraged. "The mural is an idyllic pastoral. We are depicted at natural play, not operating instrumentalities or erecting tall buildings. The necessary reference points are not present."

"Would he recognize us even if they were?" argued eleven others. They were emphatic to the point where Low turned sharply. Looking over his shoulder, he saw nothing, even though the eleven were hovering somewhere in the vicinity of his collar. He had felt their query without hearing it.

Having sensed movement, he blinked. There was nothing, only the dimly lit internal chamber and the new passage ahead. Frowning, he started forward.

Like the chamber, the new tunnel was elaborately embellished. The pyramid seemed larger on the inside than it had appeared to be from without. Some trick of alien optics, he marveled. Given what he had seen already, he was able to accept more distortions of light and space without pausing to wonder how the effect was accomplished.

Instead of glyphs and engravings, the decoration took the form of projected bas-reliefs that hovered barely a fingernail's thickness above the actual wall. The wealth of material, of potential knowledge, overwhelmed him.

Brink should be here, he knew. The passageway was an archaeologist's paradise. He studied the decorations as he advanced, trying to memorize what he could. More detailed analysis would have to wait.

Brink was preoccupied with the life crystals. Low wasn't quite ready to label it an obsession. When the scientist had finished "attending" to them, surely he would be ready to go back to work. Low felt the couple of crystals resting in his own back pocket. Their gentle warmth was comforting, but hardly seemed the stuff of madness.

An opening loomed ahead and he quickened his pace, making sure to keep a careful eye on the floor. There was no guarantee a gap wouldn't appear unexpectedly in the surface underfoot. Perhaps he also unwittingly touched the wrong section of wall, or passed through an invisible beam. He never knew what had triggered the sequence of events that followed.

"It is the end," declared a cluster of perceivers. "He is mesmerized by the beauty and mystery that surrounds him. So much so that a necessary portion of his thought-process has been neglected."

"It would not matter." A thousand flowed back and forth through the solid matter of the pyramid, the air within, the decorations Boston Low found so intriguing. "The end would be the same."

"A worthy effort," affirmed one million. "The best in a century. Perhaps those who come after will do as well." The presences were already thinking of Low in the past tense, as if he were already dead.

Unbeknownst to him, his arrival had activated a number of ancient devices. Their complex interaction was actually irrelevant. What mattered was the result.

He entered a chamber much larger than the one he had just traversed. Expansive and high-ceilinged, it occupied several stories. The instant before his arrival, a life crystal had fallen from its holder onto what at first glance appeared to be a grotesque sculpture.

But sculptures did not absorb life crystals. Only organics did that. Emitting a deep grinding sound, this one began to move. Powerful articulated limbs jerked and twitched. A skull rose. Organs of sight cleared. Alive again, it shook itself erect and began to survey its surroundings.

Low had his first glimpse of it as soon as he reached the low railing that marked a sudden drop-off. He was standing on a mezzanine overlooking a lower floor some twenty feet below. At the same time it peered up and saw him. A farrago of legs and mouths were linked by a network of exposed ligaments and tendons. There were no bones, no exoskelton, no visible eyes, ears or nostrils. Only mouths and clawed legs.

A guardian didn't need anything else.

Stretching, it caught sight of him. Eyeless, it focused on the intruder with senses unknown to Low. He took a reflexive step backward.

Contracting its astonishing network of connecting fibers, the creature sprang the full twenty feet from the floor of the lower level to land *behind* the Commander. If he hadn't ducked, it would have taken his head off. As he whirled to confront it, eerie moaning sounds arose from the multiplicity of mouths. Gathering its claws beneath it and swaying rhythmically back and forth on innumerable legs, it readied itself to pounce again. It was, he saw now, about the size of a full-grown bull moose.

With the monstrosity blocking the exit, Low was forced to retreat until he was dangerously close to the edge of the drop. Dashing to his right, he felt a cold shiver run through him as the creature immediately skittered sideways to block his path. It was the same when he darted back to his left. He could see no eyes, but it was clearly aware of his presence. Some kind of infrared sensors, perhaps, or something even more remarkable. Sundry mouths opened and closed. In expectation, no doubt, he told himself. He could turn and chance the jump to the lower level, but he had no doubt that the creature would follow.

Somehow he had to get around it. Feinting to his right, he dashed left again. The monster didn't go for it, matched him step for step. It was not only faster than he, but quicker.

It's toying with me, he realized suddenly. This wasn't going to work.

With each sideways sprint the thing came a little closer. Soon he'd have no choice but to turn and take his chances by jumping. Right into the creature's lair, no doubt. He would only be postponing the inevitable.

Fighting back was out of the question. He had no weapons, it was much too big and there were too many mouths and limbs to avoid. He'd have to get away from it, somehow.

But no matter how he darted and feinted, it continued its inexorable advance, always positioning itself between him and the tunnel. While not necessarily intelligent, it was clearly cognizant of the chamber's layout. Did it instinctively know where the exit was, or had that information been programmed into it? If the latter, then the monster had been left here for a purpose. To punish defilers of a temple, Low wondered, or to prevent them from advancing any farther?

If he ended up as brute biscuit, an eventuality that loomed

as a distinct possibility, the actual explanation would be moot.

How would a legitimate visitor identify himself to such a guardian? Did he have anything on him that might secure passage?

He dragged out the map projector and waved it. "Look, see? Local manufacture. I belong here." Giving no indication that it either understood or sympathized, the thing maintained its relentless stalk.

In quick succession Low flashed everything he had with him, from the small flashlight on his service belt to the tiny package of antibacterial tissues that was part of every crew kit. In each instance the result was the same: The creature ignored it.

Right or left? Low thought frantically. He'd have to make a choice. Even as he contemplated his rapidly shrinking options, he knew he'd never make it. The thing was too damn fast.

It was clear now why it was taking its time. If by some miracle Low did manage to slip past and make it to the tunnel, the creature would be unable to pursue. It was simply too big. It had been emplaced, or bred, or built to remain forever in this chamber. Its permanent presence here had been decreed from the beginning.

What was so important here that it required such a guardian? He was going to die without ever finding out.

The map projector was compact and heavy. Taking aim, he threw it as hard as he could. It bounced harmlessly off the creature's tough, leathery body.

Reaching into a back pocket, he pulled out one of the few objects that remained to him. But why throw a life crystal, he thought? If anything, it would probably only make the creature stronger. Could he somehow arrange things so that it would revive him after he was killed? Of course, if the monster tore him apart, it might be difficult even for one of the miraculous crystals to resurrect a mess of scattered fragments. Not to mention the impossibility of revival if the creature ate him.

Trying to divide his attention between the advancing monstrosity and his remaining choices, he peered back into the depths. That's when he saw a mate to his stalker lying curled up and quiescent on the floor below. It was motionless, desiccated and dead.

Great, he thought. *Another one.* The moaning was very near now. He thought he sensed a hint of expectation in it.

What the hell, he decided. If it didn't work, he wouldn't die any slower.

Turning, he threw the life crystal not at the creature stalking him but at the dead one below. It landed precisely in the middle of the knot of tendons and promptly sank out of sight. Whirling to once more confront the devil before him, he could only listen as the one below revived.

Standing and stretching, it angled its perceptions upward. Sensing movement, it tensed, focused . . . and sprang.

Low immediately fell to the floor. Claws outstretched, the monster sailed over him to strike the stalker head-on. Outraged moans filled the air as the two tumbled backward in an inextricable tangle of claws and legs.

Grasping mouths sought purchase within the tough hide. Claws scraped against unyielding surfaces. Powerful limbs thrashed and thrust. Like a pair of drunken wrestlers, the two guardians twisted and twitched in an orgy of determined fury.

Meanwhile a shaky Low climbed slowly to his feet. With no chance of slipping past them, he had no choice but to continue on.

How long would they continue to fight, he found himself wondering? Until one killed the other? They seemed evenly matched. Tough, fleshless torsos and limbs could take a lot of punishment. Maybe they would brawl until they exhausted themselves.

That was a dénouement he could deal with. Turning, he resumed his interrupted advance, curiosity as well as necessity driving him to the tunnel that opened into the chamber on the opposite side of the mezzanine.

He did not feel the multitude gathering above him. Even in their millions the Cocytans did not impact on the physical world. Their mental weight exerted a pressure he sensed only as the start of a possible headache, and this he attributed to his recent near escape. Had he known the truth, it surely would, so to speak, have weighed more heavily on him.

A flurry of excitement had raced through the Cocytan group-mind when Low had succeeded in bypassing the guardians. Few previous visitors had ever made it so far. For that reason none could predict what might happen next. It was a New Thing and, as such, deserving of the attention it was receiving.

"What an elegant solution," the first declaimed. "To cancel out an invincible guardian, one must utilize another invincible guardian." Even the skeptics were impressed, and so withheld their usual morose commentary.

Low felt nothing. As he advanced at a steady pace, he was unaware of the many minds that marked his progress. Accompanied by a million ghosts, he was more troubled by some dust in his left eye.

The passageway opened abruptly into another large chamber. In its center was a magnificently decorated platform atop which rested a sculpture of exquisite refinement, bathed in a pale light of a color not previously encountered. Low entered warily, ready to duck quickly back into the tunnel, but there were no guardians here, dead or otherwise. Approaching cautiously, he inspected the sculpted icon.

More than anything, it reminded him of pictures he'd seen in books on mythology. A recumbent griffin, he thought, though designed to walk on two legs instead of four. Furthermore, no terrestrial bird had ever possessed a head like that. As for the wings, they were stunted and protruded from the back in sets of three. He wasn't sure they were wings. They might have been external gills, some kind of vestigial ornamentation, or a sex attractant.

Mounting the platform, the reason for the sculpture's extraordinary detail became clear. It wasn't a sculpture but a corpse. Something about its aspect, something in the face struck him with singular force.

He felt he had finally found a Cocytan.

CHAPTER
15

He couldn't be sure, of course. In life it might prove as ravenous as the monsters he had only recently escaped. But he didn't think so. The features were somehow too sensitive, the fact that the upper limbs lay relaxed by the side of the body instead of being contracted against it, all contributed to the feeling of intelligent repose.

There was one way to find out. Dare he chance it?

What if it was nothing more than another mindless eating machine, a different sort of guardian awaiting thoughtless resurrection so that it could keep this chamber clean of intruding vermin such as himself? In the end it was the absence of predatory cutlery such as prominent teeth or claws that decided him. It might spit poison or jump on prey with both feet, but it did not have the countenance of a feral hunter.

Digging into a pocket, he removed one of the life crystals. The pale-green efflorescence was as strong as ever. Mounting the platform, he studied the calm, strong face for a long moment before placing the crystal carefully in the center of what he supposed to be the chest. As it melted into the broad torso, he retreated to a respectful distance. This time he was ready to dash back into the tunnel should the revived subject exhibit any hostile tendencies.

Both eyes flicked open simultaneously. They were wide, intelligent and intensely inhuman. Low took another step backward, marveling at the pace of resurrection. However long the entity had lain here, upper limbs laid neatly at its sides, face turned mutely heavenward, it had taken the fabulous crystal only moments to initiate the process of revivification.

How long, he found himself wondering as it rose to a sitting position? A year, a hundred, a thousand? It pivoted slowly on its hips to survey its surroundings, methodically taking in the details of the chamber, the ambient light and the ceiling overhead. Eventually, its gaze settled on the room's only other occupant. Those extraordinary eyes met Low's. Neither human nor Cocytan blinked.

Confusion, jubilation and excitement reigned in equal measure among the assembled perceivers. They were helpless to influence the course of events, which had taken a turn not even the most optimistic among them had foreseen, so their frustration nearly exceeded their elation. So strong was the outpouring of perception that several times Low found himself looking over his shoulder in search of an unseen presence. Though a million and more returned his attention, there was naught for him to see.

No longer did he have to speculate about the revived's level of intelligence. This was no mindless guardian that gazed back at him, no blindly ravening carnivore. The tripartite wings fluttered against the alien's back, serving some purpose other than flight. They could no more raise that impressive mass off the ground than could Low's arms if he flapped them until he dropped.

When the creature—the Cocytan, Low corrected himself—showed no inclination to advance, the Commander took a hesitant step forward. "Sorry for waking you up."

The being's beak parted, and sounds emerged. They might have been music or mating grunts for all Low knew. If they were language, it was quite beyond him. Though it was oddly guttural and utterly incomprehensible, he listened closely in hopes of divining some meaning. In this he failed completely.

He spread his hands wide, hoping the gesture might be understood. "It's no good. I can't understand you."

In response, the Cocytan gestured with one arm and spoke again, more softly and less commandingly this time. Double lids half closed. What this portended remained hidden from Low. He was no more adept at reading the Cocytan's gestures and expression than he had been at deciphering its language. Assuming it *was* speaking and not ululating some arcane postresurrection life chant, he reminded himself.

Robbins, now, with her experience with the Mayan glyphs and her knowledge of language in general, might have done better. Certainly she couldn't do any worse. Low spoke only a smattering of German and Russian and was fluent in nothing save math.

Unfortunately, Robbins was still wherever she was, leaving him on his own.

"Excuse me just a minute, will you?" Anticipating failure, he nonetheless removed his tiny pen communicator from his belt. It would only work if the receiving unit was activated. There was nothing to lose by trying. He lifted the communicator slowly, to show that it was harmless. The Cocytan tracked every movement. While not as imposing or threatening as the eels or the outer guardians, it was seven feet tall, broad at the shoulders, and plenty massive enough to inflict some serious hurt if it were so inclined. Low was careful to do nothing to alarm it, though it didn't act as if it could be easily alarmed.

Without much hope of success, he activated the unit and tried to contact Robbins. Would she ever remember to turn the damn thing back on?

"Just trying to get in touch with a friend of mine," he explained cheerfully. Alien eyes continued their probing. Curiously, angrily, indifferently? He could not tell. "She wandered off some time ago, and I'm probably not going to be able to get a hold of her because I haven't been able to since we split up and I've been trying ever since to—"

"Boston? Boston, is that you?" The voice was distorted by distance and intervening structures, but it was instantly recognizable. Mightily surprised, Low could only gape at the tiny built-in speaker. As for the Cocytan, its gaze might have flicked in the direction of the communicator for a second or so. Low wasn't sure.

He smiled wanly. "Guess I was wrong." Thumbing the tuner, he tried to eliminate the static. "Maggie, where are you? Where the hell have you been and what have you been doing?"

"Trying to find you," she shot back. "I've been all over these little islands."

So the scientist's supposition had been correct. "I guess we kept missing each other. Well, it's time to end the waltz. We have company."

"Company? I don't understand."

While Low spoke, he kept a wary eye on the Cocytan. It looked relaxed seated there atop its platform, silently studying both visitor and surroundings.

"At my instigation, one of the locals has decided to put in an appearance. If it's upset at having its sleep disturbed, it's keeping it pretty much to itself. We've been trying to communicate, but his knowledge of colloquial English about equals my mastery of Cocytan."

"An alien? Are you serious? A real, live alien?"

"No," Low replied sarcastically, "it's a special effect. It's sitting right here in front of me. We keep yakking at each other, without much result. It was dead, but perfectly preserved, and I revived it with a life crystal."

"Life crystal? What . . . ?"

"I'll explain everything. Where are you now?"

"Well, you know how those glass balls take you from the central island to the others? It's not hard to figure out; the machine does all the work. I crawled into one and it carried me to this huge tower."

Low nodded absently. "Brink and I have visited all but one of them. Can you describe your surroundings?"

"Sure." She proceeded to do so. "The place is full of mounted machinery and transparent cases. Some of them are lit from within. Most don't respond, but one or two react when you touch them."

The museum spire, Low decided. "I know where you are. I'll meet you back in the big chamber on the central island. I don't suppose you'll be able to make any sense out of what this creature is saying, but you can't do any worse than I am. If you'd like to give it a try, I'll bring you back."

"Oh, I think I'll be able to talk to it," she chirped brightly. "No problem. It'll be fun to try it out."

Low did a double take. "Try what out?"

"The Cocytan language, of course. At least, I assume it's the local language. Where did you think I'd been all this time? I've been studying it." She spoke as casually as if she'd been browsing a Berlitz over coffee and danish.

"How'd you manage that? Brink and I couldn't even tell the written glyphs apart from the control surfaces."

"One of the exhibits here," she explained. "It's really fascinating. Makes a CD-ROM player look like blackboard and chalk. You put this thing against your head, and I don't know exactly how it works, but it does. Direct cerebral induction?"

"Direct cerebral . . ." he hesitated. "Where'd you hear about that?"

"Read it in a magazine once. Or maybe I mentioned it in an old report. I'm not sure." She laughed. "I guess it doesn't improve your memory. But you sure learn a lot, and fast. You press your forehead against this cushion, say something and suddenly the translation's right there in your mind. The important thing is, when you step back from the machinery, the information stays with you. You could say I kind of stumbled into it. My head hit the pickup, or whatever it is, and I reacted instinctively. So the first words I learned in Cocytan were naughty ones."

This was convenient timing, Low thought to himself.

"I don't see why it wouldn't work on you also, Boston," she went on. "Although I've had some experience with other languages. Maybe it helps me to learn faster. Again, I don't know. Wish I'd had one of these when I was a grad student at UCLA. It beats the hell out of the language lab."

"It's one thing to learn a language," he told her. "Speaking it is something else. Our new host has a pretty deep voice and tends to growl a lot of words. Do you think your throat can make the necessary sounds?"

A tiny green LED atop the communicator flashed as she responded. "No problem. I've been talking back to the Educator, as I've come to call it. Tone doesn't seem to be as important as elocution. I think I can grunt with the best of 'em. Now, what's all this 'life crystal' business?"

"It's be easier to explain in person. I'll meet you back by the ceiling collapse. If I don't show up, don't wait around for me."

There was sudden concern in her voice. "What's that supposed to mean?"

"I had some trouble getting this far. I may have more on the way out. Nothing you can do about it. Just make sure that *you're* there."

"Boston?" Her tone mellowed. "I'm sorry about stomping off like that. I was angry, and frustrated, and scared, and a whole lot of other things all mixed up together. The only way I know to handle turmoil like that is to get off by myself so I can think. It worked for me in Namibia and China, so I thought it would work here."

"Forget it."

"Thanks. You know, I'm almost as famous for my temper as for my reporting."

"Now you can be famous for your translating ability."

"What about this native? Will it wait around for us to come back?"

Low glanced at the Cocytan. It was ignoring him, engrossed in its surroundings. "I don't know. If it tries to follow me out, I'm certainly not going to object. On the other hand, there's nothing to be gained by trying to coerce it. It's a lot bigger than me and I have the feeling it wouldn't take too kindly to an insistent push.

"As for how long it will stay revived, I can't say. It's been dead a lot longer than Ludger."

Her tone was incredulous. "Brink's alive?"

"Yeah, I revived him too. Why so surprised? You absorb an ancient alien tongue in a few hours, and I learn how to bring back the dead. Maybe tomorrow we'll work on anti-gravity and immortality. It would help a lot if we could ask this entity a few questions."

"That's what I do best," she replied. "Okay, I'll meet you by the rubble pile. I'm starting out right now."

"Good. Oh, and if you run into Ludger, go easy with him."

"Say again?"

"Just don't upset him. These life crystals have become something of an obsession with him. He's not acting right."

"Don't worry about me, Boston. I'm an old pro at humoring the eccentric."

"Just letting you know. Also, keep this channel open and your communicator on. We'll worry about the battery power later. I don't want to lose track of you again. I think it's important that we keep in contact from now on."

"Roger. Isn't that what I'm supposed to say now?"

"Only if you want to talk to somebody named Roger." He couldn't keep from smiling. "See you in a little while."

The fact that no appropriately snide comment was forthcoming assured him she was on her way. Which meant it was time for him to get moving as well. Hooking the communicator back onto his belt, he eyed the Cocytan as he started for the passageway.

"Listen, if you could just stay here until I return? I'm coming back with a friend who might be able to talk to you. There are many questions we'd very much like to ask you." Frustrated, he did his best to explain with his hands.

Cocytan eyes tracked the movements but gave no hint of understanding. Words emerged from the beaked mouth, elegant and incomprehensible.

"Yeah, sure." Low was backing into the tunnel. "You stay

right there, now." With that final admonition, he turned and hurried off up the passageway.

Halfway through, he plucked the communicator from his belt. "You still there, Maggie?"

"I'm on my way, Boston."

"Same here."

"Maybe when we find a way home"—she didn't say 'if,' he noted—"we can take some of this stuff with us. It's all beguiling, even if we don't know what most of it does. Any one tool would be priceless on Earth. Like for me to translate that into Cocytan?"

"Save it," he instructed her. "You can practice on our host."

"Okay. It's funny how once it's put into your head, it just stays there. Wish I could memorize news sources that well. Sometimes I—" She broke off abruptly.

"Maggie?" He brought the communicator closer to his lips. "Sometimes you what, Maggie? Come back. You okay?"

The creature was very large, very alien, extremely unpleasant to look upon and evinced no hint of intelligence whatsoever. What it was doing in the museum spire she didn't know. It hadn't been there when she'd arrived. Unlike Low and Brink, it was her first encounter with any local life-form larger than a lizard. Though Low hadn't supplied any details, she didn't think it was a Cocytan.

It looked more like a crab than a spider, she decided, though in appearance it partook a little of both. It would have been perfectly at home in a cheap 1950s horror film, except that it smelled atrocious and its contorted, bent limbs were possessed of a horrid jerking motion that was beyond the reach of cheap cinematic artifice. Big and ugly, it blocked her path with ease.

She couldn't see any eyes, though it was obviously aware of her presence and location. Hard-shelled, shiny legs twitched in her direction. As she backed away, she could hear Low yelling at her via the communicator and knew she should respond. The shock of the creature's appearance had left her momentarily dumb struck.

It had simply materialized in front of her, without any warning. Adrift amid the peace and quiet of the spire and fascinated by the enchanting Educator, she'd let down her guard. Now it was too late to take precautions.

She looked anxiously to right and left, but there was no real cover in either direction. Only exhibits and displays, none of which were large enough to hide behind. Besides, the creature obviously had a fix on her and would follow no matter where she ran.

One side of the spire boasted several unexplored doorways. All lay in the direction of the transport station. If she was lucky, one of them would connect through, allowing her to bypass the creature.

She turned and sprinted for the wall. All those hours spent in the gym were intended to keep her looking her best on the small screen while enabling her to ward off the smiling assaults of younger, up-and-coming newswomen. Now the hundreds of miles she'd spent on the treadmill were being put to more important use.

It didn't look particularly fast, she told herself as she ran. She'd outrun it, pop down a side tunnel and find another way back to the transport sphere. There was no need to worry Low. The poor man carried around an Atlas-sized load of anxiety as it was. She'd reassure him as soon as she was sealed safely inside the sphere.

Hard, unyielding digits closed about her waist. Only then did she look back, to find herself staring into a distorted mockery of a face. Twisted, curving jaws were within an arm's reach. All that was missing from the picture was ichorous drool. An overpowering stench more than made up for its absence. The monster reeked like prime carrion.

She'd underestimated its speed as well as its determination.

Although some of its movements were machinelike, it was definitely not mechanical. As it lifted her from the floor and carried her toward one of the very same dark openings toward which she'd been fleeing, she wondered why she didn't scream. Was it because she couldn't, or because the same inner drive that had taken her to the far corners of the Earth refused to concede the weakness? In any event, there was no one around to hear, and she didn't want to do anything to startle the beast. If it found the noises coming from her unpleasant, it might decide to put an end to them by, say, unscrewing her head.

She struggled futilely in its grasp. The grip around her waist was painful and she was having trouble breathing. At any moment she expected to disappear headfirst down that alien gullet. To her great relief, her captor shifted its grasp as it stepped over a floor-mounted, cylindrical exhibit, allowing her to inhale freely once more.

The largest of the openings in the wall loomed near. Low's voice continued to yammer at her from the communicator. The creature ignored it, and with her arms pinned at her sides she was unable to reach the send switch and respond. She could only listen helplessly to the Commander's frantic entreaties.

"Maggie, dammit, come back!" Low tried everything he could think of to reestablish contact, but all indications were that her unit was operating properly. Then why didn't she respond? He broke into a run. She was in some kind of trouble, but what? Had she fallen through another weakened ceiling like Brink and left her on-line communicator behind? Was she lying unconscious somewhere, unable to respond to his entreaties?

Unpleasant realization struck home. Had she encountered a guardian?

He slowed as he approached the intermediate chamber, the location of his own near demise. For an instant he heard nothing. Then the blunt, dull sounds of bodies striking each other reached him, and he cautiously leaned forward to peer out.

The two guardians were much as he'd left them, inextricably entwined and battling relentlessly. One was missing half a limb while the other bled from several deep wounds. Neither showed any sign of letting up or slowing down.

He waited until they had rolled into the farthest corner of the chamber before slipping out of the passageway. Keeping low and moving fast, he covered the distance to the other tunnel without being noticed. Or perhaps they both detected motion and chose to ignore his presence. If either let down its guard, its opponent would not hesitate to seize the opportunity. Evisceration and dismemberment would surely follow.

Elated at his escape, Low entered the smaller, narrower outer tunnel and resumed his flight. When he finally emerged back into the clear light of the spire, he nearly collapsed from relief.

No time for self-congratulation, he thought sternly. Disdaining rest, he turned and raced for the transport tunnel. Whatever trouble Maggie was in, he doubted it would wait days to be resolved. She needed help *now.* As much help as he could muster.

That meant involving Brink.

If he couldn't persuade the scientist to put aside his obsession with the life crystals in order to go exploring, he could damn sure do so with Maggie's well-being at stake. And if Brink wouldn't be persuaded, he could be dragged, pushed or shoved.

Ahead, the transport sphere gleamed on its track like a giant pearl.

It bore him swiftly back to the central island and the main chamber. There was no sign of Maggie, nor had he realistically expected her to magically appear before him, safe and sound beside the ceiling collapse. A check of the pertinent tunnel confirmed what he already knew: The transport sphere for the museum island was missing. More apprehensive than ever, he returned to the main chamber.

He didn't have to go hunting for Brink. He knew exactly where to find the scientist.

"Ludger."

The other man reclined in the rear of the storeroom where they'd first found the supply of life crystals, basking in their combined warmth. He'd removed them from his pockets and spread them out to form a narrow enclosure. Like a wizard on holiday, he lay in the midst of the pale-green framework, hands behind his head and eyes closed.

Low advanced. "Ludger, Maggie's in trouble. I'm not surmising, I just finished speaking to her via the communicators. She was talking to me and her voice went dead, like she'd been cut off. But her unit's still operating. Something's happened to her. She's in big trouble." He nudged a couple of crystals with his foot. "I need your help, Ludger. Maggie needs your help."

Exerting himself, Brink opened his eyes and sat up. Relaxed and content, he struggled to return from his self-imposed sedation. As he spoke, he rubbed slowly at his eyes, like someone awakened from a deep sleep.

"Trouble? What kind of trouble?"

"I told you." Low fought to curb his exasperation. "I don't know. We have to find out."

"Ah, but *we* don't, Commander. You handle it. I'm sure you're much better at this sort of thing than I am." He waved diffidently as he sank back to a reclining position. "I am occupied with reflection and study."

It was clear the scientist wasn't interested in helping Low, Maggie or even himself. All that mattered to him anymore was remaining close to his beloved crystals. His condition was recognizable enough: He had become addicted.

Great, Low rumbled silently. He had two companions on this world. One was in God knew what kind of trouble, and the other had turned into the first extraterrestrial junkie.

For all Low cared, once they had rescued Maggie, the scientist could spend the rest of his life in rapt contemplation of the crystals until both body and mind wasted away. But right now he needed him.

At least he's coherent and responsive, the Commander thought. Was there something in the appearance of the life crystals, in the warmth they gave off or their slightly slippery feel, that drew people inexorably to them? If he could figure out their attraction, he might be able to counteract it. Of course, if the addiction was connected to the fact that Brink had absorbed one into his body, then there wasn't much Low or anyone else could do.

Silently the Commander tried to count the number of crystals arrayed around the scientist's prone form. There seemed to be the same aggregate as before. That meant that whatever their attraction, it didn't require absorbing or consuming more of the crystals on a regular basis. The residual effect was external. In many ways that made it even more insidious.

"Look, Ludger, you can come back when we're through. I just need you to help me help Maggie."

"Sorry, Commander, but I have found all the help that *I* need," Brink responded with languorous indifference. "You know, there is a device here that I believe is designed to produce additional crystals."

"Now, how," an impatient Low inquired, "without any knowledge of the local written language, did you manage to figure that out?"

The scientist's eyes blinked open to stare up at him. Had they acquired a faint greenish cast, Low wondered, or was it only his own imagination working overtime?

"It seems fairly straightforward. There is an abundance of illustrative glyphs on the machinery. The mechanism itself appears to have been designed so that even the simplest of fools can operate it. Perhaps even such as you or I."

Low passed on the implied insult. "So how come you haven't switched it on and buried yourself up to your *tuchus* in crystals?"

"I tried, Commander. Believe me, I tried. However, when I passed my hands over the appropriate grooves, following the pattern indicated in the glyphs, nothing happened. I tried this several times and am quite sure I proceeded correctly. My conclusion is that there is something mechanically wrong with the device. I believe the problem is not insuperable." A tautness had crept into his voice.

"Think of it, Commander! Think of what it would mean to bring such a machine back to Earth. Resurrection on demand. Alleviation of all the life-threatening diseases that have forever plagued mankind. Put in a coin and receive life. A miracle machine."

"Right: if it works on everybody, and every medical problem. Meanwhile, Doctor Faustus, I'm sure nobody will touch your precious medicinal Mephistopheles if you take a few moments to aid Maggie instead of Moloch."

"Why, Commander! You are better read than I would have expected."

"Thanks. I'd like to add that I also hold a second-degree black belt in Tae Kwan Do. So get your tired Teutonic butt up off the floor and lend me a hand." As he reached for the scientist's boots, Brink quickly drew back his legs.

"It will do you no good to threaten me, Commander. Go and seek out our wayward journalist if you must, but leave me in peace."

"She's not wayward. I told you, she's in trouble."

"Journalists are always in trouble. They revel in it. From trouble they derive stories, the way a fish extracts oxygen from seawater."

Low bit down on his lower lip before replying, his words carefully spaced and intense. "Listen to me, Ludger. There are creatures on this planet that aren't cute, ground-dwelling critters. I know; I had to deal with two of them in the last spire I visited."

"Then I am certain you can deal with this crisis as well." Brink drew his knees up against his chest and wrapped his arms around them, looking for all the world like a six-year-old trying to hide in a closet. "It is more important that I remain here to look after the life crystals while I try to unearth the secret of this machine's operation."

"I'm sorry, Ludger. I don't have time to argue anymore." So saying, he reached down and grabbed the scientist's shoulder. "You're coming with me. Now."

"I am not." Brink rose to his feet and shook off Low's hand.

Though the two men were about the same size, Brink was no fitness fanatic. Whereas Low, despite his years, still retained the physical stamina that was a characteristic of his profession. That plus his martial-arts training allowed him to overpower the scientist without much effort.

Flinging Brink into a corner to keep him out of the way, Low began gathering up the glowing life crystals. Apparently the only way to induce the scientist to move was to also move the source of his intractability. Low's pockets held the crystals as readily as did his companion's.

Dazed, Brink tried to raise himself from where he'd been thrown. "No! Don't touch them! Give them back."

Low found their warmth pleasing but in no way addictive or mind-altering. Still, it was early yet. Having no one else to do so, he would have to continually monitor his own reactions.

To his surprise, Brink rushed him. Low sidestepped easily, used his hands and feet and sent the scientist crashing to the ground. Only the minimal force necessary was employed. His intention was to divert, not injure. Brink wouldn't be of much use to Maggie with a couple of broken limbs.

Breathing hard, the scientist rolled over. His expression was desperate. "Please, Commander! You don't understand. I have to—"

Disgusted, Low whirled on him, glaring hard. "You have to what?" He held up one of the sheathed crystals. "Have one of these next to you?"

Brink took a step forward, thought better of it, and stood there tottering with one hand extended. "Yes, that's exactly it, Commander. I *have* to be close to them. I can't explain it, but—"

"Fine," exclaimed Low, interrupting. "Stick close to me and you'll be close to them, right? You help me help Maggie and you can have them all back. I'll even help you reconstruct your little green playpen. What'll it be?" Following a pause, he added, "I see you eyeing that length of pipe, or conduit, or whatever it is. Don't even think of it. If you try to hit me, Ludger, I'll have to hit back hard. You won't like the result. Use your logic." He tried to lighten the proceedings.

"Besides, it's bad for crew morale. Conflict and camaraderie can't coexist." He turned to go. "I'm leaving now. Stay behind and I'll see to it that you never see these crystals again." His tone thawed.

"I know you're not entirely responsible for your actions, Ludger. It's the crystals. You've become addicted to them, somehow. Maybe because one dissolved inside you. Come on, man, use your head! Bring your analytical powers to bear. God knows they're a lot more developed than my own.

Try to step back mentally, take a look at what's happening to you."

Brink hadn't moved. Now he lowered his head along with his arm. "I know . . . *ich vergessen* . . . I know I haven't been entirely myself here lately. I see now that the life crystals have become something of an . . . an obsession with me."

" 'Something,' hell," Low replied quietly. "It's all you think about. It's driving you. With luck we'll find out why and figure a way to combat it. But right now neither of us has a clue, so you're just going to have to handle it."

"Yes. I know you are right, Commander." His head came back up, and for the moment, at least, he looked like the old Ludger Brink: confident, self-assured, good-natured and just a touch arrogant. "I will help you assist Maggie. But if she is no longer responding, how will we find her?"

Low drew the communicator from his belt and held it up for Brink to see. "These all have built-in search-and-locate functions. It doesn't matter that Maggie isn't talking. All that matters is that her unit is active. Which it is. She may not be talking, but we can still track her. She told me she was on the museum island." He clutched the compact unit tightly in his left hand. "According to this she still is. That should narrow things down a bit. Come on."

Brink offered no further objections as he followed Low out of the storeroom and back to the main chamber. Together they hurried toward the transport tunnel that led to the museum isle.

They had to walk, or rather jog, the whole way, praying as they did so that Maggie wouldn't suddenly appear in the tunnel ahead, riding the glassy transport sphere toward them. While they had no way of ascertaining its chemical composition, both men knew the rolling globe was not fashioned of thin plastic. Roaring down the tunnel, it would reduce them to pulp.

The blackness ahead remained silent. Nor did any active alien abominations come shambling out of hidden side passages to impede their progress. The lightly polished surface underfoot was perfectly smooth and seamless. Darkness might slow them, but they did not trip and fall.

Several times the Commander had to pause and wait for Brink to catch up, but overall the scientist maintained the pace surprisingly well. Either he'd done some running, Low mused, or else the life crystal he'd absorbed was keeping him going. It didn't matter to Low.

Both men were exhausted by the time they emerged from the subway. Stopping to catch their breath, they took time out to repeatedly bellow the journalist's name.

They kept calling to her as they cautiously entered the spire. Familiar cases and containers loomed around them. Only this time, instead of revelation, the sea of wonders concealed an unknown danger.

Instead of leading them deeper into the complex, as Low had expected, the communicator's locate function angled sharply to the right, pointing toward a series of holes or open doorways. When they reached the wall, Low walked back and forth until he was sure which of the openings the communicator was singling out.

"I don't like this." Pulling the small flashlight from his service belt, Low flicked it to life and entered the poorly lit tunnel. Here the light emanating from ceiling and walls was feeble, barely strong enough to illuminate the damp floor's conspicuous downward slope. Their compact beams were a welcome supplement. "Last time I was in a tunnel, I ended up playing dodge-em with a serious nightmare."

Brink was inspecting their surroundings. "Maintenance passage, I suspect. How did you escape your nemesis, Commander?"

Low smiled grimly. "Gave it a nightmare of its own. Do you hear water running?"

"Yes. Be careful. The floor is growing slippery." He sniffed. "Saltwater. This tunnel must run out under the ocean. Given the limited amount of space on each island, it would not be surprising to discover that much of this interisland complex's infrastructure exists below sea level. It is the way I would do it."

"I'll keep that in mind next time I need to build me a university, or whatever the hell this setup is supposed to be." As Low ducked beneath a leaky conduit, cold seawater dripped down the back of his neck and he found himself shivering.

"We must try to break through!" insisted several of the mind-forms which had followed the visitors' progress from the very beginning. "Otherwise they will all, despite having come so far and accomplished so much, perish here."

"Break through?" Five hundred perceptions puzzled the problem. "We have tried to break through for a thousand years. There is no breaking through."

An image formed before them all. It was a representation of the first to encounter the travelers. As a reminder of what they had once been, it was a powerful stimulant.

"We can at least try," declared the first. "Who will try with me?"

A hundred volunteered. Choosing a comparatively stable nexus in space-time, they sought out the most prominent fracture and pushed, compressing selves into self as they did so. The rip was nanoscopically slim, as they all were, but under the combined and determined effort it gave, ever so slightly.

"Look, over there." Low pointed to where flashes of light had appeared in the darkness. Fragments of fluorescence, they flowed together for the briefest of instants to form an outline, a recognizable shape. Straining, they sought to show, to reveal, to illuminate. The effort involved was inconceivably immense.

"Air currents." Brink was casually dismissive. "Phosphorescent gas. A harmless by-product of all this heavy engineering. I suspect as we move deeper, we may encounter other interesting effects."

"I expect you're right." Ignoring the frantic flickerings, the two men pressed on.

With a collective sigh of remorse, the disappointed and discouraged hundred abandoned their efforts.

"Observe." The vast host of nonparticipants was equally disenchanted. "We are no nearer solution than we have ever been. It is hopeless."

"Nothing is hopeless where there is life," promulgated a succession of the first's supporters. "Better to have tried and failed than not to have tried."

"Salvation lies not in solipsisms," riposted those who throve on doubt.

"Is there life here?" A substantial number of active onlookers posed the relevant interrogatory, which resulted in the vast majority drifting off into elaborate but wholly spurious discourse.

Only the tenacious remained proximate, following the visitors' progress with unflagging interest. "First we became irrelevant to our dimension, then we became irrelevant to this one. Now we risk becoming irrelevant to ourselves." The first was adamant. "Something must be done, or consciousness will go the way of our physical forms."

But having tried and failed to break through, there was little they could do. Philosophy was a poor weapon with which to confront muscle and sinew. As it was, they could not even assist the bipeds with a lingering notion, much less a complete thought.

"Down this way." Continuously monitoring the readout on the communicator, Low turned to his left. There was no telling how deeply they had gone, nor how far out under the seabed. Pipes and tubes, conduits and siphons snaked everywhere. Low felt as if they were descending into a bottomless bowl of steel spaghetti. No stylish use of metallic glass here, he saw. Only straightforward, prosaic metal and plastics, with hints of some dark ceramic alloy.

Water was everywhere; trickling from elderly leaks, condensing off the cold pipes, running in foreboding rivulets along the floor. He tried not to think of the millions of tons of rock hanging over his head, or the billions of gallons of seawater it was holding back.

Brink turned sharply to his right. "I thought I heard something."

Low nodded. "I heard it too." Turning in the direction of the noise, they resumed their cautious advance. Their boots splashed aside water several inches deep. Long black wriggling things squirmed away from their approach, seeking safety in the dark places.

"Watch it." Aiming his beam downward to illuminate the source of his concern, Low took a long stride forward. "There's some sticky stuff here. Mucus or something."

Brink used his own light to scrutinize the disgusting mass as he followed Low's lead, carefully stepping around the glistening heap. In appearance it had the look of glue-slathered television cable that had lain too long in the sun.

It wasn't cable.

Proof came when they turned a corner and came face-to-face with the long-absent Maggie Robbins. Unable to move, she stood facing them, wrapped up in more of the same stringy gook as neatly as a Christmas turkey. Slime was still congealing around her limbs as they rushed to free her.

Imprisoned in length after length of the gummy material, she didn't look very professional. She looked, in fact, utterly terrified. Her face was drawn, and the dark circles under her eyes hadn't been there the last time Low had seen her. They were not the result of an absence of makeup. Something had left her not only entrapped but scared out of her wits.

As they struggled to free her, her eyes kept darting in all directions. "Get away! Get out while you can." She hesitated a moment, blinking hard, before continuing. "No! What am I saying! Get me out of this gunk before it comes back!" She stared at Brink. "Nothing personal, Ludger, but aren't you supposed to be dead?"

"I was. Now I am not. It will be explained to you later." He tore at her bindings.

"Man, I sure hope so." Low had her upper arms and head

free, but she still couldn't move. Her legs were pinned to the wall and to each other.

"Before what comes back?" Brink inquired.

"Do you think I did this to myself? For a supposed scientist you sure overlook a lot of the obvious. Before the—" She stopped in midsentence and did something very unprofessional, though perfectly understandable under the circumstances. Her eyes grew wide and she screamed.

Both men whirled, and there it was: a disjointed, chitinous, crablike hulk. Ominously it had scuttled around in the darkness to interpose itself between them and the exit.

Despite the danger, Low was fascinated by the monstrosity. He could clearly see where the silken glue-saturated fibers emerged: not from spinnerets at the base of some bulbous abdomen but from specialized organs at the tips of two forward-facing legs. As it studied them, the creature rocked slowly back and forth on multiple jointed limbs. The local underground life here, Low decided, was all spasms and twitches.

That the gargoylish head was fully aware of them he did not doubt, despite the absence of visible eyes. The guardians he had left battling each other in the tomb spire were first cousins to this ambulatory nightmare. All clearly belonged to the same taxonomic family: the one you'd never invite home.

The principal differences between this beast and the tomb guardians were that this one was bigger, uglier and equipped with weaponry much more sophisticated than mere tooth and claw. It was a thoroughly revolting entity that hovered near the bottom of Mother Nature's beauty list.

"Don't just stand there gawking." Robbins would have kicked him if she could have freed a leg. "Get me out of this!"

"I am open to suggestions, Maggie." Brink was remarkably calm. Probably too busy trying to assign the creature a classification to be properly frightened, Low thought. That would come later, when it was sinking its fangs into his chest.

He wished fervently for some kind of weapon. Even a kitchen knife would have been welcome. But they had nothing, sidearms not being deemed essential equipment for spacewalks. He would gladly have traded his pension for the digger they had used to bore the original blast holes in the surface of the asteroid. Everything attached to his service belt was necessarily small and inoffensive. He supposed that Robbins carried something like pepper spray in her purse, but for some reason she had neglected to bring that along on her EVA.

All he had on him were the communicator, some generic medicinal tablets, a few food concentrates and their lights. With nothing else to point, he aimed the bright, narrow beam at the creature. Without knowing where the sight organs were located, or even what range of the spectrum they could detect, he couldn't very well blind it.

But when he shifted the circle of illumination to one side, the monster's head swiveled to follow it. Again he flashed the head and then let the beam drift to the right. Once more the bony skull turned to follow. He felt an entirely irrational surge of hope.

"The beam distracts it! Use your flashlight, Ludger." The admonition was unnecessary, as Brink had already noted Low's success.

But while it readily followed the dancing lights with whatever organs it used for sight, it would not move from its position. Similarly, it did not advance. They had achieved no better than a standoff.

"This isn't working," Low remarked.

"I commend your powers of observation, Commander." Brink favored his companion with a dry smile. "There is no point in continuing this. Eventually our batteries will be drained and the creature will have us. It is distracted by the lights but not overcome by them. Perhaps a combination of light and motion will prove more effective."

So saying, and before Low could divine his intent, the scientist splashed forward. Waving his arms, he yelled as loudly as he could. The assortment of English, German and Russian curses, not to mention a few in Latin, made no impression on the monster. But all the noise and moving light did. Sputtering ferociously, it lurched in Brink's direction.

"Ludger, no!" Low started toward him, but Brink wasn't to be dissuaded. Whether his newfound bravery was prompted by unnatural impulse or a desire to experiment, Low didn't know. More likely he just wanted to get his life crystals back.

Crabbing forward but never falling, the monster pursued the source of sound and light. Brink led it away from the imprisoned journalist. If he fell, Low knew the creature would be on him in an instant.

"Never mind him now!" Robbins shouted to get Low's attention. "If he wants to be a hero, let him. Just don't let it go to waste."

Brink was of like mind. "This reminds me of my student days, Commander, but I can't keep it up forever. No lolly-choking!"

"Lolly-gagging," Low corrected him as he turned back to Robbins. Clipping his light onto his belt, he started tearing at the sticky shackles. Robbins helped as best she could.

"I couldn't get away." Straining, she succeeded in pulling one leg free. "It was too quick for me. I couldn't—"

"It's all right," he told her. "It doesn't matter. All that's important now is getting you out of this and making it out of here."

"Okay, I'll go with that."

For all her wry commentary, Low could see that she was on the verge of hysteria. Only a lifetime of difficult experiences had kept her from losing it completely. Working his way down her legs, he almost entangled himself in the incredibly adhesive mess.

This wouldn't do, he thought impatiently. It wasn't going fast enough.

Looking around, he located several lengths of loose metal. One had a sharp edge, the other a curved tip that would make a serviceable hook. With these he was able to pry and dig much more effectively at the incomplete cocoon, particularly at the fibers that had already dried. They were strong, but one by one they eventually parted under his single-minded assault.

With Robbins pushing from within and Low ripping and tearing from the other side, one strand after another gave way, until he was finally able to fling the stiff length of metal aside and lift her clear. Dried residue covered her from head to foot, but everything worked.

His face was very close to hers, but neither of them thought anything of it. Circumstances hardly allowed for a romantic interval.

"You okay? Can you stand?"

"I think so."

"Good." He forced himself to smile. "If you'd listened to me from the start, this wouldn't have happened."

"No?" She managed to smile back. "Didn't you say we should stick together?"

"Not literally." As he stepped clear, he remembered something momentarily forgotten. "*Ludger*."

There followed a welcome, even energetic, response to their simultaneous cries.

"I'm all right! It's closer, but still unsure whether to strike first at me or the light. I'm hoping it will choose the latter. Incidentally, I must point out that I am running out of space. Any assistance would be most welcome. Don't linger."

Low took Maggie's hand and together they followed the sound of Brink's voice. He was still shouting and cursing to draw the glue-spitter's attention.

It didn't take long to find him. He'd been backed into an alcove by the spitter, which hovered on the edge of indecision. Low doubted it would remain that way forever.

"Use your light," Maggie urged him. "Lure it away."

"We can't keep doing that. Our batteries will quit. We have to try something else."

She looked up at him expectantly. "Like what?"

"Like I don't know." He scanned their surroundings. "What do you suppose that is?"

"What what is?" Turning, she saw that his beam had settled on a large, puffy pink mound attached to one wall. Thick cables supplied additional bracing, and it was covered with a thin layer of glistening mucus.

"Egg sac?" She wracked her brain for memories of anything similar. "Food storage? Sleeping nest?"

"Could be any one of those, or something else. Or all three." Picking up another metal shaft, he directed Maggie to do likewise. "Whatever it is, it's important. Look at the care with which it's been constructed, at the thickness of the support strands."

"If your assessment is correct and we attack it outright, that thing will be on us like a crow on roadkill."

"You're right." Once again Low anxiously searched their surroundings. "This way."

He led her to a nearby conduit through which a powerful stream of water could be heard rushing. Water seeped profusely from a broken seam.

"Work on that."

Under his direction they used the lengths of metal to dig and pry at the crack, until water began to flow in a steady stream from the enlarged breach. The entire conduit quivered as if ready to give way at any moment.

"Over here!" he directed her.

Bracing their feet against another pipe, they both pushed as hard as they could at the point Low had selected. Nothing happened.

"Harder! Use your weight!"

"Watch your language." More seriously she added, "What if this just snaps? It could blow up in our faces."

His expression was contorted as he strained against the heavy pipe. "You have any better ideas?"

She resumed pushing. "No. In fact, I don't even have your idea. What are we trying to do, anyway?"

"You'll see . . . I hope."

A weak cracking noise sounded above the deep rush of running water, and then the conduit snapped. The pent-up force of the liberated stream knocked them both down. With the power of a high-pressure fire hose, water shot across the gap to smash into the blob of sticky strands. Gluey filaments went flying.

Within arm's reach of Brink, who had retreated as far as possible, the creature whirled. Emitting a high-pitched keening and exhibiting far more speed and agility than Low suspected it possessed, it scrambled madly in the direction of its inundated nest.

"Ludger, this way!" Rising, Low and Robbins waved wildly in the scientist's direction.

With the monster distracted by the roaring water, Brink was able to rejoin them safely. Together they started out of the abyss and back toward the clear, compelling light of the museum spire.

Robbins quickly fell behind. "Come on, Maggie," Low urged her.

"Can't." He saw that she was limping. "Too long in one position. My leg muscles are knotting up."

The two men flanked her. Putting her arms across their shoulders, she allowed them to carry her out, using her legs whenever recalcitrant quadriceps allowed. The keening whine of the monster and the thunder of escaping water gradually faded behind them.

Eventually they reemerged into the pale luminescence and half-familiar surroundings of the spire. Robbins gingerly sat down on one of a thousand identical enigmatic containers, each of whose contents would be priceless on Earth. Wincing, she began massaging her thighs.

Low hovered close. "You doing any better?"

She smiled weakly. "I'm out of that hellhole, so I'm not too concerned about anything else right now." Experimentally, she kicked out her right leg. "It's loosening up. I'll be all right." Moving down from the lower thigh, she began working on her right calf. Low considered contributing his help, decided against it. Such an offer might easily be misconstrued. It would have surprised him to know that it would have been gratefully accepted.

"What did it want with you?" he asked gently.

"Fortunately, I never found out." She glanced at the silent scientist. "I'll bet Ludger can think of a few gruesome possibilities."

Brink considered. "Is that really what you want me to do?"

"No. Let's just assume it wasn't looking for friendly company and leave it at that." She switched her hands to her other leg.

"Its intentions might have been other than deadly. Perhaps it was merely a kind of arthropodal pack rat and wished to add you to its collection. Just because it carried you back to its nesting area and tied you up doesn't mean it intended to consume you. Possibly it was simply taken with your looks, not unlike myself."

She made a face. "You make it sound like New York." The scientist's sense of humor was as dry as the Namib. Given her spent, sweaty, gunk-encrusted appearance, he was either being mightily complimentary or highly sarcastic.

In any event, he offered no further interpretations of her unfortunate ordeal as they made their way back to the transport station. The shimmering globe awaited, a spherical genie that could only grant the same wish again and again.

On the verge of collapse, Robbins considered clicking her heels together three times, but decided against it. The quantity of goo clinging to them would probably make her boots stick together. They weren't red, anyway.

But given what she'd just been through, she was mightily tempted.

Several million powerless but hopeful Cocytans had observed and analyzed every aspect of the incident. Their individual reactions were nearly as diverse.

"They continue to elucidate unexpected depths." The first was greatly pleased.

"And utilize hidden resources." Its supporters were quietly elated.

"They have proven repeatedly that they are capable of acting and reacting with intelligence and common sense, even when under duress."

"We would not have thought of using the water ourselves." A few thousand heretofore unpersuaded slid mentally onto the side of the convinced.

"Ah, water!" Ten-and-twenty lamented the half-forgotten memory of fluid tactility. "The voluptuous feel of it, the ecstasy of liquid cool! To be able to drink again." In the absence of hearts, a heartfelt sigh nonetheless rippled through the grieving commentators. "The simple joys of physicality—all fled. The delights of experiencing without thinking—forever lost."

"Who among us would not trade eternity for the neural receptivity of a worm?" Twenty-and-ten others rode invisibly atop the rolling sphere, vicariously experiencing the sense of speed. Others followed effortlessly. Air or mud, water or stone—it made no difference to them. Nothing could inhibit or slow their progress.

Which was simply another way of reflecting on the malaise that continued to plague them. They took no pleasure in their ease of passage because nothing ever awaited them at its conclusion.

"I'm sorry." Robbins was still limping slightly as they reentered the main chamber of the central island.

"For what?" Low eyed her appraisingly.

"I told you already. Stomping off like that. Going off on my own. Stupid. I'm famous for it. It's just that I've always been lucky. I was lucky in the Yucatán, I was lucky in Burkina Faso, I was lucky in Turkmenistan."

Brink dissented. "You underestimate yourself, Maggie. You are simply very good at what you do."

"Yeah, right," she muttered despondently. "I was real good back there. If you two hadn't come along, I'd be crab cake, or whatever it had in mind for me." She shuddered, right on cue.

Low eyed Brink meaningfully. "That's right. We *two*."

She perked up. Low doubted that Maggie Robbins could remain down for very long, no matter how unpleasant the circumstances. It simply wasn't part of her mental or emotional makeup.

"Of course, one of the reasons that I've been so 'lucky' over the years is that I always travel in the company of the best people. Anyway, before something else happens, I just want to say thank you."

So she kissed him. It didn't linger or probe, but it was no wispy peck on the cheek either. As he stood momentarily stunned, his powers of review temporarily on hold, she did the same to Brink.

"Hey, c'mon," she chided them when she'd finished. "Maybe saving my life wasn't a big deal to you two, but it had real meaning for me. You ought to be pleased, Ludger. It gave you the opportunity to study another alien life-form."

Before he could reply, she turned to Low. "As for you, Commander, I know it's just part of your job description. But thanks anyway."

"You're welcome. You can thank me again if you like."

She wavered, then broke out into a wide smile. "Why, Commander Low, you *do* have a sense of humor! You just need to take it off your utility belt once in a while."

"I know. It's just that I haven't seen much to laugh about lately."

She moved closer to him, her voice dropping. "You don't get it, do you? That's when you have to laugh the most."

Brink moved to block their path. "And now, if you please, Commander, the life crystals?"

Low regarded the other man. "Listen, Ludger, why don't you let me hang on to them for you? You can have a couple to cuddle and sleep with if you want. It'd be better for you, take my word for it."

Robbins's uncertain gaze shifted from scientist to pilot. "Boston, Ludger; what's going on here?" They ignored her.

Brink had begun to tremble. For a moment Low thought the other man was going to jump him again, futile as the effort would be. The scientist ought to have learned better from their earlier run-in. Were the crystals, or their absence from his possession, still affecting his judgment?

"That was not our agreement, Commander." Clearly the other man was restraining himself with an effort.

"All right, Ludger. But I think you're making a big mistake."

"Am I?" Brink nodded in the direction of the green glow that pervaded Low's pockets. "One of these gave me back my life. What folly could there be in keeping them close to me?"

"Don't you see that they've become an obsession? Are you so far gone that you don't realize what they're doing to you?"

"Obsession? Far gone?" Robbins's confusion deepened. "Will somebody please tell me what this is all about?"

Brink held up both hands. "Our bargain, Commander. I assure you I have not gone off what you would call the deep end. I have simply developed an affection for the crystals, not an affectation. I am in complete control of all my faculties, physical as well as mental."

"Sure you are." Low's tone belied his words. But he'd given his word, and he wasn't in the mood for another fight.

Scooping crystals from his pockets, he handed them over to the scientist, who eagerly slipped them back into his own pants and shirt pockets.

"Just make sure you keep control over these things, and not vice versa."

"I cannot envision myself acting otherwise." Brink's eyes gleamed as he accepted the return of the emerald bounty.

"Thank you, Commander," he said quietly when Low was finished. "I will take these back to the room where we found them. That is where they belong." As he turned to leave, a faint greenish efflorescence rising from Low's right pants pocket caught his eye. He gestured. "Those?"

"Sorry. You've got most of them back. That's what you wanted." He patted his pocket. "I'm hanging on to these for a while."

For an instant Brink seemed torn. Then he drew himself up. "You see, Commander, my 'addiction,' as you call it, is not so very powerful as you seem to think. It is not necessary for me to possess them all." With that he turned and strode off across the wide, expansive floor, angling toward the storeroom.

Fingers gripped his arm questioningly. "Okay, now, will you please tell me what's going on here before I jump to all the wrong conclusions?"

Low ruminated before replying. "When we were trying to free you back down in that tunnel, do you remember remarking that Ludger was supposed to be dead?"

"I don't remember everything that happened down there, but I do remember saying that. Yeah, so?"

"I found a peculiar green crystal in the museum spire. You

know that some of the exhibit cases will play back explanatory projections. Well, this one showed the crystal, or one like it, performing all kinds of amazing feats, including reviving the badly injured and the deceased. Ludger being the latter, I didn't think it could do much harm to try the crystal on him. Suffice it to say that it worked. Later we found a small hoard of them in a side storeroom." He gestured in the direction Brink had taken. "Down that way."

"So one of those little green slivers you were handing over brought him back to life?"

Low nodded. "Ever since we found them, he's developed a passion for the damn things. Doesn't feel comfortable unless he's close to them. There's even a machine in the storeroom that he believes is capable of manufacturing more. It's as if he wants to drown himself in the stuff. I know he sounds and acts normal, but if you leave him alone with them for too long, he loses all drive and motivation. Doesn't want to do anything except lie around and soak up the green.

"The only way I could get him to help me rescue you was to take them away from him and promise to return them when we got back. He was pretty reluctant. The first thing he did was try to fight me."

Her eyes widened. "Ludger? He attacked you? Over a bunch of crystals?"

Low nodded again. "I know how to take care of myself, Maggie, and I'm in a lot better shape than he is. Only after he saw that jumping me wouldn't do any good did he agree to help." He gazed in the direction the scientist had taken. "Which, I have to admit, he did effectively."

She was still skeptical. "I just don't see Ludger taking a swing at you."

"I was pretty surprised myself. It shows the hold the life crystals have on him." They were both silent for a while.

"I'd never have guessed," she finally murmured. "He seems so normal. For Ludger, that is."

"I know, but you didn't see him the way I did, sprawled out on the floor with the crystals lined up around him like a bunch of jade dominoes, looking like some old Chinese opium eater. His eyes were glazed."

She was still reluctant to condemn the other man. "Hell, I've seen people get that way on coffee and chocolate."

"Maybe you're right. Maybe I'm overreacting."

"So what do we do now?"

"When we first got here, Ludger and I found another one of those plates like the kind that were used to activate the asteroid-ship. At least, it *looks* similar. I'd still like to find three more and try them on the control mound." He was apologetic. "I can't think of anything else to do."

She blinked as she remembered something. "You know, I think I've seen one."

His gaze narrowed. "You're kidding. No, you're not kidding. Where?"

Her eyes dropped. "In the museum spire. But that *thing* is in there!"

"We'll be careful. Ludger and I wandered around inside for quite a while without any trouble. Besides, I bet the creature is still preoccupied with drying out its nest. You game? If not, you can stay here, and no recriminations."

"Game? You have a funny way of putting things sometimes, Boston Low." She gazed across the wide floor. "Think Ludger will come with us?"

"Not a chance. I suppose he's earned his moment of respite. We'll let him lie among his precious crystals for a while. Can you remember where you saw the plate?"

She smiled and nodded. "I think so. It wasn't far from the entrance."

"So much the better. Let's have a look."

The plate was indeed located where Maggie had remembered seeing it—not in a case, but on a stand next to half a dozen deeply engraved slabs whose function remained an enigma to them. Were they designed to activate other devices? He made a mental note of their location for future reference. Next time they might find a control mound dimpled with square depressions instead of round ones.

The plate slid easily from its holder. No alarms rang, no doors slammed shut, and no monstrous alien guardians materialized to contest their departure. Their return journey to the central island was blessedly uneventful.

Low laid the second plate alongside the first. They looked identical, but who could really tell? On the surface they might be perfect duplicates, while their internal structure might be utterly unalike. Of course, that might equally have been true of the four plates that had initially activated the asteroid-ship, he reminded himself.

The planetarium spire yielded a third plate, the locale in itself an encouraging sign. But no matter how hard they searched, they could not locate a fourth.

Low bore his frustration silently. It was one thing to have one plate, quite another to unearth three and be unable to find the critical fourth. He munched on the last of the food concentrates salvaged from their suits. Their next priority was going to have to be to find food, not cryptic metal plates.

They rested against the wall of the main chamber while they tried to decide what to do next. A resigned Low turned to his companion.

"That's it, Maggie. I'm fresh out of ideas. Unless . . ."

"Don't expect any flashes of brilliance from me. Unless what?"

"You really think you can speak the Cocytan tongue?"

She cleared her throat and rumbled something at him. It sounded like someone with a bad chest cold trying to sing Handel. He nodded approvingly.

"Pretty good. At least, it sounded pretty good. What was it?"

"Nursery rhyme, I think, or the equivalent thereof. Part of the early teaching. What did you have in mind?"

He shifted his backside on the hard floor. "You recall me telling you that I'd found one of the locals?" She nodded. "Let's go ask it some questions. It may know where we can find a dozen plates. For that matter, it may have some better suggestions. It can't do any worse than I have."

She took his hand in hers. "Don't be so hard on yourself. I know you're used to solving every problem that comes your way, but no training could've prepared you for this." She squeezed his fingers gently. "So you want me to interrogate an alien. Why not? It can't be any harder than trying to get a straight answer out of a Beijing bureaucrat." Her expression turned apprehensive. "What does it look like?"

"Take it easy. Nothing like the tunnel crab, or for that matter, anything else we've encountered since we've been here. It's pretty nice-looking, actually. Tall, bipedal, has a face that doesn't turn your stomach, two arms with hands and fingers, along with a few accouterments I don't recognize. Its countenance is . . . I'm not quite sure how to describe it . . . noble. Yeah, that's it. Noble. You can feel it. There's an inner calmness that radiates from it."

She was eying him uncertainly. "You make it sound like some kind of god."

"No. There's nothing deitylike about it. It's just a decent sort of being that tried hard to communicate with me. Needless to say we didn't have any luck. I left promising to come right back with you, but as you know, we got diverted. Will you give it a try?"

She didn't hesitate. "In the words of the famous missing astronaut, what have we got to lose?"

"I'm not missing," he replied. "I'm right here."

"Yeah, but you're a man. Naturally you think the universe revolves around you." She climbed to her feet. "We'd better let Brink know what we're going to do."

"He won't come." Low stretched as he straightened. He was too tired to sleep.

Just as Low predicted, Brink was reclining in the storeroom, surrounded by his aura of glowing crystals. The green radiance gave him a slightly bilious look.

"I've resurrected a Cocytan," he told the scientist. "Maggie's picked up a bit of the language via some kind of cerebral transducer, or something. We've found three plates and we're going to pay it a visit to see if it can point us toward a fourth. After that last business in the deep tunnel I think it would be a good idea if we all kept together."

"Is that an order, *Commander*?" Brink eyed him noncommittally.

"No. Just common sense. But then, you don't need to heed common sense anymore, do you? You've got life crystals."

"I would put it differently, Commander." Brink smiled beatifically. "But your conclusion is accurate enough. I choose to remain here."

Maggie took a step forward. "Ludger, I'm surprised at you. No one's ever made contact with an alien species before. For that matter, this is the first time humans have run into anything as advanced as a lichen. As a scientist, I'd think conversing with an intelligent nonhuman life-form would be the fulfillment of your ultimate dream."

"Financial independence and the use of a fully equipped lab is my ultimate dream, Maggie." His expression was dreamy, distant. "So that I can study these marvelous crystals in greater depth."

"Dammit, you're a *scientist*!"

"And at the moment, a very relaxed one." He waved imperiously. "Go and chat up your Cocytan, people. If it says anything of interest, I will listen to a report when you return."

"Let's go." Low took her arm. "Can't you see he's under the influence, or stoned, or whatever you want to call it? He's thinking coherently but not linearly. His brain is glazed with green." He bestowed a look of contempt on the contented scientist, which Brink ignored with equanimity.

They left him staring mutely at the ceiling, looking for all the world like a priest who'd imbibed too much sacramental wine prior to the commencement of devotions. He might not be of any help to them in the forthcoming attempt, but neither was he likely to do any serious damage to himself.

"So this is the tomb spire." Robbins stood in the portal

that separated a familiar vaulted chamber from the transport tunnel. "Impressive."

"I thought so." He led her toward the central pyramid. "We have to be careful here. There are a couple of organic guardians. They're something like the one that caught you, only smaller and cleaner. They don't manufacture sticky capture ropes either. On the other hand, there's less room in here to maneuver."

"Whoa up." She halted. "You didn't mention anything about guardians. In case you haven't figured it out by now, I'm not interested in repeating that experience."

"You think I'd be here if I didn't think it was safe enough?"

She considered only briefly before replying. "Yeah."

"Well, I wouldn't," he responded crossly. "I promise: If it's not safe we won't try it." He extended a reassuring hand.

She disdained the hand but rejoined him. The pyramid loomed ahead. "How are you going to know if it's safe?" The floor clicked hollowly under her boots. "You said there were two of these things."

"That's right, and I left them fighting each other. They seemed evenly matched, unable to hurt each other too badly but unable or unwilling to break away either. With luck they'll still be snapping and kicking at each other. Or maybe they're both dead." He entered the tunnel.

"Or maybe," she added, following dubiously, "they've recognized each other as long-lost relatives and they're squatting somewhere up ahead waiting for the one who reintroduced them to come back."

"It's possible. But we're about due for a break, I think."

She eyed him sourly. "Now *there's* a scientific approach."

For a change, Low was right. When they paused at the entrance to the first chamber, there was no sign of the battling guardians. Not lingering to look for them, they hurried across the dangerous open area and into the next, narrower passageway. Robbins found the silence unnerving, but to Low it was bliss and balm.

Low's Cocytan was still in the sarcophagus, but it was no longer sitting up silently surveying its surroundings. The vestigial wings or gills were not fluttering slowly against its back, and the wide intelligent eyes did not turn to inspect the visitors. Low was disappointed but not really surprised. Clearly the life crystals worked differently on different beings, and this one had been dead far longer than Brink. How much longer he could not imagine.

Once again it lay on its back atop the impressive platform, arms placed straight at its sides. Mounting the platform to gaze down at it, Low found himself wishing he'd been more insistent with Brink. For all his abnormal preoccupation with the life crystals, the scientist's powers of observation and analysis were indisputably greater than Low's own. He would have had thoughts and ideas to offer.

But Brink wasn't there, and he and Robbins were. They would have to puzzle things out on their own. One option he did not consider was leaving to bring Brink back forcibly. Not only might he fail, next time entering the pyramid and reaching the inner chamber might not prove so easy.

Hesitant at first to approach too near, Robbins was now examining the length and breadth of the alien body. "It's dead."

Low made a face. "Can't fool a reporter of your experience."

She ignored the gentle sarcasm. "I wonder how many times those life crystals can revive the deceased?"

"We're about to find out." Digging into a pocket, he brought out one of the green shards he had retained from Brink's private hoard. Leaning over an oddly jointed shoulder, he placed the glowing fragment atop the Cocytan's chest in much the same manner as before. The interior of the chamber suddenly filled with darting, swirling sparks, like bits of flame that had become estranged from their candle.

Straining unsuccessfully to break through, one of the fretful, watching Cocytans drew back from reality. "This can't go on. They cannot continue to resurrect the Creator."

"Why not?" A hundred thought-forms passed through the objector, with no harm to either.

"Because the process is exhausting. The Creator had no patience when alive. In death it has less."

"Would that we could share the experience," bemoaned a thousand-and-three. "Death is so *physical*."

Alas, for every Cocytan present save one, death was no more attainable than the caress of a single sunbeam.

Low took Robbins's arm and drew her back as the crystal melted into the broad chest. It being her first encounter with the remarkable phenomenon, she looked on in mute fascination.

For the second time that day Cocytan eyes fluttered open, the beaklike mouth twitched, and an inhuman respiratory system manipulated air. For the second time the tall, muscular form raised itself laboriously to a sitting position. Turning slowly on the powerful, arching neck, the head stopped when eyes caught sight of the two humans. Under that forceful stare Robbins unconsciously moved a little closer to Low, who, without thinking, put an arm around her waist. This time she didn't shrug him off.

The resurrection was not a miracle, only a phenomenon so far beyond the capability of Earthly science as to seem like one, an *in vivo* validation of Clarke's law. Certainly it was such to the Cocytan. Rather than revel in its revivification, it remained motionless atop the platform, plainly less interested in its restored life than its tiny audience. Though he had no effective basis for such an interpretation, Low thought the alien looked bored.

"Try," he whispered to her.

Taking a hesitant step forward, Maggie let her recently acquired knowledge flow from her lips. Though it was the reaction and response they'd hoped for, it was still something of a shock when the Cocytan turned its gaze on her alone and replied.

"I can understand it." Muted awe underlined her reaction.

"Not perfectly, but I can understand. I guess I didn't spend enough time at the inducer."

"Talk to it," Low encouraged her.

She looked back at him uncertainly. "What'll I say?"

"Don't ask me. You're the journalist. You've done interviews before."

She swallowed. "This is a little different, you know."

"It doesn't matter," he murmured impatiently. "Just start a conversation. Ask if it knows where more of the round plates are. Ask it how we can get home. Ask it—"

"I can't ask it anything," she hissed, "if you don't shut up." Low obediently subsided.

It was extraordinary to hear the guttural singsong flow from the mouth of Maggie Robbins, more remarkable still to see and hear the Cocytan reply. She did her best to translate for her companion.

"I introduced us. In response it says it's called the Creator. That's the name, or appellation, that its kind bestowed upon it. As near as I can translate, anyway."

"Impressive moniker. Keep going."

She spoke again, and for the second time the entity responded without prompting. "It doesn't think so. In fact, I get the distinct impression it's not happy with the title. But it's short, and it says that it's real name is much too long and complicated for me to handle. I'm not about to argue the point."

"The plates," Low urged her. "Ask it about the plates."

But the Cocytan had its own conversational agenda and refused to be led. Robbins was compelled to explain not only who but what they were, and how they had come to be marooned on Cocytus. After a while, she was given a chance to translate for Low.

"It hasn't been dead so long that it's forgotten its sense of curiosity. It *is* somewhat interested in us." She turned back to the alien, which was speaking again.

"I cannot tell you how to reactivate the asteroid-ship, as you call it. I have no interest in that."

"But *we* have." Within the context of the complex Cocytan grammar she tried to emphasize the importance of the request. "This isn't our world, isn't our home."

"It is no longer mine either," the entity replied. "Or any other thinking being's. It is a place of cognitive death, where all that survives of the thinking are machines. Long may they thrive." The bitterness of the alien's words came through clearly. "They were built well. In the case of one, far too well."

"I'm sorry, but I don't understand. Tell me what happened here. Where are all the others? What happened to this world?"

The vestigial wings fluttered slightly, and a great sigh came from deep within the massive chest. "Very well. I will tell you. I will do my best to keep my words simple and straightforward so that you may be sure to understand. And when I have finished, I would ask that you leave me to my chosen destiny and disturb me no more."

She nodded understandingly. Low was close and anxious. "Well?"

"It's going to explain some things," she told him. "In return, it wants something from us."

He frowned. "What could it want from us?"

Bright blue eyes stared back at him. "Death."

The questions flowed fluently. It was startling how easy it was, as if she'd known the language since childhood. The words poured out of her, her mind managing the difficult translation effortlessly. Only when she encountered a word or term that had not been imparted to her by the Educator did she have trouble. It was as if she were performing simultaneous translation from the Russian with the odd word interspersed in Quechua.

"Who are you? Not a name. Tell me an individual."

"As I told you, I am called Creator, a designation I did not choose for myself. Builder would have been more appropriate. Designer, Conceptualizer. I should prefer Engineer."

She remembered to translate for Low. "It's an engineer."

"That's something." Low allowed himself to feel hopeful.

"You've been dead," she observed, unself-consciously restating the obvious.

"Pleasantly. Soon I will be again, if you will stop interfering. I long ago grew tired of life, the follies attendant upon it and the absurdities to which even the supposedly intelligent are heir."

Low responded to Maggie's translation. "Tell it we're sorry to have disturbed its . . . rest. We respect its wishes to remain dead and promise not to revive it again. Tell it we both share strong desires. It wants not to live and we very badly want to go home. But we can't do that without help.

We didn't ask to be brought here anymore than it asked to be revived."

Robbins nodded and translated. When she'd finished, fathomless alien eyes shifted slightly and came to rest on the Commander.

"Yet you are here. I see that some background is in order.

"Long ago, this world of—I will use your far simpler nomenclature for it—Cocytus was a strong and vigorous place. We discovered how to bend the material world to our needs, much as you are learning to do."

Robbins frowned. "How do you know that? You know nothing of our world."

It turned back to her. "You would not be here now if you were not technologically inclined. Only a technically advancing species would have the ability to reach one of the Messengers."

"Messengers? Is that what you call the asteroid?"

"Patience, little biped. We believed that our society and philosophy had matured along with our technology. We found a way not to exceed the speed of light but to bypass it. I cannot think of a simpler way to put it and I assure you the technical description would be beyond your comprehension."

"That's for sure," she responded. "I can't even program my VCR."

"We chose not to utilize this discovery for personal travel because search times were very long. Integral to the process is a boomerang effect. So while out-search travel times are quite long, returns take comparatively little time. Otherwise you would have aged greatly during your journey.

"We sent out many such probes to systems that harbored planets and that we hoped might also prove home to other intelligences. It is a vast universe in which to be alone and we avidly sought the companionship of other species. Each probe was disguised, camouflaged, as a natural phenomenon so as not to alarm the local inhabitants."

She took a moment to translate for Low.

"So as not to alarm, hmmm? Had the opposite effect on

us. But if it hadn't, we sure wouldn't have responded as quickly. Go on."

The Cocytan continued. "Only a species sufficiently advanced to leave behind the gravity of its homeworld would have the capability to investigate and trigger a Messenger. Once activated, each was designed to return here with its discoverers. This complex of islands was specially designed to serve as a greeting place, where representatives of other species could be met in surroundings that would intrigue but not overwhelm them."

"That explains exhibits like the museum and the planetarium," Low commented when Robbins had translated for him.

She nodded agreement. "Not to mention the language instructor. I see the point. If you're welcoming people from a primitive tribe, it's a lot kinder to introduce them first to a simple village instead of taking them off a plane at Kennedy Airport."

"The map spire. Ask it about the map spire." She complied.

"A means of showing not only our planet, but our immediate stellar vicinity, as well as the relationship between it and the visitor's homeworld."

Low muttered to himself. "Then Earth *was* in there someplace. Ludger and I just didn't know where to look."

"What?" A confused Maggie tried to make sense of his words.

"Nothing. I'll tell you later. Go on."

"We had acquired vast knowledge," the Cocytan continued, "which we were eager to share with others, if they could be found. All intelligences yearn for the company of others. In a boundless cosmos cognitive thought is a precious commodity, to be nurtured and cultivated wherever encountered. Sparks in a void must perforce stand together against the encroaching darkness. But I speak of times long vanished."

So saying, the Cocytan dropped its head in a gesture that was startlingly humanlike, though whether it meant the same or something completely different, its audience had no way of knowing.

"But something happened." Maggie's voice had unconsciously hushed. She was overcome by the Cocytan's scale of time and place. "Some disaster or cataclysm."

The alien raised a hand and gestured with surprisingly delicate fingers. "Say rather, a tragedy. Of our own making. A consequence of our drive to achieve, to surpass, to exceed."

"What happened to everyone else?" she asked. "Yours is the only body we've found preserved."

"'Preserved.'" The Cocytan ran one hand along the edge of the high platform. "None of this was my doing, nor was it by my choice. I knew nothing of it. I wished nothing more than a traditional departure from the realm of the living. I wanted to die. Instead, this was done to me."

As the Cocytan spoke and he waited for Maggie's translation, Low could not help but notice that the flickering lights had increased in both number and intensity. He fancied he heard a voluminous, ghostly moan and had to smile at the strength of his own imagination.

"This is the longest," observed a dozen thought-forms, "that the Creator has spoken with any visitors."

"It does not matter," declared sixty-three others. "Nothing will happen. It will end the same as before, and when it is over, these travelers will add their proteins and body fluids to those of their predecessors. Nothing will have changed."

"Nothing will have changed," lamented a hundred thousand of the forlorn.

"It happened after the first probes had been sent out to search for intelligent life on other worlds." The Cocytan stared blankly at the ceiling, recalling. "While they were in transit, a significant development occurred in our society. Not a natural calamity, as you propose. We had progressed beyond being subject to the vagaries of climate and geology. Furthermore, we had acquired control over our bodies. Life spans had been extended to the maximum of which our physical forms were capable.

"Yet for many, even this was not enough. As sometimes happens in science, several profound discoveries in a number of unrelated disciplines took place almost simultaneously.

"First, the life crystals, as you call them, were synthesized. At the time, they were considered to be the ultimate product of high Cocytan technology."

The Creator's expression remained unreadable. While Robbins had learned how to interpret Cocytan speech, she remained woefully ignorant of facial contortions and body language. Not that the Creator was especially expressive anyway.

Low found himself glancing frequently over his shoulder, only to find nothing staring back at him. There were only the elaborately decorated walls and the dancing lights. He forced himself to pay attention to the interview. While he couldn't understand a word of it, it was fascinating to watch Maggie and the Cocytan converse.

"These crystals, what are they?" she asked.

"For one thing, they are not crystals in the usual sense. Their appearance is incidental to their composition. Internally, they are very uncrystallike. The luminous outer sheath and inner crystalline one mask individual organic mechanisms of incredible complexity. Think of them as tiny but complete hospitals, containing everything that is needed to repair another organic life-form. With the development of the crystals it was no longer necessary for the sick or injured to travel in search of medical care. Complete treatment could be inserted into their own bodies.

"Each crystal incorporates the ability to diagnose as well as to perform any necessary medical work. Resurrection of the deceased merely constitutes a more difficult but, as you have seen, not impossible repair. It is simply a matter of rearranging and reinvigorating the appropriate molecules."

"It works on humans too," she informed it.

"The crystal's powers of examination are considerable."

"I can see something like that working on the recently deceased," she remarked, "but with someone who's been dead as long as yourself, I'd think the brain patterns would have faded beyond hope of recovery."

"What are you asking it now?" Low demanded to know.

She waved him off. "Just the basics, Boston. Hush now, or I won't be able to understand." Fuming silently at his inability to follow the conversation, the Commander went silent.

"Learning how to preserve the dead," the Cocytan explained, "is a necessary prelude to discovering how to revive them. That includes methods for the preservation of brain patterns. Although it was not my field, I believe it has to do with maintaining certain electrical flows in the absence of normal biological activity. As you can see, I was given the finest handling of which our biologists and physicists were capable. I was, as I have already mentioned, not consulted in this."

"But you're the only one." Robbins made it a statement, not a question.

"Not at all. The museum spire is full of such exhibits, if only you knew how to activate them. There are many that can be restored to life."

"No, I mean, you're the only Cocytan. The only preserved representative of the dominant species. At least, you're the only one we've found."

Was that a smile? Low wondered as he stared at the alien. Or did the twitch of beak and eyes signify something else entirely?

His thoughts drifted to Brink. "Ask it how long the benign effect of the crystal lasts." She proceeded to translate.

"It varies," the Cocytan explained, "depending on the organism. In your case I could not say. You are warm-blooded and have a closed circulatory system. Beyond that I cannot speculate on the details of your internal anatomy."

"You still haven't told us why you were singled out for this special treatment." Robbins's interviewing skills came automatically to the fore. "What makes you so unique?"

The Cocytan lingered a moment before replying. "I had the misfortune to be born brilliant."

"You don't feel honored by all this?"

"Honored?" The alien leaned forward so sharply that for an instant Robbins considered retreating. Instead, she held her ground. In her career she'd faced down all manner of threats and weapons. The feeling she received from the Cocytan was not one of menace or of friendship. Nor was it complete indifference. It ran deeper, and she determined to identify it.

"You said that your people achieved several scientific breakthroughs at the same time." Low spoke through Robbins. "You've discussed the life crystals. What were the other ones?"

The Cocytan turned to him. "There was a machine. An instrumentality called the Eye. Simple name for something so complex. I did not name it, though I was the one guilty of its evolution."

"So you were more than an engineer." Robbins spoke slowly and carefully to make sure there were no misunderstandings. "You were a scientist as well." She glanced sharply at her companion. "Boston, this one was a scientist as well as an engineer." Low simply nodded and let her get on with the translating.

"Engineering was my love," the Cocytan explained. "Science was my reason for existence. Ultimately, it became the reason for my nonexistence, for that of my friends and relations, for—" The creature broke off and began anew.

"Let me tell you about the machine.

"I did not develop the Eye by myself, of course. No mechanism so complex, so awesome in its capabilities, could be the product of one individual. But I was responsible for the underlying theorems and for much of the basic engineering.

"The concept was then taken up by others, elaborated upon and, eventually, built. It took time. Some called it magic, but of course it was no such thing. It was simply very advanced applied science.

"At the time, I was quite convinced that the mechanism ought to be built. My enthusiasm was shared by a small coterie of fellow researchers. Within what you would call the scientific establishment there was much skepticism, but the proposal was met with an open mind. Give us a concept, a design, my group was told, and it will be fabricated.

"Thus challenged, what else could I do but comply? The necessary schematics were provided." The wing-flaps on the Cocytan's back moved more rapidly. A sign of excitement, Low wondered, or agitation? Or some alien emotion that would remain forever unknown to them?

"In scope the Eye was not as grand as many other projects. We had raised cities that scraped the skies, run tunnels and temples to relaxation beneath the seas, probed the very heart of the planet. We had shrunk intricate machines to the size of cells, whose components consisted of individual atoms. You have encountered one of these yourselves, in the form of the life crystals. The Eye was a greater undertaking than some, less than others. It was simply . . . the Eye."

Robbins translated for Low, then asked, "This Eye, what did it do that was so important?"

The Cocytan shifted slightly to loosen cramped muscles. "It allowed one to enter another plane of existence, to visit a different dimension. To transcend the limitations of time and space as they are generally known. Passing through the Eye stripped an individual of physical substance, leaving only the state of *being* behind. Yet all of that individual's original self, including the physical, was compacted and retained within the being that remained, much as one might dehydrate a fruit or vegetable.

"The process was quick, painless and liberating."

"What's it talking about?" Low put an arm around Robbins's shoulder.

"I'm not sure. It's pretty complicated. Just because I understand the words doesn't mean I'm getting all the concepts. I think he's talking about being able to go into another dimension." She sought clarification.

"For purposes of explanation your interpretation will suffice, little traveler. Within this other dimension all physicalities are absent. Belief, emotion, thought alone remain. Passing through the Eye, one becomes a conceptualization of oneself. Ethereal creatures of pure id, without solid form, they still possess the ability to perceive the physical world, though not to interact with it. Solidities are no longer barriers, though the vastness of deep space remains unbridgeable."

Gesturing as it spoke, the Cocytan reminded Low of a prima ballerina. Though massive, it was not without grace.

"It was more than metamorphosis," it continued. "It was the casting off of one existence in exchange for another. In the absence of imperfect physicality, death was reduced to a philosophical concept.

"More and more of my kind chose to experience the transformation. They saw it as elevating themselves to a higher state of being. As thousands instead of dozens began to pass through the Eye, a procedure as simple in appearance as it was intricate in execution, I began to grow more and more concerned. In this I was not alone, but as the originator of the process I believe I was the only one to envision the ultimate consequences."

"You foresaw some danger," Robbins commented softly.

"Danger? What danger could there be in ascending to a higher state of being where one could no longer be killed or even injured? Where physical pain was but a memory and one could theoretically continue to live forever? Perhaps 'exist' forever is a better term, for I am not sure one should call it living.

"I tried to warn those who remained against abandoning the universe in which we had evolved. But when feelings of ecstasy and elation were generated by those who had already passed through, which was the only way they could still communicate with the physical world, the rush through the Eye became a flood. Everyone wanted entry to the new paradise.

"There was nothing I could do. I, who had been so much praised and honored, became a pariah among my kind. Or worse, I was laughed at. I withdrew into myself, into my own thoughts, as tens of thousands and more lined up to step through.

"As a scientist I have always been suspicious of easy answers. Solutions should be difficult, time-consuming and painful. The Eye was too facile. In the rush to immortality I felt we as a species were overlooking something vital. As I mentioned, there is existing, and then there is life. I was not certain that discorporeal being was also life.

"Of course, without making the journey myself there was no way I could be certain of my fears."

"Did you?" Robbins asked breathlessly.

"You do not understand. Not one who had passed through expressed any interest in returning. Satisfaction was absolute. Which only made me more uneasy.

"At that point I felt only one option was left to me. I needed to do something vivid enough to shock those who remained out of their expectant complacency. I had to propound a warning they could not ignore. They needed to be reminded of the beauty of mortality.

"So I took my own life."

Robbins gaped at the tall figure. Low had to shake her to get a response. "Come on, Maggie. What did it say? Why is it looking like that?"

"It says . . . it says that it's a suicide. It was done as a warning to those who hadn't yet made the transportation through the Eye."

"I left behind," continued the Cocytan, not caring whether the two humans had concluded their conversation or not, "a request. I demanded that my remaining colleagues not use the life crystals to revive me. In this, at least, they complied with my wishes. But unbeknownst to me I was given this elaborate burial, and my remains were preserved instead of being allowed to return to the soil from whence they sprang. How absurd! Perhaps they thought that some day I might wish to be revived so that I could pass through the Eye and join my kindred spirits, as it were. They knew of me, but none knew me."

"But you have been revived since then," Robbins suggested.

"Not by my own kind, nor by any who looked like you. Others have come. Not many."

"Other ships," Low muttered when Robbins had finished translating.

"Some have used the life crystals to revive me. They asked their questions and then they departed, leaving me in peace. None returned, and I know nothing of their fate."

"We can guess," replied Robbins.

"I am the only Cocytan left." The Creator's voice was devoid of self-pity or remorse. "This I know from having spoken with those who have revived me. I am certain that those who placed me here subsequently took their own turns in the line, until the voices of my kind were no longer heard on the surface of this world. They abandoned it to the lower forms. They used a machine to thwart evolution. My machine." The great head dropped, and this time there was no mistaking the meaning behind the gesture.

For a long time neither human nor Cocytan spoke.

"They've all gone?" Robbins inquired when she could speak again.

"All. Over, through, into: whichever metaphor you prefer will do. Within that other dimension all exist still. I have no reason to believe otherwise. Whether they also *live* I cannot say. That is a designation I reserve for physical existence. They are here now, even as we speak."

"What?" Low's eyes darted in all directions, seeking the unseeable.

"I thought I'd felt something." Robbins turned a slow circle, seeing only walls, ceiling and floor. "I've been feeling it ever since we stepped out of the asteroid-ship. A presence. And not in the metaphysical sense either." Sparks swirled urgently around her, enigmatic and undefined.

Again Low spoke through Robbins. "Does it have anything to do with these flashes of light? When they intensify, I could swear that we're being watched."

"You are," the Cocytan told them. "As alien physical intelligences, you constitute a diversion."

"How many?" Low asked.

The Cocytan considered before replying. "I see no reason why all should not be here. Watching, listening, observing, doubtless commenting."

"All?" queried Robbins uncertainly. "How many did you say made the trip through the Eye?"

The Cocytan made a sweeping gesture. "It is not so impossible as it seems. Reduced to pure thought, to a statement of oneself, existence requires very little in the way of actual space. Assuming every transposition was successful, and while I lived I never saw an unsuccessful one, the number would have been approximately three billion."

"Three *billion*?" Robbins swallowed as points of light swirled about her. "And they're all here now, in this room with us?"

"Why should they be somewhere else when they could be here? As I said, you represent an entertaining diversion."

"What's it saying?" Low demanded to know.

She turned to him. "It says that all of the Cocytans who went through the Eye are here now, in this chamber with us. You, me, it, and three billion thought-forms."

Low whistled softly. Once more his gaze flicked about the room. "Funny. Up until now I didn't feel crowded in here."

It was fortunate neither of them was claustrophobic, or remaining in the chamber would have been unbearable. As it was, they felt no pressure, no weight. Only the knowledge pressed heavily on them.

"How do you know this?" Low inquired.

"It is logical, and as a Cocytan I am more attuned to the presence of my own kind than you. I cannot be sure of the number, but it follows. I am sensitive to projections you are incapable of receiving. Not complete, coherent thoughts, mind you, but general sensations. My brethren are here, and yet they are not."

The Creator started to stand but proved unable to complete the motion. Instead, it sank back down, clearly exhausted.

"What's wrong?" The depth of her concern surprised Robbins.

"It is not good for one who has been long dead to be resurrected. The life-crystal process was developed so that those who perished accidentally could be rapidly revived. It was never intended to be used on ancient bodies like myself. Nor, as you now know, is this the first time I have been brought back. Under such circumstances the efficacy of the life crystal is marginal. I am past successful rejuvenation and find the whole process tiresome beyond measure.

"Remember that I chose death: It did not choose me. My physical form is so old that even the preservation processes employed by my misguided but well-intentioned colleagues can no longer sustain ordinary organic functions. The systems are feeble, the organs withered. I am sure that the intention was that should I be revived, I would quickly make the transportation via the Eye. It was never planned that I live for long in this precarious state."

"Are you in pain?"

Again that maybe-smile. "Only mentally."

"Then why haven't you joined them? Why don't you now?"

"For the same reason I did not do so in the first place," the scientist-engineer explained. "Immortality is an alluring concept, much better dealt with via learned philosophical discourse than actuality. Every time I am revived, I sense greater and greater unhappiness among the transposed. It is just as I feared: They are less than content with their immortal lot."

"The Creator lectures the travelers." The ten million who commented rested unnoticed on Maggie Robbins's left shoulder.

"Will they comprehend?" wondered twenty million others. "And comprehending, will they act?"

"They will not," insisted forty million more from the vicinity of Low's ankles. "Why should they? We didn't."

"Primitiveness is relative," avowed the first. "It is not related to the moment. We have had a thousand years to learn and yet are helpless to affect our own condition."

"Who could have envisioned eternity as boring?" observed fifty million more.

"From all I have been able to glean," the Cocytan told Low and Robbins, "paradise is a particularly dreary place. When one surrenders physicality, one also gives up all the sensations it is heir to. Touch, smell, taste and several other senses I do not think you possess. The ability to perceive electrical fields, for one, and to taste of the infrared. In crossing over, all are surrendered, all are lost forever."

"How do you know all this?" Robbins asked.

"Those sensations I spoke of are present even as we speak.

I perceive nothing to contradict that which I have already surmised. Each time I am revived, I sense increasing disenchantment, a desire to trade timeliness for timelessness."

"Then why don't they?" Robbins translated for Low. "Why don't they just come back?"

"Don't be ridiculous, Maggie. It's patently impossible."

"Actually," explained the Cocytan, "it is quite possible. Hypothetically, at least."

Again Robbins translated. Except for the superior smirk, which was entirely her own addition. "See?"

"Okayyy." Low turned to face the Creator. "If it's possible, and muchly desired, then when you're revived, why don't you just amble over to this Eye and throw it into reverse or whatever? Assuming the machinery is still functional, of course."

"As I have told you, my physical form is not capable of leaving this special chamber. Were I to attempt a task as elementary as rising from this platform and walking to the exit, my internal skeleton would simply collapse. My head would sink down between my shoulders to end up somewhere in the region of my pelvic girdle, crushing my internal organs along the way.

"So long as I remain atop this platform and make no attempt to leave, I am constantly bathed in what for lack of a better term I will call an energy field. It is similar to but different from that projected by the life crystals. Did you think that after a thousand years my flesh and blood would remain intact and functional without constant attention?" As an alarmed Low started to back away, it gestured sharply.

"There is no need to flee. The field is site as well as cell specific and cannot affect you." The alien visage contorted. "At this point in time, it barely affects me.

"I cannot reactivate the Eye, much less execute the necessary adjustments. It is possible that the latter were left engaged by those who stepped through last, but I do not know."

"You really think this gateway, or whatever it is, still might be operational?" Low asked through Robbins.

"As I told you, I have no way of knowing. I have not set eyes upon the device myself since I terminated my own existence. A termination, by the way, with which I am still fully comfortable and the interruption of which causes me a great deal of distress."

"We're sorry," Robbins replied, "but we didn't have any choice. We're desperate to find a way back to our own world."

"I understand. You are prey to the ills of the flesh. It must be difficult to be alive and far from one's home. Death alleviates so many petty concerns."

"Not for me," Low declared when Robbins had translated this last for him. "I've got too many questions for which I'd still like to have answers. Now, tell us about this machine."

Despite its evident fatigue, the scientist-engineer did its best to comply. "Like all devices of advanced Cocytan manufacture, the Eye was designed when not in use to shut itself down and preserve itself against decay. Unless it was tampered with or affected by unforeseen natural forces, it should remain, self-repairing and self-maintaining, awaiting reactivation should it be required. You have already seen how Cocytan machinery can sustain itself, or you would not be here now."

Low nodded. "The interisland transport system, the planetarium and many other devices are still functional."

"My people knew how to build. But they could not devise a mathematical theorem that would lead to contentment. In a delirium of expectation they cast aside everything they had built up to that time. It is a great pity.

"If the Eye could be reactivated, and if it was properly reprogrammed prior to the last of my colleagues' transposing themselves, then I feel certain many if not all would return to gladly engage the normal progression of life and death they unwittingly left behind. Among them would be many who could be of assistance to you.

"As for myself, there is nothing more I can do for them. I did too much while I was alive. My punishment is that I am not to be left in peace. And yet, perhaps I may be of assistance to you. Not out of any personal fondness, you understand, for you are nothing to me but an inconvenient interruption, but because your departure would assure my continued rest."

"Help us," Low urged the alien, "and I swear we'll never bother you again." It was an easy promise to make.

"Your desire to return home." The enfeebled scientist-engineer strained to remember distant schematics from an even more distant time. "I recall the activation mechanism that was used on the probes. I believe it involved . . . ," and a long string of untranslatable engineering terms followed.

A brief physical description, however, left no doubt as to what the Cocytan was referring to.

"The four plates," Robbins told an expectant Low. "It's describing the four-plate system."

"We have three. Tell it we have three." She did so.

"Then the matter is simple. I would think there would be others here, in this spire. Before it became my resting-place, it was a museum of travel. Search near the entrance. I think you will find what you are looking for."

So saying, it raised its feet from the floor, leaned back, and resumed the traditional Cocytan resting position, prone on its back, winglets outspread to both sides.

"I tire of this new life, as I have tired of all that have gone before. I choose not to think. Leave me now, and if you would respect my intelligence as I have respected yours, do not inflict the pain of consciousness on me again. It is time for me to not be." The slim, magisterial head turned slightly toward them.

"Go now, and I hope you find your way home. My entire species could not."

"We don't know how to thank you." Robbins spoke quickly, conscious of the gravity of the moment.

Eyes full of wisdom flickered as the life force began to wane. The voice was an echo of what it had been earlier. "You are not home yet. When you reach your destination, thank me then." Eyes closed, the voice silenced and breathing ceased. Once again, the great scientist-engineer was not.

Robbins wiped at her eyes. "I hope we didn't impose on it too much. I wouldn't like to go away thinking we'd caused it any pain."

"I wouldn't worry about it." Low was firmly prosaic. "It's dead now. Again. That's what it wanted." He turned to look in the direction of the exit. "Now maybe we can get what we want."

They left the tomb then—a silent, lifeless, but somehow not at all tragic place. They were forced to pause for a while in the passageway while the contentious guardians fought their way across the central chamber. As they sprinted across the deserted floor, Low wondered if the two combatants would fight until their internal mechanisms ran down, or if one would finally succeed in overpowering the other. It might happen tomorrow, next week or next year. Or the salutary effect of the life crystals might simply give out. It didn't matter, since he hoped he would never have to return to this island.

It took less than twenty minutes to find the necessary fourth plate. As soon as they had it safely extracted from the exhibit in which it had been half buried, something deep inside moved him to turn and face the pyramidal sarcophagus. Raising the edge of his stiffened right hand slowly to his forehead, he snapped it down smartly in the first formal salute he had performed in many years. Then he turned to Robbins.

"Right. We can go now."

Low hefted the precious plate as they made their way back to the transport tunnel. By now he felt as comfortable in the rolling sphere as he did on the subway back home. No, that wasn't quite true, he corrected himself. He felt more comfortable. There were no aggressive panhandlers, no forlorn students, no gang-bangers and no graffiti.

As they raced silently and comfortably toward the central island, he stared through the transparent wall of the spinning sphere and squinted, half imagining he could see destination signs painted on the dark walls. It was an ephemeral, childish fantasy, but one he was able to enjoy for several minutes.

An unusually pensive Robbins interrupted his reverie. "You know, Boston, we were pretty selfish back there, all wrapped up in trying to figure out a way to get back to Earth. There were so many questions we could have asked the Cocytan. So many things people have wondered about for thousands of years that it probably could have resolved with a shrug or a few words."

"Like what?" He continued to squint at the tunnel walls.

"Oh, like, what is the meaning of life? How big is the universe?"

"Where are the cookies?" he added, making her smile. "I didn't know telejournalists pondered such weighty matters. I thought if it wasn't sexy, or with it or of the moment, then it wasn't relevant. Reflection isn't something I associate with modern news coverage."

If she was hurt by his appraisal, she didn't show it. "It has nothing to do with modern news coverage. Those are questions *I* would've asked, if I'd thought of them in time."

Low shook his head dubiously. "I never heard a journalist ask questions like that."

"Who would you ask them of?" She reminisced. "The people I'm told to interview, the stories I'm assigned to cover, don't have much in common with the great questions. All I'd have to do is devote one show to a story on 'the meaning of life' and I'd find myself back in Topeka reading the morning farm reports so fast, it'd make your head spin. Which is where and how I got my start, by the way.

"The network isn't interested. They don't like for their reporters and anchorfolk to appear too much smarter than the individual on the street. You think an audience would watch?" She didn't wait for him to respond, and he knew that he wasn't expected to. "That doesn't mean that I can't be interested."

He opened his eyes all the way. The fanciful station signs

for Fisherman's Wharf, Chinatown, the Financial District, Berkeley and points east vanished from his imagination and his inner eyelids at the same time.

"I'm sorry, Maggie. I've been underestimating you and overcategorizing you ever since the start of the mission."

"Forget it. Not only am I used to it, I'm guilty of it myself. For example, when we started out, I thought you were a stiff, humorless, dry, emotionless robot. Now I see that you're not dry at all." She grinned and he returned the favor.

She had a beautiful smile, he decided. Perfect teeth, as you would expect from an internationally famous telejournalist. Accumulated grime and sweat couldn't detract from the beauty of her skin. Her hair was a mess, but her eyes glistened like sapphire cabochons. Her lips were . . .

He turned away. Light had appeared at the end of the tunnel, signifying their approach to the central island.

Among the millions of monitoring thought-forms confusion, surprise and jubilation reigned in equal measure.

"They have spoken with the Creator and have found the fourth plate! They will use it to return to their world, and all will be as it has been."

"Perhaps," cautioned the iconoclastic first. "Have patience. We have been patient for hundreds of years. Time yet to see."

"Truly," chorused ten million supporters. "Patience we have in infinite quantity. Time still to dream."

"Let us again discuss the physics of luck," suggested ten thousand, and that prompted a renewal of an earlier debate.

The keen buzz that unexpectedly filled the sphere confused and startled its passengers, not to mention interrupting Low's contemplation of Robbins's features. Then he realized that the sound arose from their pen communicators. They were being called.

Pulling the unit from his belt, he spoke sharply into the pickup. "Ludger?"

"It would have to be, wouldn't it, Commander?" The scientist's words were labored and weak. "I regret to report that I am experiencing some difficulty."

Low exchanged a glance with Robbins before replying. "Take it easy. We're on our way back to the main island. What's wrong? Did you misplace one of your precious crystals?"

"No." Clearly Brink was under too much strain to respond to Low's sarcasm. "But I was about to, and that is the source of the problem. I find myself unable to move. I am also," he added tersely, "in considerable pain."

"Hang on. Our sphere is arriving."

It took only a moment for the transport to dock at the station. The door cycled open and they exited hurriedly. Brink wasn't waiting to greet them.

Low raised the communicator. "We're here. Where are you?" There was no sign of the scientist. Wind whispered through the gigantic chamber, a querulous intruder from outside.

"I am on the surface," came Brink's reply. "Afraid we might be overlooking important external sites in our preoccupation with what we found below, I decided to hike out and survey the area immediately surrounding the opening into the large chamber. I should have been more careful."

"You still haven't told us what's wrong."

"You will see. Climb out and I will give you directions."

"We're on our way."

Together he and Robbins struggled up the rubble pile and managed to make the jump from its peak to the nearest solid ground. It felt strange to be back in sunlight after being so long underground. After hours spent in the company of mysterious alien artifacts, relentless organic guardians and the resurrected Creator, he experienced the plain wind-swept rocks and low scrub as heartbreakingly normal. Squinting at the sky, he found himself speculating on the length of a Cocytan day.

"All right," he informed the communicator, "we're out." He oriented himself. "We're facing the setting sun."

The scientist's reply was shaky. "Turn forty-five degrees to your right and you will be facing me. I am not far. Please hurry."

It took a bit of scrambling up a broken slope. Nothing difficult, which they both managed with comparative ease.

"There he is." Robbins spotted their errant companion first.

As they approached, nothing seemed out of the ordinary. Brink was lying on his left side against the rocks, his right arm resting against him, looking for all the world as though he was relaxing and enjoying the view. But as they drew near, they saw there was no sign of his left forearm. It was hidden by the crack in the hillside into which the scientist had thrust it. They hurried to his side.

"What's wrong, Ludger?" Even as she asked, Robbins was straining to see for herself.

Sweat dappled the scientist's face, though the temperature was on the cool side. "As you see, my hand and wrist have become stuck."

"How did you manage that?" Robbins tried to find a better angle.

"I was holding one of the life crystals." He smiled weakly. "If you just hold them gently and don't press them against your body, you can feel their warmth without absorbing them. It is a most invigorating sensation.

"Climbing this slope, I slipped slightly and lost my grip. The crystal fell into this hole. It isn't deep, and I thought I could dig it out. When I attempted to do so, the rocks above shifted and, as you see, pinned my arm. I cannot pull free. Every time I try, the rocks above slide down a little more. It really is very painful. I am afraid that most of the bones in my left hand are broken to one degree or another.

"Fortunately, I was able to reach my communicator with my other hand."

Low had completed a circuit of the scientist's predicament. "Just hang in there, Ludger. We'll get you out."

But try as they might, with both of them digging, they

were unable to free the scientist's pinioned arm. When Low tried to use a long, narrow rock to lever the others, it only made the situation worse. The hillside immediately above was unstable. If much more rock shifted, the scientist's neck as well as his arm would be at risk.

"I am afraid I cannot contain myself much longer." Brink was trembling now, and perspiration had enveloped his entire body.

"Go ahead and scream if you want," Robbins told him tightly. "In my work I've had to listen to plenty of screams."

"It's not that," Brink wheezed. "Nothing so melodramatic. I am just afraid that I am going to pass—"

He slumped back against the hillside before he could finish the sentence.

Low straightened. "We've got to get him out of there. I'm worried about steady bleeding. But if we're not careful, this whole section of hillside is going to come down. Then we're liable to have to dig ourselves out."

Robbins wiped sweat from her forehead and looked up at him. "One of the alien machines from the museum?"

"This isn't a complex piece of engineering. We ought to be able to make do without anything that exotic. Besides, he's already in shock. By the time we figured out what device to bring and got it back here, he's liable to be dead. What we need is a big jack, and I don't remember seeing anything that straightforward. For all we know, there might be half a dozen portable antigravity lifters waiting in crates by the entrance, but it could take weeks to find one and puzzle it out."

Robbins put her ear against the scientist's chest. "He's still breathing, but not well." She straightened. "You're right, Boston. We need to do something quickly."

Instead of rapid excavation they tried removing the confining rock slowly, one handful at a time. Occasionally Brink would regain consciousness, but he was no longer coherent. Raving in three languages, he would moan and flail about with his free hand before relapsing into a coma.

It didn't matter whether they removed a little dirt and detritus at a time or a lot. Whenever it seemed they were making some progress, more rock would suddenly slip down to mock their efforts. Blood was now visible on the scientist's left arm, seeping up from the breaks below to stain the sleeve.

"It's no good." Low sat back, weary from his efforts. "We've got to get him out of there *now,* or he's going to bleed to death. Do you hear me, Ludger? Do you understand? We don't have any more options."

The scientist's eyes flickered unsteadily.

"*Ich . . . verstehen.* I understand, Commander. Do what you have to do." Low and Robbins might be tired, but the scientist was completely drained.

Low bent close. "If we don't do something right now, Ludger, you're going to bleed to death."

"Don't want . . . to die." Somehow he summoned a feeble grin from the depths of his distress. "As you Americans say, been there, done that."

Removing a small packet from his belt, Low tore it open and pressed two tiny pills against the other man's lips. "Can you swallow these? I'll find some water if you need it."

"No water. Need schnapps." Opening his mouth and making a great effort, Brink leaned forward slightly and sucked in the pills. Low and Robbins looked on as he swallowed.

"Concentrated general anesthetic," Low told her. "Part of every suit's emergency kit."

"What now?" She eyed him expectantly.

"We build a fire." In response to her look of confusion he added, "I'll need something to cauterize the wound."

"Cauterize . . . ?" Her eyes widened. "You're not kidding, are you?"

Low met her gaze without blinking. "You got a better idea?"

She shook her head slowly. "Not only don't I have a better idea, I don't have any ideas at all. You're sure you know what you're doing?"

"No," he replied curtly, "I'm not." He pulled a coil of glossy alien metal from a pocket. Unfolded, it was roughly two inches wide, a foot long and honed on one edge.

"Used this on the glue strands when we rescued you from the spitter-crab. Thought it might come in handy later." His gaze shifted back to Brink. The scientist was resting peacefully, the powerful anesthetic having already started to work. "This wasn't what I had in mind." He began to remove the top of his flight suit.

"What are you doing?"

He bunched the material tight. "I don't know what the alloy is, but this strip is plenty sharp. If I tried to hold it with both hands and saw away, I'd cut my own fingers to ribbons. I think it will work. It'd better. Let's try to find some debris that will burn."

"You know, I think I do have a better idea," she murmured. "What about using one of the crystals . . . after you're through?"

Low considered, then nodded admiringly. "Should've thought of that. All right, you stand by with a crystal. But I want a fire going in case it doesn't work."

Once they had a fire blazing hot, he inserted one end of the long lever stone he'd used earlier into the glowing coals and waited for it to heat up. When he was satisfied, he picked up the strip of alien metal, using his bunched-up shirt and undershirt in lieu of gloves.

"You sure that will cut . . . through?" Robbins asked quietly.

"It'll cut, all right. I just hope it doesn't snap when I'm half done." Approaching the motionless Brink, he took up a predetermined position, nodded at Robbins and went to work. She waited nearby, cradling in both hands one of the life crystals they'd taken from Brink's overfull pockets.

Working as fast as possible, Low had no time to wonder how his companion was coping with the gory spectacle. She claimed to have been in numerous wartime situations and seen much worse. He hoped she'd been telling the truth.

Despite the tourniquet they'd tightened around Brink's upper arm, blood came fast and copiously. The metal strip cut cleanly until he reached the bone, then more slowly. His hands were growing slippery from the blood and he was afraid of losing his grip. Then he was through the bone and sawing rapidly again.

"Finished!" Exhausted, he flopped back against the rocks. Robbins immediately jammed the glowing green crystal against the bloody stump and held it there.

Mere seconds passed before the journalist felt the shard beginning to flow between her fingers. Drawing back, she watched in awe as it seemed to melt into the open wound. Pale-green light enveloped the scientist's severed arm from slice to shoulder. Bleeding slowed, then stopped altogether.

"It's working!" More than anything, the process reminded her of the time-lapse photography she'd seen used on occasion by the news division's editing team. "I can *see* it healing."

A weary Low spread his bloodstained shirts out on the rocks to dry. "Don't jump to conclusions."

"I'm not," she objected. "Come and look for yourself. It's like magic."

"Runes of the witch doctor." Low mumbled to himself as he struggled over to join her.

No spurting blood, no dangling tendons, no gleaming-white bone greeted his tired eyes. Clean flesh covered the end of the stump, pink and fresh.

"Too bad," he commented.

She made a face. "Too bad? What did you expect?"

"I didn't expect anything, Maggie. I hoped for full regeneration, for the arm to grow a new hand. I guess even the life crystals have their limits." He ran bloodied fingers over the smooth terminus. The new skin was so perfect, you couldn't tell that the limb had ever been damaged.

"Interesting. It can restore life but not individual body parts. I'll bet we could have reattached the severed hand if we'd been able to dig it out." He looked longingly at the narrow crevice in the rocks that had caused all the trouble. It would take days to excavate the sundered appendage, and that was assuming the loose scree didn't come crashing down to trap them while they were working.

Brink didn't need two hands anyway, Low rationalized. He was an idea man.

Robbins's thoughts had traveled along similar lines. "Hey, he doesn't have any reason to complain. It beats the alternative."

They stayed close to the scientist all through the night. The strange constellations were a welcome sight, sparkling and twinkling in the unpolluted air. There was no need to rush to shelter since after dark the temperature dropped only a few degrees before steadying.

By morning the scientist had recovered sufficiently to share water and a couple of handfuls of scavenged berries, which Low prayed contained nothing toxic enough to knock their feet out from under them. They ate comforted by the knowledge that in the event of poisoning, a life crystal apiece could probably cure them.

Brink managed well with his one remaining hand. "It's all right," he assured his companions. "I told you to do what you had to do, and you did. At least I am alive."

"You know what my biggest fear was?" Low told him. "That the shock would kill you and I'd have to use one of the crystals to revive you . . . with your hand still trapped in the rocks."

Brink was thoughtful. "Perhaps the crystals are not all identical. It may be that different kinds contain different instructions and we are not perceptive enough to distinguish between them. Possibly some are not capable of full resurrection. Hence the lack of any digital regeneration." He held up his stump.

"It was my fault. I had, and still have, plenty of the crystals. I should have let that one go."

Robbins put a comforting hand on his arm. "Don't blame

yourself. You couldn't have known the rock was going to shift like that."

"She's right." Between the bloodstains on his hands and arms and the pulpy residue from the berries darkening his lips, Low looked first cousin to a condor.

"No, I blame myself." Brink paused, trying to find the appropriate words. "I have to thank you both. Recently I have been somewhat . . ."

"Obsessed?" Low supplied the word without prompting.

The scientist smiled thinly. "As good a term as any, Commander Low. I still feel their pull"—he patted his overstuffed crystal-packed pockets—"but I think I can control my interests now as opposed to having them control me."

"Good. Then maybe you're ready for another piece of good news. Remember me telling you that I'd found a preserved Cocytan? Well, while you were sunbathing in crystal light, I used a couple to resurrect it. Twice. Maggie was there the second time. We learned a great deal about this world and what happened to it."

"I should like to have seen that." A glimmer of the old inquisitiveness shone in the scientist's eyes.

"You had your chance," Low told him. "We promised it that we wouldn't revive it anymore. In return, it told us where to find more of the activation plates. We have four of them again. Whether they'll work on the asteroid-ship or not is anybody's guess, but at least we've been given a chance."

Brink nodded solemnly. He no longer appeared agitated or nervous. His most recent brush with death and the subsequent amputation had left him chastened. Nothing like losing an important appendage to put things in perspective. Or perhaps his newfound calm was a salutary side effect resulting from the absorption of the life crystal. Low didn't really care. He was simply pleased with the result. It might well take all of them to make it off this world, and he was glad to have the scientist back on the team.

"If you will lead the way, Commander, I will help as best I can." Brink gestured in the direction of the main chamber.

"What about 'attending' to your life crystals?" Low inquired challengingly.

"These?" Brink patted his bulging pockets. "They're not going anywhere." He started off in the direction of the break in the chamber ceiling. "We are wasting time. I suggest you both keep up with me, since my capacity to wave to you has been significantly diminished."

They gathered up the four plates and hauled them to the tower mound containing the four matching cavities. Whether inserting the plates would activate the asteroid-ship or some other system they had no way of knowing, but there was no place to put the plates inside the asteroid. The original control pylon had metamorphosed and sunk into the floor, taking the original four plates with it.

One at a time, Low carefully placed them in the vacant recesses. When the time came to insert the fourth and last, he directed his companions to move back. Then he inserted the plate and hastened to join them.

Side by side they watched and waited. The plates sat neatly in their receptacles. Light poured through the distant fracture in the ceiling. Somewhere up above, a representative of the local fauna squealed inquisitively.

Nothing happened.

"Maybe if we alter the order of placement," Robbins suggested. "We might have inserted certain plates into the wrong orifices."

"I don't think there is a wrong order." Low did his best to sustain his companions' spirits, not to mention his own. "There's nothing to indicate that a particular plate goes into a certain cavity."

"We are fools for expecting this to resolve our situation." Both of them turned to Brink. "What did you expect? For this chamber to turn into a giant spaceship and carry us homeward?" Arm outstretched, head flung back, Brink turned a slow circle.

"The machine is broken. We have been spoiled by finding so many mechanisms still capable of functioning. It is unreasonable to expect everything to work. Unreasonable!" Lowering his arm and straightening, he looked back at them as he staggered to a stop. His eyes were wild.

The beneficial side effects of his amputation were already wearing off, Low saw sadly.

"Perhaps it requires more than four plates to activate it, whatever this damned console controls." Brink held up his foreshortened arm. "Perhaps it is missing a part, as am I."

Robbins looked around sharply. "Did you feel that?"

"Feel what?" Low was baffled, and he didn't want to be baffled. He wanted to be simultaneously sorry for and angry at the scientist.

Then he didn't have to ask. The floor had begun to tremble. The distinct yet subtle quivering ran up his feet and into his body. It was accompanied by a deep electronic hum, like the moan of some huge hibernating creature stirring from a long sleep.

The ceiling did not crumble, the floor did not crack. The chamber simply continued to vibrate in harmony with the unseen source. Nor did it begin to rise skyward and accelerate toward the distant Earth. Not for the first time Low noted how different the interior of the great chamber was from that of the asteroid-ship.

He turned his attention to the gap in the roof. Rocks and gravel spilled over the edge, adding to the height of the rubble pile beneath. There was no more sign of impending collapse than there was of a hidden port sliding sideways to seal the opening.

Robbins's attention was directed elsewhere. "Over there!" She pointed excitedly.

Following close on the heels of their elevated expectations, Low found the sight decidedly anticlimactic. The fifth and last high, arching doorway had finally opened. In appearance it was identical to the four he had accessed with the aid of the compact robots.

They advanced cautiously on the newly revealed portal. Beyond lay no sleek Cocytan starship or gratuitous alien wonder. The sight was depressingly familiar: another spherical transport station that was an exact duplicate of the four they had already utilized. Low's gaze took in the same gray walls, the same unmarked dark tunnel, the perfect pearllike sphere resting alongside the loading platform.

The vibration in the floor ceased. Looking back, he could see that the four round plates, acquired after so much effort and with such high hopes, still rested neatly in their respective recesses. They could be removed, he decided, as easily as they had been inserted.

It was hardly what Brink had been hoping for. The disappointment hit him harder than either of his companions.

"Another tram." Brink swore softly. "How exciting. Perhaps this tunnel terminates in Orlando. The Cape or Disney World, I would not care. Heidelberg would be better still. But I think not, I think not."

"I guess its destination is pretty obvious." Low sighed tiredly. "The fifth island. The only one we haven't visited yet." He frowned. "I wonder why such an elaborate setup to operate this doorway? Why hide it like this? There must be something special on the fifth island. Something even more remarkable than the Creator's sarcophagus."

"A used-starship lot, no doubt." Brink giggled. It was clear his sanity was continuing to slide, the slip no doubt accelerated by yet another failure, another disappointment. "The starships are free, but you have to turn over an important body part in return for a map."

"Ludger, get a hold of yourself." Low started toward the other man. "Use one of the crystals if you have to."

Brink backed away. "Might as well make yourselves comfortable," he told them derisively, "because we're going to be here for a long time, I think. Probably just this side of forever. We're never going to leave this world, you know. Never, never, ever. In a thousand years or so some other cursed, unfortunate visitors will trip over our skeletons and wonder what we were doing here and why we failed to leave. Cocytus, oh yes, how true I named it!

"Now, if you will excuse me"—he executed a mock Prussian bow—"I have to go and find a nice, cozy burial site. Do not ask me to share. Each must find his or her own."

Babbling in German, he whirled and sprinted madly away from them.

"Ludger!" Low took a couple of steps after the other man before slowing to a halt. It would do no good to run him down and tackle him. As mad as he was at the moment, he might be capable of inflicting serious damage on anyone who tried to restrain him, and that would do none of them any good at all.

"Ludger, please!" Robbins had come up alongside Low. Her entreaties were no more effective than those of the Commander.

"It's no good, Maggie." Low put an arm around her. "Let him go."

"Go where? He could end up hurting himself again, and next time we might not be able to find him."

Low tracked the running man's progress. "I think he's headed back to his crystal sanctuary. If he stays in there, he should be all right. Either he'll come to his senses or"—Low shrugged—"he won't."

She wasn't satisfied. "But we have to go after him, we have to help him."

Low eyed her quizzically. "Why? When you stomped out on me, I didn't go running after you, and you came to your senses."

Her gaze narrowed. "I never lost my senses." Angrily, she shrugged his arm off. "I was upset and I needed time to think." She gestured in the direction the fleeing scientist had taken. "Ludger's gone over the edge. He's not responsible for his actions. There's a difference."

"Then he'll climb back up, or he won't." Low was insistent, if not obdurate. "I'm not going to waste what time and energy I have left trying to wrestle him back to reality. For one thing, we're all out of concentrates and we have to find a suitable food source." He turned. Brink was now out of sight.

"Really, he'll be okay. He's carrying a king's ransom in life crystals. I wonder if they can cure madness? If so, he'll heal himself. He has a better chance of doing so than we do. Eventually he'll get tired, or hungry, or both. Then he'll remember who and where he is and come looking for us, wearing that same sheepish grin he flashed after we saved him the last time.

"Meanwhile, since we've nothing better to do, we might as well make a visit to the fifth island. Who knows? Maybe it's a giant preserved Cocytan supermarket. At this point I think my stomach's willing to try thousand-year-old dehydrates." Turning, he headed for the beckoning portal.

"But why the elaborate door key? That's what I don't understand."

She fell into step alongside him. "Maybe we'll find a key to the key."

He snorted skeptically. "I'm getting sick and tired of finding keys. I want to go home."

Her eyebrows arched as she cast him a reproving look. "Now who's out of patience?"

He didn't reply. His shirts stank of Brink's blood, he was hungry and tired as well as depressed, and worst of all, he didn't have a clue how to tell Maggie how he really felt about her.

The transport sphere behind the fifth arch functioned exactly like the other four, its entrance cycling behind them before it commenced its slow, steady acceleration down the blank tunnel. While he had no means of measuring their velocity precisely, Low did his best to time the duration of their journey. It coincided closely with the previous four, which put it in line with the estimated travel time to the fifth and last island.

When it finally rolled to a halt, they exited and found themselves confronting another spacious, high-ceilinged chamber crammed with unrecognizable instrumentation. The individual devices were larger than anything Low had previously encountered save for the Creator's pyramidal sarcophagus. That didn't mean they would be of any use.

From the outside, the machinery appeared simplistic, no doubt in contrast to highly intricate interiors. Dominating everything else and rising toward the peak of the spire was a massive, irregularly shaped console. As big as a house, it took some time to circumnavigate. Low hunted for individual controls while Robbins kept an eye out for circular depressions that might accept metal plates. Neither search was successful.

What they did find sticking out of the far side of the mass was an assortment of projections tipped in glass, crystal or some other translucent material. When they touched these, or attempted to manipulate them, or passed their hands over the ends, nothing happened.

It was Robbins who picked out the image from the wealth of elaborate glyphs and engravings.

"Doesn't mean anything." Low made no effort to hide his continued disappointment as he studied the schematic she had found. "It's just a picture of a bunch of Cocytans."

"You're looking at it, Boston, but you're not seeing it." She traced the surface of the detailed representation with a fingertip. "See how they start out wholly and perfectly rendered and then gradually fade away to nothingness?"

"So? Part of the image is well preserved and part has worn away."

"No, no, don't you see?" Her excitement contrasted sharply with his lassitude. "There's a steady progression, right to left, from fully rendered forms through transitional stages right down to minimal outlines. Furthermore, the material on the left is as smooth and polished as the material on the right."

"What's your point?" he muttered impatiently.

She took a step back and gestured at the massive mechanism. "Don't you get it? This is it, this is the machine!"

He blinked, his apathy sloughing away. "You mean you think this is the *Eye*?"

"That's what the diagram says to me. Believe me, after you've spent months staring at thousands of Mayan glyphs, certain ways of illustrating things visually catch your attention." She stepped back to examine the inscrutable bulk. "The only thing is, the Cocytan spoke of stepping *through*, and I don't see anything like a door or portal or screen." She encompassed the exterior with a speculative wave. "It all looks solid, except for this one slot over here."

Moving to their right, she pointed out a dark hole in the otherwise unbroken flank of the machine. It displayed the same elaborate starburst design that embellished a number of other devices throughout the chamber.

"What could go in there?" Low bent forward to study the opening. "It's much too small to take one of the plates. Maybe some kind of key, or card."

"There's only one thing we've found that might qualify as a universal tool." When he looked puzzled, she gestured at his pocket.

He felt of the remaining sheathed crystal within. "You're serious, aren't you?"

"Why not? They resurrect people, and aliens. Why not machines?"

"From an engineering standpoint that doesn't make any sense. You use a socket wrench on a car, not on a person."

She smiled slyly. "Even if that person has an artificial hip joint that needs tightening?"

He considered. "Maybe you're right. Maybe I'm thinking too much like a human again." He studied the slot. "If the machine's well and truly dead, dumping anything in there isn't going to hurt it. If it's still capable of activation, well . . . I left my Eye ignition key in my other pants." He grinned admiringly. "You're a pretty observant gal, Robbins, you know that?"

"If I wasn't," she replied evenly, "I'd have been dead twenty times over these past ten years." She stepped aside to give him better access to the slot. "Go on, just do it."

Taking the shard from his pocket, he moved to deposit it in the waiting opening . . . and hesitated. "Wait a minute. Why are we bothering with this, not to mention probably wasting a life crystal? There's no spaceship here, no way home."

"We're doing it because we can," she told him, "and because it might bring us some help. The Creator can't do anything else for us. Maybe this machine can. Maybe it'll let us talk to the Cocytans in the other dimension and they'll know how we can reactivate the asteroid-ship. If not, maybe they can tell us where to find food, or how to get somewhere besides these islands."

He took a deep breath. "As I've said before, I don't have any better ideas." Then he turned to her. "Here. This is your idea. You do it."

"Okay." She took the life crystal, turning it over several times in her fingers, feeling the warmth of it while admiring the uniquely cool green glow. Then she slid it into the opening and gave it a little push. It disappeared silently within.

Low quickly stepped forward and put his eye to the slot. "I can't see the glow anymore. It's definitely gone somewhere."

"You could say that." She put a hand on his shoulder and drew him back.

Lights were coming on throughout the length and breadth of the mechanism. Pulsing just beneath the waxy, translucent surface, they formed circles and streaks of intense color. Some burned steadily, others blinked sequentially, while still others raced back and forth like fiery predators seeking electronic prey. Occasionally two of the latter would collide in a shower of controlled sparks.

Low commented laconically. "I'd say that did something."

"That's not all it did." Robbins had turned. "Have a look, Boston."

Instrumentalities were coming to life throughout the

chamber. It seemed as if every device in the spire had been activated by the insertion of the single crystal. Deep-throated hums and whirrings filled the air.

"There!" she shouted, pointing. "Something's happening."

Before their rapt gaze a vast section of wall slid slowly aside on hidden bearings. When it finally halted, they walked toward the new opening. It was no false projection. Standing in the portal, they could smell the sea and hear the slap of waves against unseen rocks below.

Behind them, more and more machinery continued to come on line, throbbing with the muted power they had come to associate with Cocytan technology.

Separated from the islet by a substantial stretch of ocean and directly in front of them lay the central island. It was easily recognizable as such from its size as well as from the familiar bulk of the asteroid-ship nestling in its rocky repository. Two of the other islets were also clearly visible, their gleaming spires stabbing at the sky. Beneath the one off to their left, Low mused, the Creator lay sleeping his final sleep, dreaming the slow dreams of the deceased and blissfully unaware of what was taking place close at hand. He had no more advice to give them, and they were once again truly on their own.

Inquisitive as ever, Robbins commented on her observations. "What's supposed to happen next?" She looked back into the room. "Seems like an awful lot of power and paraphernalia just to open a window."

Low considered the chamber. So many bright lights and indicators had come to life that he had to shield his eyes against the multihued glare.

"Right now we're standing in a line between the big machine and the central island. I think it would be a good idea if we moved." He took her hand, and together they stepped aside.

Less than a minute later a high, dominating whine filled the vaulted chamber and a beam of light ten feet in diameter erupted from the front of the combined mechanism. They dropped to the floor, overwhelmed by the unexpected radiance.

"Don't look directly at it," Low warned her. "Cover your eyes and move away from it."

Robbins had her eyes closed and had turned away from the source of the luminescence. Stars pinwheeled inside her eyelids. "If I cover my face, how the hell am I supposed to tell which way to crawl?"

As soon as his outraged optics had recovered somewhat, Low opened his eyes and let them focus on the floor. When he had his vision back, he found he was able to look in the direction of the projector so long as he kept his glance averted from the beam itself.

"Take it slow and it's not so bad." He took her arm and led her forward. "Let your vision readjust gradually."

When they reached the portal that separated the interior of the spire from the transport station, they finally turned to survey their handiwork. The entire room was alive with light, every single piece of machinery regardless of size having been brought back to life. The incredible beam leaped through the observatorylike opening in the far wall to soar across the ocean.

Floating high above the center of the main island was the resurrected Eye. It hung suspended in a crosshatch of tremendous beams, one emanating from each of the five surrounding islets. Resembling an immense flat disk, it slowly rotated through a complete arc every minute or so.

"Not bad for one small crystal," Robbins murmured.

Low squinted at the stunning sight. "Looks more like a disk than an eye. Maybe the designation's more apocryphal then descriptive." He stepped back into the room, shielding his face against the brightness all around. "There's some kind of transparent film around it. Looks like a giant soap bubble. You can't really see *it,* but you can see the sunlight reflecting off the surface."

"I wonder what happens next?" she mused.

For once Low had nothing to say. Thoroughly engrossed

in the sight, they stood and watched for some thirty minutes before the beam began to fade. No warning flicker preceded the diminution of intensity. The light simply dimmed until it vanished altogether. All five beams faded in concert. When they were no longer discernible, the disk ceased its methodical rotation and sank down into some hidden repository deep within the central mountains of the island.

Then all was as it had been before Robbins had slipped the life crystal into the slot. Somewhere an indigenous flying creature cried out to the lowering sun. A hidden instrument whirred one last time and died. It was hushed within the room. Only the lofty cleft in the far side of the spire wall remained to indicate that anything had taken place within.

They stood and listened to the distant harmony of the waves.

"It didn't work," Low commented finally. "I mean, it worked; it just didn't do anything."

"It just stopped." Robbins was scrutinizing the far reaches of the chamber, her eyes traveling from one now-silent instrument to the next. "We didn't touch anything and it stopped."

"Probably designed to shut itself down when nothing happens," he decided, "or . . ."

"Or what?" she prompted him.

"This is a lot for one crystal to operate. Maybe it needs more power to bring it fully on-line."

Her eyes widened as comprehension dawned. "Ludger."

Low nodded. "Exactly. And he's gone crystal crackers again. Or maybe we'll be lucky and he's come around by now. I'm hoping that deep down he's too rational and too logical to go completely psychotic."

"I'll talk to him." She exuded confidence as they headed for the transport sphere. "I've extracted coherent statements from men in combat and from politicians on the run. I think I can handle one addicted scientist."

"You've never tried to persuade one of the living dead," Low reminded her.

She smiled as they mounted the platform and entered the sphere. "Like I said, I've handled politicians on the run."

Unseen, unfelt and unperceived, three billion anxious thought-forms accompanied them.

They found Brink easily enough. As Low suspected, he had made his way back to the small storeroom where they had originally unearthed the hoard of crystals. When they arrived, they found him tinkering with the device he had claimed could reproduce them in quantity.

"Any luck?" Low inquired as the two of them caught sight of the scientist.

Brink glanced up briefly before returning to his work. He didn't seem surprised to see them.

"I believe that I am making some progress. The overall layout of the machinery is straightforward, but I do not have the engineering skills, or rather the machinist's, to effect the necessary repairs."

Gesturing for Robbins to remain behind, Low moved closer and peered into the depths of the device. Brink had achieved a small miracle in successfully opening the machine. Or perhaps, the Commander told himself, a concealed catch had simply responded to the scientist's touch.

Exposed to the light, the appliance's innards were a mass of unfamiliar color and components. There was nothing resembling a simple cable, chip or circuit board.

"I can't see where a drill or screwdriver would fit into this thing."

"Of course not," agreed Brink condescendingly, "but there are places here and here"—he pointed to gaps in the alien sequence—"where I have been able to remove entire components." He indicated a pile of small globes and ellipses that had been placed off to one side. "I have tried activating the device without them as well as reinserting them in various combinations. So far nothing has worked." He held up his stump. "It would go faster with two hands."

Might as well be playing with toy blocks, Low thought to himself. He took another step forward.

"Here, let me have a look."

Kneeling, he made a show of inspecting the mechanism's interior, acting as if he knew exactly what he was doing. In reality, he was sizing up the other man. There were circles under the scientist's eyes, a combination of eyestrain, lack of sleep and proper nutrition. Possibly there were other side effects he wasn't seeing, a consequence of Brink's recent demise and revivification. Physical strength had never been the scientist's forte, but madmen were capable of extraordinary feats of resistance. Low knew he would have to move carefully.

"We could try two of the globes here instead of one of the ellipses," he suggested.

"Anything! Anything at all!" The eagerness in Brink's voice could not mask his desperation. Were the effects of the crystal that had brought him back to life finally beginning to wear off?

Low picked up one of the globes and juggled it casually in his palm. "It's like this, Ludger. Maggie and I may have found a way to get some invaluable information. Maybe about returning home, maybe about surviving here. We don't know yet. We don't know because we haven't been able to fully activate the machinery in question."

"That is too bad." Brink's response was a mixture of admiration and indifference. "Nothing can exceed the importance of learning all we can about the crystals, of course."

"Oh, to be sure." Low exchanged a glance with Robbins. "In fact, this machinery we found seems to run on them."

"I am not surprised. The crystals are *allgegenwärtig*. They can do anything."

"It seems that way, doesn't it? Why, you should see what we managed to accomplish using just one of them. There's no telling what we could achieve with a handful or more. " He tapped the top of Brink's crystal-maker. "If we can get this thing up and running, we'll split the production with you."

"That seems reasonable." Brink agreed readily.

Robbins observed the byplay silently, wishing she could do something to help. Low appeared to be managing without her, though, and she kept quiet, waiting for the proper moment to intervene.

"Let's see what we can do here, then." Feigning eagerness, Low knelt and began to fiddle with the mechanism's interior.

A flash of light caused Robbins to jerk reflexively, and Low hastened to reassure her.

"Relax. False alarm. That part didn't fit there, but I don't think it caused any damage. We'll try it in this cavity on the other side instead."

Some time later he rose from the open device. "You know, everything's so sensibly laid out, I wouldn't be surprised if the damn thing *did* work." Bending forward, he ran a finger along a groove in the surface.

Lights began to glow within. The last thing Robbins had expected was for Low to get it working. How it produced crystals that contained more energy than the device itself utilized she couldn't imagine. Obviously it drew upon unknown and unseen sources.

The small bin attached to the back of the mechanism slowly began to fill with glowing, sheathed crystals. When it was full, the device stopped. Nothing Low could do, from removing the fresh product to trying different hand passes across the control surface to realigning the internal connections could induce it to start up again.

Meanwhile Brink had gathered up the new hoard. Low confronted him.

"Looks like that's the best we're going to be able to do, for a while at least. We'll take our share now, Ludger."

"Really, Commander," replied the scientist even as he was edging toward the doorway, "you can't honestly expect me to turn them over to you to squander on some frivolous experiment? If this device has produced its limit, then that means there will be no more."

Low moved to block the other man's path. "It doesn't matter what we want them for, Ludger. You agreed to the split."

"I don't believe my statement has the force of law here, Commander." With the doorway blocked, Brink reversed direction and began working his way back through the stacked containers and piles of machinery.

Low pursued, trying to avoid forcing the issue. Sooner or later the scientist had to run out of space. As the dangerous dance proceeded, he kept up a continuous soothing patter, trying to persuade the other man to see reason. Robbins chipped in with her own arguments, but despite her experience had no better luck in convincing the jittery scientist to act rationally.

The storeroom terminated in a dropoff that overlooked another level below. Brink halted, teetering on the edge. There was no ladder, no elevator, no way to make the descent. Clutching crystals to his chest without pressing them inward, he glared back at his tormentor.

Low halted. "Look, Ludger, we haven't got time for this. Maggie, watch the door. If he gets past me, try to slow him up."

"Boston, are you sure that—?"

"Just do it, okay?"

She nodded and assumed what she hoped Brink would see as a determined stance.

Crouching slightly, Low commenced a slow advance, one hand extended palm-up in front of him. "Come on, now, Ludger. Hand them over."

"No." Brink's heels hung over emptiness.

"We just want our half. You can smother yourself with the rest, for all I care." He was very close now, and still the scientist showed no sign of moving.

When he had approached to within arm's length, Low reached for the glow of an overflowing pocket. As he did so, Brink convulsed and tried to dart past. Low grabbed, and the other man swung with surprising force. The Commander ducked and pulled, dragging both of them to the floor.

Rabid, maniacal energy drove the scientist's swings, but he was wild and undisciplined. Brilliant as he was, he had no idea how to fight. It still required all of Low's strength to ward off the mad flurry of blows, so much so that he was unable to land a single solid punch of his own.

He finally managed to roll clear, using his legs to kick free of the tumultuous embrace. Life crystals spilled from Brink's pockets, littering the floor with emerald magic.

"*No!*" The scientist scrambled to his feet, staggered, and put his right foot down on emptiness. Robbins screamed as Brink went over backward, disappearing from view. Several seconds later they heard the heavy, sickening, inevitable *thump.*

They rushed to the edge. Their companion's crumpled, bent body lay directly below the drop. Blood spread out beneath the twisted corpse to form a dark oval frame. In falling, Brink's head had struck the edge of a pyramidal projection. Not only was his neck broken, the skull had been shattered. Bits and pieces of brain and bone lay everywhere.

"Didn't mean to do that," Low muttered tersely. "Didn't mean for that to happen."

Robbins put a hand on his shoulder. "He would have thrown you over if he could."

"I know, but that wasn't the real Ludger Brink I was fighting with. Hanging around all those crystals for so long did something to him. Altered his personality." He eyed the softly glowing shards warily. "We'd better watch out they don't start to act on us as well.

"I don't think there's much chance of reviving him with a crystal. The important parts are in too many pieces." His eyes met hers. "It's done and there's nothing we can do about it. At least now maybe he's at peace." He indicated the scattered shards. "We might as well pick these up and use them the way we planned."

The transport sphere returned them to the fifth islet. As before, a single life crystal reactivated the entire complex as well as raising the Eye above the mountains of the central island.

Averting their eyes from the fantastic beam, they focused their attention on the unprepossessing slot in the side of the primary mechanism.

"Ready?" Low held a second crystal above the opening.

"Why not?" She smiled. "What's the worst thing that could happen?"

"This whole island could blow sky-high and there'd be no one around to revive us."

"If the whole island goes, then we'll end up in more pieces than poor Ludger. At least if that happens we won't have to worry any longer about finding food or returning home."

Gazing back into the expressive, open face he had come to know so well, he debated whether or not to kiss her. Not the right moment, he decided. He chose not to consider the possibility that there might never be any more moments as he fed the next crystal into the waiting slot.

Consequences manifested themselves immediately. The beam deepened in color and intensity as a subtle vibration passed through the floor. Lips compressed tightly, Low continued to feed life crystals into the mechanism at sixty-second intervals.

Could the device be overloaded, he found himself wondering? From their position alongside the central mechanism they couldn't see the central island. He passed the remaining crystals to an attentive Robbins.

"Keep dropping them in. I need to see what effect this is having on the nexus."

"All right." She resumed fueling the machine as she watched him make his way to the gap in the wall.

He kept his head low and his eyes three-quarters shut and averted as he passed beneath the beam. Considering its strength, he thought it remarkable that he felt no heat or vibration. What would happen if he stuck his hand into it? Would the Eye fall and shatter? Would it swerve and tremble? Or would his hand simply disintegrate like wheat straw in a furnace? He decided against performing the experiment.

Robbins called out to him as she dropped another crystal into the slot. "See anything?"

Standing in the opening beneath the beam, Low shouted back over his shoulder. "Everything looks the same to me! Maybe the bubble effect enveloping the lens is slightly more solid! It's hard to say. Might just be a disturbance in the atmosphere. You still loading crystals?"

"Every minute," she yelled back. "Why don't we just dump them all in at once?"

He turned to peer back into the chamber. "Maggie, I'm not sure that's such a good—"

He never finished the sentence. The concussion was deafening. It blew him off his feet and out through the gap. He landed hard on the rocks outside, bruising his face and arms.

Rolling over, he caught his breath before climbing to his feet and stumbling back toward the gap. Lights danced before his eyes and he couldn't hear a thing. Overhead, the beam had turned a deep purple that appeared solid as steel, but he wasn't interested in the beam anymore.

"Maggie!" He fell to his knees, cursing his recalcitrant legs, and forced himself erect again. "Maggie, talk to me!" Dazed and bleeding, he staggered into the chamber. "Where the hell are you? What happened?"

There was no reply.

Not far from the base of the primary mechanism, which appeared undamaged, he found her lying facedown on the floor. A glance revealed that the feeder slot had sealed itself shut. Sated, he decided, just like a carnivore after a big feed. As his hearing began to return, his ears rang as if he'd just finished a year as chief apprentice bell-ringer to Quasimodo himself. He turned her over. Her eyes were closed.

Too stunned to cry, he slipped his arms beneath her and carried her back to the gap in the wall. She'd been so tough, so enduring, that the lightness of her body surprised him. Laying her down gently just inside the opening, he cradled her head in his hand and raised it so that she could see. Her eyes fluttered open.

"Look, Maggie. Can you see? Can you see what we did? What you did?"

Across the intervening ocean the slowly rotating lens had accelerated tremendously on its luminous axis. So fast was it spinning that it resembled a globe instead of a lens.

Or an eye.

It was a deception of speed, of course. There was no rigid gray globe out there, hovering above the center of the main island at the nexus of the five beams. It was simply the original lens, spinning so fast that it gave the illusion of solidity. If it had rotated in his direction and blinked, he wouldn't have been surprised.

"Worked," she whispered. He had to strain to hear the single word.

"Yeah, it worked, all right." With his other hand he took her fingers in his and squeezed gently. "Kill or cure. You shouldn't have done it, Maggie."

A hand reached up to caress his lips with shaky fingers. "Please, Boston. Don't be angry." She smiled, and he could sense the effort it required.

"Don't worry. If you . . . if you slip away, I'll use one of the life crystals to bring you back."

Her fingers dropped to coil tightly around his wrist.

"There are no more, Boston. I put them all in the machine, and the machine took them." She struggled to see. "It's kind of pretty, isn't it? With all the lights?"

"Yeah. It's real pretty." His voice choked.

"But no return ticket. Our asteroid-ship hasn't moved." She smiled again. "Hell of a bang, wasn't it?" Her back arched slightly as every muscle in her body tensed. Her eyes squeezed shut.

"Maggie?"

She slumped back against him. "It's . . . okay. I've been in this position before, you know."

"You mean, lying down?" He tried to smile back, without much success.

She could only laugh with her eyes. "You astronauts. Always kidding." She tried to punch him, but couldn't raise her arm high enough. Blood began to run from her nostrils. "I think I'm dying, Boston. I feel all broken inside."

The concussion had blown him clear through the gap in the wall. Much nearer the source, what had it done to her? He was afraid to feel along her ribs for fear of what he might find.

"You're not going to die, Maggie. You're not going to leave me here alone."

"What, another order?" She coughed, and what came up finally started his tears flowing. "Don't try to fool an experienced reporter." For an instant her eyes seemed to focus. "Listen to me, Boston Low. If you can get home, if you can find a way, you do it. Promise me."

"I promise." He wiped angrily at his eyes. "Brink still had some life crystals on him when he went over. I'll find a way down, come back with one—"

"No." Her strength was fast ebbing, but her voice remained strong. "No life crystals for this girl reporter, Boston. No resurrections."

"But it worked for Brink. It'll work for you."

"No. He wasn't the same . . . after. You saw it. The crystals took him over, remade him as well as revived him. I don't want to be remade. Who knows what would have happened to him if he'd lived? He might have gone a little madder each day. Or maybe one day, without warning, the crystals just stop working and you fall over. No thanks. None of that for me. I'd rather die peacefully than live like that."

He found himself shaking his head in disagreement. *"You're not going to die."*

"Right. I'll just lie here and relax. Keep holding me, Boston. It feels right."

Silently they watched the convergent beams, which showed no sign of diminishing, and the spinning lens, which gave no indication of slowing. Was the reaction now self-sustaining? What was taking place deep within the complex interlinked instrumentation? Could he turn it off now even if he wanted to?

None of it mattered. Not even finding a way home was important anymore. All that mattered was the woman lying in his arms, her eyes half-closed as she continued to breathe shallowly.

"Hey," she blurted abruptly, "take it easy."

"I didn't do anything."

"You're beating up on yourself. You didn't do anything, Boston. No regrets, *comprende?* You wouldn't have liked living with a journalist anyway. We talk all the time, and I'm told that female journalists are the worst of the lot."

He dredged up a smile. "I'm surprised to hear stereotypes from you, Maggie."

"What the hell. When the muse fails, you fall back on clichés." She coughed again, harder this time, her body wracked by the spasm.

His touch light, he brushed hair from her forehead. "I think I could've gotten used to it. We would've managed. I could have done the heroic deeds and you could have reported on them."

"S'truth. Here I am sitting on the story of a lifetime and I can't get a word out. Probably doesn't matter. My regular audience wouldn't believe a word of it."

"Pictures, Maggie. Video."

She smiled up at him. "Special effects. Morphing. People believe what they want to believe." Her fingers tightened against him. "It hurts, Boston."

"I'm sorry." He didn't know what else to say. He knew there must be something else, but he couldn't think of it. It was ever so at such moments.

"The beams. Find out what they're for. Find out for me. It's part of the story, you know. You can't leave out critical parts of the story. Bad journalism."

"I'll try. I'm just a little ol' jet jockey, but I'll try. You can help me find out. Right? Right, Maggie?" Her eyes had closed again. That's when he thought of the right words, but by then it was too late. It always was.

"I love you, Maggie."

She died there in his arms without saying another word. There was no eloquence to it, no beauty in it, as the poets postulated. She just went away.

He laid her down gently on the unyielding floor, her lifeless face illuminated by the final product of a science so advanced, it embodied concepts humankind could not contemplate even theoretically. While the chamber throbbed with electronic life, the only one that meant anything to him lay lost at his feet.

He thought about ignoring her request, considered racing back to the main island to retrieve one of the remaining life crystals from Brink's body. Her words refused to leave him, stuck in his mind, and he knew that she would curse him for bringing her back, for subjecting her to the potential tyranny of crystal addiction.

So he left her there, her beautiful silent face turned toward the alien sky. Left her the way she always wanted to be left from the time they'd first met: with the last word.

Rising, he turned to squint directly at the beam. Beyond lay the transport tunnel, its ever-efficient sphere waiting to carry him back to the central island. He started walking . . . away from it.

Many of the machines boasted assorted indentations and projections. Once more he found himself wondering what would happen if he made actual contact with the beam. If it was deadly, death would come instantaneously. His eyes watered and he had to wipe at them continually as he scrutinized the projection. It was only light, of course, but even light could exert pressure. And he'd never seen a light like this.

What lay at the end of the light, at the terminus of the beam? It was no rainbow and the spinning lens no Valhalla. He'd promised Maggie that he would find out.

Using various projections and indentations, he climbed easily to the top of the primary mechanism. Looking down the length of the beam, he could see the distant cryptic illusion that was the lens, the Eye. What if he could reach it, what then? Probably it would knock him silly, send him flying off onto the rocks.

Seen from above, Maggie Robbins was more lovely than ever. She lay as he had left her, unawakened and still. It wasn't a bad dream.

Find out what the beams are for, she had implored him. It might only take a nanosecond to find out.

Closing his eyes, astonished at how calm he was feeling, he stepped forward off the edge of the machine. He did not die. His leg was not incinerated. Instead, he found himself standing on the light, his boots sinking into it an inch or two. Bouncing tentatively on the balls of his feet, he took an experimental step forward. It was like walking on deep foam rubber. He would have compared it to walking on air, except that he *was* virtually walking on air.

Well, now, that's interesting, he thought. He knew a couple of physicists who would have given a year off their lives just for the privilege of studying the phenomenon.

He resumed walking. The beam continued to support him, buoying him up by who knew what implausible stretch of applied photonics. His feet sank no farther into the light.

Increasing his pace, he left the spire behind and soon

found himself striding along high above the alien ocean. There was no breeze. He was no tightrope walker, but the beam was plenty wide, and to say that he was accustomed to high places would have been an egregious understatement.

Besides, he didn't much care if he fell. The drop of a hundred feet on either side of the beam didn't concern him. Ignoring it, he maintained his steady pace, occasionally jamming his hands into his pocket and whistling softly as he walked. The spire receded behind him as the illusory gray globe of the Eye drew near. Gradually, a new revelation manifested itself.

The Eye sang.

Actually, it was more of a very high-pitched whine, an unsurprising by-product of the spinning lens. But he preferred to think of it as a song, albeit a one-note threnody. Close now, he could see that the lens was not revolving on a single axis but on many, like a gyroscope. Within the sphere of rotation, light was bent, making it impossible for him to see through it. In addition to the serene whine, it exuded a faint dampness.

He glanced back. The fifth islet looked small in the distance, its glistening spire a needle looking to pierce some low-lying cloud. Below he could see the broken terrain of the central island, the quiescent asteroid-ship, even the hold through which access could be gained to the vast underground chamber. It all seemed so mundane, so irrelevant. Like his life, he mused.

With a sigh he turned back to face the Eye. Maggie wasn't the only one who always wanted to see what lay on the other side of the mountain. As nonchalantly as if he was crossing Market Street, he stepped forward into the vaporous maelstrom.

The sphere vanished. So did the island, and the sea, and the sky. So, too, did any sense of up or down, left or right. Looking in the direction he believed to be down, he wasn't really surprised to see that he wasn't there anymore. If he'd been able to access a mirror, he would have discovered that he no longer possessed eyes with which to see. Instead of seeing, he perceived.

Looking (or rather, perceiving) around, he settled on something that had neither mass nor shape but that was there nonetheless. It was *there* by virtue of its selfness, adrift in the same waxen pale as himself. The cosmos had become solid cloud flecked with presence.

Reaching out with what would have been his arms had he still been in possession of such limbs, he found he could move closer to the presence. Contact was made. He felt a coolness in his mind instead of on his skin, which extraneous envelope he had discarded along with the rest of his physicality. Pulling back, he sensed and felt nothing. There *was* nothing to sense in this place: no heat, no light, no smell. One could only perceive.

Effortlessly, he moved away from the intermittent gray flicker he perceived to be the Eye. Looking down, he found that he could perceive the central island, the ocean and the creatures that dwelt within. He saw everything all the way to the heart of the planet and, looking out, all proximate space as far as the Cocytan sun. Everything was incredibly obvious, though viewed through the veil of newfound perception.

He sensed other thoughts moving close and prepared to receive them. When they chose to manifest themselves, they were as clear and sharp in his mind as any speech.

"We have been observing you for some time, by your standards," declared one. Without head or ears, he understood it perfectly, and turned to confront it.

It was a Cocytan, though not one boasting beaked skull and vestigial wings. Rather, it was the essence of a Cocytan, perceived whole and complete. A presence against which he could measure his own existence. He was unexpectedly glad to have it confirmed.

Others crowded near, though there was no sense of crowding. Some were cool, others decidedly warmer. He perceived each of them individually, just as they perceived him. Behind the first there were others. Dozens, hundreds, millions and more. Astonishingly, he found he could perceive each and every one of them, both separately and as a group. He did not try to comprehend how he was able to do this. For the moment, it was more than enough simply to accept.

"Where am I?"

"In our place." The one he perceived as nearest to him replied. There hung about it an aura of great satisfaction. "In the other dimension. Resign yourself to it. It is remarkable that you have succeeded in coming among us, but now you will never go back. We have been searching for the way back for a thousand years."

"So this is the fourth dimension." Low turned, or perceived that he was turning. It didn't matter which way he looked: Everything looked the same unless he focused on the physical universe. The dimension of which he was now a part encompassed the entire cosmos yet was not restricted by it.

Brink should be here, he found himself thinking. Not me.

"You have come through the Eye." Was that a dozen of the thought-forms addressing him, he wondered, or a million? "Reactivation was always believed possible, but not likely. The movements of the Creator, when revived, were circumscribed by the exigencies of the tomb. Others have come and gone on the physical plane, and all failed. Until now. Until you."

"Thanks." He knew he ought to feel flattered by this homage from an ancient race, but he did not. He didn't feel much of anything. "Were there many who tried before me?"

"Not so very many. Some. All perished without activating the Eye, much less achieving this dimensionality. Their skeletons, and exoskeletons, and other hard body parts lay scattered among the islands."

"Quite a place," Low murmured. "I feel like I can go anywhere, do anything."

"Our range is limited, but within that span perception is boundless," he was told. "Great knowledge is to be had. Existence is endless, and pain banished. Thoughts have consequence. Physical force is irrelevant."

They showed him, and despite his melancholy he was awed. The whole world, the entire system with its sun, planets, comets, asteroids and related bodies—all were within easy reach. He could penetrate and examine anything at will, be it living or dead. From the cells of a strange swimming invertebrate to the molten heart of the planet, from the eye of a flying creature to the center of the yellow-white star, he could cast himself with ease.

All this was open to his perceptions. But he could not feel, taste or smell so much as an errant weed.

"Enough," he thought suddenly. "I've got to go back."

"But you are back," they informed him. "Within this dimension, all points are tangent." And he saw that it was so.

"No. Back to the real world. Back to the physical dimension. Don't you miss it yourselves?"

"Breathing," declared one or a billion. "The sting of dust molecules against retinas. The heaviness of air. Moistness, dryness. The common sensations. These are what we miss most."

"Then why don't you go back? Doesn't the Eye work both ways? Can't you simply step back through it now that it's been reactivated?" Shifting his perception, he noted that the requisite instrumentalities continued to function efficiently, that the beams still shone and the lens still rotated.

"Would that we were able." This time he knew that it was only one addressing him. The first. "Unfortunately, the way has been forever lost. In this dimension of insubstantiality and indirection, there are no landmarks, no signposts. We can perceive the workings of the Eye down to the tiniest component, we can observe the beams and note their confluence, but for all that we cannot locate the Eye itself. It is the one actuality that is closed to us."

"We have searched for a thousand years," the distraught thought-forms echoed, "without finding. The Eye cannot be perceived from this side, cannot be found."

"One would think that the laws of probability . . . ," began a thousand others.

Orienting himself, Low perceived amid the whiteness and the veiled physicalities a grayish splotch. "But I don't understand. It's right there."

"Of course it is," exclaimed the weary millions. "It has always been 'right there.' It is simply that we cannot locate, cannot perceive."

"Well, *I* can." Low was adamant. He moved himself.

"Impossible!" ten thousand thought-forms chorused.

"Can it be?" The first moved close, to examine the new arrival from the inside out. "His neurology differs. He is similar, close, yet different. *Not* Cocytan."

"A blind spot?" theorized the nearest others. "Active and transparent, fixed yet motionless?"

"I'm telling you," Low asserted, "it's right here!" The grayish patch was tenuous and indistinct, but real.

"We perceive nothing," the first insisted. "Were that it were otherwise."

"You'd give this up to come back?" Low manifested a gesture. "All this knowledge, this opportunity?"

The first confronted him, as much as it was possible to do so given the limitations of their immediate environment. "Listen well, traveler. Immortality is Hell."

"Then follow me."

So saying, he entered the gray splotch. He felt a light buffeting, as if he'd suddenly opened the door to his home on a blustery day.

He was standing on the beam that emanated steadily from the fifth islet. The gray globe grew misty behind him.

The breeze struck again. Standing at his shoulder, seven feet tall, was a Cocytan. More massive than the Creator, bright of eye and dynamic of countenance, it inhaled deeply. Much to Low's surprise, he found he could understand the words when it addressed him.

"In the other place knowledge is absorbed as easily as is food in the physical world. Much was implanted in your thoughts while you were among us. Food!" it exclaimed, as though contemplating all the jewels in the universe. "To eat again. To consume, and process." Eyeing the muscular form, Low found himself wondering if the Cocytan were vegetarians.

A second alien stepped through the vortex of the Eye, followed by a third.

"Come." The first gently urged Low downward, back toward the fifth islet. "Now that the way is known, it will not be lost again. We must make room for the others."

Looking back as he retraced his steps, Low saw Cocytan after Cocytan emerge from the Eye. They paused to stare at the sky, the sea, one another. Soon more were stepping out onto the four other light-bridges and making their way toward the other islets. Cries of delight and booming calls of homecoming echoed across the sky.

He wondered how long it would take for all of them to make the transition. Three billion, the Creator had told him. Would the machinery that powered the Eye continue to function long enough? He put the question to the Cocytan accompanying him.

"Worry not, traveler. Among the first to come through are many who were engineers and builders. They will take control of the mechanism and see to its maintenance. The bridges will not be allowed to fade nor the Eye to dim." Even as he spoke, long-limbed Cocytans were striding past Low on either side. Their strange singsong speech filled the air with what he could only think of as exclamations of sheer joy. A number leaped and pirouetted with remarkable grace, heedless of the potentially fatal plunge to the ocean below. Others simply paused to inhale deeply of both fresh air and a restored reality. Upon successive reemergence, several embraced. Their joy and delight could not help but communicate itself to Low.

Vividness of expression is more than possible, he thought, without the use of any language at all.

"Where are you going to put everybody?" Low wondered. "Even the central island isn't very big."

"There are transportation systems that lead to the nearest continent and from there to the rest of Cocytus. Like so much other carefully tuned machinery, it has been waiting patiently for a return we had come to believe would never take place. I infer that you did not discover them. It is as well. Had you been presented with all of Cocytus to explore, it is likely you would not have found the key to the Eye.

"After transportation, communications will be restored, for on this plane of existence we can no longer simply think at one another. You cannot imagine, cannot conceive of, what an enchantment it is to utilize ordinary speech again." Alien eyes gazed down at him.

"You cannot imagine our debt to you, Boston Low. What we owe you can never be repaid."

"Hey, it's all right. To be perfectly truthful, I didn't think I was embarked on any kind of good deed. My intentions, my thoughts, were . . . elsewhere. So don't give me any credit for it." The spire that overtopped the fifth islet loomed near. "In the other dimension your physical forms were still preserved?"

"As was yours," the Cocytan told him. "In the other dimension all memories of the physical world are preserved. And like memories there, they do not age. Now we have regained them at last, along with our heritage." A powerful, multidigited hand came to rest on Low's shoulder. "And also, I think, some new friends. You have no idea how much anxiety you caused us. We could observe you but not help, scrutinize but not contact, monitor but not warn. Many sensations were denied to us in the other dimension, but frustration was not one of them."

As they entered the spire, Low could see numerous Cocytans busying themselves among the instruments and machines. They worked smoothly, efficiently, as if they had left their professions only yesterday. Watching them operate, it was impossible to believe they had been absent from this place for a millennium.

"Since the beginning of our civilization," Low professed, "my people have wondered about the existence of a Heaven."

"Heaven." The Cocytan ruminated. "A paradise beyond and outside the realm of physicality. We found a way to exist without physicalities, but we did not find a Heaven. Perhaps your people may have better luck."

As they made their way through the chamber, which now rang to the cries and calls of busy Cocytans, Low tried to avoid the place where Maggie's body lay. Again the strong hand rested upon his shoulder.

"I feel a tenseness within you."

Low looked up at his new friend. "Can you read minds too?"

"No, but you forget that we have been observing you ever since your arrival on our world. There was little we missed. Your body language as well as the one you speak was learned. You grieve for your female companion, do you not?"

Low could only nod.

"She could not have known how dangerous it was to stand so near to the center when final attainment was achieved. Why do you not speak to her now?"

"Because she's dead," Low replied bleakly. "Because she gave her life to—"

"Hey, I don't give my life for anything. Well, maybe for the right story."

Low gaped. Maggie was coming toward him. She had been concealed behind a pair of Cocytans. Her eyes sparkled, and there was a spring in her step he hadn't seen since they'd first boarded the *Atlantis*.

There wasn't a mark on her.

"But how . . . ?" He gawked at his tall alien comrade.

Then she was in his arms, and he didn't have to worry

about whether the time was right for kissing. She made sure of that.

When at last she drew back, he could only gape and marvel. "I thought . . . I thought you didn't want to be brought back? I thought you didn't want to have anything to do with the life crystals?"

She was laughing at him. Dead one minute, giggling uncontrollably the next. Who said the universe had no sense of humor?

"Did I say anything about life crystals?" She indicated the two busy Cocytans behind her. One made a gesture in their direction that might have been a wave. "It seems that they've developed a number of different ways of doing the same thing. It's just a matter of adjusting the crystal, or fine-tuning its inner frequency, or something. I don't pretend to understand, even in translation, but they promised me there would be no side effects."

"And the result?"

"What, already worried about me keeling over in the middle of visiting friends? The resurrection is permanent for the duration of my normal life span. Which, I am told, is now greatly enhanced. You can get the same treatment, and we'll live long enough to be feted as famous old geezers."

Not knowing what to say, Low glanced back at his newfound friend. "It is true," said the Cocytan. "A properly attuned crystal will maximize your natural life span. We should like that. It will enable us to honor you that much longer."

"We'll go on and on, Boston," she told him, "until our cellular machinery finally gives out. Maybe I can even finish that book I've always wanted to write."

"I thought your people were rejecting immortality," Low told the alien.

"Immortality, yes, but not a long and healthy natural life. The physical dimension offers too much to enjoy."

As if to confirm these words, Low and Maggie embraced for the second time, even more tightly than before.

The pair of Cocytans who had revived her looked on with interest. "Are they mating?" wondered one.

"I do not think so," declared the other. "I envy them their exquisite combination of emotional resonance and surface tactility."

"Most touching." The voice was cool, analytical . . . and familiar. Low and Maggie turned as one.

"Ludger?" the Commander exclaimed.

"Do you know anyone else on this world by that name?" The scientist came toward them. "As you can see, I seem to have developed an aversion to protracted death."

"But you look . . . so old." Maggie stared at the otherwise fit and healthy scientist. His hair had thinned and whitened and his skin looked as if he'd just emerged from twelve hours spent in a hot bath.

For the second time he made her a present of his formal bow. "Thank you so much for the compliment. I have been . . . on tour, I think you would say it. The realm of the deceased is a fascinating place, though I wouldn't want to live there. I have learned much, in exchange for which a decade or so of life seems little enough to sacrifice. It is not as if I had any choice in the matter." He turned to confront Low.

"If I recall correctly, Commander, we had a little disagreement."

"I didn't push you off that platform, Ludger. You fell."

"I know, and I apologize most profoundly for my actions. I was not myself, but rather under the influence of the life crystals." He gestured at his face, and Low noted the profusion of wrinkles and lines. "My appearance, I am told, is the result of their improper application. A lesson that I will more easily be able to impart to others, should the occasion arise."

"He will still live a long time," the Cocytan standing behind Low declared.

"I do not mind the premature aging." Brink smiled. "It will give me status among my peers. In the professional circles in which I move, you're not considered experienced until you've reached the age of sixty." He chuckled. "Wait until those old fossils read my report on *this* expedition."

"So you won't need to take any more of the crystals?" Low asked him.

"No." Brink smiled broadly. "I have been . . . attended to. They performed what I like to think of as neural chiropractic on me. I don't need any more green."

"And now," announced the Cocytan, "I believe you would like to return to your home."

"Return home?" Low shook his head in disbelief. It was altogether too many miracles to deal with at once. "But how?"

"By the same means that brought you here. The asteroid-ship retains a record of your transference. It is easily reprogrammed."

"You mean, we could have done that all along?"

"No." The Cocytan's tone was somber. "You never could have done it. The mechanics are far beyond you. But not beyond your capacity to understand. With a little instruction, you will be surprised at what your kind can accomplish. And we will be glad to share. Not because we owe you, which we do, but because it is in our nature."

"Let's get going," Maggie insisted. "I have a *story* to file."

"You're not afraid?" Low slipped his arm around her waist. "It's a long way home, and an old piece of machinery."

She took his hand in one of hers and Brink's in the other. "Now, why should I be afraid of a little faster-than-light hop? I've already been dead, and Ludger twice. If one of us ought to be afraid, Boston, it's you."

But he wasn't afraid. He wasn't afraid at all. Not with a royal Cocytan retinue to escort them from the chamber.

The only thing Boston Low had ever been afraid of was ending up alone.